TOM CLANCY
EXECUTIVE POWER

ALSO BY TOM CLANCY

The Hunt for Red October
Red Storm Rising
Patriot Games
The Cardinal of the Kremlin
Clear and Present Danger
The Sum of All Fears
Without Remorse
Debt of Honor
Executive Orders
Rainbow Six
The Bear and the Dragon
Red Rabbit
The Teeth of the Tiger
Dead or Alive (with Grant Blackwood)
Against All Enemies (with Peter Telep)
Locked On (with Mark Greaney)
Threat Vector (with Mark Greaney)
Command Authority (with Mark Greaney)
Tom Clancy Support and Defend (by Mark Greaney)
Tom Clancy Full Force and Effect (by Mark Greaney)
Tom Clancy Under Fire (by Grant Blackwood)
Tom Clancy Commander in Chief (by Mark Greaney)
Tom Clancy Duty and Honor (by Grant Blackwood)
Tom Clancy True Faith and Allegiance (by Mark Greaney)
Tom Clancy Point of Contact (by Mike Maden)
Tom Clancy Power and Empire (by Marc Cameron)
Tom Clancy Line of Sight (by Mike Maden)
Tom Clancy Oath of Office (by Marc Cameron)
Tom Clancy Enemy Contact (by Mike Maden)
Tom Clancy Code of Honor (by Marc Cameron)
Tom Clancy Firing Point (by Mike Maden)
Tom Clancy Shadow of the Dragon (by Marc Cameron)
Tom Clancy Target Acquired (by Don Bentley)
Tom Clancy Chain of Command (by Marc Cameron)
Tom Clancy Zero Hour (by Don Bentley)
Tom Clancy Red Winter (by Marc Cameron)
Tom Clancy Weapons Grade (by Don Bentley)
Tom Clancy Command and Control (by Marc Cameron)
Tom Clancy Act of Defiance (by Andrews & Wilson)
Tom Clancy Shadow State (by M. P. Woodward)
Tom Clancy Defense Protocol (by Andrews & Wilson)
Tom Clancy Line of Demarcation (by M. P. Woodward)
Tom Clancy Terminal Velocity (by M. P. Woodward)

TOM CLANCY
EXECUTIVE POWER

BY ANDREWS & WILSON

SPHERE

SPHERE

First published in the United States in 2025 by G. P. Putnam's Sons
(an imprint of Penguin Random House LLC)
First published in Great Britain in 2025 by Sphere

1 3 5 7 9 10 8 6 4 2

Copyright © Clancy Media LLC 2025

The moral right of the author has been asserted.

*All characters and events in this publication, other than those
clearly in the public domain, are fictitious and any resemblance
to real persons, living or dead, is purely coincidental.*

All rights reserved.
No part of this publication may be reproduced, stored in a
retrieval system, or transmitted, in any form or by any means, without
the prior permission in writing of the publisher, nor be otherwise circulated
in any form of binding or cover other than that in which it is published
and without a similar condition including this condition being
imposed on the subsequent purchaser.

A CIP catalogue record for this book
is available from the British Library.

HARDBACK ISBN
978-1-4087-3289-2

TRADE PAPERBACK ISBN
978-1-4087-3288-5

Printed and bound in Great Britain by
Clays Ltd, Elcograf S.p.A.

Papers used by Sphere are from well-managed forests
and other responsible sources.

Sphere
An imprint of
Little, Brown Book Group
Carmelite House
50 Victoria Embankment
London EC4Y 0DZ

The authorised representative
in the EEA is
Hachette Ireland
8 Castlecourt Centre
Dublin 15, D15 XTP3, Ireland
(email: info@hbgi.ie)

An Hachette UK Company
www.hachette.co.uk

www.littlebrown.co.uk

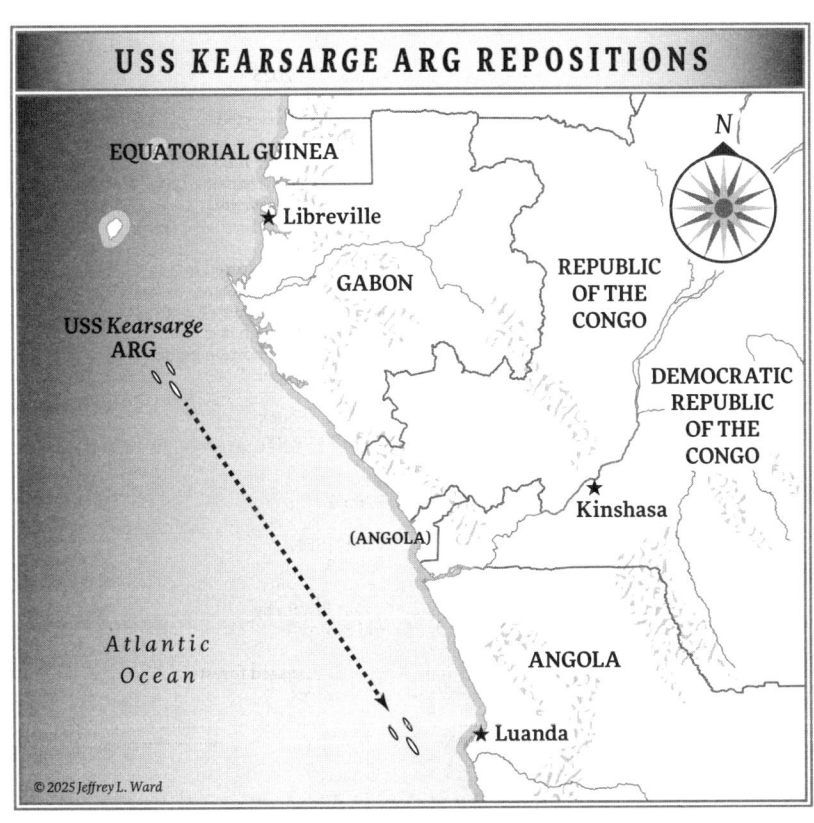

PRINCIPAL CHARACTERS

WASHINGTON, D.C.

Jack Ryan—President of the United States
Arnold "Arnie" van Damm—White House chief of staff
Mary Pat Foley—Director of national intelligence
Scott Adler—Secretary of state
Robert Burgess—Secretary of defense
Admiral Lawrence Kent, USN—Chairman of the Joint Chiefs of Staff
Major General Bruce Kudryk, U.S. Army—Joint Chiefs of Staff
Dr. Cathy Ryan—First Lady of the United States
Dr. Sally Ryan Kartal—Ophthalmic surgeon
Commander Dennis Knepper, USN—Executive officer

LUANDA, ANGOLA

Kyle Ryan—Defense Intelligence Agency
Ambassador Patricia Gonçalves
Madison Bennett—Executive assistant to the ambassador
Julio Tejada—Regional security officer (RSO)
Freddy Vincent—CIA chief of station
Lieutenant Commander Katie Ryan—Office of Naval Intelligence

PRINCIPAL CHARACTERS

Intelligence Specialist Second Class "Bubba" Pettigrew—Office of Naval Intelligence

Lieutenant Junior Grade John Conza—Office of Naval Intelligence

Captain Anthony Miles, USN—Commanding USS *Kearsarge*

Colonel Ricardo "Rick" Crocker—22nd MEU commander

Major Merriweather, USMC—1st Company commander

Captain Nick Camperos, USMC—Alpha team leader

Captain Josh Dane, USMC—Charlie team leader

President Francisco Luemba

Victor Baptista

General João de Souza—Chief of the general staff of the Angolan Armed Forces

GLOSSARY

AOR—Area of Responsibility
ARG—Amphibious Ready Group
BDU—Battle Dress Uniform
BRI—Belt and Road Initiative
BUD/S—Basic Underwater Demolition/SEAL training
BZ—Bravo Zulu (military accolade)
CASEVAC—Casualty Evacuation
CCP—Chinese Communist Party
CDR—Abbreviation for Commander (O5)
CENTCOM—Central Command
CIA—Central Intelligence Agency
CIC—Combat Information Center
CLO—Community Liaison Officer
CO—Commanding Officer
COC—Combat Operations Center
CONUS—Continental United States
CSO—Combat Systems Officer
DC—Damage Control
DDG—Guided Missile Destroyer
DIA—Defense Intelligence Agency
DNI—Director of National Intelligence
DOD—Department of Defense

DWS—Defensive Weapons System (remotely controlled, belly-mounted variation of the GAU-17 7.62 minigun on the MV-22 Osprey aircraft)
Eighteen Delta—Special Forces medical technician and first responder
EOC—Emergency Operations Center
EXFIL—Exfiltrate
FARP—Forward Area Refueling/Rearming Point
FOB—Forward Operating Base
FST—Fleet Surgical Team
GOE—Grupo de Operações Especiais (Angolan Special Forces)
GPI—Global Peace Index
GRS—Global Response Staff (the clandestine CIA protective operations force responsible for the security of CIA personnel)
GWOT—Great War on Terror
HUMINT—Human Intelligence
HVT—High-Value Target
IC—Intelligence Community
INFIL—Infiltrate
JCOS—Joint Chiefs of Staff
JLTV—Joint Light Tactical Vehicle
JO—Junior Officer
JSOC—Joint Special Operations Command
JSOTF—Joint Special Operations Task Force
KIA—Killed in Action
LCAC—Landing Craft Air Cushion
LCPO—Leading Chief Petty Officer
LFOC—Landing Force Operations Center
LHD—Landing Helicopter Dock (amphibious assault ship)
LPD—Landing Platform Dock (amphibious assault ship)

GLOSSARY

LPO—Leading Petty Officer
MAGTF—Marine Air/Ground Task Force
MARPAT—Marine Corps digital camouflage pattern
MARSOC—Marine Corps Special Operations Command
MAW—Marine Air Wing
MEDEVAC—Medical Evacuation
MEU—Marine Expeditionary Unit
MPLA—Popular Movement for the Liberation of Angola (political party)
MSOB—Marine Special Operations Battalion
MSOC—Marine Special Operations Company
MSS—Ministry of State Security
NCO—Noncommissioned Officer
NMIC—National Maritime Intelligence Center
NOC—Nonofficial Cover
NSA—National Security Agency, or National Security Advisor
NVGs—Night Vision Goggles
ODNI—Office of the Director of National Intelligence
OIC—Officer in Charge
ONI—Office of Naval Intelligence
OPORD—Operations Order
OPSEC—Operational Security
PFU—Patriotic Front for Unity
PLAN—People's Liberation Army Navy (China)
POTUS—President of the United States
POV—Point of View
QRF—Quick Reaction Force
ROE—Rules of Engagement
ROTC—Reserve Officer Training Corps
RPG—Rocket-Propelled Grenade
RSO—Regional Security Officer

SARC—Special Amphibious Reconnaissance Corpsman (a Marine special operations medic)
SAW—Squad Automatic Weapon
SCIF—Sensitive Compartmented Information Facility
SDV—SEAL Delivery Vehicle
SEAL—Sea, Air, and Land Teams, Naval Special Warfare
SecDef—Secretary of Defense
SF—Special Forces
SIGINT—Signals Intelligence
SIPRNet—Secret Internet Protocol Router Network (a secure communication network used by the U.S. Department of Defense)
SITREP—Situation Report
SOCOM—Special Operations Command
SOF—Special Operations Forces
SOG—Special Operations Group
SOPMOD—Special Operations Modification
SQT—SEAL Qualification Training
SWO—Surface Warfare Officer
TAD—Temporary Additional Duty
TAO—Tactical Operations Officer
TOC—Tactical Operations Center
TOS—Time on Station (usually referring to the time a combat aircraft can remain on station before needing to refuel)
TS/SCI—Top Secret/Sensitive Compartmentalized Information
UAV—Unmanned Aerial Vehicle
UNITA—National Union for the Total Independence of Angola (political party)
USN—United States Navy
VTOL—Vertical Take-off and Landing
XO—Executive Officer

PART I

Few men have virtue to withstand the highest bidder.
—George Washington

1

URASHA APARTMENT COMPLEX, UNIT 3B
SÃO PAULO DISTRICT
LUANDA, ANGOLA
2222 LOCAL TIME

Kyle Ryan sat in the dark, his face lit by the blue-gray glow of his laptop computer screen.

"Pull Me Under" by Dream Theater played in his headphones as he worked the keyboard with methodical, tenacious effort. His mind was fully immersed in the slipstream of data and the task at hand. In this state, his body felt separated—his consciousness tethered only by a biological umbilicus providing the fuel and oxygen necessary for computation. In this state, his body was nothing but a distraction. Only when hunger, dehydration, bladder pressure, or exhaustion reached an alarming level would he stop to address the constraint.

Bodies were such a bother.

Sometimes he wished he didn't need one.

He'd argued he could do this work remotely from Defense Intelligence Agency (DIA) headquarters in Virginia, but his boss had maintained otherwise and sent him to Angola. As usual, his boss had been right. The data and communications infrastructure in Angola would never have supported remote configuration. The hardware required for that did not exist in theater. This is why he and the hardware team were building out the infrastructure they needed in situ, including dedicated antennas, multiband transceivers, relays, cameras, and power supplies. And all of this was being done without permission or knowledge of the Angolan government.

Their new stealth communications and surveillance network would operate entirely independently from any existing or future Angola Telecom infrastructure. AT's recent partnership and multimillion-dollar contract with Chinese telecom giant Huawei meant that all traffic living on the state-owned network would be subject to Chinese scraping and interrogation. The DIA certainly couldn't risk or tolerate that. The Chinese were eating America's lunch in a raging cyberwar that no one wanted to admit was happening. Just because the bullets being fired happened to be electrons instead of lead slugs didn't make it any less real or any less important to national security.

And when the DIA put out a call for capable volunteers to fight this war, like the Ryan that he was, Kyle raised his hand.

While he performed device configuration routines and programming, his teammates bickered like little brothers on the comms circuit.

"Dude, what the hell are you doing?" Cockburn said in Kyle's headset. "You're on the wrong roof."

"No, I'm not," Waddle fired back.

"*Yes*, you are."

"Bro, I'm not. Check yo-self before you wreck yo-self."

"Seriously? That's your go-to—Ice Cube?" Cockburn said.

"I do what I do. You like it, great. You don't, go listen to somebody else. I'm stickin' with the people who stick with me."

"Who said that?"

"Ice Cube, obviously, fire dick."

"You're a toddler, you know that, right?" Cockburn fired back.

"Takes one to know one."

For Kyle, their bickering idiocy was the concentration-wrecking equivalent of being tapped repeatedly on the shoulder by a bony index finger. He sighed, stopped what he was doing, and shifted his gaze from the laptop he was working on to a second laptop, whose screen saver had activated due to inattention. He tapped the space bar to wake the machine, then pressed his thumb on the fingerprint sensor to authenticate. The display refreshed from the log-in screen to a bird's-eye view of the one-square-mile area of Luanda where they were working. On the map, he saw one green dot with the tag COCKBURN and another a block away labeled WADDLE. Kyle wasn't sure which team member's surname was more ridiculous. And though it was something he rarely reflected on, whenever he was in the company of Cockburn and Waddle he was glad to be a Ryan.

"I can settle this debate," Kyle said, looking at the monitor. "Bravo is technically on the correct roof."

"Ha, take that, Hot Willy," Waddle said. "I told you I knew what I was doing."

"I said *technically*, Bravo. You're on the right roof, but you're installing the dish in the wrong place," Kyle said, addressing Waddle by his call sign before either man could chime in with a retort. Despite all the smack talk and clowning around, they were professionals and never used their actual names on comms. "It was supposed to be positioned in the northeast corner; you're on the southwest corner. So, in one sense, Alpha makes a point—you'd be closer to the correct install location if you were in the same quadrant on the wrong building next door."

Kyle fully expected a snarky celebratory comment from Cockburn, but the hardware tech didn't say anything.

"Well, that's a first—burnt weenie is speechless," Waddle said as Kyle watched Waddle's green dot moving across the roof to the correct corner.

A long, awkward static-filled pause followed.

"I think you hurt his feelings," Kyle said, breaking the silence and cracking a smile.

"Dude, no reason to get all sensitive. You know I'm just messing with you," Waddle said, shedding his wise-guy bravado for the first time all night.

Cockburn didn't answer.

A twinge of uncertainty flared in Kyle's chest as he shifted his attention from Waddle's green dot to Cockburn's position indicator. The field tech had been walking north on Rua Cristiano dos Santos, and his dot had been moving on the map accordingly, but now the icon had gone still.

"Alpha, sitrep. You all right, buddy?" Kyle said, eyes locked on the dot.

No reply came.

"Bravo, this is Omega—comms check," he said, hailing Waddle, just to make sure his transmission was going out.

"I hear you Lima Charlie, Omega," Waddle answered. "I'm going to check on Alpha. I should be able to see him from up here."

"Copy that. Good idea."

Kyle turned back to Waddle's green dot, which had reversed directions and was now moving south on the rooftop toward the edge of the building. He looked back at Cockburn's position indicator and saw that his dot was now moving in little fits and starts into an alley between two rows of buildings. For this operation, he had neither a satellite nor a drone providing imagery. This was not a spec ops evolution. He and his team were cyber division, not shooters.

"Bravo, it looks like Alpha is on the move," he said, picking up the bottle of fruit punch–flavored Bodyarmor sitting on his desk. "He seems to be ducking down an alley."

"What the—" Waddle said, but his transmission abruptly cut off. At the same time, Kyle also heard what sounded like a gunshot, followed by a thud.

"Bravo, sitrep?" he said, snapping upright in his chair and dropping the bottle without taking a sip. "Bravo, do you copy?"

Waddle didn't answer, and the green dot on the roof had stopped moving.

Fear blossomed in Kyle's chest and the primitive fight-or-flight subroutines he so rarely accessed in the depths of his brain activated and took control. For complex multifactor problems like strategy and programming, the amygdala lacked the processing power to compete with the cerebral cortex. But for situations like this, it had no equal. It cut through analysis paralysis like a blowtorch through butter. The *how*, the *why*, the *what-ifs* . . . none of these things mattered. The amygdala processed the events of the past two minutes and simplified the logic into terms that even an ADHD brainiac like Kyle Ryan could not misunderstand:

His team had been identified and targeted.

Cockburn and Waddle were dead.

All that remained was a simple, binary decision: *Run or die.*

Every fiber in his being wanted to bolt out of the apartment like a man on fire, but duty compelled him to perform one final task before evacuating. He pressed and held Ctrl + Alt + F1 for three seconds and a pop-up window appeared:

Authenticate to erase all data.

Kyle swiped the pad of his thumb across the fingerprint reader. The window refreshed.

To proceed, press the "Y" key. To abort, press the "N" key.

He tapped the Y key, whirled, and sprinted to the front door, leaving everything in the apartment exactly where it lay. As he grabbed the doorknob, the invisible hand of caution stopped him from turning it. What if a gunman was waiting outside in the hallway for him? Or in the stairwell?

"Shit," he muttered, wishing he'd paid more attention to the layout and details of the apartment building both inside and out.

If his survival came down to a gun battle, then Kyle knew he was already dead. First and foremost, he wasn't armed. And even if he were, he was no match against a professional. Yes, he was a U.S. Naval Academy graduate and had fulfilled all mandatory firearm handling and shooting requirements, but he was no shooter. Unlike his older brother, Jack Junior, Kyle didn't inherit a single strand of Marine Corps DNA from his dad. During plebe summer, a midshipman upperclassman had berated Kyle with the line *"It's obvious there ain't a single ounce of Navy SEAL in that skinny-ass body of yours, Ryan."*

As it turned out, the jab was true.

A warrior, Kyle was not.

But there was *one* thing he could do better than his big bro and probably ninety-nine percent of the people on the planet, and that was run very long distances very fast. As a junior, he ran a sub-twenty-four-minute 8K at the Paul Short Run cross-country course at Lehigh University, placing second at the meet. Even now, despite the constraints of his job, he was religious about logging twenty-five miles a week. A sub-six-minute-mile pace for Kyle was child's play.

Too bad he couldn't outrun a bullet.

Despite the ominous feeling that he was destined to cross paths with a hit squad sent to kill him, Kyle had no other viable option but the stairs. A sniper had most certainly whacked Waddle and Cockburn, so going out the window and climbing down the outside of the building was a nonstarter.

To escape, he'd need speed, lots of cover, and luck.

Most of all luck.

With a shaky exhale, he twisted the doorknob and pulled the door inward, opening it just enough to listen. Holding his breath, he heard all the typical sounds of apartment living barely muted by improperly insulated walls and cheap doors: a baby crying, music playing, a television news program . . .

What he did not hear was the pounding of booted feet or the barking of orders from a SWAT team.

Feeling the crush of time, he opened the door wide enough to stick his head out for a glance right and left. Finding the corridor deserted, he exited the apartment and sprinted to the stairwell at the end of the hall. Without pause or hesitation, he plowed into the metal fire door with all his weight, giving the slab a massive shove inward. To his surprise, the door slammed into someone just on the other side, knocking the person backward and sending them tumbling heels over head down the concrete stairs. Kyle gasped, momentarily mortified for injuring some innocent civilian or building resident, but then his eyes ticked to a pistol the man had dropped on the top landing.

He knelt to pick up the weapon as the would-be assassin came to rest a half flight below. The shooter was dressed in dark civilian clothes and wore a black N95 face mask—the same kind people wore during the pandemic—which concealed his features. The man's head was cocked at an unnatural forty-five-degree angle, and his wide-open eyes were staring unblinking off into the distance.

Kyle looked at the pistol in his hand.

The make and model were unfamiliar to him, but that wasn't surprising because he wasn't a "gun guy." He was experienced enough to know it was a semi-automatic model, looked similar to a Glock, and likely held 9mm bullets. He confirmed the weapon was loaded by pulling the slide back and looking in the ejection port to see a round in the chamber. Then, weapon in hand, he descended the stairs. As he approached the downed assassin, a part of his brain questioned whether the man was really dead. What if he was faking and at the last second reached out and grabbed Kyle's legs? But the logical part of his brain knew this would be an absurd tactic and was nothing more than the product of having watched too many horror movies as a teenager with his sister Katie. Nonetheless, he gave the dead guy a wide berth as he quick-stepped around the body on his descent.

It all felt very surreal, almost make-believe, as he made his way down the switchback staircase—six half flights—to the ground level. He'd never been in a situation even remotely like this before. His coworkers had been murdered, and now the people who'd done it were coming after him. Escaping the building alive was his first objective, but then what? His amygdala had been crystal clear with the order to *"Run,"* but light on specifics. Where was he running to? Shockingly, the answer immediately came to him, his midbrain offering a simple, obvious, uncomplicated solution:

The U.S. embassy.

At the bottom of the stairwell, he paused, forced to make his next blind decision. The landing had two exit doors—the emergency exit leading outside and the regular door leading to the ground-floor hallway. His heart was pounding at what felt like a thousand RPM in his chest—not from exertion but from fear. He wasn't sure what side of the building the exterior door opened out to. He didn't know which cardinal direction he'd be facing when he stepped outside. He'd not paid attention to where Cockburn had parked the rental car, and he doubted he could find his way back to it. And if he abandoned the car and ran to the embassy, he wasn't sure which route to take to get there.

There were so many damn unknowns . . . Too many.

With such imperfect information, how could he possibly execute a good strategy?

"What would Jack do?" he mumbled.

But Kyle already knew the answer to that question. Jack would do exactly what he always did—keep moving and figure it out as he went along. Oh, and God help the poor son of a bitch who tried to get in his way.

"But I'm not Jack," he heard himself say.

He stuffed the pistol into his waistband, hiding it from view with the flaps of his untucked shirt. Hands shaking, he walked to the interior door leading to the ground-floor-level apartments. Pretty sure he was about to die, he opened the door and stepped into the hallway. A middle-aged African male was walking toward him, head down, looking at his mobile phone as he walked. Kyle performed a quick threat assessment—slight build, civilian clothes, no mask, no hat, no visible weapons or conspicuous bulges.

Nothing about the man said operator or assassin, but then again, wasn't the ability to hide in plain sight a hallmark characteristic of great tradecraft?

Kyle moved his right hand into a ready position while drifting to the far side of the hall to give space for the passing. The man looked up from his phone—seemingly just registering Kyle's presence for the first time—and made eye contact. Kyle nodded. He nodded back and returned his attention to his phone as they passed each other, left shoulder to left shoulder. Kyle lengthened his stride and turned his head to keep the man in his peripheral vision as he opened range. The man did not look back and disappeared into the stairwell Kyle had just exited.

A wave of relief washed over Kyle, but the feeling lasted only a split second.

If the man went to the third floor, he would find the body . . .

"Shit."

Just then, a mental screenshot of the map program he'd been using all night popped into his mind's eye—his subconscious apparently finally deciding to join the party. Kyle did not have a photographic memory, but right now it sure felt like he did because he could literally see the map as clearly as if he were sitting at his computer. His internal compass instantly recalibrated as his sense of orientation and direction solidified. As if an app was running in his brain, a route populated on the mental map from the apartment building to the U.S. embassy: *Exit the rear of the apartment building into a mid-block alley, head south, and cut between two other buildings to Rua de Benguela, then sprint one thousand meters west and dogleg to reach the embassy at the corner of Rua Ndunduma.*

For the first time since this nightmare began, Kyle felt a flicker of confidence.

Body on autopilot, he turned right to exit the apartment building via the rear door. On reaching it, he forced himself not to think about or second-guess the decision. He pushed the door open, ducked low, and took off in a sprint. A suppressed gunshot cracked somewhere and a sniper round slammed into the door behind him. The narrow alley was only ten feet wide and he crossed the gap into cover—a narrow slot opening between two adjacent buildings—which he reached before the shooter could get off another shot. He ran the length of the slot and emerged onto Rua de Benguela, which ran perpendicular to the cut-through and parallel to the alley. He turned right and kicked it into high gear. The pistol immediately worked itself loose from his waistband and he grabbed it an instant before it fell. His only option was to grip it in his right hand while he ran, which at this late hour didn't matter because not a soul was out on the street to notice the crazy white American agent running for his life. Powered by fear, adrenaline, and an inexplicable sense of obligation to his family to survive, he pushed his body to the limit. His fastest mile split in cross-country was 4:24. He tried to remember the feel of that pace and find it now.

Parked cars zipped past him on the left in a blur as he streaked down the dimly lit street.

He'd not heard a second sniper shot . . .

Yet.

He hoped and prayed the sniper would need to relocate from his original perch to a different one to achieve a line on the current track. If a supersonic round did punch a hole in his skull, at least he wouldn't feel it. There were worse ways to go out of this world, that was for damn sure.

The squeal of rubber on asphalt cut through the quiet like a falcon shriek.

Risking a fall, he glanced over his left shoulder mid-stride and clocked a pair of headlights approximately four hundred yards behind him. Forget the sniper, he was being hunted. In the movies, they love to show people running away from cars that can barely seem to catch up. A ludicrous proposition because an elite athlete running at a four-minute-mile pace was only traveling at fifteen miles per hour over ground. At sixty miles per hour, a vehicle was doing four times that speed. The hunter would quickly catch up to the hunted.

The engine of the closing SUV roared as the driver accelerated.

Kyle knew he had only one advantage over his enemy.

Size.

He scanned the row of buildings ahead, looking for an alley too narrow for the SUV to follow him into. However, Luanda wasn't a big American city like New York or Boston. Most of the buildings were jammed right up against one another in an architectural hodgepodge of asymmetrical disunity, and so it was with the stretch of storefronts beside him. The businesses were buttoned up tight for the night, with steel bars safeguarding the ground-level windows and roll-down security gates blocking the doors. The next intersection with a north-south cross street was fifty feet ahead. He could make this intersection, but definitely not the next one, which was a full block away. If he turned here, the SUV would be able to follow him easily. If he kept going straight, maybe there'd be an alley or a cut-through he could exploit.

But maybe there wouldn't be.

His mental map was useless when it came to this decision.

As he reached the cross street, he glanced over his shoulder and saw the SUV had only closed the distance between them by half. Maybe he could make the next intersection . . .

"Fuck it," he said between huffs and decided to roll the dice.

Suddenly, he remembered something. When he'd burst out of the apartment into the back alley—that alley, the east-west alley, ran straight through. North-south access between buildings was limited and irregular, but every block was bisected by a parking alley that connected the cross streets.

He changed his mind at the very last moment, turning right and heading north at the intersection. Kyle didn't consider himself a religious person, but he said a silent prayer that he was right about the alley. Halfway down the block, salvation beckoned and he turned hard left down the parking alley. His pursuers could follow him, but not at speed. The narrow alley was packed full of impediments—dumpsters, parked cars, and other junk. On passing a six-foot-tall stack of wooden shipping pallets, he stopped, whirled, and tipped it over, sending the pallets sprawling across the alleyway.

Squealing tires told him the SUV had reached the intersection and made the turn. He sprinted to the closest dumpster and hid behind it. The game had just changed from chase to hide-and-seek. In a straight-up race to the embassy, he'd lose. Now his strategy was to evade and move in bursts. If they didn't spot him on their first pass, they might drive past the alley and turn west in the direction of the embassy, expecting to intercept him on Rua Ndunduma. If they turned down the alley, his life depended on finding a slot alley between buildings before they caught up and gunned him down.

Breathing hard, he resisted the compulsion to peek around the edge of the dumpster to see what was happening. He thought he heard the vehicle drive past the alley, but he couldn't be sure. He held position and waited for a ten count, trying to listen over the huffing sound of his heavy breaths. Feeling the crush of time and the compulsion to move, he glanced around the corner of the dumpster. To his horror and dismay, the SUV was stopped at the end of the alley—idling with the windows rolled down and the driver and rear gunman passenger scanning for him.

In an epic moment of catastrophic timing and coincidence, Kyle and the driver locked eyes. The driver shouted and pointed at the dumpster, which the gunman strafed with automatic-rifle fire. Had Kyle's reflexes been a millisecond slower, the barrage would have turned his head into pulp. Bullets pummeled the opposite side of the steel dumpster as Kyle crouched in cover, waiting for the barrage to end.

The instant the machine gun went quiet, Kyle took off in a crouching sprint on a vector that kept the dumpster between him and the SUV. Behind him, he heard the roar of an engine and tires on pavement as his pursuers turned and gave chase. Head down, arms and legs churning, Kyle pushed himself harder to eke out a little more speed, but his body was already at the limit. The sound of cracking and splintering wood echoed in the alley as the SUV ran over the pile of pallets he'd tipped over.

He scanned for a cut-through between buildings, but every building was built snug tight against its neighbor. Panic welled inside, and he unleashed a flurry of f-bombs as he ran for his life. The end of the alley where it intersected the next cross street was at least forty yards away. Once they got around the dumpster, he'd be an easy kill.

Then he saw the tree.

The next building had a rear courtyard—with a large tree in the middle—protected by an eight-foot-tall wooden privacy fence. He had no idea what was on the other side of the fence or if the courtyard had a front exit, but this felt like his only shot and so he took it. Behind him, he could hear the SUV barreling down the narrow alley in pursuit, sideswiping parked cars as it did.

"I want to live, damn it," he heard himself say as he ran right at the fence.

On reaching it, he jumped, and with all his might hoisted and rolled his torso up and over the wooden slats with athletic grace and efficiency that took him by surprise as he was doing it. His landing, however, was the opposite because lining the other side of the fence was a row of clay planters growing various flowers and vegetables. Not expecting this, his lead foot landed on the edge of a large pot, tipping it and causing him to tumble. He crashed to the ground, landing in a pile of ceramic shards, dirt, and tomatoes. At the same time, automatic gunfire ripped a line of holes through the fence at chest level.

Grunting in pain he scrambled into a low crouch, the realization not lost on him that he would probably be dead if not for the tumble. Ducking as low as possible, he ran north through the little garden courtyard desperately seeking freedom. The apartment building, or whatever it was, had a separation between it and the neighboring building. The slot alley had an iron gate blocking access to the courtyard from the other side, but once he hopped it, he'd have a straight shot to Rua Ndunduma. On reaching the gate, he spied a padlock on the latch, forcing him to climb yet again. Behind him, he heard yelling and wondered if the shooter in the SUV was going to pursue him. He mounted the fence, rolled over the top, and landed in a deep crouch on the other side of the gate.

Facing backward, his question was answered.

Through the bars, he saw a pair of gloved hands gripping the top of the wooden privacy fence, followed by a head. Kyle raised his right hand to fire at the assassin, but found he was no longer holding the pistol.

"Shit . . ."

He had lost the weapon when he hopped the privacy fence, and somehow it hadn't even registered in his conscious mind.

The masked killer kicked a leg up onto the top of the wooden slats.

Without a second's hesitation, Kyle whirled and sprinted for his life. In the slot alley, there was no cover. Nowhere to hide. Any strafe down the chute would cut him to ribbons because it was simply impossible to miss. With each stride, his right ankle was starting to complain. He must have strained it on the landing, but that's why nature invented adrenaline. He harnessed the pain and pushed himself even harder.

Ten yards to safety.

Seven . . .

Five . . .

He imagined the shooter was over the fence by now, but he didn't dare look back.

Three yards to the gap . . .

Jaw clenched, he dug deep and summoned every ounce of strength and power his body could muster. Three strides later, he exploded out of the alley like a cannonball blast. He immediately juked left around the corner of the building. He expected to hear the staccato crack of gunfire lighting up the alley, but no gunfire came. At first, his brain considered this a win, but a moment later he recalculated the scenario. The shooter had probably stopped climbing the fence and returned to the vehicle . . . which would be tearing down the alley to the next intersection to intercept him on Rua Ndunduma before he reached the embassy.

"With my luck, I'll be gunned down on the street five feet from the embassy."

As the words left his mouth, he realized that he was—both metaphorically and literally—running the race of his life.

A race *for* his life . . .

He had contemplated the nature of death plenty of times, but he'd never feared it. Maybe because of his youth or his pedigree as a Ryan, death had always felt one step removed. For Kyle, death was, and always had been, something that happened to *other* people. But right now, death felt near. Proximal. Tangible. It felt as if the Grim Reaper was running stride for stride beside him. Or maybe, more accurately, a few strides behind . . . like Dillon Harper. Harper had been Kyle's main competition on the Naval Academy's cross-country team, challenging Kyle on every course and forcing every contest to end with a sprint to the finish.

"Ten percent more," he heard himself bark in between breaths. "Just give me ten percent more."

Strangely, his body heeded the order without complaint or question, like a dutiful Marine. He felt his stride lengthen, the muscles in his legs accept the additional burn, and the cadence of his heart rate accelerate beyond what felt safe or even possible. He'd already been running at a pace that felt beyond his personal best, but this felt like a speed that if he kept it up for too long his body would tear itself apart.

A half block ahead he saw the corner of the embassy grounds.

One hundred yards to freedom.

One hundred yards to safety.

The next twelve seconds would determine the rest of his life.

The squeal of tires and the roar of an engine ahead to his left announced the arrival of his adversary. Like the Grim Reaper himself, the entity who'd killed Cockburn and Waddle was faceless, hiding its true identity under a cloak and mask.

And this infuriated Kyle.

For some reason, it mattered. He wanted to know.

He *needed* to know.

The SUV rounded the corner on an intercept course, and based on quick mental math, Kyle predicted they would both arrive at the embassy at the same time.

Fifty yards.

A pair of Marines standing guard at the front gate came into focus. At this hour, the embassy was closed for business. The gate was shut, and the Marines were posted inside the perimeter fence. But their presence sent a message beyond just vigilance. These men were more than mere sentinels.

They were symbols . . . of safety and strength.

"Help," Kyle shouted in between gasps. "I'm an American!"

Despite being winded, his voice projected with a volume that surprised him. He watched both the Marines turn to look at him through the bars.

Forty yards.

"American intelligence officer . . . Open the gate!" he bellowed. "They're trying . . . to kill me!"

Kyle watched the gunman materialize in the rear passenger window of the SUV with a machine gun.

One of the Marines shifted his gaze from Kyle to the intercepting SUV. At the same time, the assassin fired a strafe at Kyle—a strafe that by all rights should have cut him down, but miraculously the bullets ripped past behind him.

Thirty yards.

What happened next, Kyle did not expect and certainly was not protocol. One of the Marines opened fire on the SUV and his shots connected. The vehicle swerved, changing direction toward the gate. This caused the second Marine to raise his rifle and fire. The first Marine fired again and the barrage of bullets blew out the windshield, headlights, and front tires.

The SUV swerved again, this time erratically and farther left.

The rear gunman, who no longer had a line on Kyle, fired a volley at the Marines.

The Marines returned fire with extreme prejudice, emptying their magazines.

Kyle, for his part, was only twenty yards from the gate, but still running straight toward the line of fire. He didn't care. All that mattered was getting on the other side of that gate. The SUV was slowing down, but on a crash course with the embassy's perimeter wall. Both Marines swapped magazines, then one opened the gate, while the other took a knee and covered the SUV. Kyle could no longer see the gunman in the passenger window, but that didn't mean the threat was neutralized.

Time shifted.

Ten yards.

The Marine manning the gate locked eyes with Kyle and waved him in, his arm making circles and his mouth moving to form what looked to be the words *C'mon! C'mon!* but Kyle's mind no longer registered any sound except his own panting breath.

Five yards.

Kyle felt the Grim Reaper gaining on him, challenging him for the finish line.

Three yards.

In his peripheral vision, the masked assassin materialized in the SUV window and, impossibly, Kyle's heartbeat quickened even more.

A muzzle flare flashed in the window just as the covering Marine saw the shooter and unloaded a volley of rifle fire.

Lungs on fire and leaning for the ribbon, Kyle barreled through the gap in the gate, crossing the finish line and stepping onto sovereign American soil. After just another step, his legs gave out entirely, done with his demands, and he stumbled, rolling through and out of the fall. Time seemed to freeze for a moment, and he felt engulfed in blackness, the only sound his own raspy breathing. When his vision cleared and his wits returned, he stared straight up into the face of a Marine looking down at him.

"State your name," the Marine said, covering him with his rifle.

"My name is Kyle Ryan . . . I'm an American intelligence officer, and the rest of my team has just been murdered."

2

**PRESIDENT'S RESIDENCE
THE WHITE HOUSE
WASHINGTON, D.C.
1711 LOCAL TIME**

Jack Ryan stood in front of the mirror in the dressing room off the presidential bedroom and held up two ties, one at a time, in front of the dark blue suit he wore. Then he shook his head and chuckled as he realized they were the exact same damn tie.

"Which tie do you like?" he called out to his wife, Cathy, who was just outside the door, in the bedroom, ready to read her in on the self-deprecating joke.

Then, quite suddenly, he felt so overwhelmed by an inarticulable sense of dread, that the tie in his left hand slipped out of his grip and fluttered to the floor.

"What's the other choice?" Cathy asked from behind him, and he realized that he still held the one in his right hand up to the collar of his starched, white shirt. Their eyes locked in the mirror and a cloud of concern spread over her face. "Jack, what's wrong?" she asked and placed a hand on his shoulder from behind. "Are you feeling okay? Are you . . . are you having chest pain?"

Ryan broke the stare and looked at himself in the mirror, and realized instantly why she might think he was having a heart attack. His face had become pale, drained of all blood, and his mouth hung open. He snapped it shut and forced a smile onto his face.

"Yes . . . I mean, no," he said and tried to give her a reassuring laugh, but it sounded strained even to him. "That is, yes I'm feeling fine, and no, I'm not having chest pain." He turned around and put his hands on her hips, the tie still draped in his right hand. "You look amazing," he said and kissed her cheek.

"Thank you," she said somewhat dismissively, then, "Now tell me what just happened. You looked like you saw a ghost or something."

"I'm not sure, to be honest," he said. "Have you ever gotten that sudden sense of, I don't know—dread maybe?"

"Yes," she replied immediately, her face solemn. "When you were in South America years ago and again just before a plane crashed into the Capitol. Do you think everything is okay? Should we check on our kids?"

Ryan felt a sudden, almost visceral need to do just that. But instead he took Cathy's hands.

"I think everything is fine," he said. "It's been a long day and my brain might be looking for any excuse at all to beg out of this state dinner." His color must have returned and his face become more normal, because his wife's shoulders visibly dropped and she let out a sigh. "And anyway, as you just pointed out, *you're* the one with the mystical antenna. You would feel something before I would. Whatever weird, gut feeling I just had is more likely related to something that will piss me off at the cabinet meeting tomorrow."

Now Cathy laughed for real.

Still, something just felt . . .

Wrong.

He looked at his watch and saw that the time was five thirteen. Ryan wasn't superstitious, but he'd never been fond of the number thirteen and uncharacteristically wondered for the briefest of moments if this was a bad omen. He pushed the absurd thought from his mind and took a deep breath, exhaling slowly to try to calm his nerves and recalibrate as he reached for the tie on the floor.

If something terrible had happened in the world requiring his attention, he would have already been interrupted by a White House steward or a phone call from Arnie van Damm, his chief of staff, or the DNI. Mary Pat Foley had no problem interrupting him regardless of the hour, should the situation warrant.

"Which one do you like better?" he asked, straightening up and holding the two identical ties side by side at his collar.

She laughed again.

"Those are the same tie, Jack," she said, touching his face and then kissing his cheek. "So, why don't you go with the one on the left?"

"I like that one better, too," he quipped.

She returned to the bedroom and whatever she'd been doing, and Ryan turned back to the mirror and pulled the tie to the right length under his collar, then his hands whipped through the rote motions of tying an overhand Windsor knot.

Cathy was here with him, Katie was almost certainly still at the office, and Jack Junior was on leave after a tough couple of months. Sally was at home with her baby girl at this hour. That left Kyle . . .

It suddenly occurred to him that he didn't know exactly where Kyle was. But the youngest Ryan was some sort of cyber expert—not exactly the kind of billet that puts you in harm's way, right?

He'd learned long ago not to ignore his feeling of intuition, but whatever might be going on, he had every reason to believe his kids, at least, were safe.

If it was anything other than just bad tuna at lunch, he had the most amazing team in the world working for him, so he'd find out soon enough.

Being the President of the United States brought enormous responsibility and with it power, but more important, it surrounded him with the best people. Whatever was happening, he knew he could trust those people to respond decisively and inform him immediately.

For now, he supposed, his biggest stress was dealing with the president of France and his young wife when what he'd prefer to do was cuddle on the couch with Cathy and watch an old movie.

Such was the life he'd somehow found himself in.

A knock at the door drew his attention as he exited the dressing room and his heart skipped a beat as Cathy shot him a look.

He gave her a reassuring shake of the head and another smile. But the dread returned.

"Sorry to disturb you, Mr. President," Arnie van Damm said when Ryan opened the door to the sitting room outside the bedroom.

"Not at all," he said, hearing his pulse at his temple. "What's up?"

"I'm not sure, Mr. President," van Damm said. "We have early reports that there may have been some Americans' deaths in Luanda, sir."

"Angola?" he asked, then felt a twinge of guilt at the relief he felt. This must be what his gut was warning him about, but there was no way any of the Ryans were in Angola. "What kind of deaths?"

"Early to say, sir. But . . ." Arnie shrugged. Ryan could always count on van Damm to be forthcoming and honest. "It sounds like it might have been a covert DIA mission that went awry."

Ryan gave a tight-lipped nod. They had been conducting operations in Angola to counter the Chinese dominance there for some time, but he wasn't read in on any specific operation that was ongoing.

"Keep me in the know, Arnie," he said. "Are you still making the dinner?"

"Unless this gets me out of it, sir," van Damm replied with his own smile.

"It doesn't."

"Then I'll see you there, Mr. President," his chief of staff said, glancing at his watch. "But I'll try to learn more about what's going on before I do."

Ryan shut the door as van Damm left.

That must be all there was to it, but, for some reason, he still felt unsettled.

"Jack," Cathy called from back in the bedroom, "which shoes do you like better?"

"Coming," he said. His mind shifted to his goals for tonight's dinner, which mostly involved shoring up support from France for a multinational coalition to invest more heavily in the African continent. Sending aid was one thing, but it was time to invest in the emerging nations of the continent in a way that would lead to financial independence for those nations and strategic partnerships with the West.

Because they had plenty of adversaries in the region already working to fill political and, more important, economic voids. And he had no intention of letting poverty and hunger turn eastern Africa into the next Afghanistan.

3

OFFICE OF NAVAL INTELLIGENCE (ONI)
NATIONAL MARITIME INTELLIGENCE CENTER (NMIC)
4251 SUITLAND ROAD, WASHINGTON, D.C.
1742 LOCAL TIME

Lieutenant Commander Katie Ryan glanced at the date and time stamp in the upper left corner of her computer screen and made a little *tsk* sound. Normally she would be settling into her cozy office to enjoy the quiet as most staff headed home, make herself a tea, and start digging into all the little threads around the world that had piqued her interest during a chaotic day. Those little pesky things that made her go "huh" as she went from one meeting or briefing to the next and oversaw the operation of her team all went into her little gray notebook—the one Kyle had given her last Christmas with *Dad Jokes* on the cover and a cringey joke at the top of each page—and then evening was where she followed those little threads to see where they might take her. It was, actually, her favorite part of the day because free from distraction she could let her mind run wild on all the little "huhs" that made it into her book.

On a normal day.

But this was *not* a normal day.

She looked at the time stamp again and chewed the inside of her lip.

Today, her celebrity crush was coming into town. Well, she supposed that CDR Dennis Knepper wasn't a celebrity in the traditional sense. If he was doing his job well then no one outside of the Navy would have any idea who he was. In fact, outside of the circles in naval intelligence, the White House, and of course the tight-knit submarine community, no one in the Navy would know who he was. But in those circles, he was the XO of the badass submarine that had stopped a nuclear attack on the East Coast of the United States by a madman, rogue Russian submarine captain.

With a little help of a fish-out-of-water intelligence officer . . .

She smiled at the thought and tapped her finger on the notebook. If she left now, she should be a few minutes early, but traffic anywhere even near the Beltway was completely unpredictable. In her experience, she could predict that it would not go her way if she was running late. She literally defined Murphy's Law when it came to D.C. Beltway traffic.

She moved her mouse and her computer came to life.

I'll just take a quick look . . .

She typed her username and password to access the SIPRNet. In the scrolling brief, she could see super-short summaries of events occurring worldwide and information relevant to the intelligence communities of both the United States and her allies. It was like a scrolling news feed of classified briefings at her fingertips. If anything hit a nerve, she need only double-click the header and open a more detailed brief as well as an initial assessment from the posting agencies.

It wasn't unusual for Katie to sit at her desk for a couple of hours or more in the evening, filling her mind with the events of the world, most of which were secret from the general public. It was a fantastic bunny hole—her version of losing herself in social media, which was something she never did.

Bomb maker identified in Yemen supplying the Houthis . . .

Resistance leader captured in India . . .

Increased pirate activity in northern Indian Ocean expected with rise in . . .

Chinese cyber facility likely located in East China Sea . . .

DIA assets in Luanda attacked . . .

She was about to click on the last link when her phone chirped. She picked it up and smiled at the tag—DN—and tapped the green button to accept.

"Hi there," she said, leaning back in her chair with a contented smile on her face. "Let me guess—duty calls, and you're headed out to sea to save the world again?"

"Nope," Knepper said with a laugh. He sounded eager . . . maybe even excited. "Just checking to see if you are on time, on target. Traffic on 95 North was a little lighter than I expected, so I might be arriving a few minutes early. But I can grab a drink at the bar if you're running late. I've got all night . . ."

She glanced at her watch. The drive to Old Town Alexandria was only twenty to twenty-five minutes without traffic, but this wasn't the best time of day to be driving. Still, she should be headed against the rush-hour traffic. If she was in her car in the next ten minutes, she might arrive a few minutes early herself.

"Nope, I'm headed out now," she said. "I should be there with time to spare."

"I'm really excited to see you, Ryan," her submarine officer, maybe-boyfriend said, and his soft tone sounded like he really meant it. "I mean . . . I missed you."

Even though she was alone in her office, she felt her face turn warm with a blush.

"I missed you, too, Knepper," she said, teasing him about how he always used her last name. "I'll be there as quick as I can."

"Can't wait," he said.

She hung up and started gathering things to shove into her bag. She'd already changed out of her Navy uniform into a flowery sundress and comfortable shoes. She let her hair down and decided she could pull a brush through it on the drive.

She glanced again at her computer screen.

DIA assets in Luanda attacked . . .

She was vaguely aware that she chewed the inside of her cheek for a moment, a nervous habit when she was thinking something through, which she hated but still kept doing.

What did DIA have going on in Luanda? She knew that the NSA had been barking about China's efforts to dominate telecom and, therefore, cyberspace for the last six months. Sub-Saharan Africa was an increasingly important region for the West, and not just because of the rich carbon reserves. Angola itself was estimated to have nine billion barrels of oil reserves and nearly eleven billion cubic feet of proven natural gas. But the strategic location on the Atlantic Ocean as a gateway to the rest of Africa was equally as important. The U.S. had been pouring money in the form of both aid and business investment into the nation, but it was no secret they were losing the battle for influence to China, who was investing far more heavily. There were rumors going around of a deal with the Angolan government to further grow China's footprint in the country—not just economically, but perhaps even militarily.

She looked at her watch again.

Then she opened her gray *Dad Jokes* notebook and on a fresh page she put tomorrow's date and scribbled:

DIA OP IN ANGOLA?

She circled it twice, then closed the notebook and logged out of her computer. She turned to leave, but stopped and fished a tiny, travel-size mouthwash out of her desk drawer. She took a swig, swirled it around, then bent over and, very unladylike, spit it into the circular trash can beside her desk.

Then she hustled out of her office with an excited flutter in her chest at the prospect of seeing Dennis.

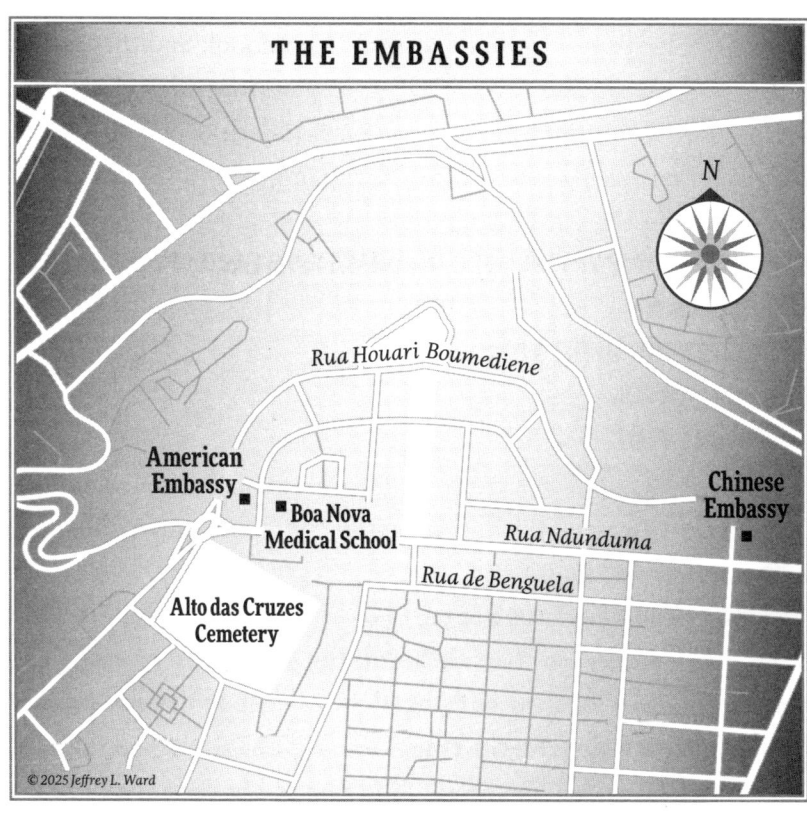

4

SENSITIVE COMPARTMENTED INFORMATION FACILITY (SCIF)
U.S. EMBASSY
R. HOUARI BOUMEDIENE 32
LUANDA, ANGOLA
0019 LOCAL TIME

Kyle drummed his fingers on the conference room tabletop, alone and waiting.

The SCIF was not particularly well-appointed. It had a drip coffee maker on the sideboard, but no Keurig or sink. The mini fridge was stocked with bottled water, but the compressor was definitely failing on the thing because it was noisy as hell and not very cold inside. The chairs didn't have wheels, adequate seat cushions, or a tilt function. In other words, they were shit. But most annoying of all, the room was warmer and more humid than it had been outside, which, to Kyle, seemed to violate the laws of physics.

In short, he was safe but miserable.

His natural ability to "not sweat the small stuff" was normally much higher, but two of his teammates had just been assassinated on his watch, and he was struggling with it. His mind was oscillating like crazy between the first three stages of grief—denial, anger, and bargaining. He couldn't stop thinking about how he'd fucked up and everything he could have done—no, *should have* done—differently.

"If I'd just stopped Waddle from walking to the edge of the roof, maybe he'd still be alive," he mumbled.

The magnetic lock clicked, snapping him out of his ruminations and self-flagellation. The door opened, and two men walked in. Half of the duo Kyle had already met—Julio Tejada, the embassy regional security officer (RSO) who was the senior law enforcement officer at the embassy and security advisor to the ambassador. The other arrival was dressed in a gray camo hoodie, blue jeans, and a pair of black retro Air Jordan 5s. He sported a Benson Boone–style mustache and wore his medium-length brown hair gelled back.

Kyle pegged him as CIA.

"Hey, I'm Freddy Vincent," the dude said, walking up and extending a hand, "the chief of station here."

"Kyle Ryan," Kyle said, standing only long enough to shake hands with the CIA lead, who Kyle guessed wasn't a day over thirty-five. That the chief of station was so young made a statement, but Kyle wasn't sure if that statement was good or bad.

Freddy and Julio dropped into chairs, and they both leaned in and propped elbows on the table.

"Julio read me in on everything," Freddy said. "I'm sorry, man. Fucking terrible."

Kyle shook his head. "Yeah . . . I'm gutted."

"All right, well, I think the first order of business is damage control and plugging any holes that need plugged. What do you think, JT?"

"Agreed," Tejada said.

Kyle shook his head. "*I think the first order of business is retrieving the bodies of my teammates. We're not leaving Waddle and Cockburn out there. Not like this.*"

"I hear you, and recovery is a priority, but before we do that, I need to better understand the threat. JT and I can't do our jobs until you read us in on what group you're with and your tasking," Freddy said.

Kyle balked, frozen with indecision. On the one hand, the clock was ticking, and they didn't have time to wait for the wheels of bureaucracy to turn. On the other hand, the group he worked for in the DIA was highly compartmentalized and his boss was a hard-ass when it came to OPSEC.

"Look, dude, I get it. You don't know shit about me and whether you can trust me . . . But I don't know shit about you, either. You're not one of ours—I know that—or I would have been read in on your operation in my sandbox," Freddy said, his tone very relaxed and matter-of-fact. "So, whatever phone calls you need to make so that we can work together, I'm asking that you do that now. I don't think any of us want to wait until morning to clean this up."

Kyle's brain, as it was apt to always do, distilled the scenario into a simple binary decision:

0—Follow the rules and lose control of the bodies and the narrative.
1—Break the rules and have a chance of recovering his teammates and maybe even all the sensitive hardware and personal belongings in the apartment.

He chose 0.

"I'm with a group in the DIA that, how do I say this . . . preps the cyberspace battlefield prior to potential future conflicts," he said. "And I'll answer your next question preemptively to save time. My team was tasked to covertly begin the build-out of a secure cyber communications infrastructure package in Luanda and other strategic locations."

Freddy shot a knowing glance at Tejada, then looked back at Kyle. "And I'm sure your proximity to the Chinese embassy was entirely coincidental."

"Obviously not," Kyle said.

"I was being sarcastic."

"I know."

Freddy ran his index finger over his thin mustache. "Are you with DIA/ST or Mission Services?"

"Yes," Kyle said, not feeling obligated or obliged to get into the weeds on his group's dotted-line existence on the DIA org chart.

Freddy and Tejada both chuckled.

"I guess what I don't understand is why you guys didn't partner with us on this one. I mean, this is really a job that should be in *our* wheelhouse, not the DIA's. The DoD has no permanent military presence in country. The Angolan military is certainly not a concern . . . So why would the DIA care about prepping the cyber battlefield here?"

It wasn't any of the CIA's business or concern what his head shed prioritized and what they didn't. And therein lay the problem. During the global war on terror and in the years since, the DIA and CIA had increasingly found themselves operating in the same sandbox—both metaphorically and literally. Both agencies were chartered with gathering intelligence on foreign governments, militaries, and non-state actors. But where the CIA's mandate was broad—covering all aspects of foreign intelligence, including political, economic, and social—the DIA focused exclusively on military and defense intelligence collection activities. Even though the Office of Director of National Intelligence (ODNI) had visibility to what each agency was doing, teams from the DIA and CIA were sometimes like two birds hunting the same worm. Kyle was pretty sure that wasn't the case this time, but he decided to answer Freddy's question implicitly.

"As you know, the DIA is tasked with collecting intelligence on two kinds of military threats—current and emerging."

"Ah," Freddy said, the light bulb illuminating momentarily, but then going dark. "But . . . China doesn't have a military presence here, either."

"Not yet," Kyle said.

Freddy nodded, the answer seeming to satisfy him. He turned to Tejada. "I'm going to send Isaacson and a team to collect the bodies and sterilize the apartment Ryan was using. Cool?"

Tejada looked troubled. "Are you going to tell the ambassador, or should I?"

"I already did."

"What did she say?"

"She said, 'Keep me posted and don't kill anyone.'"

Tejada laughed. "Dude, we got lucky with her. She gets it, you know?"

Kyle logged this interesting little detail that Freddy had already prepped to do the right thing *before* this debrief. He'd wondered why it had taken as long as it did for the station chief to show up, and now he had his answer.

Freddy turned back to Kyle. "Do you have any idea who targeted your team? I find it hard to believe the Chinese would send a hit squad because you're installing comms hardware."

"Agreed. I have no idea who hit us," Kyle said. "This was classified as a low-risk operation. It didn't even warrant a security detail."

"Is there anything new or fresh that's come back to you since your debrief with JT?"

"No. And like I told Tejada, the dude in the stairwell was wearing a mask."

"Did he have mono or double-crease eyelids?"

"I'm sorry, I don't remember," Kyle said. "I was running for my life."

Freddy nodded. "Roger that, I just wanted to know what my guys are going to be up against."

"Do you have a GRS contingent stationed here?" Kyle asked, referring to a Global Response Staff.

"I wish, but no. But we do have a four-man ground branch team that just came back from doing a thing in Kinshasa. We're lucky they're still here, because they were scheduled to fly home the day after tomorrow. This oughta be a cakewalk for these guys."

"I want to go with them," Kyle said, sitting up and leaning in.

"Absolutely not."

"They're ground branch. I'll be fine."

Freddy laughed, then his expression turned serious. "You've been targeted, Ryan. Your teammates were assassinated. According to your own statement, Waddle was taken out on a rooftop by a sniper. By accompanying the team you would not only be intentionally putting your head back into the crosshairs but you'd be endangering their lives as well by making them targets by association." He paused and his eyes bore into Kyle's face like twin laser beams. "I know you're President Ryan's son. We should assume the group that targeted your team knows this, too. And if they don't, it's my duty to keep it that way. My number one priority right now is to keep you and your NOC safe. So, it's a hard no, Ryan. You're staying right here until we get this situation sorted."

Kyle had expected this, and Freddy was right, but damn it, he had to try. Cockburn and Waddle were his teammates, and for some reason, participating in the recovery operation felt obligatory. He exhaled and surrendered with a grudging nod.

"Good, then it's settled," Feddy said, and turned to Tejada. "Tell Isaacson he's got a green light."

Tejada scooted his chair back from the table and stood. "On it," he said and left the SCIF.

"If you want to join me, you can watch the op from the EOC," Freddy said as he slid his chair back from the table. "We got a decent coffee maker in there."

"All right, thanks," Kyle said, then catching Freddy's eye added, "I'd appreciate it if you don't run this up the phone pole to the very tip-top. I'd rather not have POTUS involved."

The ask earned him a wry grin from the station chief. "I'm flattered that you think I have sway with the brass, but *that* decision is way above my pay grade. What the CIA director and DNI do or do not discuss with your dad is entirely out of my control."

Annoyed, Kyle stood and let his body language serve as his reply.

"Come on, Ryan," Freddy said, unfazed and with a politician's charm. "Let's go round you up a decent cup of coffee and something to eat. I promise you'll feel better."

"All right."

As he followed Freddy out of the SCIF, his mind was a whirlwind of anger, guilt, and uncertainty. He was upset about the failed operation. Upset that an adversary had potentially pierced his NOC. Upset that he'd lost teammates. And upset about how the entire event could derail his career, let alone his life.

He wondered how often his brother, Jack Junior, had struggled with these emotions that were all quite new to him. Not that Kyle would ever ask. Kyle kept his feelings and his thoughts about his feelings to himself.

His current gig was one of the few things in his life that he felt like he'd truly earned on his own. The idea of being banned from fieldwork and sentenced to a career of office work was bad enough, but getting plucked from the DIA and "promoted" into some safe bureaucratic job in the administration would be like a knife to the gut. He was pretty sure that his dad didn't even know what he did in the intelligence community, or that instead of re-upping for O-4 he'd resigned his commission and joined the DIA as a GS-13. He'd told no one about that. Not his dad . . . not even Katie.

And boy, when they found out, they were going to be pissed.

5

EMBASSY DISTRICT
LUANDA, ANGOLA
0034 LOCAL TIME

From the passenger seat of the idling up-armored Chevy Suburban, Daryl Isaacson raised the high-tech monocle spotter scope to his right eye and scanned the alley for threats. Seeing none, he switched from night vision to thermal imaging mode and checked for heat signatures. Kyle Ryan said this alley was where DIA agent Kevin Cockburn had last been seen.

Isaacson had been asleep when he'd gotten the call from Tejada. He knew before he picked up his phone that somebody had died. Call it cosmic intuition, operator's Spidey sense, or two decades' experience serving overseas and downrange . . . he'd just known. When the RSO read him in on the details, it turned out that not one person had died, but two. And they hadn't just died, they'd been assassinated five blocks away from the embassy and their bodies were still out here and in need of recovery.

"See anything?" asked Grant Hickman, the driver of the SUV. Like Isaacson, Hickman was a former Green Beret who'd spent fifteen years working in Special Forces before joining the CIA ground branch as a contractor. They'd known each other during their Army years, and it had been Isaacson who'd convinced Hickman to follow him over to the dark side. They'd been assigned to the same unit since day one.

"I got nothing," he said and swept his scan to the rooftops.

During a debrief with Freddy and Tejada, Ryan said his teammates had been taken out by a sniper, but he'd not actually witnessed the killings. Isaacson hated freakin' snipers. With modern firearms and optics, even an amateur shooter posed a lethal threat, and he had no intention of putting himself or any of his guys in the crosshairs of a shooter who'd already logged two kills tonight.

"You want me to drive down this alley—see if we spot a pair of boots sticking out from the bottom of a pile of garbage?" Hickman asked.

To an outsider the comment would have come across as incredibly callous, but Isaacson didn't take it that way. Hickman had a heart of gold, but he was also about as pragmatic and nononsense as they came. If Cockburn and Waddle were dead, then they were dead, and dancing around the topic wasn't going to bring them back.

Isaacson shook his head. "Not without checking these rooftops first."

In real life, *bulletproof* was a relative term. The Chevy was armored, but that didn't mean she was impenetrable.

"Three, One—sitrep on Monty?" he said into the thin black boom mic positioned at the corner of his mouth, using the pet name for their recon quadcopter.

"Monty is . . . in the air," Lou Mills came back. Behind the fellow operator's words Isaacson could hear the high-pitched whine and Doppler fade of the little drone as it zipped away and into the night.

"Roger that. Standing by for intel," he said and lowered the monocle.

"You want me to sweep the buildings near your pos before or after the rooftop where Waddle was last located?" Mills queried.

"The buildings by us first, then look for Waddle," he said.

"Check."

"Dude, this whole thing is fucked up," Hickman said and stuffed a pouch of wintergreen snuff into his bottom lip.

"I thought you quit," Isaacson said, cocking an eyebrow.

"I did—this is Smokey Mountain," he said and showed Isaacson the can, which was printed with the label:

SMKY MTN
TOBACCO-FREE CAFFEINATED POUCHES

"Shit, I didn't even know they made such a thing," he said with a dubious look.

"Wanna try one?"

"What do they taste like?"

"Sorta like the real thing, sorta not. At first, I didn't like it, but now I think I prefer it." Hickman held out the tin.

Isaacson was tempted and about to reach for one of the little white pouches, but a call from Mills came in: "Rooftops and fire escapes clear on both sides of the alley."

"Roger that," Isaacson said and spun his index finger in a little loop beside his temple.

"Hooah," Hickman said, whipping the steering wheel clockwise, and moving his foot onto the accelerator.

The big SUV turned off Rua de Benguela and into the narrow,

nameless alleyway. As his teammate eased them forward, it occurred to Isaacson that once inside the alley there was no turning around. If things went to hell, they only had one exfil option and that was reverse.

Relax, dude, his inner voice said. *This is Angola, not Mogadishu.*

Before his last assignment, he'd not known much about the sub-Saharan East African nation. When he'd checked the Global Peace Index, Angola had been ranked 82 out of 163 countries, positioning it as *moderately safe* among African nations. According to the agency's unpublicized metrics, Angola was categorized as a mid-tier nation with an asterisk. The asterisk indicated that Langley analysts predicted the country was at risk of entering a period of increased geopolitical instability, terrorism, and homegrown violence during the next twelve to forty-eight months. The asterisk was the reason Isaacson and his team of ground branch brothers had been offered the assignment to augment the embassy staff. So far during his eleven-month tenure, he'd not witnessed a single act of violence in country.

Not a single act of violence until now . . .

"There," Hickman said and pointed over the steering wheel with his gloved left hand as they reached the midpoint of the alley.

Sticking out from behind a pair of trash cans, Isaacson spied a pair of boots.

"Shit," he said, his voice a hoarse growl.

He hated the fact that Hickman's suggestion had proven prescient. No . . . what he really hated was that this proved the CIA analysis team right and that tonight's event was likely to be the first in a series of incidents and attacks that sent yet another African nation spiraling down the toilet of conflict and human misery.

Hickman eased the SUV past the trash cans, then stopped. "Want me to put the tailgate up?"

Isaacson, who was not normally skittish, hesitated.

"What's that look for?" Hickman asked.

"I got a bad feeling about this," he said, checking their six out the rear window.

"Mills cleared the rooftops. We're good, boss."

Isaacson took a deep breath and swallowed the feeling. Then, yanking the door handle, said, "Let's go."

He jumped out the passenger side of the SUV and swept around the rear of the vehicle, giving a wide enough berth to avoid smacking into the tailgate, which was coming up. When he reached the body, Hickman was already kneeling by the torso. The former Green Beret had his mobile phone out with Cockburn's headshot displayed.

Hickman looked up to meet Isaacson and answered the unspoken question. "Looks like our guy . . . At least what's left of him does."

Isaacson frowned. He'd seen and dealt plenty of lethal violence during his tenure as an operator, but that didn't make seeing it again any easier to stomach.

"I need you to grab a towel for me from the back," Hickman said.

Isaacson cursed to himself as he grabbed a dark-colored towel from the cargo bay of the Suburban and tossed it to Hickman. Instead of watching, he checked the alley in both directions, then scanned the rear-facing windows and fire escapes.

"One, Three—I found Whiskey," Mills said in Isaacson's headset, using the assigned phonetic designator for Waddle. "KIA on the rooftop where they said he'd be."

"Copy. And we found Charlie," Isaacson said, referring to Cockburn.

"Check," Mills came back, the single-word utterance laden with melancholy.

Isaacson felt it, too. He didn't know either of these guys, but that didn't make it easier. Cockburn and Waddle were American field agents working on the pointy tip. It didn't matter that they worked for the DIA and he worked for the CIA, they were kindreds.

They were brothers.

"Ready," Hickman said.

Isaacson stepped up and grabbed the dead DIA man's legs while Hickman lifted under the armpits. As they loaded the corpse into the back of the SUV, Isaacson couldn't help but stare at the half-missing head wrapped in a towel. He also couldn't shake the feeling that supersonic death was incoming for his head at any second. Whatever outfit had targeted Ryan's team was not only professional but not afraid to pick a fight with the United States of America.

And that did not bode well for anybody involved on the other side.

Hickman looked up expectantly after getting Cockburn's body into a position that left room for a second corpse.

Isaacson gave a solemn nod. "All right, let's go get Waddle."

6

EMERGENCY OPERATIONS CENTER (EOC)
U.S. EMBASSY
R. HOUARI BOUMEDIENE 32
LUANDA, ANGOLA
0045 LOCAL TIME

A lump formed in Kyle's throat as he watched the live feed from the quadcopter.

The large center monitor at the front of the EOC displayed the "bird's-eye view" video feed from the drone's high-res camera as it hovered over the rooftop of the building where Waddle lay motionless. His body was sprawled in an awkward position—torso prone with arms out wide, but his hips and legs were rotated to the side. A swath of blood and gore painted the roof deck behind his blown-out skull.

Despite desperately wanting to pull his eyes from the horror, Kyle could not.

Minutes earlier, he'd listened while Isaacson and Hickman recovered Cockburn from the alley, where his body had been dumped in a pile of trash.

But seeing this was much, much worse.

"It's my fault," he murmured.

A strong hand gripped his shoulder, and he turned to find Freddy glaring at him.

"Don't," the CIA station chief said.

"But if I had only—"

"*You* didn't pull the trigger," Freddy said, cutting Kyle off. "Luanda is not a combat zone. And you were not conducting combat operations. Do you get what I'm saying, Ryan? You and your team are noncombatants who were targeted by a hit squad. There's no culpability on your part. Do not play the *woulda, shoulda, coulda* game . . . Trust me, I know what I'm talking about."

"And why should I?"

"Because I've been down that road once or twice myself, and there's nothing but misery at the end."

Kyle nodded.

Freddy was right.

He, Waddle, and Cockburn were DIA cyber, not Navy SEALs on a shit-hot raid to bag a high-value target. *They'd* been targeted, not the other way around. In his mind, he already knew and accepted this. But recognition of the facts didn't make it any less agonizing.

"I appreciate what you're trying to do," Kyle said at last. "Thank you . . . But I'm just so angry."

"We all are. Which is why I'm going to launch a full-scale investigation into what happened. We're going to find out who did this and make sure that justice is served."

"Thank you," he said again, ready for the conversation to be over. But Kyle could tell from the fire in Freddy's eyes that this wasn't just a hollow promise made in the moment. The CIA man meant what he was saying, but whether the chain of command supported the plan was another thing altogether.

Freddy turned to Tejada, who was sitting at a control terminal. "JT, I'm thinking we might want Mills to run a quick sweep around the perimeter of the building before One and Two arrive, just in case."

"Good idea," Tejada said, then cued his mic and gave the order to Mills. "Three, this is Dugout—conduct perimeter scan with Monty on the target building before One and Two arrive to exfil Whiskey."

"Copy," Mills said.

A beat later the feed swerved as the drone operator piloted the quadcopter down and away from the roof and into a surveillance run.

"Bullpen, this is One—three mikes out. Camera's up."

"Roger, One," Tejada said, clicking away at his keyboard.

A new live-stream video appeared on the rightmost monitor of the three large screens at the front of the EOC, replacing the previous feed, which was from an external security camera watching the embassy's main gate. Kyle quickly identified the new feed as belonging to a body or helmet cam, because the POV was looking out a moving SUV windshield. At the bottom of the frame, in white blocky letters, was a mission clock in military time and the name ISAACSON, D.

"I didn't know ground branch operators wore body cams," Kyle said, turning to Freddy.

"They don't. This protocol was Isaacson's idea," Freddy said. "Unlike most shooters, he wants us to see what he's seeing. He views our eyes as a tactical advantage and situational backup."

Kyle rubbed his chin. "I see the upside, but uh, it also could be a liability. What if the feed gets hacked? Now the adversary can ID everyone on the team."

"Yeah, that came up in the discussions, but the guys have a

solution for that," Freddy said, chuckling, and keyed his mic. "One, show me Two."

The video frame spun left and showed the driver of the SUV, Hickman, whose face was now covered by a black mask overlayed with a chilling Punisher skull.

"See, problem solved," Freddy said.

"Yeah, that works." Kyle looked at the center monitor and noticed a white SUV drive into the frame and park on the street in front of the apartment building where he and his team had been lodging. The SUV then slid out of frame as the quadcopter conducting a sweep arced around the corner. "Go back!" he said, pointing at the screen. "Have the drone reverse course. Hurry."

"Three, Bullpen—reverse Monty," Tejada said. "We think we saw something before you made the turn."

"Roger that," Mills said on comms. "Where do you want to look?"

"A half block to the east. A white SUV just pulled up and parked in front of the apartment building I was operating out of. It's the third building down from the one where Waddle is . . ." Kyle said, his voice trailing off.

"Three, did you hear that?" Freddy said, and Kyle saw that Freddy had his mic cued.

"Copy," Mills came back, and the drone camera put the white SUV in frame just in time to catch two pairs of masked men exiting the vehicle, then sprinting toward the building.

"There!" Kyle said, pointing at the screen, feeling stupid as he did it because they could obviously see it, too.

"Ghost, Bullpen—be advised you've got four shooters entering the primary building." Tejada whirled in his chair to face Freddy. "What do you want to do? Pursue or abort?"

Freddy didn't answer Tejada and instead turned to Kyle. "You scrubbed your PC drive, but left everything else behind when you fled, correct?"

"Everything but my passport," Kyle said.

"What about Waddle and Cockburn? Were they carrying their IDs or did they leave them behind?"

"I have no idea," Kyle said.

"Doesn't matter. They can collect DNA," Tejada said.

"Assuming they're that sophisticated," Freddy said.

"Bullpen, Ghost One—what do you want us to do? Abort, monitor, or engage?" queried Isaacson, his voice impatient and echoing over the loudspeaker.

Freddy blew air through pursed lips, then locked eyes with Kyle—his look seeming to say, *A promise made is a promise kept*.

"It's risky. I'm sure the data wipe worked. You don't have to do this," Kyle said, and meant it.

A cocky grin curled the CIA station chief's lips. "Ghost, Bullpen—happy hunting, and don't forget to tell these assholes that Uncle Sam says hello."

"Hooah," Isaacson said, and the view from the body cam appeared to zoom forward as the big SUV accelerated toward the target.

7

EMBASSY DISTRICT
LUANDA, ANGOLA
0047 LOCAL TIME

Kalemba was not screwing around. One of the targets had escaped and now he would be blamed for whatever fallout ensued. With gritted teeth, he crossed the threshold into the apartment. A quick scan confirmed that the agent who'd escaped had panicked, and in his panic, left behind his computer and personal belongings.

Maybe something good will come out of this after all, he thought, scratching at the three days' scruff on his neck.

The order to eliminate the three-man team had surprised Kalemba. They were not arms dealers, human traffickers, mercenaries, or known enemies of the Luemba administration. They hadn't even been armed. He'd surveilled the trio extensively before the hit and concluded they were most likely Americans installing communications and surveillance equipment. If he was right, then best-case scenario, his crew had just murdered two contractors employed by the U.S. government. Worst-case, they'd assassinated two field agents from one of the American three-letter agencies. This worried him, because when the Americans found out what he'd done—and they would find out—they would deliver retribution. None of the world's superpower nations took kindly to the meddling in their operations and murdering of their assets.

Kalemba didn't know the client who'd contracted them for the hit. His employer—who was based out of Kinshasa—never shared such details. The only criteria that seemed to matter to Mukadi was whether payment was guaranteed. Kalemba wouldn't be surprised if the man accepted contract work from factions on the opposite sides of the same conflict. The Congolese mercenary was as shameless as he was ruthless.

He walked over to the table where the technician had left his laptop computer. He flipped open the screen and the user log-in page illuminated. Surprised the agent had not smashed the machine, Kalemba closed the screen, picked up the computer, and tucked it under his arm. Finding nothing else besides empty cups and mostly drained water bottles on the table, he continued his survey of the apartment. Next, he wandered into the closest bedroom and spied a backpack on the floor beside the bed and a black roller suitcase propped open atop a luggage stand. He decided to start with the backpack. He sat on the mattress, set the computer down beside him, and searched the bag.

Tucked inside an interior zipper pocket he found a passport book embossed with a golden shield and eagle on the front.

"*Merda*," he muttered, opening the cover flap to look at the ID page. The face staring at him belonged to a serious-looking Caucasian male whose listed age of thirty-three looked consistent with the photograph. "Jack Bauer . . . from Maryland."

His stomach sank.

Not good. Not at all.

"What did you find, boss?" Henrique asked from the doorway.

He wagged the passport at the shooter. "Americans."

Henrique let out a low growl, expressing his displeasure at the news.

Frowning, Kalemba put both the passport and laptop computer into the main compartment of the backpack, zipped it closed, and slung it over his shoulder. He stood and was about to tell Henrique to search the other bedroom, when gunfire erupted in the hallway outside the apartment.

He pulled his pistol.

"We make our stand here," he said, signaling for Henrique to shut the door and prepare to defend the breach. Then he cued his radio to call for backup, praying that Armando's squad wasn't already dead.

8

EMBASSY DISTRICT
LUANDA, ANGOLA
0102 LOCAL TIME

Isaacson slipped out the passenger-side door of the Suburban. The instant his boots hit the pavement his body sunk reflexively into a combat crouch. After decades of operating, he didn't even have to think about it; the body mechanics came as natural to him as breathing. The combat crouch was not an easy position to sustain—maintaining the required tension in the glutes, hamstrings, and quads took both physical endurance and will power. But over the years, he'd come to anticipate and even crave the burn.

The burn made him feel alive.

Keeping his head below the roofline of the armored Chevy, he quick-stepped aft and swept around the rear end. On reaching the driver's-side back bumper, he took a knee and sighted around the SUV's hindquarters. Facing the front side of the apartment building, he scanned for threats with his Wilson Combat SBR Tactical assault rifle. The weapon had been the ultimate present to himself—tricked out with a custom paint scheme, Whisper suppressor, and an EOTECH holographic hybrid sight with magnifier. Methodically, he swept his floating green dot over the main entrance, windows, and roofline.

Satisfied, he said into his boom mic, "Two, One—covering. No visible threats."

This report gave Hickman the green light to exit the driver's side, which was exposed because it faced the target building.

"Check," Hickman said and exited the vehicle.

"One—Three and Four are set," Mills said in Isaacson's ear.

"Check," he said and took off after Hickman, who was quick-stepping across the sidewalk toward the main entrance.

The plan was simple and straightforward. They'd breach and secure the building working as two teams of two, which matched the number of tangos that Bullpen had seen on the drone feed moments ago. Mills and Levitt would breach from the rear, while he and Hickman entered through the front. Most likely, the bad guys had no idea that Isaacson and his guys were hunting them. The enemy squad had arrived first on the scene, with orders that almost certainly were to search Ryan's apartment and recover all electronics and personal items of interest.

Isaacson figured that his counterpart—the team leader of the adversary force—would be operating with an offensive mindset. He was the infiltrator . . . which meant he might be giving less thought than normal to playing defense. This might give Ghost squad—the call sign for the ground branch team—a leg up.

Of course, if I were him, Isaacson thought, *I'd leave a team in the lobby or position shooters in the third-floor hallway just in case.*

A moment later, his back was pressed against the wall outside the apartment building's front door. He locked eyes with Hickman, who nodded that he was ready.

"Three—One and Two are set. Ghost is set to breach on your mark," he whispered into his mic.

He absolutely hated ops in occupied civilian residence structures. The mere prospect of dealing collateral damage twisted his insides into knots. This apartment most certainly housed families and children. No one in this building deserved to be wounded or killed by an errant bullet.

None of this is their fault.

He forced himself to shake it off.

They had a job to do and that was that.

I'll be careful.

Having never surveilled this building before and with no schematics or photographs to study in advance, Isaacson didn't know if the front and rear entrances were in line or offset. He had no idea about the geometry of the space, or if there was even a lobby at all. This was an apartment building in Luanda, not New York City. Odds were good it didn't even have a lobby, just a first-floor hallway. Isaacson's default protocol for situations like this was for the rear shooter pair to call the breach and enter a split second before the front-door team. Because it was human nature to pay more attention to the front door, if the bad guys did have a lobby sentry team, this breach pattern was more likely to surprise and distract them.

Every millisecond of uncertainty in a firefight gave Ghost squadron an advantage.

"On my mark . . . three . . . two . . . one . . ." Mills said on comms.

Isaacson and Hickman rolled inward, around their respective corners. Hickman kicked the front door in, and Isaacson surged across the threshold, sighting over his SBR. He cleared right and immediately came face-to-face with a masked tango. Call it bad luck or Murphy's Law, the bad guys had indeed posted a pair of sentries in the lobby, and they were hanging out just inside the front door. In a fluid movement, Isaacson juked right and clear of the shooter's barrel line while firing three rapid rounds center mass to drop the surprised warrior without return fire.

The second tango standing on the other side of the hall had whirled to face the back door on hearing Mills and Levitt breach per the plan. Twin muzzle flashes, accompanied by twin suppressed burps, flared as one of them dropped the second shooter with a headshot before he could engage.

In Isaacson's left peripheral vision, Hickman had entered and was clearing left, the western section of the hallway behind Isaacson.

"Clear," Hickman said a heartbeat later.

"Clear," came the call from Mills, who, along with Levitt, was securing the east end of the hallway.

Isaacson stepped forward and visually interrogated the first tango he'd shot. The damage his three 5.56 rounds to the chest had inflicted on the shooter would be fatal, but the man was still alive and moving. When the man's right hand went for his radio, Isaacson put a suppressed round in the dude's forehead.

"Clear," he said, his voice a low growl.

When he looked up, his teammates were coalescing into a defensive formation safeguarding the hallway and awaiting his next order. He spied a sign with a stick figure on stairs located fifteen feet down the hall next to a fire door. He chopped a hand forward and the now four-man assault team moved in a diamond formation toward the stairwell with Levitt in the lead. On reaching the stairwell, Levitt took position to open the door, with Hickman and Isaacson side by side, ready to breach.

Isaacson held up three fingers, then pointed up, reminding his team the target apartment was on the third floor. Mills nodded, swiveled, and dropped into a kneeling firing stance to cover their six.

"Three, two, one, go," Hickman said, and Levitt opened the door.

Hickman and Isaacson surged into the stairwell at an offset stagger. Hickman cleared right while Isaacson cleared vertically, sighting up the switchback staircase. Finding the first flight and landing clear, Isaacson ascended, stepping fast and light, but not skipping treads as he did. On reaching the first switchback landing, he paused, then peeked his head around for a glance.

"Clear," he said, and Hickman surged around him to take the lead and the inside railing track.

Isaacson fell in a stride behind, taking the outside track.

They used this lead-switching, clearing protocol all the way up to the third-floor landing, where they held until Mills and Levitt arrived. Having arrived first, Isaacson squatted behind the door, which was hung for in-swing. He gestured for Mills and Levitt to breach the hall once he pulled the door open.

Expecting resistance, he mouthed, *Stay frosty* to his teammates, who nodded.

Mills counted down the breach.

On the zero beat Isaacson pulled the door open. His fellow operators surged through the gap and disappeared. He'd expected immediate gunfire, but none came. Hickman went next, and finally it was his turn. Savoring the burn in his legs, he pressed up from a squat into a combat crouch and surged across the threshold and into the hallway.

As he did, the song "Wishlist" by Pearl Jam began to play in his brain.

This phenomenon happened to him on most ops and had been

going on for fifteen years. Why this song, he had absolutely no friggin' idea. Maybe it was the repetitive guitar riffs, or the steady, predictable beat, or maybe Eddie Vedder's syncopated, subdued baritone growl . . . Whatever the reason, this song put Isaacson into a weird tactical-flow state. Like a movie soundtrack in his head, his movements hit on the beats and the next measure provided a propulsive fluidity to his combat sequences.

And the lyrics . . . Could they be any more ironic when accompanying a man performing such violence of action?

Isaacson took a knee beside Hickman, sighting east down the clear and quiet hallway.

He felt a tap on his left shoulder and swiveled his head around for a look. Mills pointed to a partially open door, five units down on the right side of the corridor facing west. The hallway location matched the description Ryan had provided of the two-bedroom apartment's position in the building.

Isaacson chopped a hand toward the door.

Showtime.

The four-man team quick-stepped down the corridor with Mills and Levitt in front. On reaching the target apartment, they fell in as pairs bookending the doorway. In Isaacson's head, "Wishlist" continued to play in the background, providing comfort and cadence rather than distraction. Since he and Hickman were on the handle side of the door, they would breach first. As longtime teammates, no discussion was necessary between them about who would clear where. He'd go left, Hickman would go right, and Mills and Levitt would shoot the gap up the middle.

With his gloved left hand, Isaacson gave the silent countdown: *Three . . . two . . . one . . . go.*

Like a coiled viper, he launched his body through the doorway. Fueled by adrenaline and hyperfocus, his brain instantly mapped the room the second he crossed the threshold. He registered zero shooters directly in front of him as he swiveled left to clear his corner, his gaze laser-focused through the targeting reticle of his holographic sight.

Finding it vacant, he swiveled back to front as Hickman cleared right. In his peripheral vision, Levitt and Mills swept up the middle in matching combat crouches. The modest apartment had an open common room with a sofa and TV area to the right and a kitchenette with a small dining table straight ahead. Two doors—one right and one left—almost assuredly led to the two bedrooms.

With the common room secured, Ghost squadron separated back into pairs to clear the bedrooms. His Spidey sense suddenly on fire, Isaacson pulled a flash-bang from his kit, armed it, and lobbed it through the gap in the door of the left-side bedroom. The nonlethal grenade exploded a heartbeat later with a blinding pulse of light and concussive *whump*.

Isaacson, with Hickman a half step behind, charged into the bedroom.

Clearing left, he found a target—a crouching black-clad operator with a rifle—a mere five feet away. With mechanical precision, he placed his green floating dot on the shooter's face and squeezed the trigger. The suppressed round split the target's head, and the body crumpled into a heap against the wall.

Bidirectional gunfire exploded to his right as Hickman engaged a second tango that managed to return fire. Isaacson swiveled, aimed center mass, and delivered two rounds to the shooter's chest. Hickman's round, fired first, had already found its mark—ending the tango's cerebral operations—but not before the shooter managed to get off a shot of his own.

Isaacson watched the body pitch backward, then quickly scanned the rest of the bedroom for additional threats. Seeing none, he quickly entered the small attached bathroom and cleared it, too.

"Clear," he barked.

"Clear," came the call from Mills on comms from the other bedroom.

With the combat finished, he turned and reentered the bedroom, where he saw Hickman looking down at his kit. "Dude, you okay?"

"Took a round to the chest," Hickman said, probing a spot on the upper left chest of his vest. "Not sure if it punched through..."

Isaacson slung his rifle and rushed to his friend and teammate's side. Using his teeth, he yanked off his right glove, then jammed the hand under Hickman's vest to check for blood.

"How's your pain?" he asked as he probed and pressed, watching Hickman's face for a reaction. Over the years, he'd seen plenty of guys get shot with high-velocity rounds. In many of those cases, the operator did not know how badly they'd been wounded. Adrenaline and injury were strange bedfellows.

"Just a little tightness. I think I'm good to go," Hickman said.

Isaacson pulled out his hand and checked his naked fingers, which were wet and crimson. "It punched through."

"Well, that sucks," Hickman said, as if he'd just dropped his ice cream cone instead of being shot in the chest.

"You guys good?" Levitt said, popping his head into the room.

"Hickman took a round to the left chest, just outside his SAPI plate. Gonna need a medevac," Isaacson said, and his brain shifted into overdrive as he prioritized everything that needed to happen. "Grab the backpack. It looks like the computer's in it. Then I want you to photograph these two dudes and meet us at the truck."

"Check," Levitt said and got to work.

Mills, who'd since appeared in the doorway, said, "I'll help you carry him down."

"Dude, I don't need to be carried," Hickman said. "I'm good. I'm in the fight."

"Right now, maybe, but not in five minutes, when you have a hemothorax and your lung is filled with blood," said Mills, who was an 18 Delta combat medic back in his active-duty SOF days. He looked at Isaacson. "We need to get him to Josina Machel Hospital ASAP."

"Whoa, are you *trying* to kill me?" Hickman asked. "Hell no. I'd rather have Mills operate on me in the truck than go there."

Isaacson ignored the comment and looked from Hickman—who was beginning to go pale—to Mills. "Is there an elevator in this building?"

Mills shook his head. "Didn't see one."

"I'll help him down the stairs, you lead and cover," Isaacson said.

"Check," Mills said.

"Ghost sitrep?" Tejada's voice said in Isaacson's ear.

"Bullpen, Ghost—target apartment secured. Four tangos KIA, but we have one urgent surgical."

"One, this is Bullpen Actual," Freddy Vincent's voice said. "We saw. Already working a helo medevac option from the embassy to Kinshasa, where there's a task force FST and a jet to take them to the next-level care."

"Copy all," Isaacson said, feeling a small measure of relief.

"Long flight, boss," Mills said, his voice serious.

"Too long?" Isaacson asked.

Mills gave Hickman a tight smile, but they were all professionals here.

"By the time we get to the embassy we'll know," the medic

said. "If he's still stable, he can probably go with just a chest tube. If not, that means he's bleeding in his chest, and we go to Josina."

"Fuck that," Hickman said.

"We got ya, bro," Isaacson said, the fear in Hickman's voice unmistakable. "You're gonna be fine either way."

It was situations like this why he wore the body camera. Freddy and JT had seen and heard the entire exchange; they were already working a plan in parallel to his own actions.

"What about Waddle?" Hickman said. "We can't just leave him. I'll be fine in the truck."

"Waddle is already dead, bro. You're not. But you will be if we fuck around here much longer. After we get you airborne, we'll come back for Waddle." He circled behind Hickman and hooked the operator's right arm over his shoulders. "Now stop arguing and do as I say."

Hickman grumbled something, but he did as ordered and leaned on Isaacson.

Levitt, who'd been busy working while the plan coalesced, said, "Got the photos, computer, and the backpack."

"Perfect timing. We're out of here," Isaacson said.

With his mind full of unanswered questions and his friend's life literally in his hands, CIA ground branch team leader Daryl Isaacson led his team out of the apartment building toward safety. Whatever group had targeted Ryan's unit had somehow managed to deal yet another blow to team America.

Teeth gritted, he made a silent vow:

Whatever it takes, I'm going to find out who did this and make them pay.

9

MILK & HONEY SOUTHERN-INSPIRED KITCHEN
4531 TELFAIR BOULEVARD
CAMP SPRINGS, MARYLAND
0917 LOCAL TIME

Katie stared at the laminated menu, torn between a half dozen decadent-sounding options in the brunch section. Across the table, her older sister, Sally, sat sipping her water and waiting patiently for Katie to make up her mind.

"What are you thinking?" Sally asked, a polite nudge, since Katie had already told the server once that they needed more time.

"I'm torn between the cheesecake flapjacks with fruit or maybe the jumbo smothered chicken and biscuits, but . . . I'm also thinking about the kale and watermelon salad with grilled chicken."

Sally laughed.

"What's so funny?" Katie asked, looking up.

"You."

"Me?"

"Yes, you," Sally said, grinning large. "You didn't pick this place so you could have a kale salad. You picked it for the good stuff. So, order something you actually want to eat."

"I know," Katie said with feigned exasperation and put down the menu, "but if I do, I'm going to feel guilty all day."

Sally reached out and patted the top of Katie's hand. "Oh, sweetie, you haven't changed a bit."

"Well, what are you getting?"

"The Wharf Scramble."

Katie found it on the menu. "Oh, Sally, that's healthy. Now I have to get the salad."

"It's not *that* healthy," Sally said, which was true. "Tell you what, I'll switch. I'll get the cheesecake flapjacks, you get the smothered chicken and biscuits, and we'll share."

"Really?" Katie said, perking up.

"Absolutely. It's not every day I get to have brunch with my little sis," Sally said. "Eating out is supposed to be fun, not a chore. This can be a cheat day for both of us."

"Perfect," Katie said, loving Sally for being so cool. Then her brain-to-mouth filter glitched and she said, "Don't take this the wrong way, but I feel like you've definitely become more relaxed and chill since you became a mom."

Sally looked taken aback for a moment.

Katie grimaced. "I'm sorry. I didn't mean it like it sounded."

Sally's expression softened and she chuckled. "Yeah, that's something I've been working on . . . I guess becoming a mom changes your perspective on what's really important and what's not."

Katie nodded. Sally had, for as long as Katie could remember, checked all the first-born stereotypes: type A personality, highly motivated go-getter, perfectionist, and parent pleaser. She'd followed in their mom's footsteps, becoming a doctor and going into pediatric surgery. She'd been the first and only Ryan sibling to get married and have children, something that Katie knew pleased her parents immensely. Mom was always gushing over little Genevieve, the newest member of the Ryan family.

Well, she's technically a Kartal, the administrator in Katie's head said, since Sally had given up her maiden name to take Davi's family name as her own.

"Yeah, I can see how becoming a mom could do that," Katie said, returning to the conversation.

For everyone else on the planet, having a kid would increase their stress ten times, she thought with a grin. *I guess for "Stressed-out Sally," the only way to go was down.*

"What are you grinning at?" Sally asked, but the arrival of the server saved Katie from having to confess her and Kyle's secret nickname for their big sis growing up.

After ordering the entrées and getting their coffees and waters topped off, they picked the conversation back up.

"Speaking of relationships and having kids, Mom tells me you're seeing someone," Sally said with an impish smile.

Katie felt her cheeks blush, her mind going back to her wonderful evening with Dennis. Her stomach fluttered like a teenager with a crush. "Oh, she did, huh? What did she say?"

"That his name is Dennis, he's a naval officer, and that Dad supposedly had him vetted by Mary Pat before letting him come to the house."

Katie rolled her eyes. "All true, except I'm still not sure if the ODNI vetting thing is real or if that was Dad just trying to be funny."

"Either one is plausible," Sally said with a laugh. Her phone—which was sitting screen side up—dinged with a new text message notification. She shifted her gaze to read it, then returned her attention back to Katie.

"Everything okay?" Katie asked.

"Yeah. I'm on call, so I have to be available, but this is something I can handle later."

"Do you like being a doctor?" Katie asked, realizing she'd never asked her sister that before.

Sally nodded. "I'm a surgeon, but yeah, I do . . . I like helping people, especially kids."

"It's pretty cool what you do. I've never told you that before, but it's true."

"Thanks . . . Pediatric surgery is rewarding, but it can also be difficult when something goes wrong," Sally said, and the look on her face suddenly turned haunted, as she stared off into the middle distance. She snapped out of it a moment later and said, "But I'm not letting you change the subject, you sneak—I want to hear about Dennis."

Katie squirmed in her seat. "Sure, he's the XO on the *Blackfish*, er, the USS *Washington*."

"That's a submarine, right?"

"Yeah. A Virginia-class fast-attack submarine stationed in Norfolk."

Sally's eyes narrowed as she searched her memory. "Virginia class—that's the kind that sneaks around and carries nuclear missiles, right?"

Katie shook her head. "Well, they definitely sneak around, but they don't carry nuclear missiles. You're thinking of the other kind of submarine—the SSBN—which the Navy calls 'boomers.' The kind of submarine that Dennis is on can carry missiles, but not the nuclear kind."

Sally nodded. "Is it dangerous—what he does?"

Flashbulb memories of standing on the conn of the *Blackfish* while in a torpedo battle with the Russian submarine *Belgorod*, fighting a fire, and almost sinking below crush depth paraded before her mind's eye. "It can be, I suppose," she said, forcing a pleasant smile onto her face, "but under normal circumstances, submarine operations are very safe."

"Mm-hmm," Sally said with a skeptical eyebrow that reminded Katie of Dad. Sally might be a Kartal in name, but she was still a Ryan by blood.

"Anyhoo," Katie said, "I really can't talk too much about what he does. They call it the silent service for a reason."

"I know, I know . . . it's classified. The Ryan family motto," Sally said. "But that's not what I'm asking about anyway. I don't care what he does underwater, I want to know about your relationship. Spill the tea, sis . . . What's he like?"

If she was blushing before, now her cheeks were on fire. "Well, he's funny and smart—ridiculously smart, actually—and you know, I think he's hot . . . Even though he could definitely use a tan."

"I'm assuming pasty white comes with the job? I can't imagine they get a lot of sun underwater."

They both smiled at this.

"Yeah, we were joking about it the other day. Dennis said he put a request in with the captain to have a tanning bed installed in the torpedo room, but the skipper shot it down."

"And you said Dennis is the XO?" Sally said. "Remind me what that is again."

"XO stands for executive officer, which means he's second in command below the CO, or commanding officer."

"So, what happens next, he gets promoted to be the captain when the current captain's assignment is finished?"

"Not exactly. After he finishes his XO tour, he'll have a shore-based assignment, and, assuming he screens for command, he'll start the pipeline to become a captain of a submarine himself."

"But not the *Washington?*"

"No, probably not. It's almost always a different sub."

"Do you think he'll become a captain?"

"Dennis? Oh yeah, most definitely." She smiled, remembering him in action and how calm and collected under pressure he was. She crossed her fingers and held them up. "He's waiting to hear if he made the cut . . . Fingers crossed."

"So, are you guys pretty serious? I mean, what happens if he gets assigned to a submarine in, say, Hawaii?"

Katie sighed. That was the buzzkill topic she preferred not to think about. "I don't know. I guess we'll cross that bridge if and when we come to it."

She and Dennis had danced around that very conversation at dinner, in fact. Neither one wanted to bring it up, but it was there. She supposed that meant that they might be getting serious, but her sister was right to ask the question. Was it really even possible that they could make this work with her in the ONI and him deploying constantly on secret submarine missions? There were plenty of families that made the sacrifice of service work, but their situation might just be next-level.

"So, it's not that serious between you guys?" Sally asked, as if taking a cue from Katie's internal monologue.

"I don't know," she said, her tone more defensive than she intended. "I mean, I like him, but it's hard because we both love our jobs. Relationships in the Navy are complicated."

"I get it," Sally said, eyes down, then she grinned and met Katie's eyes. "I'm just excited for you, that's all. I've only met Dennis that one time, but he seemed pretty cool. And Davi and I would loooove for Genevieve to have a little cousin to play with."

Katie swatted away the comment. "Whoa, we are light-years away from the cousin-making department."

"I'm just sayin' . . . Mom and Dad would love another grandbaby."

Thank God the server arrived with their meals, which ended the baby-making discussion.

"Wow, this looks amazing," Katie said, gazing at the homestyle feast of epic proportions laid down in front of them. "How do you want to do this—each eat half and swap plates or divvy up and share halves now?"

"I'm definitely in the divvy-up-and-share-now camp."

"Me too," she said, and they got to work dividing the entrées.

"Have you heard from Kyle lately?" Sally asked as she slid half the stack of pancakes from her plate onto Katie's.

"Not lately," Katie said. "You?"

Sally screwed up her face at the question. "Are you kidding me? Little bro has never once reached out to me. I'm lucky if I get a hug from him at Christmas."

Katie gve a knowing half smile. If dictionaries had pictures, the word *insular* would have Kyle's headshot beside it. "That's just Kyle."

Sally paused mid-bite, holding her fork in the air with a hunk of pancake and peach quivering on the tines. "You know what, it just occurred to me . . . I don't even know what he does in the Navy. Does he work at the ONI with you?"

Katie shook her head.

The truth was, *she* didn't know what Kyle did in the Navy or what group he was with these days.

And I have TS/SCI security clearance, and Dad is the President, for God's sake.

The last professional intersection she'd had with Kyle was when he was working TAD at Task Force 59 and shuttled some critical information her way. But even then, it had all been digital and they'd not actually spoken. She knew Kyle was doing something tech- and cyber-related, but nothing more. This wasn't surprising because Ryans had a knack for worming their way into highly compartmentalized assignments—so compartmentalized that the other Ryans didn't or couldn't know about their work. This always made for interesting conversations during holiday get-togethers—full of innuendos, cryptic questions and replies, and lots of winks and nods. If someone had "Covert Lingo Bingo" cards, then the Ryan family dinner table was the ultimate place to play.

"But don't you have, like, super-duper top secret clearance?" Sally pressed.

Katie bobbed her head from side to side. "Yes, but that's not how it works. Everything in the intelligence, cyber, and covert operations spheres is highly compartmentalized."

"But you *do* know what he does, right?"

"I swear, in this case, I really don't."

"Assuming I believed you, answer this," Sally said, pressing. "If you *did* know, would you tell me?"

"No," Katie said and stuffed a big bite of chicken and biscuit in her mouth.

Sally let out an exasperated groan. "You're just as annoying as Dad."

"So, I've been told."

The rest of the brunch zipped by in a flash with the conversation shifting to Genevieve and all things baby. Sally picked up the check, despite Katie's protests, and they parted ways with a big sisterly hug.

Feeling overstuffed, Katie walked the parking lot to her Grand Cherokee and climbed into the driver's seat wishing she'd ordered the kale and watermelon salad. She was so bloated, she unbuttoned the top button of her trousers . . . But both entrées had been delicious.

"Trade-offs," she mumbled with a smile as she flipped down the visor to check for food in her teeth using the vanity mirror.

Seeing none, she freshened her lip balm, flipped up the visor, and started the Jeep's engine. Brunch had been Sally's idea, which had taken Katie entirely by surprise. Kyle wasn't the only Ryan who was too buried in work to connect with family. For years, Sally had been persona non grata. During med school, her residency, and the beginning of her practice, she was way too busy to hang out. Katie totally got it and never begrudged her sister for that. Hell, she never begrudged anyone for chasing their dreams, but the effort her big sis had made to connect felt good. The age gap between them had always made it a challenge for Katie to bond with Sally during their youth. Now, as adults, it didn't matter.

I finally have a big sister.

She synched her iPhone to the vehicle's infotainment system, put the transmission in drive, and pulled out of the parking lot. She had decided to swing by work and check in on the high-side feed, maybe circling back to whatever had happened in Angola. It had been gnawing at her since last night. She had a few hours to get a deeper dive in before she would meet up with Dennis again. They were going to do the D.C. thing for a couple of hours before an early dinner and then something special he had planned—a surprise, despite her reminding him she wasn't a fan of surprises. She hadn't made it a quarter mile down the road before the phone rang. The caller ID indicated it was her boss, Captain Ferguson, calling from the National Maritime Intelligence Center. She took the call on speaker, hands-free.

"Commander Ryan," she said.

"Katie, it's Russ," Ferguson said. "I need you to come in."

"Well, sir, as luck would have it, I'm on my way as we speak," she said.

She'd not chosen Milk & Honey for brunch by accident, as it was located less than five miles from the office. Like every member of the Ryan clan, she was a workaholic and went in most weekends for at least half days.

"Okay, good," he said, but his tone didn't *sound* good.

"Did something happen?" she asked, her already unsettled stomach going tense.

"Not over the phone. I'll fill you in when you get here."

"Roger that, sir," she said.

"Find me in the SCIF," he said and ended the call.

"Well, that answers that question," she said with a shrug and steeled herself for whatever flying-monkey circus she was about to get thrown into next. Whatever it was, she silently hoped it didn't mean missing out on whatever it was Dennis had planned.

10

U.S. EMBASSY MISSION IN ANGOLA
R. HOUARI BOUMEDIENE 32
LUANDA, ANGOLA
1634 LOCAL TIME

Kyle felt out of place for so many reasons as he stood inside the doors of the loading dock at the rear of the American embassy building. One reason was that this solemn moment called for him to be attired in something more than just blue jeans and a long-sleeve Under Armour T-shirt. He would have given anything to be standing at parade rest in Navy summer whites in this moment. It wasn't the first time he'd missed the uniform in the few months since he'd left the Navy, but it was by far the most intense. For most of his life, Kyle had felt out of place among his peers, but that had disappeared when he had matriculated to the United States Naval Academy. Sure, he still didn't socialize quite the same as most of his classmates—something he knew his parents thought he was oblivious to, but he wasn't. It had never been that he lacked the ability to form close friendships. Instead, what he lacked was the motivation to put in the considerable amount of effort to make them work. But at the Academy, things had been different. Kyle knew a lot of people, maybe even his sister Katie—he'd never asked—who loved the prestige of having attended the Academy, but found the rote and structure and ceremonial customs oppressive. For Kyle, those had been the things that felt the most liberating. He had loved every moment of being at the Naval Academy. Even the rigor of plebe summer had been worth the pain for the instant feeling of inclusion. At the Academy, he was part of a community joined by shared purpose and shared commitments. It had removed much of the stress he always felt outside of the Navy. He didn't need to worry about if his clothing choices were outdated or quirky—everyone proudly wore the uniform that represented their shared life's journey.

Since leaving the Navy to join the cyberwarfare task force run by the DIA, he'd lost much of that. He felt like an outsider once again, not quite part of the spook community. He lost the sense of brotherhood that he cherished in uniform—something that would probably surprise most who knew him, including his family.

"You okay, Ryan?" He turned to see the embassy RSO, Julio Tejada, standing beside him, hands clasped in front of him.

Kyle glanced again at the two flag-draped metal coffins that waited by the closed roll-up door at the back of the loading dock. Then he clenched his jaw and let out a long, slow breath.

"I'm good, thank you," he said softly.

"We can give you a few minutes alone, if you need it. Sometimes it helps to—you know—say goodbye in private," Tejada said.

"No," Kyle said, feeling uncomfortable suddenly. "That won't be necessary."

He did close his eyes for a moment, though, intending to say a short prayer. Then, when nothing from the litany of memorized prayers from his youth came to him, he simply mouthed, *I'm sorry*, and opened his eyes again.

"Lieutenant Ryan?" a soft woman's voice asked, and he turned around, immediately recognizing the woman from his briefings back in Virginia.

"Madame Ambassador," he said with a nod. "And I'm not a lieutenant anymore, it's just Kyle now, ma'am. I'm so sorry for all the trouble . . ."

Suddenly and unexpectedly he felt, to his horror, tears well up in his eyes. He clenched his jaw and quickly blinked them away.

"That is not at all how we feel, Kyle," she said gently. For a moment she reminded Kyle of a younger version of his mom for some reason, though Ambassador Gonçalves looked nothing at all like her. "We are sorry for your loss."

He didn't know what to say, having never even imagined himself in such a moment, so he just turned back to the flag-draped caskets as Tejada moved toward the garage door, joined by Daryl Isaacson and his teammates Mills and Levitt. Tejada pressed a button beside the door, and it began to rattle up on the track.

As his eyes adjusted to the sudden intrusion of sunlight, he saw two black Chevy Suburban SUVs backed up to the loading dock, rear-hatch doors open and rear seats folded down to receive his friends. And in that moment, he realized that's what Bryce Waddle and Kevin Cockburn had been—friends. They had been DIA teammates, to be sure. But Kyle realized now that they felt like so much more. He brushed away the fresh tear that spilled out onto his left cheek with the back of his hand and shuffled forward to join Isaacson, Mills, and Levitt at the door. As he did, Freddy Vincent, the CIA station chief, appeared from behind him with two United States Marines in tow, both in tightly-squared-away

MARPATs, the camouflage sleeves rolled perfectly over their biceps.

Kyle joined the ground branch team at the casket to the left, squatting to take the handrail at the right rear corner as Vincent, Tejada, and the two Marines mirrored them on the other side. It suddenly occurred to Kyle that he didn't have any idea whose body was in which casket. His brain reassured him that it didn't matter at all, but for some reason not knowing suddenly filled him with terrible anxiety. Kyle could feel his pulse pounding in his temples and he squatted in formation with the ground branch operators and prepared to lift the body of his teammate—whichever one it was. His brain argued in confusion with his heart over why he suddenly trembled with uncertainty.

Then his mom's voice came to him in his head. Just as when he was a child, she reassured him that everything was okay. Cockburn and Waddle knew he was there, that he was with them, and that was all that mattered.

As they raised the casket and began to move toward the loading dock, his brain assured him that the thought was nothing more than the retrieval of processed and stored information based on synaptic connections that were both formed and strengthened as the memories of his mother were developed from short- to long-term memories. In this case, the emotional context added an additional layer to the memory, meaning it had long since moved out of the hippocampus.

Still, in this moment, Kyle ignored the reasoning and just let the memory of his mother soothe his anxiety as he crouched behind Isaacson at the lip of the loading dock. The operator stepped into the bed of the truck, squatting low, and helped slide the casket forward as Kyle and Levitt fed it to him and Mills.

Kyle decided, completely irrationally, that the casket contained the body of Bryce Waddle. Rationally he knew that there was no way he could know if that was true and that his cerebral cortex simply invented that to calm the emotions firing off in his limbic system. But for now he didn't care. He'd liked both men, but had felt closer to Waddle for some reason.

He stood now, having passed the last rail to Isaacson. The operator shuffled out of the back of the Suburban and rose beside him.

Somehow, gratefully, the man seemed to know it was better to say nothing.

Kyle turned robotically and headed toward the door at the other end of the large storage room.

"Hey, Ryan," Isaacson called after him, and Kyle turned and faced him.

"Yes?"

"We'll find out who is responsible for this," the CIA operator said, fire in his eyes. "And when we do, we will find them and make them pay."

"Yes," Kyle said simply. "I know we will."

If he knew anything at all about his dad, the man who wore another hat as the President of the United States, it was that President Ryan would do everything in his power to make sure that was true.

"Thank you," he added as the memory of his mother returned. She had always been the best at helping him normalize his responses in these difficult interpersonal situations.

The CIA man nodded and Kyle went out the door. He needed to touch base with his boss back in Virginia and find out what was next for him.

11

OFFICE OF NAVAL INTELLIGENCE (ONI)
NATIONAL MARITIME INTELLIGENCE CENTER (NMIC)
4251 SUITLAND ROAD, WASHINGTON, D.C.
1041 LOCAL TIME

The drive from Milk & Honey to the NMIC took Katie only fifteen minutes, but in relative time it felt like an hour. She hated knowing that something big had happened but not being read in on what that big thing was. She knew it was something big because otherwise Ferguson wouldn't have called her in. Just the other day, he'd chastised her for being a workaholic and encouraged her to stop burning the midnight oil and working weekends. But she couldn't help herself. The intelligence business was like a drug. Maybe for some people ignorance was bliss, but not for her. She was a Ryan and "need to know" was coded into her DNA.

God bless everyone in the world who doesn't have a security clearance, she thought with a chuckle. *I couldn't make it through a single day.*

Just stepping inside the NMIC lowered her blood pressure,

which was most certainly the opposite biological response for everyone else who worked there. She loved her job and actually preferred being in the office. She recognized a few familiar faces—other weekend warriors—and exchanged waves as she jogged to Captain Ferguson's office. When she arrived, she looked through the glass window and saw her boss at his "duty station"—the little round table he preferred to work at instead of his desk—with two laptops open and what looked like two cups of coffee.

She knocked on the doorframe.

He looked up and waved her in.

"Open or closed?" she said, pausing as she crossed the threshold.

"Open's fine," he said. "Have a seat."

On hearing this she deflated a little because "open door" meant the situation was not particularly sensitive.

"On your second cup already, huh?" she said, nodding at his twin coffees.

"Technically, I'm still on my first cup," he said with a grimace. "Ruined the first one by accidently using the hazelnut-flavored creamer. Do you like hazelnut, Ryan?"

She shrugged. "Not my go-to, but it's fine, I guess."

"I think it tastes disgusting. Hazelnut and rye bread—if both those things were banished from existence the world would be a better place for it," he said, chuckling.

"But if you banish rye bread, then what happens to Reuben sandwiches?"

"I don't eat Reuben sandwiches."

"Are you kidding me? A nice toasted, melty Reuban, dripping with every bite—it's heaven."

"They're an abomination, the Frankenstein's monster of sandwiches. Every ingredient in a Reuben is weird—corned beef, sauerkraut, rye bread, Swiss cheese, Russian dressing. Seriously, only a mad scientist would mix these things together."

"I guess I see what you mean . . . But Swiss cheese? What can you possibly have against Swiss cheese?"

He shook his head; he was a man who would not be swayed. "It tastes weird. Tangy and stale . . . Anyway, I didn't call you in to talk about sandwiches, Ryan."

"Yeah, I know, sorry," she said, leaning in. "What's going on?"

"There's been an incident in Angola," he said.

"What kind of incident?" she asked, and immediately thought of the high-side brief she had skipped reading in favor of meeting up with her crush, Dennis Knepper. The thought filled her with regret, but she wasn't sure why. Then that thought made her think of the plans they'd made to hang out on the D.C. Mall that now seemed likely to be put on hold.

"I sent you everything on your high side to review, but the long and short of it is that the DIA had a small cyber team operating covertly in Luanda. That team was targeted by a hit squad and two of the three members were murdered."

She blew air through her teeth. "And the third member?"

"Escaped to the embassy."

"Do we know who's responsible for the hit?"

"No, and that's where you come in," Ferguson said with a closed-lip smile. "I'd like you to do your thing on this one and see where it takes you."

She screwed up her face at him. "*Do my thing?* What exactly do you mean by that, sir?"

He chuckled. "What I mean is, I want you to do what you do best—find the relevant bunny hole and dive in headfirst like you can't help but do. Instead of trying to corral you in, Ryan, I'm giving you free rein to run wild. The CIA and DIA are certainly going to do their own independent investigations and offer their assessments, which will be routed to the DNI, but Admiral Kohler and I want to see what you can dig up. The DIA are our military brothers and sisters—the intelligence community outside of the ODNI and part of DoD. This is our lane more than theirs. You have a knack for looking outside the box, so put that skill to work."

"Don't you mean *thinking* outside the box, sir?"

"No," he said with a grin. "I meant it how I said it."

He picked up his coffee, took a sip, then screwed up his face and spit it back into the cup. "Damn it, that was the wrong one," he growled, shoving it away and out of reach.

She smiled, unable to help herself.

He grabbed the other paper cup and took a swig from it.

"Better?" she said.

"Much."

"Is there anything else, sir?" she said, preemptively scooting her chair back from the table.

"No, that's it for now."

She picked up the hazelnut-contaminated coffee from his desk. With a wry grin, she said, "I'll throw this out for you, sir."

"Thanks," he said, grinning back.

On her way to her office, she detoured to the break room to dump Ferguson's coffee and make herself a cup. As it brewed, she sent a quick text to Dennis, letting him know she'd been called into the office and might be running late. He replied with a thumbs-up and then a heart emoji, which made her smile and, for some reason, blush.

Five minutes later she was in her office, where she greeted her yellow-petaled orchid—which she'd named Josie—and got to work. As was typical for her, time evaporated as she familiarized herself with the sub-Saharan West African nation of Angola.

Known for its natural resources, especially oil and diamonds, Angola was a Portuguese colony until 1975. Following its hard-fought independence, the country tumbled into a bloody civil war that lasted twenty-five years. In the decades since, the prevailing MPLA (Popular Movement for the Liberation of Angola) party had tried to manage the human toll of war—an estimated half million dead and a million others displaced—while simultaneously working to rebuild its infrastructure. Like so many African nations, Angola was characterized by high levels of poverty and inequality, with wealth and power concentrated among a small number of connected elite.

One of the interesting details that caught Katie's eye was that the MPLA was originally formed as a Marxist-Leninist party and received substantial support from the Soviet Union in the form of weapons, training, and financial assistance. This was not unusual during the Cold War era, when the USSR worked diligently to expand its influence in Africa and Central America by backing leftist movements. Also not surprising, she learned that the United States had backed the National Union for the Total Independence of Angola (UNITA) and its unsuccessful effort to unseat the MPLA from power in the civil war. In the two decades since the brokered peace, UNITA transitioned from a military party to a political one—abandoning violence for civil action. While a democracy on paper, the hard reality was that the MPLA government employed all manner of authoritarian practices to maintain control.

Angola's current president, Francisco Luemba, espoused himself as an anti-corruption crusader, but he was not afraid to embrace his inner dictator when it suited him. Katie stared at a photograph of the man walking down a row of Angolan soldiers standing at attention in their forest-green dress uniforms. Luemba looked both regal and smug, something that the rich and powerful worldwide seemed to have an undeniable knack for. The third president since the civil war, Luemba had been in power for nearly nine years. Despite his authoritarian leanings, he had made demonstrable strides in bolstering the economy and modernizing the country through a major infrastructure-development campaign.

Instead of looking west to the U.S. for aid and foreign direct investment, Luemba had turned east to Communist China. From the facts and figures she had available, she estimated Angola had received upward of twenty-five *billion* in foreign direct investment via China's Belt and Road Initiative. She made a list and categorized Angola's BRI projects into one of five categories: energy, transportation and logistics, telecommunications, residential and commercial construction, and the creation of special economic zones to spur growth of industrial parks. To offset what the FDI required for such a sweeping and multi-disciplined tsunami of activity, the Angolan government had assumed debt upward of twenty billion, with repayment structured around future oil sales. This arrangement created a close link between Angola's oil and gas reserves and its ability to service its debt to China.

Katie leaned back in her chair and stretched, glancing at the time in the corner of her computer screen and only mildly surprised that hours had passed as she searched and collated her intelligence information on Angola. She reached for her phone to send Dennis a message that she wasn't going to have to bail on their plans after all. Just as she picked it up, it chimed and the screen lit up, revealing two messages—one just incoming and the other from an hour ago.

> Save the world, girl.
> If you finish in time, we can meet for dinner instead.
> If not, looking forward to tomorrow.

She smiled, though the thought of brunch at her parents' tomorrow gave her a twinge of anxiety. This would be the first time she'd ever invited a guy to the "family brunch," but she'd done it without thinking through the subtext of the invite. Was that strange? Her relationship with Dennis was becoming something... Exactly what, she wasn't sure. She really liked him, and her conversation with Sally had her wondering if they had a future, and what that future could be.

She sent him a thumbs-up and a blue heart emoji, then dove back into her work.

Having educated herself on the geopolitical basics, she spent the next several hours doing exactly what Ferguson had asked her to do... looking for rabbit holes. One particular project caught her eye—the Port of Lobito Modernization and Expansion Initiative. Unlike all the other BRI initiatives, which had splashy, self-congratulatory press releases and propaganda articles in Angolan and Chinese media outlets, the Port Lobito project did not.

As the old saying went, the silence was deafening.

"What are you guys up to?" she murmured as she began to profile the port.

Situated in the Benguela Province, Porto do Lobito was the second largest seaport in Angola. Geographically speaking, Lobito was strategically located in the center of the Angolan coast just over three hundred miles south of the northern capital of Luanda, allowing it to service the central and southern regions for the export of minerals and agricultural products. More interesting, however, the average depth of Lobito Bay was between forty-five to sixty-five feet, making it suitable for handling deep-draft vessels, including bulk carriers, ULCVs, and . . .

Warships.

The thought might not have occurred to her had it not been for a particular statement made by the commander of the People's Liberation Army Navy, Admiral Jun Wong, in an interview he'd given two weeks after the Operation Sea Serpent incident, where the U.S. Navy had helped defuse and narrowly stave off a Chinese invasion of Taiwan. When asked by a *China Daily* reporter how he felt about the United States operating so aggressively in the East and South China Seas, Wong had responded:

"The Americans believe they own the world and so they patrol our oceans and seas with impunity. Very soon, our submarines and warships will challenge them for hegemony from forward operating bases around the world."

The comment had burned itself in her brain—not just the bravado, but the specific phraseology.

"'Very soon, our submarines and warships will challenge them for hegemony from forward operating bases around the world . . .'" she said, repeating it from memory as she entered the latitude and longitude for Porto do Lobito into the search field for ONI's database of satellite imagery.

Was she trying to find meaning and nuance where there wasn't any, or had the admiral accidentally tipped his hand? In this boast, he'd put a stake in the ground by declaring China's intention to build forward operating bases. Right now, they only had one, the PLA Support Base in Djibouti, which was located at the confluence of the Red Sea and the Gulf of Aden on the other side of the continent.

"I wonder . . ." she mumbled as she dug into the satellite imagery looking for clues.

Zooming and scanning, she methodically worked her way through dozens of images until she found what she was looking for.

"Gotcha," she said triumphantly.

She took a screen capture of the zoomed image—five Chinese men in uniform being given a tour of what looked like a new series of berths being built on the mainland side of Lobito Bay, formed by the peninsula that stretched out like a long, pointy finger from south of the port city. She indexed through all the imagery from that satellite pass and took multiple screen captures of the delegation as they were led around the construction zone. Based on the time stamps, the official tour of the future forward operating base lasted about twenty minutes.

With a heavy exhale, she leaned back in her chair and stared at the final image on her monitor—a snapshot frozen in time of one of the Chinese PLAN officers pointing east.

"So, you want access to the Atlantic," she said, talking to herself, "and Porto do Lobito is how you intend to get it."

She settled in to hunt for confirming data, knowing that Dennis—a submariner who often deployed for weeks or months on short notice—would understand that duty called.

Besides, she thought with a smile, *I'll get to see him tomorrow.*

12

PATRIOTIC FRONT FOR UNITY (PFU)
SAFE HOUSE AND COMMAND CENTER
RUA DR. LUÍS PINTO DA FONSECA
LUANDA, ANGOLA
2231 LOCAL TIME

Victor Baptista frowned at the kneeling man begging for his life.

"Kalemba swore he had everything under control," said Baptista's soon-to-be-retired urban operations lieutenant.

"But everything wasn't under control was it, Armen? The Americans sent a CIA ground branch team to investigate," he said, the iron sights of his Beretta 92 fixed and unwavering on Armen's forehead.

Armen shook and began to whimper. "But how was I supposed to—"

Baptista pulled the trigger.

The pistol roared and flashed fire as he executed the weak and worthless sack of human garbage. Armen's eyes went wide with surprise, and his head jerked back as the round punched a hole through his skull. The body remained upright for a full second before falling to the side in a heap on the plastic tarp.

Baptista shifted his attention to a second man, who was also kneeling in the middle of a plastic tarp. "What do you have to say for yourself, Pedro?"

Pedro Oliveira was relatively new to the movement, having joined within the last year. Baptista knew most everyone who worked for him by name—remembering names and faces was a gift he'd had since he was a child.

The underling, who was shaking uncontrollably, somehow managed to speak. "I will do better next time, Mr. Baptista. I swear . . . I will not fail you again."

Oliveira did not deserve to die for his role in last night's failure, but in West Africa fear was a prerequisite for being respected. To successfully pull off the coup he was about to undertake, Baptista needed absolute loyalty from the rank and file.

He needed men who were willing to die for him.

However . . .

Mercy and benevolence were an equally important part of the leadership equation. Which was why he had decided that Pedro would be allowed to live.

"I believe you, Pedro, which is why I will give you a second chance. But fail me again, and you will find yourself back in this basement." He bent forward at the waist, his forehead nearly touching the young man, who reeked of sweat and fear. "Except next time you'll be kneeling where Armen was. Do you understand me?"

"Yes, yes, thank you, Mr. Baptista, thank you," Pedro blathered. "I promise you won't regret it."

"And I'm going to hold you to that promise," he said, and with all eyes on him, he used the decocker to safe the Beretta.

"Clean up the mess and burn the body," Baptista said, turning to his lead enforcer, Jorge Cardosa.

"Yeah, boss," Cardosa said.

Baptista holstered his weapon in the black leather shoulder rig he always wore and headed for the stairs leading up and out of the basement. He'd spent the past twenty-three years imagining this day and the last eight years planning it. Like so many of his brothers who filled the upper-echelon ranks of the Patriotic Front for Unity, Baptista was former UNITA. And like his brothers, he harbored a deep and festering resentment for the United States of America. He despised American diplomats, but he loathed the Central Intelligence Agency most of all.

Liars and manipulators, every last one of them.

UNITA had been closer than anyone realized to ousting the MPLA and seizing control of the country in 2001. Had that happened, Baptista would already be prime minister—a position dissolved under the Angolan president in 2015 in favor of a cheap imitation of American political structure. But no . . . America abandoned UNITA in its moment of greatest need after their leader was killed in combat. Baptista attempted to rally the ranks in Jonas's absence, but the CIA did not back Baptista's bid for power.

"Our priorities have changed," the then American CIA station chief had explained to Baptista with false humility. "We're fighting the war on terror now. Iraq and Afghanistan—that's where the administration intends to focus its resources and attention. I'm sorry, Victor. I really am."

It had taken Baptista the next two decades to consolidate power, form the PFU, build his war chest, and grow his ranks. The coup to seize control of the government and oust Luemba would be dangerous and bloody, but Baptista knew his plan was perfect. He'd considered every move and countermove. He had dozens of spies and agents inside the government, military, and police force on his payroll who would undermine and degrade Luemba's response. But most important, he had Chinese reassurance that they would not intervene . . . provided he agreed to honor and continue all BRI projects signed under the Luemba administration *and* guarantee China exclusive rights to mine rare earth minerals in Angola. He had formed a valuable relationship with the deputy Chinese ambassador to Angola, cultivating it over time based on their mutual adversary—the Americans. When he had shared his vision with Deputy Ambassador Sima, whom he knew, of course, was almost certainly Ministry of State Security (MSS) rather than any kind of diplomat, the response had been favorable. China would need to keep their hands clean, he had been told, and could not provide direct resources. What they could provide, however, was money in exchange for financial guarantees that would keep American interests out of Angola—something Luemba would never agree to, preferring instead to leverage the Chinese-American competition to his advantage. If Baptista promised to do no business with America on mineral rights and other things, Baptista's new government would receive far more investment. And, in the meantime, Sima had promised that his government would do nothing.

Which was exactly what Baptista needed from them. No response militarily. No international outrage. No condemnation. China promising to do nothing was of great value to Baptista and meant that taking over the government would have long-term viability.

He'd agreed unconditionally. In exchange for the presidency, he would promise almost anything.

Once I'm in power, then I can reevaluate all options.

He exited the stairwell and walked to the operations center, where he would personally oversee today's kickoff operation. Seizure of the American embassy was the first step to creating chaos and destabilizing the capital city. With Luemba distracted and his military and police forces dispatched to Embassy Row, Baptista's main army would then seize control of the Palácio Presidencial—the Presidential Palace.

The timing of this had been meticulously choreographed by Baptista. Luemba would be addressing the National Assembly at the National Assembly Palace, the new complex that had housed the government's legislative branch since 2015, and even better, his token woman pawn of a vice president, Rosine de Carvalho, would be in attendance as well. Baptista had plenty of allies within the National Assembly—the exact number would shock both the Americans and President Luemba. There was no reason to attack the Assembly itself, since his allies inside that body would best serve him in his transition to power from within. Violence against the Assembly would cause more harm than good, though it was tempting, since there were many enemies inside worthy of violent revenge.

But no. His was the long game and he knew he best consolidated power by overtaking the executive branch, eliminating Luemba, and allowing the system he had in place inside the Assembly to do what needed to be done and rally the legislature behind him. He had two powerful allies in the Supreme Court to back him up as well, should it come to that.

It would not.

Fear was the most powerful weapon in Angola. And he most certainly had that on his side.

The attack on the embassy would be massive and effective and achieve multiple goals. First, it would create chaos and disrupt communications between the embassy mission and the American President. It was no secret that the CIA ran its operations from the American embassy, and his teams would have instruction to kill anyone suspected of being CIA and to take out the power and comms in the building. They would also take hostages, which would be an important bargaining chip guaranteeing his safety in the first, delicate days of his rise to power.

And it would sate his need for vengeance against the American CIA for betraying him. Without that betrayal, he would have been in charge all these years, as they had promised.

Lastly, and most critically to his coup, as the feigned protests became violent ahead of the actual attack, the Angolan security forces would immediately move to transport Luemba and Vice President Rosine de Carvalho to safety at the Presidential Palace. Luemba and Carvalho would be together, and they would not arrive safely at the palace. He would have two teams in place along the route from the Assembly to Luemba's palace on Rua Pedro Furtado. Should the first team be defeated, the thinning of the security team would mean the second would succeed for certain.

And the next time Luemba walked into the Presidential Palace, it would be to bow before Baptista and beg for his life like the coward and dog he was. Baptista would hear his pleas. But once his life no longer guaranteed Baptista's safety and his power was ratified by the Assembly, then Luembo and his puppet vice president would be executed.

The Chinese would be a great deterrent to American retaliation. He would also immediately "rescue" the American hostages who had been taken by the "protesters" and return them safely. He would round up those who had attacked the embassy and appease the Americans with swift executions of those responsible.

Of course, those actually executed would be political enemies he substituted for his loyal army of followers.

His plan was perfect and there was no one now who could stop him.

He may have lost twenty years of power to the fickle and feckless Americans, but he would more than make up for it with the years of power that lay ahead. And the deals he intended to broker with China would make him a very rich man.

As his men mopped up the blood and brains in the basement, Baptista allowed himself a rare smile.

His lifetime of work was finally coming to fruition.

13

**THE RYAN HOME
CHESAPEAKE BAY, MARYLAND**
1812 LOCAL TIME

Ryan smiled at Cathy in the kitchen and gave an apologetic little shrug as he replaced the phone in its cradle. She gave him a genuine smile in return and kissed his cheek.

"I'll fix you some tea when you come back," she said.

He remembered again, as he did a hundred times a day, why he loved this woman so very much. He headed to his office, which also served as a SCIF, wondering what had happened in the world that was now intruding on his rare weekend at home. He hoped that it was nothing that would bring him back to the White House for what was left of the weekend, because Katie was supposed to come to dinner with her new beau, Dennis, tomorrow, and Sally had seemed strangely eager to attend as well.

He closed the door behind him and slipped into the comfortable chair behind the large desk. He picked up the secure, encrypted phone and simply said, "Yes?"

"Sorry to bother you, Mr. President." The voice of his chief of staff, Arnie van Damm, didn't hold the tight cord that meant a trip to the White House, and Ryan felt his pulse slow a touch. "I knew you would want to be in the loop, sir."

"Of course, Arnie. We're twenty-four seven. What's up?" Ryan asked and leaned back in his chair.

"Well, sir, we have a development in Angola. There was an attack on a covert DIA team that I'm afraid left two men dead."

Ryan felt a band tighten around his chest. Nothing about his job as President weighed on him as heavily as the loss of men and women from the military and intelligence communities. It was the very best of America that volunteered to put themselves in harm's way for their country and neighbors, and the sting of loss never dulled for him.

Of course, now having three of his four children answering that very call elevated it to a new level, he supposed. When Katie had been aboard the USS *Washington* . . .

"What do we know?" he asked.

"Not much just yet, Mr. President," van Damm said. "The team was apparently from a cyberwarfare task force setting up hardware systems to bypass the Chinese telecom network in Luanda. They came under fire and two were killed. A third made it to the embassy unharmed, so we have CIA in country sorting things out as we speak."

"You're not suggesting the Chinese targeted our team, are you?" he asked, suddenly feeling a swell of anger. After what had happened in the Taiwan Strait and on the out island of Taiwan, there was no way he would tolerate more American losses at the hands of the Chinese. And he believed that he had an understanding with CCP secretary general Xu Chao. More than that, Chao owed him far more than the other way around.

"No, sir. We don't really know much just yet," van Damm admitted. "The Chinese do have a significant presence in Angola, which we are working to balance, as you know. But there is a lot of violence in Angola right now and a rising political opposition. We simply don't know yet what happened. Director Foley has sent you a full brief, sir, but is available to talk if you prefer."

"Yes, connect me to her, Arnie," Ryan said.

"Of course, Mr. President."

The phone took on a hollow tone and he could just hear the clicks and magnetic hum as the ODNI checked the security of the encryption.

"I thought I might hear from you, Jack," Mary Pat said a moment later. "I was planning to call you, but I was hoping to have more details before I did because I knew you'd have questions and I don't have answers to those questions yet."

"No problem, Mary Pat," he said. "What *do* we know?"

"Not much," she said and read him in quickly on the events of the last few hours, including the attack and the subsequent recovery of the bodies. "We do know that the ground branch team met with resistance during the recovery and one man was injured."

"Are the Chinese involved?" he asked bluntly.

There was a pause while she either considered this or considered how to respond.

"I don't know, Jack," she said. "All I have is initial reports so far. I can tell you that the shooters that engaged our ground branch team were locals, but I don't have identifications on them yet. We will be doing a deep dive over the coming hours. It is possible, of course, that these were managed assets of the MSS, but there is no evidence of that yet. But, Jack, do you really believe that the Chinese would brazenly assassinate an unarmed cyber team on foreign soil?"

He knew Mary Pat well enough to know that she was looking more for his reaction to the question than for information. She would have her own thoughts on that subject.

"If they were executing the op using an airtight cutout, then sure. They've made no secret of their desire to dominate African finance, trade, and infrastructure. They have BRI projects in practically every country on the continent. If they thought we were working to jeopardize that investment, I think they would do what they needed to do so long as they thought they could get away with it."

"Yes, but only *if* they thought they could get away with it," Mary Pat emphasized. "They are far too dependent on world opinion right now, especially after the action in the Strait of Taiwan."

Ryan thought hard about that. The more important question was probably the why. He did not put anything past the CCP's MSS, but there would have to be a pretty big motive to justify the risk.

"Do you know what military assets we have operating in the area, Mary Pat?" he asked.

"I thought you might ask," she said, and he could actually hear her smile. "The *Kearsarge*'s ARG is deployed in the area with the 22nd MEU aboard. They're conducting training operations in the South Atlantic off the coast of Gabon."

Ryan thought for a moment. Nigeria remained a hot spot, but then again, the entire continent was becoming a powder keg. Well, not becoming—it had been that way for decades, he supposed. Only the actors changed. If there was one constant in sub-Saharan Africa it was violence.

"I want to reposition them south toward Angola," he decided out loud. What had happened might be a random act of violence in a region where such things were common. But it might also be a prelude to something more. And this DIA team were certainly not the only Americans at risk in Angola, including American civilian business interests and a robust embassy presence. "I'll connect with the secretary of defense and Admiral Kent."

"I can let them know, Jack," Mary Pat said.

"Thanks," Ryan said, and glanced at the door to his study, eager to get back to spending time with Cathy, but wanting to be sure he was doing all that needed to be done for now. "It might make sense to forward-deploy additional intelligence assets, too. Maybe we embed an intelligence task force aboard the *Kearsarge*."

"I had thought the same thing," Mary Pat said. "Tell Cathy I say hello."

"I will, Mary Pat," he said. He got the subtext—his DNI and friend was reassuring him that there was nothing more for him to do and his very talented staff was working on things. "And let's get some answers."

"We will, Jack," she promised. "And I'll get the names of the fallen and wounded to you as soon as I have them."

"Thank you," he said softly. Mary Pat knew better than anyone how important it was to him to know the names and stories of those who sacrificed for their country. He never, ever wanted it to stop being personal. And he would want to speak to the families when the time was right. "Keep me in the loop, Mary Pat."

"You know I will, Jack," she said.

And then she was gone.

Ryan replaced the phone and leaned back in his chair, clasping his hands in his lap and closing his eyes. He let out a long sigh, then said a silent prayer for the souls of the fallen.

He gave himself a few moments to compartmentalize his emotions, then rose and headed for the steel-reinforced door of his office.

His evenings alone, at home with his wife, were far too rare to let this one go to waste. And capping the weekend off tomorrow by seeing Katie and her new crush was something he was looking forward to as well. While no man could measure up to the standard he'd set for his youngest daughter, he had to admit—to himself at least—that submarine XO Commander Dennis Knepper came pretty damn close.

Ryan smiled and forced thoughts of Luanda from his mind and tried to focus instead on being present for Cathy, the love of his life, knowing that the best people in the whole world were working on the problem.

14

BRIDGE
USS *KEARSARGE* (LHD 3)
SOUTH ATLANTIC OCEAN
201 NAUTICAL MILES OFF THE GABON COAST
2345 LOCAL TIME

United States Navy captain Anthony Miles stared out across the flat, squared-off bow of his warship and let a slight smile creep up at the corners of his mouth. The truth was, he absolutely loved his job. When he had graduated from Vanderbilt University on a naval ROTC scholarship he had ranked surface warfare officer as his number one pick. He was well aware of the running joke that the SWO community was filled mostly with Academy and ROTC graduates who had *not* selected for pilot or submarines, but for Miles, standing on the bridge of a mighty warship had always been his dream billet in the Navy. The only surprise had been that he loved it far more than he could possibly have imagined. Five years of service to pay for his undergraduate degree had morphed into a career.

No, more than just a career—command at sea had become his passion.

When he'd entered the pipeline to become a surface warfare officer, Miles had imagined himself aboard the cutting-edge, Arleigh Burke–class DDG destroyers. In fact, when he was assigned as a junior officer to the USS *Bataan*—a Wasp-class amphibious assault ship just like the *Kearsarge*—Miles had been bitterly disappointed. Then he'd made his first deployment and everything changed. He'd always known that the role of the surface Navy had been to deliver ordnance on target from the very pointy tip of the spear. The surface fleet was the literal definition of power projection and the Navy's presence in the world's hot spots determined the safety and stability of the world. What he'd learned on his first deployment, however, was that, from both a strategic and tactical standpoint, there was no more versatile, deadly, effective, and feared weapon in the American arsenal than the might of the United States Marine Corps Marine Expeditionary Unit. Tomahawks were powerful and sexy, nukes gave nation-state enemies pause, but few things brought about real change like Marines arriving on the scene from the sea, with the might of their infantry, armor, artillery, and airpower with them.

The Navy was about power projection, and no one projected power better than an amphibious ready group (ARG) and her embarked Marines. Miles had stayed in the "Gator Navy" ever since, knowing he would one day command an LHD (landing helicopter dock ship). Assuming his command tour went well, he hoped one day the Navy would see fit for him to lead as an amphibious ready group commander, or Phibron. The billet was currently occupied by Commodore Andy Ho, a man who Miles both liked and respected. Commanding the ARG was no small task, considering it included an LHD, an LPD (landing platform dock ship), an LSD (landing ship, dock), and the embarked Marines and all their additional assets brought to bear.

"Bridge, Combat—Captain, request you pick up, sir," the speaker box beside him squawked.

Miles picked up the handset. "This is the captain."

"Skipper, we just received new tasking," the on-watch CSO said from the combat information center. "Colonel Crocker requests you come to the LFOC," she said, referring to the landing force operations center, a separate SCIF-level space occupied by the MEU for their battle operations.

That Crocker was read in on the tasking before Miles was served as a minor annoyance. The relationship between the Phibron, the LHD skipper, and the commander of the MEU was tricky and kinetic. It was made more complicated by the fact that all three of them shared the same rank—O-6, so two Navy captains and a Marine Corps colonel. That was intentional, he knew. Which commander took on the role as lead while the others were in support was a dynamic thing in the amphibious ready group. Having a Phibron well-versed in the operations of the LHD, the embarked Marine Air-Ground Task Force (MAGTF) and her aircraft, and the MEU was very helpful when it happened, but that wasn't always the case. In Miles's case, Captain Beckham was a great guy, but had never himself commanded an LHD, so he wasn't always read in on what Miles could and couldn't do.

Fortunately, Crocker had been amazing. There were only a few months of workups available to blend together the MEU and ship's crew before deployment, but he and Crocker had spent many hours together even before that and had become teammates and friends.

"Roger that, on my way," Miles said, slipping out of his captain's chair with a surge of excitement at getting new tasking, a feeling that never seemed to get old. He turned to the officer of the deck. "Ping me in combat when the Black Sheep are ready to recover."

"Yes, sir," Lieutenant Junior Grade Ashley Richards replied, her voice confident.

Miles liked Richards. She was a solid JO and would make it far if she chose to make the Navy a career. He had no doubt that she would perform perfectly, and intended to let her keep the conn during the recovery of the F-35Bs from the VMFA-214—the Black Sheep—which were due back from their training evolution and combat air patrol within the next thirty minutes. The *Kearsarge* had been one of the first of the East Coast LHDs to have her flight deck reinforced to accommodate the next-gen fighters that were replacing the aging AV-8B Harriers.

He descended the ladder well to the O2 level and strode over to the door to the CIC, beside which stood an armed United States Marine, his back straight, his eyes locked on the wall across from him at the presence of the ship's captain. Miles had noticed that his sailors were more squared away when in the presence of the Marines. Professionalism, as they say, is often contagious. He punched in his code to unlock the heavy metal door, heard the click as the magnetic lock released, and entered.

"Captain in Combat," a young sailor announced sharply.

"As you were," Miles said, scanning the room. "Is the commodore here?" he asked, looking for the Phibron.

"No, sir," replied the TAO, who stood behind a sailor at the table-size digital dead-reckoning tracer, or plotter, where he was no doubt walking the young man through deconflicting surface contacts. "I believe he returned to his stateroom and wanted to be part of plans for something that is coming up. Shall I summon him, sir?"

"No, it's okay," Miles said. He'd hoped to connect to see what was up, which was why he was cutting through the CIC on his way to the LFOC, but Crocker would have the gouge, it sounded like.

He crossed to the far bulkhead and then passed through another door that separated the Navy CIC from the Marine LFOC.

Colonel Crocker looked up from beside Major Merriweather, the younger officer in charge of the 1st Company, 3rd Marine Special Operations Battalion, as Miles entered. Merriweather's two dozen Marine Raiders from the 3rd MSOB were what made the MEU special operations capable for this deployment.

"What's going on, Colonel Crocker?" Miles asked, using the formality he knew the Marines preferred, despite sharing both rank and command with the Marine officer. Theirs was a truly symbiotic relationship, since neither could exist without the other.

"Skipper," Miles said, straightening up beside Major Merriweather. He then gave the 3rd MSOB commander a nod, indicating Merriweather should brief the captain.

"Sir, we've received orders to be prepared to respond to an emerging threat in the Angolan capital of Luanda," Major Merriweather said. "It would appear that a covert American team was targeted and killed last night. The situation is under investigation, but it seems that someone believes this may potentially be a prelude to additional violence toward Americans and our allies in the region. The United States mission in Angola is located at the embassy in Luanda and we have both civilian and government interests in the area. The State Department is elevating the threat condition as we speak."

Miles put a hand on his hip and glanced at the map on the large screen behind Merriweather, noting their position south of Lagos and the distance to Luanda—though he was quite familiar with both already. Obviously, there must be orders for the *Kearsarge* and the rest of the amphibious ready group to reposition south. They were nowhere near in range to support an operation in Luanda from all the way up here.

"The commodore is probably looking for you to share tasking as we speak," Crocker said, correctly reading his irritation. He handed him a tear sheet containing an operations order from the Pentagon, ordering the ARG to reposition south. "He asked us to put together several possible mission packages for violence in the capital, but I'm sure was coming to you next."

"Are they evacuating nonessential personnel out of Luanda?" he asked, trying to envision what type of response might be needed and waving off the colonel's attempt to cool his annoyance. They were all well-versed on the threats and geography of their area of responsibility, but the rather vague "potential violence to Americans and allies in the region" didn't give him much to work with. Delivering an entire MEU and all of their assets was a completely different evolution than delivering a rapid-response, special operations team from the 3rd Raiders.

"Not that we know of yet, sir," Major Merriweather replied.

"As usual, we're not receiving much in the way of detailed information just yet," Crocker noted. "I'm going to have Major Merriweather's team prepare for predictable contingencies, including securing the embassy mission in Luanda, and I'll have the team on ready alert once we're in striking distance, Captain Miles."

"Which I can have us positioned for off the coast in twenty-four hours," Miles asserted. "Fifteen to sixteen hours can place us approximately here," he indicated a rough area north and west of Luanda in the South Atlantic Ocean. "That's our first reasonable infil distance, but it will be hard to provide ongoing support for at least another few hours after that, other than cycling your F-35s and getting troops in and out via the MV-22s."

"That's what I was guessing," Crocker said, though they both knew he had more likely made the calculations on his own down to the minute. "If we steam directly toward Luanda from our present position, we can deliver air support from the Black Sheep sooner than that, but we don't have range for much more until then, I agree. I'll have the officer in charge from the VMFA-214 detachment prepare his guys to sit Ready Five beginning in eight hours?"

"Sounds right," Miles agreed. "We have two aircraft to recover, but we can have them on deck in under thirty." He glanced at his watch. He picked up the radiophone beside the plotter. "Bridge, CIC—this is the captain."

"Officer of the Deck," came the serious voice of LTJG Richards.

"Officer of the Deck, once we recover aircraft we'll be repositioning south at flank speed. I'll have CIC deconflict surface contacts ASAP."

"Bridge, aye, Captain," Richards said.

Miles ended the call and then gave Crocker a nod.

"Give me forty-five minutes," he said. "Once I get things locked in, we should meet in plans to get some options together. I'll make sure the air boss and Lieutenant Benson are there," he added. The air boss was responsible for all air operations off the ship, working with the MAGTF officer in charge and Benson, who was the limited duty officer in charge of all operations in and out of the well deck—the submersible deck where the landing craft, including the big-ass "hopper," their nickname for the LCAC hovercraft—were launched and recovered. Miles liked having all of his experts present at every plans meeting so that potential problems with capabilities were deconflicted before planning got too far along. "And I'll get the commodore there as well," he added, giving Crocker a grin.

"Oorah," Crocker replied.

Miles passed back through the door to Combat and joined his TAO and his junior sailor at the DDRT.

"Deconflict surface contacts and plot me a course for right here," he said, tapping a point north and west of the Angolan coast in a straight line from where the green square labeled OS, for own ship, sat at the front of a diamond head of other green squares, the rest of the ships of the *Kearsarge* ARG. "We'll be traveling at flank speed. Send all fires up to the bridge right away."

"Aye, aye, Captain," the young sailor, whose name tape read BILLINGS, said and got to work.

Miles turned back to his TAO.

"Yes, sir," the TAO said.

Miles headed back for the door, intent on getting to the bridge, where he would let Richards gain the experience of recovering the aircraft, but making sure there was no delay.

Whatever the hell was going on in Angola must be real for the President of the United States to reposition the ARG.

He needed to make sure his warship was ready to respond when asked.

Crocker and his men were the weapons he'd use, but it was the *Kearsarge* that would deliver those weapons when asked.

15

OFFICE OF NAVAL INTELLIGENCE (ONI)
NATIONAL MARITIME INTELLIGENCE CENTER (NMIC)
4251 SUITLAND ROAD, WASHINGTON, D.C.
0343 LOCAL TIME

Katie arched her back and glanced at the time stamp in the upper right corner of her desktop computer, then both of her eyebrows shot up. Once again, time had become a liquid for her, and she was shocked to see that it was already nearly morning. She reached for the mug on her desk and took a sip of the over-steeped, now-cold tea and wrinkled her nose. She considered going to the break room, where they had invested in an automatic cappuccino machine. Espresso might help her in this last hour of organizing her brief for Captain Ferguson at 0600, but it might also make it impossible to take a power nap afterward—something she would desperately need before brunch with Dennis at the Ryan house on the Chesapeake Bay. She chewed the inside of her cheek, deciding.

Her phone vibrated on her desk with an incoming call.

"Lieutenant Commander Ryan," she said after tapping the green accept button.

"Doesn't sound like I'm waking you, Ryan. Please don't tell me you never left the office," Ferguson said.

"Guilty as charged, sir," but this shouldn't surprise him. She'd earned the reputation of being a "quirky night owl," as Petty Officer Pettigrew had once described it to Lieutenant Conza.

"They've done studies, you know. It turns out sleep is good for you," he said with a smile.

"Meh," she said, playing it up. "I'll sleep when I'm dead."

"Well, I might have to pull rank to change that," he said, then his voice turned serious. "I'll be in at five. That will give us an hour to go over things with you before the brief."

"No problem. I'm not going anywhere."

"Yeah, about that," Ferguson said, his voice preemptively apologetic. "As it turns out you . . ."

Katie let out a long sigh, but away from the phone, hopeful he wouldn't hear it. "Am I going somewhere, sir?" she asked, but of course she already knew the answer.

"You are, Ryan," Ferguson said. "I have both Petty Officer Pettigrew and Lieutenant Conza heading in for the brief, and after we're putting the band back together. Given your team's success in Taiwan, the ODNI wants an expanded intel presence aboard the *Kearsarge* amphibious ready group to augment the intelligence team from the N2 shop and the intelligence team from the 22nd MEU. Someone seems to think that things might be about to explode in Angola. The *Kearsarge* is steaming there now to be the contingency for whatever is going on."

"Yes, sir," she said. "I have a go bag with everything I need here at the office."

"That's good thinking, Ryan," Ferguson agreed. "Your team will be leaving the NMIC by oh-eight-hundred for Joint Base Andrews. You'll fly to Cabinda, where the *Kearsarge* will send an air asset to get you aboard the boat."

So much for the family brunch . . .

But if the director of naval intelligence was rushing her and an intel team all the way to Africa, then something big was going on. Or, at the very least, there was the potential for something big that had someone's antennae up. She suspected that everything she'd learned overnight about Angola might well be supplemented by all she now knew about China since the events in the Taiwan Strait. She resisted the urge to ask what the hell was going on, knowing Ferguson wouldn't—and certainly shouldn't—share it over the phone.

She'd have to wait until he got here.

"I'll be ready, sir," she promised.

Ferguson hung up, and she turned back to the computer.

Here she was at the NMIC, surrounded by the most advanced cyber technology available in the Navy world, but still, somehow, she had to go to sea. One day she would ask her brother Kyle—the Ryan family's very own cyber expert—when technology would finally reach the point she could be an intelligence analyst from the safety and comfort of her office.

16

**NORTHWEST CORNER OF THE ALTO DAS CRUZES CEMETERY
JUST SOUTH OF THE U.S. EMBASSY MISSION
SOUTH SIDE OF RUA NDUNDUMA
LUANDA, ANGOLA
1357 LOCAL TIME**

Baptista raised the binoculars to his eyes, scanning the crowd that grew by the minute outside the main entrance of the American embassy, where several hundred people had now completely stopped traffic in both directions on Rua Houari Boumediene. The crowd had been whipped into a frenzy by the agitators he had embedded among them, and they were now shouting "Death to America" in both Portuguese and Kimbundu. This was easily achieved, as his followers had a hatred of America bred into them from the time they began training with the PFU, and the nonaffiliated crowd members were easily swayed by the constant propaganda campaign that blamed everything from the cost of eggs to the death of children from disease on the capitalistic Americans and their greed.

He raised his radio to his mouth.

"What is the situation at the back?" he asked.

"It is not likely we can squeeze any more people into the back road," said Jimen, his newly minted operations lieutenant, who was in position to direct the operation to the east from the fifth-floor room he occupied in the medical school building overlooking the embassy compound. "Roka has them in a frenzy and they are beginning to throw rocks and bottles now. It will already be difficult to move our vehicles into position after we take our prisoners. There is a line of American Marines in the parking lot beyond the fence, but they are not engaging yet, though they are heavily armed."

Baptista could not see the east side of the compound from this angle, his view blocked by a large, private residence compound just north of the corner of the cemetery. Nor did he need to. Once the incursion began, he fully intended to be elsewhere. His allies inside the Angola military would be preparing for the second stage of the operation, and he wished to greet *former* president Luemba once he was in custody. It would be a sign of strength for him to lead his prisoner into his own palace residence personally.

He moved his binoculars upward and scanned the roof of the embassy. As expected, he saw two heavy-machine-gun teams assembling at the east and west sides of the roof.

Once the attack was in full swing, they would lose many people, but the videos and pictures of dead civilians—stripped of their weapons, of course—that had been massacred by the American Marines would play very well on the international media.

But they cannot kill enough people to prevent the breach.

Baptista smiled. Just as the armed men in the crowd outnumbered the American Marines by more than ten to one, the total crowd would soon approach a hundred to one. And that was before he sent his highly trained, expert operators in behind the initial attack.

Let the Americans thin the herd with their security teams from the roof. Then, when it was safer, he would send his assault team in from the south entrance by the pool house. The mob outside was there to keep the Americans in a fight for their lives, nothing more, and to allow his real team access to the building.

His precision team would find and capture the American ambassador and take at least a few other hostages.

They would kill everyone else, but the captured American VIPs would be a highly valuable bargaining chip.

"Commence the escalation," he ordered. "Rocks and Molotov cocktails. Then fire some rounds inside. Once the Marines engage, then and only then do we blow the walls, throw our grenades, and enter."

"Understood," Jimen replied.

"We are ready at the front," came the voice of his young but highly capable team leader organizing the action at the front of the embassy.

"Do it," Baptista said into his radio.

A moment later he heard the shouts increase and the crack of rifles fired into the air. He could barely hear the din of the rocks and bottles pummeling the compound or the bloodthirsty shouts of the mob.

Baptista turned to the man beside him.

"Move to the fence, Duden," he instructed the leader of his elite assault team. "When the machine gunners are engaging the mobs on both sides, make your breach quickly. You know your mission, my friend."

"We will succeed," the man said, then a huge smile split his weathered face. "I will see you at the palace with the American ambassador, *President* Baptista."

"I will see you there," Baptista said, containing his excitement.

More than two decades he had waited for this day.

The day he not only rose to power but put the Americans in their place.

17

COMBAT INFORMATION CENTER (CIC)
USS *KEARSARGE* (LHD 3)
SOUTH ATLANTIC OCEAN
TWENTY NAUTICAL MILES SOUTHWEST OF SOYO, ANGOLA
1519 LOCAL TIME

Colonel Ricardo "Rick" Crocker, USMC, stood with his hands clasped behind his back beside the reinforced door of the combat information center. He was well aware of the impact his presence, as the commander of the special operations capable 22nd Marine Expeditionary Unit, or MEU (SOC), had in the CIC in this moment—reaffirming the idea in the minds of the young sailors manning the stations in the tight quarters that their ship and the ARG were going to war. The sailors at the various stations beneath the large-screen monitors of the C4I integrated command and control system looked tense and focused, perhaps a bit more so than his other visits to the CIC during training evolutions.

He smiled. The sailors now had the intensity in their faces that his Marines carried every day while deployed.

He caught the eye of Captain Tony Miles, the skipper of the

Kearsarge, as he leaned over the shoulder of the very young and tense operations specialist, who worked on the digital dead-reckoning tracer, where his captain watched him plot a course through the various surface contacts. Miles gave Crocker a nod.

"We're steaming southeast at flank speed to give you the shortest infil time possible, Rick," Miles said, his look serious. He stood up and patted the young sailor at the DDRT station on the shoulder and headed over to meet Crocker by the door. "We have a few surface contacts to deconflict, but nothing I'm concerned about," he said. "What's your window?"

"I have Major Merriweather building out a mission set with his team leader now," Crocker answered. "I anticipate launch of the combat team in under thirty, and my air assets from the wing are preflighting as we speak. The air boss is working with your flight operations to make sure that goes smoothly."

Miles was relieved that his air boss, a Navy helo pilot named Commander Marc DeLaurier, was already on it. Moving aircraft around on the flight deck to maximize the efficiency of getting the air assets up was no small feat. Having the F-35s aboard was a real value add, but it complicated things immensely, since they needed space to launch from their positions on the aft port side of the flight deck. They were technically VTOL aircraft, but pure vertical launch was tricky and very fuel inefficient, so they generally did more very-short-distance takeoffs, which required significant cleared deck on the port side. As a result, the Ospreys were packed in tight formation forward of the island, just inches apart, and the 53s had been repositioned to the LPD, the USS *Arlington*.

"That was my next question," Miles said. "Air operations."

"We'll launch two Osprey with Alpha and Charlie Raider teams," Crocker said. "Two Zulus will provide close air support and once they're inbound, we'll send up a flight of two F-35s from the 214th as well. I have the UH-1s in reserve with a third Osprey as a quick reaction force with two rifle platoons and an additional scout sniper team."

He watched Captain Miles nod and saw the man's gears turning as he planned his ship's movements. Despite the sometimes brutal interservice rivalry between Marines and Navy sailors, the truth was they were purely symbiotic. Nowhere was that truer than in the ARG.

And Miles seemed to understand as well or better than most that the embarked Marines were always the true mission of his ship. The *Kearsarge* existed to deliver the world's most lethal combat force to the battlefield, nothing more. Every other capability of the LHD and other ships of the ARG were simply designed to preserve that capability.

As for Crocker, he liked and respected Miles and his team and worked hard to view his MEU from their point of view—a weapon that the Navy deployed against the enemy. To the sailors, the Marines on their ship were not much different than the Tomahawks aboard an Arleigh Burke—a weapon in the United States Navy's inventory to deploy against the enemy. Except these weapons came aboard, ate their chow, took up space, and crowded the gym.

When the relationship was kept in that balance it worked. And when it worked, the ARG truly was one of the most lethal weapons in the United States arsenal.

"I'm trying to get you close, Rick, but your AH-1 Zulus won't have much loiter time, I'm afraid."

Miles was thinking through the problems and was right. His AH-1Z Vipers—the lethal attack helicopters similar to the Army's deadly Apache—were no good if they couldn't stay on station to deliver ordnance.

"We're using the new auxiliary fuel tanks, so that buys some time," Crocker said. "And we're setting up a second pair to launch fifteen minutes behind them and I'll have the F-35s on station. I'm also holding two 53 Kilos on alert five on board the *Arlington*, ready to go, so we can send them in for dust-off if we get outside the Osprey's TOS."

In fact, the CH-53K King Stallion helicopter might even be more capable for recovery, Crocker had decided, green-lighting Major Merriweather's pitch. The Ospreys would deliver his special operations team from the 3rd Raiders much more quickly, but nothing carried more shit farther than the new CH-53 variant.

And they had no idea how many people they would need to carry, should evacuation of the embassy become necessary. Two of the 53 Kilos could haul an additional forty people on top of the assault force.

Crocker's look turned somber. "And we've got the FST setting up to receive any casualties."

The fleet surgical team was comprised of Navy doctors, nurses, and medics. Assigned to the Marines rather than the ship, the FST could forward-deploy with the troops when needed to set up a damage control surgical hospital. In this case, they were most effective with the additional resources of the USS *Arlington* and would be set up to receive casualties on board the ship.

"Sounds good, Rick," Miles said. "What else can we do for you?"

"Loiter close and stay safe," Crocker said with a smile.

"Done, my friend," Miles said and shook Crocker's outstretched hand. "Let me get things squared away and I'll meet you in the LFOC shortly."

Then the skipper of the *Kearsarge* headed back to work.

"OS2, get me the XO on the bridge," the captain said to a young sailor at a station beside him. "And let's update the surface contacts out to four thousand yards along our route. You never know what kind of assets these assholes might have out here."

"Aye, sir," the sailors replied almost simultaneously from the DDRT console.

Crocker turned and departed via the heavy door that secured CIC.

He glanced at his watch as he headed down the passageway toward the ladder well that would lead him back to the LFOC. Crocker realized that he was thoroughly enjoying life aboard the Navy's premier Marine force platform. Most of his career as a JO and one hundred percent of his time in combat had been spent in the deserts of Iraq or in the mountains and valleys of Afghanistan. He was a poster boy United States Marine, perfectly content in the plywood huts that housed the operations centers in the middle of the desert. But he was nearly fifty, and there was a certain luxury to shipboard life that, while he might never admit it to anyone other than his wife back home, he thoroughly enjoyed.

He arrived at the bottom of the ladder well, made the single turn, and nodded to the Marine standing sentry beside the door to the LFOC. The Marine straightened up and stared at a point on the wall across from him.

"Good afternoon, Colonel Crocker," the Marine said.

"Oorah, Marine," Crocker said. Then he punched his code into the door's magnetic lock. It clicked open and he entered the bustling space, where his Marine leadership was planning the combat operation to put down the violence at the United States embassy in Luanda and rescue the Americans there if needed.

Similar to the CIC, the low blue light in this space gave it a cool, tactical feel that was quite different from the dusty plywood COCs of the Middle East. Multiple large-screen displays added to the vibe. The center screen was currently streaming a satellite image of the American embassy in downtown Luanda, less than a half mile inland from the Luanda Bay, formed by the mainland and a thin fingerlike peninsula of land extending northeast.

Crocker's eyes ticked to the screen just beside the monitor displaying aerial imagery streaming in real time. This appeared to be a drone feed, and it showed that the mob around the embassy had clearly grown and were now throwing rocks into the compound. A number of the men held rifles and had bandoliers of ammunition on their shoulders.

"Looks like this could go sideways really damn soon, gentlemen," Crocker said, hands on his hips.

"Yes, sir," Major Merriweather said and turned to Captain Nick Camperos, the team leader for Alpha, and the HQ master sergeant, Andy Miller. "Tell the colonel what you've got, Nick."

"Yes, sir," the captain who led Alpha team said, no hesitation or uncertainty in his voice. "Captain Dane and I have planned the initial assault set." He tapped on the laptop in front of him and the image behind him zoomed in as he turned and looked, moving a pointer with the mouse on the table. "This building here, sir, is the dormitory for the medical school just east of the embassy compound. It's got a well-protected roof with raised concrete waists around two patios on either side of center. From here it is separated from the embassy compound only by this two-lane road here, Rua Engenheiro Armindo de Andrade."

"Sniper roost," Crocker said, seeing where Camperos was going.

"Yes, sir," Camperos said. "Crossing sight lines covering most of the compound and short distances. We'll have Eagle One insert overwatch teams from both Alpha and Charlie here and here." The pointer indicated the two patios on the roof. "Then One will insert Alpha on the east side down here at the south end of the compound, on this grassy area just north of Ruan Ndunduma, while Eagle Two inserts Charlie team here," he said, moving the pointer to the roof of the embassy. "We have good comms so far with the embassy security team, so they'll provide eyes and ears and additional security on the crowd."

"That crowd is getting big and riled up, Captain," Crocker said.

"Yes, sir," Camperos said. "Which is why the Zulus lead the charge, with two passes on both sides. Show of force, obviously, to keep them down, but my understanding is the ROE allows deadly force for hostile action."

"It does, but remember we're operating under the assumption that the members of this mob are civilians until proven otherwise," Crocker said. "So, brief the pilots as such. What is your contingency if there is a breach of the compound before you arrive?"

"We thought of that, sir," Camperos said. "If there is a breach before we arrive, we'll still insert our overwatch as briefed. Depending on the situation on the ground, we will then insert Alpha onto the roof of the embassy, where the security Marines have two SAW teams already established, and we'll put Charlie north of the front entrance to flank the crowd to the east. If the situation is escalated outside, I may instead put all elements inside the compound and call for the QRF to infil."

Crocker nodded. The young officer had clearly thought this through.

"Bring everyone home, Captain."

"Yes, sir," Camperos said. His eyes held the fire of a blooded warrior. "Preflights are about done, and the crews will be here for final brief any moment. Captain Dane is with the teams getting kitted up and loaded out. We can be wheels up in the next fifteen."

"Do it," Crocker said, folding his arms across his chest. "No one left behind, Captain. And that includes the embassy staff."

"Oorah," Camperos said.

Crocker looked at the screen and set his jaw as he watched someone from the mob hurl a Molotov cocktail over the wall, where it exploded in the courtyard, black smoke rising from the spreading flames.

This was going to be a real shit show, but Merriweather's Raiders were the perfect team for the job.

18

EMBAIXADA DA CHINA EM ANGOLA (CHINESE EMBASSY IN ANGOLA)
LESS THAN A HALF MILE NORTH OF THE AMERICAN EMBASSY
56WX+C5, LUANDA, ANGOLA
1612 LOCAL TIME

MSS agent Sima Liang tapped a silver pen on the corner of his laptop, trying to decide what, exactly, he had to report. The truth—and therefore the problem—was that he had almost nothing to report, at least nothing that provided answers instead of more questions. His gut told him what was unfolding at the American Embassy. He could literally see the angry crowds filling Rua Houari Boumediene, the road along the west side of the embassy, from the rooftop of their much more modern building. Little separated the two compounds, except the construction along the south side of their complex, where more buildings were rising up to accommodate the growing presence in Luanda. And, of course, he was listening in real time to the communications from the Americans. There was plenty of encrypted signals yet to decode—no doubt from the rather paltry CIA presence at the American embassy—but the initial call for help and the attempts at communicating with the Angolan National Police were easy enough to translate. The mob at the embassy was turning violent.

And for some reason, the Angolans were not responding.

It was a reasonable conclusion that Baptista had launched his takeover of the palace. While Sima put the man's chances initially at less than one in ten, he'd reconsidered that over the last twenty-four hours. He had assets inside the Angolan military, of course, and there was evidence that Baptista's claims to have the support of significant leadership inside the Angola armed forces were not bullshit after all. That crazy son of a bitch just might pull his coup off, if that proved to be the case.

He stopped his pen tapping and leaned back, trying to put all the pieces together. Was it possible the protests outside the American embassy were Baptista's doing—a giant, well-planned distraction to thin out the police and military security forces ahead of his attack on Luemba? If so, he had underestimated the man's intellect and cunning.

The door to his small office opened with a metallic click, and his chief of HUMINT operations, Wang Wei, entered without knocking. His face looked concerned.

"What is it, Wei?" he asked his teammate and friend, using his given name. On paper Liang was the deputy ambassador tasked with corporate engagement, but as the lead agent for the MSS team, he had cultivated a tight-knit unit reminiscent of his time in the 72nd Special Forces Brigade of the PLA. He missed that brotherhood and had tried his best to replicate it on every assignment since assuming a leadership role in the field.

"The mob is growing at the American compound, Liang," his teammate said, his face heavy with worry. "They have now filled the entire street behind the embassy as well and are throwing stones and bottles. Why are they doing this? What have the Americans done to anger the people? I don't understand."

"I am confused as well. We did not see any of this coming, Wei." He gestured with his head and Wang Wei closed the door to the soundproof room. "If this is related to Baptista's plan, I am at a loss to see how it helps him. At first, I thought that perhaps the protest was a distraction only, but it would seem it is growing out of control. That is insane. If they know anything about President Ryan, they must know he will respond swiftly and decisively if any Americans are injured."

Wang paced a moment in front of the desk at which Sima sat. The man was brilliant, but had no military background, which Sima liked. It gave him a different perspective at times.

"You are right," Wang said. "And most especially if someone is killed or, God help us, is taken. If this is Baptista, he will start his very short reign of power as an enemy of the United States."

"I also wonder what the Americans knew that we did not, Wei," Sima said.

"What do you mean?" Wang asked.

"Well, we know that the *Kearsarge* amphibious ready group has been steaming at full speed toward us. Perhaps they saw this coming when we did not?"

Wang shook his head.

"Impossible," he said with confidence. "Our signals intelligence suggests that they were moving into the area as a precaution, nothing more."

Sima sighed and pulled at his chin. Their intercepts of American signals in the region were quite robust. Wang was right. Surely they would have heard something.

"But this is still bad news for whoever is behind this," Wang said. "We know that the American ready group is special operations capable. They will be more than prepared and skilled to respond. And if they determine that Baptista was involved, he will be dealt with in short order."

Sima looked thoughtful. So many questions. Either way, it was good that he had maintained an operational distance from Baptista. The money he had provided was significant, but through multiple solid cutouts. The Americans lacked the sophistication to ever trace it back to the PRC. He had provided nothing more except promises for the future. It was good he had not offered more, it now seemed. Still, if Baptista took power, he might well be a more manageable pawn than Luemba had slowly become. Trillions of dollars, yet still Luemba wooed American corporate presence, playing them against one another for his own economic and personal financial gain.

But if Baptista's coup failed, then it was well that China appeared neutral.

"Thank you, Wei," he said. "Keep the team on this, and let me know anything you find, right when you find it."

"Of course," Wang said, and bowed before leaving and shutting the door behind him.

Sima reached for the phone and pressed 2 on the speed dial. The line connected, then he waited until the clicks and whirs in the background stopped, signaling the encrypted call was secure.

"What is going on there, Agent Sima?" a voice demanded. Director Chou from Beijing sounded more concerned than curious.

Sima gave a quick overview of the situation, including the breach of the embassy moments ago.

"Is this the PFU leader?" Chou asked.

He hesitated only a moment.

"I believe it might be, sir," he said.

"You *believe?*" Chou said, his voice oozing incredulity. "We pay you to know far more than that."

"Yes, sir," Sima said, admonished. "I simply mean we cannot yet confirm it, but I also do not believe in coincidences. It seems likely that this may have been a false flag to distract from Baptista's plans to seize power. If he makes a move, we will know immediately, as our assets inside the government, the National Police, and the military leadership are very well placed. Unfortunately, I cannot say the same for our ability to develop assets inside the PFU. What we know of them comes only from our contacts in Luemba's government and the military."

"And from Victor Baptista," Chou pointed out. The insinuation was not lost on Sima.

"Yes," he admitted. "However, I did not feel I could adequately probe the details of his plans from my NOC as deputy ambassador, Mr. Director. My plan was to introduce him to one of my agents as a 'facilitator' of the Chinese interests, but that has not happened yet."

"Perhaps it won't matter," Chou said. "Whoever the culprits, President Ryan will use this as an opportunity to grow his footprint in Luanda as security for his embassy. If Baptista is behind this, and they find out, that will be the end. Unfortunately, it will not be business as usual for us for a time if this should occur, Liang. Violence against the Americans and then a coup? The region will be under high scrutiny by Western governments as well as the media. We must take a posture of neutrality."

"I agree," he said, and meant it. "But if Baptista is successful, then in time it will most certainly accelerate our plans for Angola, if managed correctly."

"And we trust you to manage it just so, Liang," Chou said, and

Sima felt relief in the implied confidence in his tradecraft. "But if it proves otherwise, we must have nothing that can point back to Beijing."

"Understood. I am already seeing to it." He thought for a moment. "Perhaps I can even reach out to the Americans and offer aid from our embassy security team."

Chou laughed on the other end of the line.

"And that is why we trust you, Sima Liang," his boss said. "Very good thinking. At least make somewhat of an effort we can point to. That will play very, very well on CNN and the BBC. Keep me informed, Liang."

And the call was dropped.

Sima smiled. He would slow-walk this offer of assistance and see where things went. It would not be strange for them to not yet be aware of what was going on. They were diplomats, not spies, after all. The thought made him laugh out loud.

If the Americans intended to land Marines at the U.S. embassy, the last thing they needed was a handful of pistol-wielding embassy security guards in suits helping out. And he most certainly would not be sending any of his MSS operators out the door.

He needed them here.

Time would tell what happened with the leadership of Angola. The truth was, he didn't really care. He was tired of the sub-Saharan violence and politics; he was ready to go home to China.

Or perhaps he just needed a vacation.

Miami. He would book a trip to Miami once this was all behind him. That would recharge his batteries for dealing with the Angolans. Outside of rare earth minerals and access to the Atlantic, he'd found the country had very little to offer.

19

U.S. EMBASSY MISSION IN ANGOLA
R. HOUARI BOUMEDIENE 32
LUANDA, ANGOLA
1735 LOCAL TIME

Kyle sat on the edge of the bed in the small but comfortable private room he'd been assigned. He'd slept for nearly twelve hours and on waking felt completely out of sorts—detached from his normal circadian rhythms. Disassociated from reality, or at least the reality he'd occupied yesterday. Sunlight cut like yellow-orange blades through tiny gaps between the edges of the window blinds, creating a pattern on the floor.

It was almost dinnertime, but he had no intention of joining the mess. He didn't want to be around people right now.

Everything that had happened yesterday seemed like a dream. No, not a dream . . .

Like it had happened to someone else.

As he often did when he was deep in thought, he sat with both feet flat on the floor and his palms on his thighs. When they were little, Katie used to call this his meditation pose, but of course she knew him well enough to know that it wasn't a pose that signaled relaxation or even deep contemplation. When they were a bit older, she'd confided in him that it was his face that gave it away—what the Ryan family called Kyle's stress face. He didn't know what that face looked like. He wasn't one to look in the mirror other than to square away the Navy uniform he'd been so proud to wear.

He blinked his eyes open when the images of his dead teammates intruded into the gray stillness of his mind, making his heart rate and breathing increase. He wondered if his big brother, Jack Junior, ever felt this way. Jack talked very little about what he did, but they all knew he was a clandestine operator. Kyle imagined that his brother had suffered loss like he was experiencing many times. Yet somehow, he always seemed cheerful, engaged, and, well . . . *Jack*.

Kyle wondered if his brother ever struggled with guilt.

Kyle's brain rationalized quite easily the mathematics of all that had happened and with the equations balanced he knew without a doubt that he had done nothing wrong. There was nothing he could have done differently—other than die as well—and, therefore, there was no reasonable explanation for feelings of guilt.

But he found himself struggling with those feelings nonetheless, and the emotional paradox was almost as frustrating as the feeling itself. Kyle lived in a binary world—ones and zeros. On or off. Right or wrong.

But perhaps there were variables he was not considering that would allow him to let go of the uncomfortable emotions. He needed to search for that variable, because until he could release these unfamiliar and uncomfortable feelings, he would not be able to clear his mind to make decisions that needed to be made. At the top of that list was just what he should do next. In the last twenty-four hours he had wondered more than once how easy it might be to simply return to his life as a naval officer. He missed the structure, the stability, the predictability, and the pride of the uniform. But he also wondered how well he would live with the feelings of failure that he believed would follow him if he left the task force now.

A knock on his door made him startle—another strange and unfamiliar reaction that had become common the last day or so.

"Come," he said simply.

The door opened, revealing a woman about his age, dressed in a gray pantsuit with a tablet clutched to her chest, her hair pulled back tight in a bun.

"Sorry to bother you, Lieutenant Ryan . . ."

"It's Mr. Ryan," he corrected. His tone wasn't meant to be harsh, though he was aware he was often misunderstood as being rude.

"Of course," the woman said, not apparently bothered by his tone. "Mr. Ryan, I'm sorry to bother you. I'm Madison Bennett from the embassy staff. I wanted to let you know that your departure to the airport will be delayed. We anticipate this will be for only a short time."

"Is everything all right?" he asked, rising. Honestly, they could delay his departure by several days and he would be okay with it. He had nothing to do here now, but was in no hurry to return to the offices at Joint Base Anacostia-Bolling back home in D.C., either. In fact, he would prefer the solitude of his small room at the embassy mission in Luanda until he got his emotions under control and a plan for his next chapter, as his dad would call it.

"Yes," the woman said, her face impassive. He rather suddenly and unexpectedly noticed that Madison Bennett was quite beautiful. Perhaps it was the way she remained all business as she adjusted her glasses on her nose. "A protest has formed outside the embassy and, out of an abundance of caution, our RSO, Mr. Tejada, prefers not to send your car out through the crowd until this situation resolves."

"Is there a danger?" he asked, confused why a rather commonplace thing like a protest outside an American embassy abroad seemed to fill him with dread.

"No, Mr. Ryan," Madison replied. "Not that I have been made aware of. Perhaps I can arrange for something to eat for you?" Her face softened, almost as if she might be aware of the struggle he was having, a thought that made him even more uncomfortable. "I'm aware that you have had a difficult couple of days, Mr. Ryan. If you prefer to stay here, may I bring something to your room?"

He studied the woman carefully for a moment.

"No," he said. "I'm fine, I think. I do wonder if—"

There was a loud sound that, to Kyle, seemed likely to have been an explosion. Not like a bomb or a grenade, but something more like a Molotov cocktail.

"What was that?" Madison asked, looking over her shoulder into the hallway and appearing, for a moment, rattled.

Kyle was about to answer her when a new, much more powerful explosion rocked the building, making the lights in his room flicker and dust to fall from the light ballast overhead.

"Come in and shut the door," he said, his voice a command rather than a request.

Madison did as he instructed, closing the door and then backing away from it into the room.

"What is it they are protesting?" Kyle asked, moving now to the window along the back wall. He used the hanging wooden stick, rotating it to move the little gear that opened the shutter slats.

"I . . . I'm not sure. The crowd has been gathering and growing all day," Madison said, regaining some of her composure. It was pretty clear she was organic embassy staff and not part of the CIA mission operating out of the embassy. "We've had a handful of protests before, but I've never seen anything like this."

Kyle peered through the slats. His room faced east. Outside the street that ran up behind the embassy was a legitimate two-lane road, but Isaacson referred to it as the alley. Right now, that alley was packed with people. No—not just people, but with military-aged men, many of whom were lifting rifles over their heads. Those who weren't had their hands in fists and all were shouting angrily.

Then he heard gunfire. It was a few single shots, but then the cracks of rifles were followed by several long, sustained bursts. This was followed by shouts in English, the Marine security contingent calling out movement, Kyle thought.

He felt a tap on his shoulder and turned.

Madison's face remained composed, but her eyes were full of fear, and she was trembling.

"What do we do?" she asked. "We have to get out of here, right?"

Kyle patted her awkwardly on the shoulder as his mind reeled. He looked out again, and the mob was clearly working itself into a frenzy. But no one in that crowd seemed to be aiming or firing their weapons.

The attack must, therefore, be coming from the front and/or the sides of the complex. What that meant for their escape he was unsure.

Another burst of gunfire reminded him that he was completely unarmed now. Not that having a pistol would protect him or the woman in his room from the danger outside, he supposed. But it might make it easier to fend off attackers who might breach the building for a time—maybe long enough for whoever there was who might come to their rescue to arrive. He knew that there was not a large presence of military or intelligence community operators in Angola, but there must be a QRF. His team's emergency plan had been to make it to the embassy. But what was the embassy's emergency plan?

"Mr. Ryan?"

He turned to face Madison again and found her struggling to control her fear. Her bottom lip quivered a little.

"You're CIA, right?" she asked, hope trumping fear for a moment.

"No," he said. "I'm with a different group, but I will do everything I can to keep you safe, I promise."

She bobbled her head in nervous agreement.

There were more than a hundred people in the road between the embassy and the six-story building behind them. That meant the total number could be more than five hundred, maybe even a thousand.

Kyle had no idea what the size of the Marine security detachment at the embassy was, but it wasn't enough to resist that, he didn't think. They would need help, and they would need it fast. But from where?

"Listen to me, Madison," he said, taking the woman gently by the arms. "We are not going to be able to safely escape the embassy. We need to secure here until help arrives. We'll shelter in place for now. How many Marines are attached to the embassy?"

He could see her mind working to find the information and was not surprised when she finally did.

"There are two teams of sixteen Marines attached to the embassy, plus a command staff for the unit of four people—an officer, who is a major, a master sergeant, and then an admin Marine and a Navy medic, who is a senior chief. Then we have the CIA team, which is only a few people who you already know."

"Is there a GRS team assigned here?"

She shook her head. Kyle noticed that just having something to focus on seemed to bring a calm to the young woman.

"No," she said. "The security risk here doesn't warrant a GRS team." She looked past him, her eyes widening as she saw the mob in the alley, which seemed to Kyle to have doubled in size in the last few minutes. "Though it would seem that assessment was clearly in error."

"Clearly," he said, and tried but failed to share a smile with her.

The time of the riot couldn't have been timed better—or worse, depending on your point of view—because Isaacson and his four-man team were either at the airport or airborne with Cockburn and Waddle on a plane headed back to CONUS. Having, or not having, the ground branch operators to augment the organic Marine security force could be the difference between life and death if the embassy fell under siege.

He moved away from the window and grabbed the wooden chair from the small desk. There wasn't even a closet in the room to hide in, nor a bathroom, as there was a shared bathroom in the hall for the ten rooms on this floor. With Isaacson's team gone, they were mostly empty, though he knew some civilian contractors were on the floor as well.

He moved toward the door with the chair, looking up, hoping to see a drop-panel ceiling that they could perhaps find a way to climb up into to hide.

"We'll barricade the door, and then—"

Another explosion rocked the building, and more gunfire sounded.

This time there was no mistaking that the exchange of gunfire was from inside the building. He thought it might even be very close.

Shouting in the hallway seemed to confirm his fear.

He was about to jam the back of the chair under the doorknob when he saw the shadows of feet underneath the door and someone pounded loudly, shouting something he couldn't understand.

"Help me with this," he said, keeping his voice low, to Madison.

But before they could implement the block, the door burst open with enough force that it knocked him backward, where he fell on his ass hard enough that it brought both pain in his hip and an electric stinger down his right leg as the chair twisted out of his hand and slid across the floor, hitting the corner of the bed.

Madison finally let go of her full emotions with a scream that ripped through the middle of him.

Kyle looked up to see two men entering the room, both in Army-style fatigue pants and tank top T-shirts. Both leaned forward over rifles he thought were probably the AK-47s everyone talked about.

The taller of the two men stared at them, eyes wide, then shouted something that Kyle thought must be Kimbundu, since it clearly wasn't Portuguese. He raised his hands and tried to stand, but the man kicked him hard in the left side and pointed his rifle squarely in the center of his face.

Kyle didn't feel nearly as much fear as he might have imagined as it dawned on him that he was very unlikely to live through this encounter.

Madison said something in Portuguese that he thought meant "We don't understand," but the man released his grip on his rifle to backhand her, hard. The blow was enough to drive her into the wall, where she collapsed onto the floor.

At the sight of the man then brutally kicking the young woman, something snapped inside of Kyle and he exploded to his feet, driving himself right shoulder first into him. He heard an animal-like scream that some distant part of his brain calmly and clinically noted was somehow from him as he drove the man over onto his back, the rifle loose from his grip.

He straddled the man's chest and raised both hands together in one big fist over his head to crush the face of the man beneath him.

He heard Madison scream, "Kyle!"

Then enormous pain exploded in the back of his head simultaneously with white light that he knew was in his brain, not his eyes.

As he collapsed into the darkness, his last thought was that the only logical explanation for the white light was because the butt of the other man's rifle had impacted him in the occipital region, where vision was controlled by the brain.

Then he saw and felt nothing but blackness.

PART II

Government is not reason; it is not eloquent; it is force.

Like fire, it is a dangerous servant and a fearful master.

—George Washington

20

**SITUATION ROOM
THE WHITE HOUSE
WASHINGTON, D.C.
1253 LOCAL TIME**

One of the hardest things Ryan experienced as POTUS was watching crises from the relative comfort and quiet of the Situation Room while his fellow Americans were fighting in harm's way. It had always been the most difficult part of his work with the CIA when operators on a screen, often depicted as thermal images, moved through a battle because of *his* analysis. Later, as CIA director, men and women had been put in harm's way based on his recommendations. Now, as President, it was on his orders.

"There are more attackers moving into the compound from the breach to the north at the front," General Bruce Kudryk noted. Everyone could see the group of men moving tentatively through the breach in the wall, but Kudryk couldn't help himself, and Ryan imagined the combat veteran, career Army officer who now served on the Joint Chiefs of Staff felt an even stronger pull than he did—the need to be in the fight himself. Kudryk had distinguished himself in Somalia early in his career and time and again in Iraq and Afghanistan as an officer who led from the front. Together they had watched the team come out of the cemetery to the south of the complex, cross the four-lane road, and breach over the walls and into the compound with ease, once the escalating violence at the east and west sides of the compound had engaged the security forces. Ryan didn't need an expert to tell him this was a well-designed and professionally choreographed attack. Hell, he had been that expert for years before fate had led him to the White House. The team from the south was inside the building before the Marine security force even knew they were inside the wall—well before they could reposition from where they were under constant fire from the crowd out front.

This is no mob of protesters. These are professionals, using the mob as a cover.

"Why aren't the Marines firing?" someone asked from behind Ryan.

Just as the question was posed the machine-gun team on the east side of the embassy roof fired, the flames from the M249 licking out silently from the barrel on the feed that Ryan assumed to be a satellite. Dirt kicked up from in front of the group inside the wall and they moved back, but muzzle blasts lit up from the crowd outside the wall, clearly directed at the team on the roof.

"They missed," the same woman's voice said, a staffer for someone, Ryan guessed.

"They didn't miss," Kudryk snapped in irritation. "They're following their ROE. That was a warning shot to push the crowd back. These are highly disciplined Marines. They won't just mow down a crowd of civilians without knowing who is a threat and who is not."

"Let's clear this room, please," Ryan ordered. "Only essential personnel."

He left it for his team to decide who was and was not "essential" to any decisions that needed to be made as the attack unfolded. There were murmurs around the room as his key personnel, the NSA, the secretary of defense and secretary of state, his military advisors, and of course his DNI, Mary Pat, ordered their various staffers to leave the room. Moments later Ryan was left with just his core, trusted team.

"Do we have thermal?" Kudryk asked.

"Not until the Predator arrives, sir," the technician running the video feed replied.

Ryan got it. He, too, wanted almost desperately to see what was going on inside the walls of the embassy compound. They had watched two teams of eight to ten men enter the building after engaging with the Marines in the courtyard while the machine gunners were still scrambling to get into position. He had watched at least two wounded Marines being dragged to safety by their comrades. That was at the main entrance of the compound and that team of Marines was still engaged in an intermittent gun battle from the other breach point at the gate. The crowd had literally pulled the gate out of the wall by hooking chains to it behind two pickup trucks. Now insurgents or terrorists or whoever the hell this mob was made up of were crouched behind the wall at either side of the wide-open gate, occasionally blindly firing into the compound, then receiving return fire from the Marines huddled at the corner and inside the recessed entrance by the carport.

The breach in the wall on the north side of the wall running along the main east entrance of the building was a new development—the result of explosives of some sort that had opened a gaping hole, but had also clearly injured a number of the protesters who had been nearby. Two people were motionless on the ground and others had already been dragged away.

"Who the hell are these people, Director Foley?"

"Well," Mary Pat said, her voice tight but calm, "it appears that the majority of the mob are just angry Angolans who have been whipped into a frenzy by someone. My guess is that most of them are separate from the small core of breachers who infiltrated the building. Those are who we need to get a line on."

"My people haven't gotten any hits on the few bits of usable facial rec we've collected," CIA director Jay Canfield grumbled. "And now that the main players are inside . . ."

"Predator will be on station in less than ten, sir," the tech at the computer terminal behind Ryan said.

"And there must still be plenty of agitators inside the crowd to keep things on track. And the armed crowd at the rear wall of the compound will have core people as well, I'm guessing," Mary Pat said.

"No more guessing," Ryan snapped. "We need to know what the hell is going on. This looks both staged and coordinated, so let's figure out who is pulling the strings, people."

"We're working on it, Mr. President," Canfield said.

Ryan had no idea who had killed two DIA operatives or why, but he didn't believe in coincidence, so it seemed likely that the murders would turn out to be linked to whoever was responsible for the attack on the embassy. And he felt certain that both events were linked, but more importantly that there was something else in play, some other objective that they just had not figured out yet. While the Chinese seemed likely players for the attack on the DIA operatives running a counter-signals intelligence operation, the outright execution of Americans seemed an incredible escalation. And they would have no motive he could see for the attack on the embassy in Luanda. No matter how many cutouts they used to keep any shadow involvement covert, he simply couldn't arrive at the endgame that justified the risk.

In any case, right now he needed his team focused on one thing only—the safety of the Americans inside the embassy.

"Where the hell are the Marine Raiders?" Ryan demanded. He was watching in real time as the sovereign property of the United States was being overwhelmed and Americans were being shot. God only knew what might be happening inside. He could only pray that the Marines and the embassy protection detail were keeping the ambassador and her team safe.

"Only twenty miles out, Mr. President," Robert Burgess, his secretary of defense, said after whispering a moment with Admiral Kent, his JCOS chair. "Just a few more minutes."

Ryan clenched his jaw and forced himself to remain quiet. He had the best, most capable team in the world, and they were laser-focused. The chief executive grumbling and demanding things in the background would hurt more than it would help.

Movement just north of the compound on the road behind the embassy caught his eye.

"What's going on there?" he asked, pointing to the screen. "To the north of the crowd at the rear of the complex."

"Zoom in, Spencer," Canfield said, directing his technician. "Separate camera, separate screen. Just north of the crowd on Rua Engenheiro. See it there, a bit north of the cross street?"

"Got it," the tech said, working magic on his computer to redirect the imagery from the satellite in low orbit. A second screen to the right of the main screen flickered to life and Ryan leaned in. Two high-top vans, like Sprinter vans, were moving south, arriving now at the cross street, south of which the crowd was packed tight, blocking the road. But an armed man walked in front of the lead of the two vehicles and the crowd parted as they approached, like the Red Sea, filling back in behind them.

"What are they bringing to this fight?" the SecDef asked grimly. The vans could contain anything from additional shooters to RPGs or many things even worse.

"Not bringing," Mary Pat said. "Retrieving. Look at the rear loading dock."

Ryan watched as two figures arrived on the ramp of the loading dock. They looked skyward, as if looking right into Ryan's eyes, and even on the grainy image Ryan could tell they were smiling. Then they unfolded something, a blanket maybe or . . . no, it was a large tarp. Two more men must have been out of view inside the loading dock, because the tarp spread out and then began to move down the cement stairs, just as the vans arrived at the rear. The lead vehicle accelerated suddenly and hit the gate in the wall hard, pulled forward, and repeated the move. The second blow knocked the gate all the way to the ground and the vehicles entered the lot behind the main embassy building, stopping bumper to bumper.

All Ryan could see was the large tarp covering whatever was below as it fluttered in place by the first van's passenger side. After a few moments, the van began to pull away and the tarp moved to the second van. Three seconds later, the tarp collapsed and was pulled into the second van's side door.

Then both vans pulled through the gate and headed north through the crowd.

"Raiders are two minutes out," Kudryk announced, urgency in his voice.

"Track those vans," Mary Pat said. "Under no circumstances are you to lose them, even if we lose eyes on the embassy."

Ryan understood, as did everyone in the room. The men had just removed something—or more likely *someone*—from the embassy. And if they lost these vans, they would never find whoever was taken. Ryan's thoughts went for a moment to Patricia Gonçalves, the talented career diplomat he had named ambassador to Angola.

Dear God, no . . .

"Yes, ma'am, Madame Director," the tech named Spencer said. He tapped his keyboard, and a red box formed around each van. The right screen now remained centered on the two moving vehicles, switching to a split screen. Ryan felt relief to see that the main screen still showed the aerial view of the embassy.

"Larry, update the ROE," he said grimly. "Deadly force for absolutely anyone else who tries to enter the compound. And I want prisoners from those who assaulted the embassy."

"Yes, sir, Mr. President," Admiral Kent said, but his failure to relay the order suggested he had already given it on his own.

"First pass from the AH-1 Vipers. Raiders will be on station any minute, Mr. President," Kudryk said.

Ryan watched as the crowd looked upward, and people began to panic and run. The combat helicopters could decimate the crowd in moments if he ordered it, and the crowd knew it.

21

LEAD MV-22 OSPREY FROM VMM-162
CALL SIGN EAGLE ONE
1,500 FEET OVER THE SOUTH ATLANTIC OCEAN
EIGHT NAUTICAL MILES WEST OF LUANDA, ANGOLA
1818 LOCAL TIME

United States Marine captain Nick Camperos, Alpha team leader, Mike Company, 3rd Marine Special Operations Battalion (Raiders), scanned the faces of the elite Marines in his charge from his nylon bench seat aboard the fast-moving, tilt-rotor aircraft and felt both pride and confidence. Just a moment earlier, he'd received an update on his ROE, loosening the indications for deadly force. The head shed—and the President he so admired in the White House—had signaled a commitment to ensuring he had what he needed to complete his mission of defending the embassy and rescuing the embassy staff and safely bringing all his Marines home.

"Two minutes," came the call in his Peltor headset, and he held up two fingers to the two Marine scout sniper teams at the edge of the aft ramp of the Osprey. They could easily have fit both Alpha and Charlie teams into a single Osprey, which could bench up to two dozen Marines or more than thirty if they assembled on the floor instead of the benches. But for rapid infil with fast-roping insertion, that would rather defeat the purpose. Part airplane, part helicopter, the tilt-rotor assault aircraft could travel at over 275 knots and had a range of nearly nine hundred nautical miles, making it the fastest delivery vehicle at his disposal. But to utilize its capabilities, he needed it to hover just long enough to get his Raiders onto the X, while minimizing how long it stayed stationary and vulnerable in the air.

"Raider One, Viper One—first pass is scattering the crowd, but you've still got hundreds on the ground on both sides of the embassy," came the call of the lead AH-1 assault helicopter on the shared frequency.

"Copy, Viper," he replied. "Insertion in under two minutes."

"Raider, be advised we saw no tangos in the cemetery to the south on our pass."

"Raider One," Camperos replied in acknowledgment.

He wasn't surprised. Whoever was watching the scene from heaven—the CIA, he assumed—had relayed that multiple SUVs had exited the area on the east side of the cemetery several minutes ago.

Just like al-Qaeda and ISIS—the bosses leave the kids to do the dirty work once things heat up.

He felt the deceleration and heard the disquieting sound of the engine nacelles, with their powerful Rolls-Royce AE 1107C turboshaft engines, transitioning from horizontal to vertical, turning the enormous twin propellers into helicopter rotors for their hover. The weird change always sounded like an impending engine failure to Camperos, but he'd gotten used to it over time during workups.

He gave his two scout sniper teams comprised of four highly

trained Marine snipers a thumbs-up where they crouched beside the jump master at the ramp.

Then he heard the unmistakable *ping, ping* of small-arms fire impacting the aircraft.

"Well," the pilot said with a slow, relaxed southern drawl, "looks like they're shootin' at us. Clear to engage, gunner."

"Gunner," came the reply.

Camperos looked to where a gunner sat at a console, remotely operating the DWS turret on the belly of the bird. The defense weapons system was beautifully designed with sensors, day and night vision cameras, and a computer through which the gunner controlled the turret mounted on the belly of the MV-22. The turret contained a GAU-17 minigun firing 7.62mm ammunition at a rate of thousands of rounds per minute.

A moment later he felt the floor vibrate as the gunner let loose a half-second-long burst of 7.62 at whatever the target he had identified as firing on them. Without waiting to see if the fire had been suppressed, the rope was out the back, and his four Marines left the bird in under five seconds.

"You got 'em scattered now, gunner," came the voice of the pilot, just as the rope was released and the Osprey banked right and climbed, circling around to infil the rest of Alpha team.

"Viper is making a guns pass," came the pilot from the lead Apache.

He didn't know if that meant he was shooting to kill or just keeping heads-down, but the timing would be perfect as the Osprey pilot completed his two-hundred-and-seventy-degree clockwise turn. As mission lead, Camperos had already made the call to insert both Alpha and Charlie on the roof of the embassy, the crowd having grown way beyond what a dozen Marines could engage—even the highly capable operators of the 3rd MSOB.

"Charlie is Whiskey," he heard Raider Two—Josh Dane, who led Charlie team—say, indicating they were on the roof already.

"Eagle Two is clear," came the voice of the pilot at the controls of the other MV-22B Osprey as he cleared the roof to allow Eagle One to insert Alpha team.

Camperos led his team aft to where the rear ramp was still open and a new rope bag had been secured above and positioned on the starboard side of the ramp. A second bag stood ready at the port side, where his HQ master sergeant, Enzo Fuentes, mirrored his position in that corner. 1st Squad, led by Staff Sergeant Earl Briggs, lined up behind Camperos's rope bag, and 2nd Squad lined up on the port side with Fuentes, led by Staff Sergeant T. J. Ward.

It took only a moment for the Osprey to stabilize into a hover and Camperos and Fuentes kicked their heavy rope bags out the back, where the rotor wash from the powerful twin rotors above them instantly whipped the two ropes aft. The hurricane-level prop wash was why they couldn't fast-rope out the forward side doors.

The crew chief of the MV-22B stood between the columns of warriors and checked the team as, one by one, they gripped the thick rope in gloved hands, stepped out into the air, and locked boots on as well, with only a second and a half between each Marine. When 1st Squad's Navy combat medic—a special amphibious reconnaissance corpsman—stepped off for his turn, Camperos locked onto the rope and began his slide.

As he descended, he scanned the rooftop, relieved to see Alpha team already moving to cover the crowd outside the embassy with Dane's Charlie team, except for Sergeant "Moose" Elkins, who lay prone on the end of the rope, using his full body weight to secure it in the heavy downwash from the Osprey.

Camperos's feet hit the ground and he moved quickly away, tapping Elkins on the shoulder as he did and then raising the MK18 compact assault rifle he still preferred to the 7.62 FN SCAR most of his Raiders carried now. He moved swiftly in a combat crouch as the rope hit the roof behind him and the sound of the Osprey faded as it departed expeditiously. Fuentes fell in behind him, clearing around them as they moved, and together they reached the wall beside a door leading into the stairwell of the embassy, just as they'd been briefed. Beside the door he took a knee next to Captain Dane and the Charlie team master sergeant, Kurt Moore.

"We got two machine-gun nests as advertised," Dane said, pointing to the team by the far waist wall and then above them on the next level of the tiered roof. "We're taking intermittent small-arms fire and there's a security detachment pinned down in the courtyard. Unknown number of shooters still inside, but estimated to be two dozen or so on the initial assault. No one knows how many left with the vehicles that just headed north from the rear of the building."

Camperos nodded.

"Leave your second squad up here to augment the security Marines," he said. Merriweather had made him assault leader for this mission, but he and Dane worked best when they worked together. "Then three teams of five, we clear from top to bottom. Civilians are sent up as we find them, securing them on the top floor until we decide about evacuation. We're center building here, so two five-man teams go north and south, then the third leads south down the stairwell and we rotate. Oorah?"

"Oorah," Dane barked.

Camperos called Briggs and Ward, who each brought their other four men to the door. They quickly briefed the assault and then he crowded in with Briggs and 1st Squad beside the door, with Dane and his squad on the other side of the door.

Camperos chopped a hand, Kurt Moore yanked the door open, and Moose Elkin led 1st Squad through the door.

They moved with the rhythm and pace of a well-choreographed ballet, a result of hundreds of hours of training and drills, as well as real-world combat operations together. No one spoke; they simply cleared their corners to the left and right. The following two members in the formation moved straightforward to the stairs of the landing, clearing down. Brian Gerard, their Navy medic, and Camperos surged to the stairs leading down to the next landing. They held security one level down the stairs, while the team assembled by the door to the top floor of the embassy, which was mostly residential spaces according to the brief.

They repeated the breach, this time clearing the corners and forward in the hall, then holding security while Dane and his team surged onward as a diamond formation a few yards until they reached the first two doors.

Camperos noticed the doors were open and took a moment for a silent prayer, hoping they had been left ajar by embassy personnel rushing to evacuate to the basement, where a reinforced safe room could accommodate all civilian staff during an attack. He watched as Dane and Moore simultaneously breached the left and right doors, then led his four-man team forward, leaving Moose and Pav to secure the stairwell door past the open entrances.

As he passed, he glanced into the room where Dane shouted, "Clear." His throat tightened at the sight of two bodies on the floor: a man in jeans and a polo shirt and a woman in workout gear, both clearly dead in large puddles of blood.

"Two angels, fifth floor," he heard Dane say in his earpiece.

Then he arrived at his door, steeled himself, and chopped a

hand straight ahead before leading the breach through the partially open door, clearing left as Briggs moved right, then sensing more than seeing Gerard and McFall surging between them.

"Clear," he barked.

He thought the room was empty, but then heard Gerard's tight voice countered that assumption.

"One angel in the corner, fifth-floor residence," his combat medic said.

They headed to the door, knowing that the LFOC back on the *Kearsarge* would be carefully cataloging the body count.

Dane had leapfrogged past them and already was calling "Clear" of the next room on the right as Camperos exited. Motion down the hall caught his eye, and he raised his MK18, dropping the holographic sight onto the figure coming out of a room halfway between Camperos and the door at the far end of the hall. The figure threw his hands up in the air and dropped to his knees, head down.

"We're United States Marines," Camperos barked. "Keep your hands where we can see them!"

At the words, the figure—a man, he could see now—raised his head, mouth open and eyes wide, and his shoulders sagged.

"Oh, thank God," the man said, sobbing. "I . . . I heard so many gunshots. So many people were screaming. I . . . I hid under the bed . . ."

Camperos dropped his weapon to forty-five degrees and motioned with his head for Gerard to move forward to the man. The medic sprinted up as Camperos scanned left and right, searching for threats.

"I'm an American," he heard the man say as Camperos helped him to his feet, though the medic ran a hand over the victim first, checking for weapons or an S-vest.

"It's okay," Gerard said gently. "We've got you. You're okay now."

The door at the far end of the hall, leading to the north stairwell, burst open. Camperos quickly adjusted his holographic sight to the two figures entering. Instantly recognizing the threat, he shouted, "Get down!" as his finger reflexively moved inside the trigger guard of his weapon. He shifted right to clear a line of fire past Gerard and the American victim he was assisting.

Gerard reacted immediately, pulling the American to the ground and shielding him with his own body. Just then, the bright light of twin muzzle flashes registered in Camperos's vision before the sound of gunfire reached his ears. Camperos squeezed the trigger in rapid succession, watching the lead assaulter pitch backward as the 5.56 rounds hit their mark. He was aware of rounds whizzing past him from behind as another Raider fired at the second enemy shooter.

A split second later the hallway was quiet except for the final *tink* of a spent casing bounding off the floor and the two enemy shooters were down. He locked eyes with Gerard, who was still lying on top of the civilian he'd just saved.

"Holy shit, boss," Gerard said with a crooked grin.

"Secure him in the first room by the south stairwell while we clear this hallway," Camperos ordered.

Gerard quickly complied, hustling past Camperos with the shell-shocked embassy staffer in tow. Camperos brought his rifle up and formed up with the rest of their stick to continue clearing rooms. As he moved down the corridor in a combat crouch to the next door, dread filled Camperos as to who or what they would find next.

22

SOMEWHERE

Kyle opened his eyes . . .

But the world was still dark.

It took his sluggish brain a beat to realize why.

There was a black hood over his head. He was lying on his right side on a hard, uneven surface. His hands were bound together at the wrists in front of him with some sort of rope or cord. His ankles did not feel bound, but he moved his left leg slightly and confirmed that they were. His skull throbbed terribly as if someone had his head in a vice and was alternately tightening and loosening the crank. The epicenter of the pain seemed to be located at the back of his head. Lying very still, he called upon his remaining four senses to help him paint the picture that his eyes couldn't see.

He felt motion.

And he heard tire noise.

Which meant that he was in a vehicle. This supposition was confirmed a moment later when the vehicle hit a bump, and the jolt bounced him on the metal deck he was lying on. Due to the lack of wind noise, he concluded he was in the back of a cargo van or SUV rather than the bed of a pickup truck.

It took him a beat to reconstruct the events that had led him to this moment.

Once he did, dread settled over him like a cold, wet blanket.

He was alive, but every future experience awaiting him was likely to be more negative and unpleasant than the one preceding it. Such was the nature of being a hostage. He'd been taken instead of being executed, which meant the men who'd knocked him out must have concluded that Kyle had some level of value as a bargaining chip. Whether the kidnappers knew he was the President's son was an unknown and important variable he needed to solve. It would probably go better for the other hostages if his pedigree remained a secret for as long as possible. Because from the kidnapper's point of view, possessing one extremely valuable bargaining chip made the other chips seem more disposable by default. Also, policing one hostage and serving his biological needs was easier than managing those of many.

From a self-preservation perspective, these thoughts helped tamp down Kyle's fear.

But knowing that others might be sacrificed in his place created an altogether different kind of angst in him. His mind went to Madison Bennett, the last person he'd seen before being knocked unconscious. She'd been alive then. He remembered hearing her scream as everything went black. He was desperate to know if she'd also been taken and whether she was hooded and bound and lying on the floor beside him, but he resisted the urge to whisper her name. He didn't know what kind of people he was dealing with, and the last thing he needed right now was a rifle butt to the face. The hood would come off at some point, and when that time came, some of his questions would be answered.

Eventually, the van stopped.

Commotion and conversation ensued, the latter in a language

he didn't understand. Then the van started moving, but not for very long before stopping again. This time, he felt the clunk of the transmission being shifted into park and heard vehicle doors opening a beat later. Someone nudged Kyle in the middle of his back with either a boot or a rifle butt.

"You, wake up," a male voice said in accented English.

Kyle stirred and let out a legitimate groan as his head pulsed with the movement.

"Sit," the voice commanded.

Kyle did, and this time his head throbbed so severely that he felt momentarily nauseous. The analytical portion of his mind determined he was likely concussed from the blow.

Someone grabbed his wrist binding and pulled him forward.

Kyle obediently scooted on his backside, feet forward, until his heels slid off the end of the floor. He kept scooting until he was sitting at the edge of the cargo compartment. He lowered his feet, knees bent at a ninety-degree angle, and the soles of his shoes made contact with the ground.

"I'm trying. Stop pushing me," a woman's voice said.

"Madison?" he asked, reflexively turning his head to the left.

"No talking," the male voice barked.

"Kyle?" said a female voice, definitely Madison, but this was followed immediately by a thud and a yelp of pain.

"I said no talking!"

Anger flared in Kyle's chest, and he almost lashed out, but his analytical brain quickly retook control. He couldn't do anything to help her blindfolded and bound. Now was not the time to challenge or antagonize his captors. Number one, he didn't even know who his captors were; and number two, right now he was severely physically and strategically disadvantaged. But hopefully, with time that would change. He needed to be patient, accumulate data, and look for an opportunity to gain and apply leverage.

Eventually, someone would make a mistake.

If there was one thing you could count on assholes to do, it was to overestimate their perceived advantage.

A hand grabbed the rope binding between Kyle's wrists and jerked him forward.

"Stand," the male voice commanded.

Kyle stood, but without any visual feedback, his already compromised equilibrium wasn't up to the task, and he lost his balance. Strong hands grabbed him by the shoulders and steadied him on his feet before he could fall. A flurry of conversation unfolded between two men, probably in Kimbundu because it didn't sound like Portuguese. An arm wrapped around his shoulders and urged Kyle on.

He complied.

As he continued shuffling, he counted his steps and memorized the turns as he was led into a building. After about twenty seconds of walking, Kyle's escort halted him.

"Stairs down," the man said in heavily accented English.

Kyle probed the ground in front of him with his right foot and felt the first drop-off. Relying heavily on the support of his escort not to lose his balance and fall, Kyle took the first step. Then he brought his back foot down onto the tread. Instead of alternating feet, Kyle repeated the process carefully, feeling with his right foot for the next tread. He'd been navigating staircases since he was a toddler without difficulty, but it turns out that being blind and unable to use your hands on a railing turned this simple, basic task into a challenging one. He descended the concrete staircase methodically—right foot first on each of the fifteen treads—and arrived in what he assumed was a basement. The air smelled earthen, and the temperature felt a few degrees cooler than before.

His guide, who'd been conscientious on the stairs, keeping Kyle from falling, now gave him an impatient shove in the back and barked at him.

"Walk."

Kyle walked.

Underfoot, he noticed the ground change from concrete to dirt. As he shuffled forward, he heard men barking orders at the other hostages from the embassy. It was impossible to tell, but using fuzzy logic he deduced that three others were with him. The way that sounds echoed, the uneven quality of the dirt floor, the way the air felt increasingly stale and stagnant—it didn't take long before Kyle understood he was not in a basement but a tunnel. He continued dutifully counting steps and turns, but after ten turns and two hundred steps, he realized it was pointless. He wasn't being led through a simple tunnel, this was a warren—a warren he'd likely never find his way out of.

Eventually, he was halted by his minder.

"Stairs, up," the gruff voice said.

Kyle felt for the first tread. Finding it and settling his foot, he stepped up. Climbing was easier than descending, and he made his way to the top of a wooden staircase without too much difficulty. At the top of the stairs, he was escorted into what he assumed was a room on the first floor of a building, where he was directed to sit on what felt like an unpadded wooden chair. Then someone bound Kyle's torso to the chairback with a heavy, coarse rope.

His relocation to this remote site did not bode well. Not only did the tunnel system mean the location was likely hidden and would be difficult for the Americans to find, it also meant the next stage of his journey as a prisoner was about to begin.

Torture.

Kyle had originally assumed his kidnappers had taken him for ransom purposes, but he could easily be wrong about that. Maybe the men who'd grabbed him were Islamic extremists. Instead of ransoming Kyle for money or other geopolitical means, maybe he was meant to be camera fodder.

He felt himself shrink in the chair, subconsciously trying to become small and insignificant. The black cloth hood he wore had a tight weave, and he couldn't make out anything through the fabric. The only thing he could tell was that this room was a little brighter than when he'd been unloaded from the van. Not being able to see amplified his sense of vulnerability a hundredfold. The man who'd escorted him to the room could be holding a club, ready to swing at Kyle's face with punishing effect. Or he could be holding a machete, ready to flay flesh from Kyle's body in strips.

Or chunks.

He shivered with terror at the gruesome thought.

No, not shivered—spasmed. His entire body shook as if he'd stuck his finger in an electrical outlet. Inside the hood, the rank odor of his breath and perspiration was beginning to nauseate him. Was *this* what people called the stench of fear?

The anticipation of the unknown—this was the driver of his fear, and he told himself to make his mind a blank slate. He forced himself not to anticipate.

He forced himself not to predict.

The man who'd delivered Kyle to the room departed. Kyle knew this because he heard the man walk out and then shut and lock the door. Alone and motionless, he listened. A moment later, he heard another door slam. He guessed that room was nearby, possibly next to his own, and it was probably where they'd put Madison.

"You are probably wondering why you have been spared," a male voice said in accented English loud and confident behind Kyle.

Kyle jerked with a start against his bindings and let out an involuntary string of curse words that would have made his brother, Jack, laugh and his mom give his backside a whack with her palm.

The speaker chuckled. "Thought you were alone, hmm? Well, surprise . . . you're not."

Kyle heard padded footsteps, then felt a metal point gently trace the back of his right hand and up his right forearm to the elbow. The pressure was light, not enough to slice or even scratch his skin, but enough to leave no doubt that the instrument was a knife.

"You don't talk much, huh?" the man said, and the knifepoint departed.

Kyle said nothing.

"You work at the embassy, Jack?" the man said, using the name on Kyle's NOC.

"Temporary assignment," Kyle said, his voice sounding surprisingly calm and melancholy to him, like that of a veteran inmate on death row.

"What type of temporary assignment?"

"I'm a telecommunications technician. I was helping them with their network," Kyle said.

"Good, I need someone good with communications in the coming days," the man said.

Kyle decided whoever this man was that he was important. High-level lieutenant in the terror organization that raided the embassy, or possibly even the boss. His English was practiced and easy and he spoke with the immense ease and confidence that comes only with power and authority.

"How well do you know Ambassador Gonçalves?" the man asked.

"Can you take off my hood, please?" Kyle asked.

"It is terrible inside the hood, isn't it? The inability to see what is about to happen makes the fear so much worse."

And the knifepoint was back, this time pressing against the inside of Kyle's upper left thigh, six inches below his groin. Kyle resisted with all his might the urge to move his leg away from the knifepoint, which had poked through the fabric of his pants and punctured his skin. He felt a dribble of blood run down the inside of his leg.

"Tell me everything you know about the ambassador, and I will consider removing the hood. What type of woman is she? Cooperative or defiant? Stubborn or open-minded?" the terrorist said with a casual demeanor as if they were having a business lunch together.

Kyle hesitated, then answered truthfully. "I don't know the ambassador, but from what I understand she's a woman of integrity and courage. I suspect she'll disappoint with regards to whatever illicit agenda you're hoping to achieve with her kidnapping."

"I would have thought you'd try to be a little more useful given your situation. If you're of no value to me, why should I keep you alive?"

"I'm sitting here asking myself the same question."

The terrorist said nothing for a beat, then he laughed. "You've got balls, and you make me laugh, which is more than I can say of most men in your situation. I want you to spend the next hour thinking about how you can make yourself useful. When I return, I expect you to give me something of value."

The knifepoint pressure disappeared from his thigh, and Kyle heard the interrogator walk toward the door.

"For me to help you, I first need to know what it is that you want," Kyle called as the door lock shifted.

"Regime change," the terrorist replied simply, and before slamming the door added, "and for your government to let it happen."

23

SAFE ROOM/SCIF
BASEMENT OF THE U.S. EMBASSY MISSION IN ANGOLA
R. HOUARI BOUMEDIENE 32
LUANDA, ANGOLA
1935 LOCAL TIME

Camperos and a young Marine with a clenched jaw and wet eyes stood beside a metal door as the man who had identified himself as the embassy RSO punched a code into a panel. There was a loud click as the magnetic lock released and Camperos and Staff Sergeant Briggs took a step back as the large door swung inward. Camperos tapped his finger against the trigger guard, keeping his MK18 assault rifle down at a forty-five, but ready to bring it to bear. RSO Tejada had not been at the door when it was secured. He had been in comms with the people inside, he said, but there was no way to verify they were not under duress until they cleared the room.

Camperos surged in behind Briggs, aware of the two security Marines behind him, breaking right and clearing the right corner. Then he turned forward, where a dozen or so personnel in civilian attire were huddled, looking shell-shocked, around a large table in the center of the room.

"Ambassador Gonçalves?" he pressed, scanning the group.

"She isn't here," a man in suit pants and a white T-shirt said. "I'm Jim Theron, her CLO."

"What's a CLO?" Camperos asked, interrupting the man and scanning the terrified faces in the room. One woman was sobbing openly, her arms wrapped tightly around her waist to hold a cotton robe over what looked to be pj's.

"Community liaison officer," Tejada answered for the man. "I don't see the ambassador nor her executive assistant, Maddie."

"Maddie was on the fifth floor, checking on a visitor who was supposed to be leaving for the airport," the woman in the robe said. "I never saw her when we got the word to report to the safe room."

"Was the ambassador with her?" Camperos asked.

"No," the CLO said. "She was in her residence, I believe. We had a meeting scheduled."

"We are securing the compound, and you are safe now," Camperos said, forcing the hard edge out of his voice. He could still hear scattered, muffled gunshots above them, but it was hard to tell if it was incoming or outgoing. "We need to know who is here and who is missing. We also need to know anyone you may have seen who was . . . injured or anything else as you made your way here. We have the situation under control."

Another burst of gunfire above them seemed to make a counterpoint and made the woman jump.

"Listen up, people," Tejada said, reaching for a legal pad beside a computer station along the wall. "I know most of you, but I need everyone to write down your names and positions on the top page here. Then on the second page, write down the names and positions of anyone from the staff you saw upstairs, where you saw them, and how they were, okay?"

"Okay," the man named Jim Theron said. "Where is Freddy?"

Tejada turned to Camperos.

"Freddy Vincent is the CIA station chief," he said. The RSO turned back to the group. "Freddy was with me and is okay. He's working with my team and the Marine detachment upstairs."

"Were there other CIA operators in the fight?" Camperos asked. If there were ground branch operators here, that would be a real asset. But Tejada look pained.

"We had a ground branch team here, but they were off station at the airport when the attack came. They took wounded during an operation to secure materials after the attack on the DIA cyber team and were evacuating. Freddy had a small team here of two analysts, a cyber dude, and one case officer. They may have secured in their own SCIF, which is on the ground floor, and the case officer, Ellen Baker, was likely in the fight, if I know her."

"And the DIA team?"

Tejada shook his head. Camperos watched the woman in the robe try to write her name with a shaking hand, but then drop the pen on the floor. Another woman in workout clothes picked it up.

"I can do that for you, Riley," she said gently.

"The DIA team wasn't working out of here," Tejada said. "A small team of three, but two were killed, which sort of kicked off this shit show time-wise. The survivor was still here, but he's no shooter, just a tech guy, I think. He was the one who was supposed to be leaving for the airport that Riley was talking about—the one Ambassador Gonçalves's executive assistant, Madison, was checking on when the attack began."

"So, combat assets are your RSO team and the Marines, plus a CIA case officer?" Camperos asked.

Tejada nodded.

"But my team is really just the Marine security detachment and one other DSS agent, and he's out of station right now. Understand, this was not considered a high-risk station."

"All good," Camperos said, and patted the man on the back.

He counted fifteen people inside the safe room including Tejada, so that meant there were forty-seven others, not including the DIA guy, which made forty-eight. He'd kept a mental tally of the survivors they'd secured and moved to the fifth floor, which he thought was twenty-nine. There were sixteen angels, meaning dead, but he thought at least two of the bodies found were likely bad guys, so call it fourteen.

He needed to account for at least five others.

And one of them was the ambassador and another her executive assistant.

"When are we leaving?" the woman named Riley asked in a shaking voice.

"That's for the ambassador to decide," Camperos said, then glanced at Tejada, who gave him a grim look. "Or the President. But we will begin evacuating wounded immediately and the rest of your noncombatants will likely follow soon after. We'll secure here for now until we know better what the next steps are."

"Okay," Riley said and slipped back into a chair.

"Charlie One, Alpha One," Camperos said, keying his mic. "Sitrep?"

"Charlie One," came Dane's response. "Building secured. My Second Squad is still rooftop with the organic Marines engaging scattered shooters in the crowd. My First is at the front augmenting the security force."

"Copy," Camperos said. "Alpha Nine, One."

"Go for Alpha Nine," HMC Gerard replied immediately.

"Nine, secure the wounded for dust-off where you are. Have Five bring anyone not injured to the sublevel safe room for now."

"Nine, copy," Gerard replied.

Camperos turned to Tejada.

"Work on the list for us, sir," he said. "We're gonna make a pass to find the ambassador and any other missing."

"You got it, Captain," the man said.

But his face said that he knew what Camperos also suspected.

The ambassador would not be found.

Because she, and maybe some others, had been taken.

24

OFFICE OF THE DIRECTOR OF NATIONAL INTELLIGENCE (ODNI)
1500 TYSONS MCLEAN DRIVE
MCLEAN, VIRGINIA
1450 LOCAL TIME

Director Mary Pat Foley set her leather satchel-style briefcase on her large oak desk and then leaned across to press the button on her phone.

"Yes, Director Foley?"

"Hot tea, Jerrod," she said. "And then thirty minutes undisturbed, please."

"Of course," Jerrod said. "Can I bring you something to eat, Director?"

She smiled. Jerrod had become quite paternal the last few months, constantly reminding her to take care of herself. But then Jerrod knew precious little about the path she'd taken to this office. She knew she was getting older, like they all were, and twenty-nine-year-old Jerrod didn't see the young woman who, with her husband, had run clandestine operations behind the Iron Curtain for years. He didn't see the woman who had managed assets against the Russians and East Germans in East Berlin, or even the deputy operations director of the CIA, who had run scores of deep, dark operations around the world with a younger Jack Ryan and John Clark. No, to Jerrod she was a tough but older bureaucrat who loved her tea.

She thought she maybe loved that about him.

"That would be great, Jerrod," she said. "Bring me something."

"Of course, Director Foley," Jerrod said, sounding very pleased that he was taking good care of her.

Mary Pat hung her coat on the coat stand in the corner and then slipped into the oversize leather chair behind her desk, firing up both laptop computers already open there. She logged in, then typed in the twenty-character codes to access SIPRNet—the high-side, classified network.

She had work to do—work that would be mostly assigned to her best agencies and task forces, perhaps, but she wanted a deep dive to get familiar first. The truth was she yearned to be back in the Situation Room, watching things unfold in real time on the big screens. But the work she needed to do was better, and more efficiently, done here. As the computers began the searches based on her key words, she pressed 3 on her speed dial and cradled the phone against her shoulder.

"Good morning, Director," came the crisp answer after half a ring. "How can I help you?"

The voice of Tammy Butler, the current CIA director of operations, was confident and calm, but held the strain of someone who knew the shit was hitting the fan in Africa.

"Tammy, do we have numbers yet from Luanda?"

"Yes, ma'am," Butler replied, and Mary Pat could tell from her voice it was bad. "Was just about to send it to you on the high side. We have eleven confirmed dead, including one agency analyst, Ollie Meiser—a great guy and top analyst with nine years and a wife and toddler back here at home. The rest of the dead are embassy staff. Seven wounded including two critical—also organic staff except two Marines, one of whom is the second critical. And we have four unaccounted for."

Mary Pat nodded. It was grim, indeed, but she worried it might be a much larger number of kidnapped and dead.

"The ambassador?" she asked, but her sixth sense had already answered that one.

"Afraid so, ma'am," Butler said. "Both her and her executive assistant, Madison Bennett. The fourth person was a DIA operator on assignment passing through the embassy. All I have is the NOC he used at the embassy, but I'll have an ID from Daniel any time now, I expect."

"Let me know," Mary Pat said. Daniel Weingard was the interim operations director at the DIA, likely to be made permanent, she'd heard from Robert Burgess, the SecDef. The DIA was a distant cousin for her. Unlike the rest of the IC, which fell under her direct authority, the DIA was their own, independent intelligence community reporting directly through their chain to the SecDef, as they were part of the DoD. The relationship was solid, and so far Weingard had been a team player, but it wasn't required, since she wasn't in his chain of command.

"Of course, Director Foley," Butler said. "What do you need from me? We still have our station chief, Freddy Vincent, on station. He doesn't have much of a team, but I'm prepared to augment whenever you pull the trigger."

She understood. One of the mission dead was one of Butler's own. She wanted a piece of the fight.

"When the dust clears the President will give more direction, Tammy. But you know President Ryan—he's one of us. He'll do whatever it takes to get our people home."

"Yes, ma'am," Butler said and sounded like she believed it.

"I expect I'll be back with you very quickly," Mary Pat said, then broke the connection.

As she did, Jerrod entered, balancing a tray with a big mug of tea and an assortment of sliced fruit and little coffee cakes. Just where the hell the kid found this stuff was a curiosity for her, but she suspected he had a stash somewhere prepped for days like these. Just as he set it down, the phone on her desk chirped instead of rang—a hint that this was a high-side call, coming in encrypted.

"Thank you so much, Jerrod," she said, but the kid was already hustling for the door. He knew what the chirp meant, too.

"Foley," she said as she looked at the digital screen. It was a 202 number—so an inside-the-Beltway office—but she didn't recognize it.

"Director Foley, it's Dan Weingard," a strong but tired voice said. She had met Weingard only a few times, but they interacted at least indirectly often since he was director of operations for the DIA.

"Dan, thanks for calling. I'm sorry for the loss you had."

"Thank you, ma'am," Weingard said. "I imagine you heard, we've lost the third member of that team now as well. Our surviving operator is among the four missing from the embassy attack."

"Yes, I just heard," Mary Pat said. She knew exactly what Weingard was going through. She had spent a lifetime at the CIA, from field officer to station chief to operations director to director. The losses got harder as you climbed the chain, not easier—at least for the good ones, and she suspected Dan Weingard was one of the best. "You should know we'll use every asset in the IC and your DoD to recover your man."

"I know you will, and I appreciate that," Weingard said. Something in his voice suggested there was another shoe about to drop. "But that's not why I'm calling. Look, I just wanted to give you a heads-up, Director. Our missing agent is Kyle Ryan—the President's son."

The shoe was much, much bigger than she had anticipated and when it dropped it took her breath away.

"What? How is that possible?" she asked. "Kyle Ryan is a naval officer . . ."

"He was, ma'am," Weingard said. "He came over to us a few months ago. We respected his request to keep the transfer private."

Now her mind was reeling. Did Jack know his son had moved to the DIA? She was almost certain he did not. She couldn't imagine him not mentioning it to her. At first, she felt angry, but then realized she respected Weingard for the move. His agent had requested secrecy and Weingard had honored that, even knowing something like this was possible.

"I appreciate you letting me know, Dan," she said, finding her breath again. "I'll have to let the President know immediately."

"Of course," Weingard said, sounding genuinely surprised she would even imagine otherwise. "I was planning to reach out to let him know personally, but wanted you to know first. Respecting Kyle's request was my call and I take full responsibility."

"I admire that, Dan," she said, and she did. "And President Ryan will as well. But I would ask that you let me notify him, okay? The President and I go way back."

"Of course," Weingard said, and Mary Pat wondered if he felt a little relieved to have the burden shifted to her. "But do let him know this was my call and I stand by it."

"I will, Dan," she said. "And I'll keep you in the loop."

"And I, you," he replied. "We should coordinate our efforts and assets on this one."

"I agree," Mary Pat said. "I will call you soon."

And then the DIA OPSO was gone.

Mary Pat let out a long slow breath and leaned back in her comfortable leather chair. She closed her eyes a moment and then opened them and reached for the phone.

"Yes, ma'am?" Jerrod answered immediately.

"I need the car around again," she said. "I'm heading back to the White House."

"Right away, Director," Jerrod said and clicked off.

Mary Pat ignored the tea and snacks and rose, grabbing her coat and slipping her bag back onto her shoulder.

This was a conversation that would need to happen in person, and as soon as possible.

25

CABINET ROOM
O ESCRITÓRIO DO PRESIDENTE (OFFICE OF THE PRESIDENT)
PALÁCIO DA CIDADE ALTA
RUA PEDRO FURTADO
LUANDA, ANGOLA
2011 LOCAL TIME

Francisco Luemba, the president of Angola, scanned the faces of the ranking officials sitting around the conference table in the Cabinet Room. In this moment of crisis, not one of the men or women present had the courage to look him in the eye. Not one of them had the courage to answer his question.

So, he asked it again.

"Will someone please explain to me how the American embassy could come under attack in our capital city, and not a single one of you acted in your official capacity to stop it?" he said, his voice booming.

Still, no one answered.

"If I could fire all of you right now, I would," he said, shaking his head.

Finally, someone broke the silence.

"Mr. President, if I may speak freely . . ." said José Silva, the director general of the Serviço de Investigação Criminal, Angola's national agency responsible for criminal investigations, law enforcement, and maintaining public order.

Luemba waved his hand in a dismissive *Too little, too late* gesture, but he signaled for Silva to speak nonetheless.

"The SIC counterterrorism division is working the problem, and we have identified three individuals in the riot crowd who are members of the Patriotic Front for Unity," Director Silva said. "I think Victor Baptista should be our primary suspect in this attack."

"You think? You think!" Luembo said with disdain, raising his voice. "I don't give a damn about what you think, I care about facts. I care about results. If Baptista and the PFU are behind the attack, then find him and put him in shackles. Or better yet—put a bullet in his head!"

Silva nodded. "Yes, Mr. President, I have agents scouring the city for Baptista as we speak."

Luemba turned his gaze to the lone empty seat at the table, which belonged to General João de Souza, chief of the general staff of the Angolan Armed Forces. While Luemba held Silva responsible for the intelligence failure leading to the attack on the embassy, he blamed de Souza for what could only be described as a complete security collapse. Why were counterterrorism squads from Forças Especiais Angolanas not marshaled in time to support the American Marines and prevent the fall of the embassy? Why weren't a dozen M113 armored personnel carriers loaded with Army infantrymen and military police officers not sent to secure the scene? Luanda was the nation's capital city. The military could have easily put down this uprising, but hadn't reacted in time.

Why?

Luemba had many questions, and he needed the military's top general to answer them. He'd been told by his own chief of staff that General de Souza had declined this emergency cabinet meeting because he was busy leading the military's response at the Ministério da Defesa Nacional—the central command and headquarters of the Angolan Armed Forces. But so far, Luemba had seen or heard nothing of the sort. Had the Cidade Alta been secured? Had Luembo's order for martial law in the city been implemented? Luemba could accept de Souza's absence, but why had he not sent a deputy in his stead? A liaison from the general's staff should be present to answer these critical questions. He was about to turn to Admiral Cardosa—the head of the Angolan Navy—for answers when gunfire echoed in the corridor outside.

Marta Almeida, the minister of trade, screamed and several other cabinet members dropped out of their chairs and ducked under the table. Luemba, who was seated at the head of the table, instinctively popped to his feet and defiantly faced the closed double doors that separated the Cabinet Room from the hallway outside. As he did, two members of his security detail converged on him—one from either side—to drag him backward and shield him with their bodies.

A moment later, the double doors flung open and General de Souza marched into the Cabinet Room flanked by a dozen soldiers in full combat gear, who Luemba recognized as belonging to the Grupo de Operações Especiais (GOE), Angola's most elite special operations unit. The relief Luemba felt from seeing de Souza almost instantly turned to dread as the look in the general's eyes told the Angolan president everything.

This was not a security precaution.

It was a coup.

Most of the special operators turned their weapons on the members of the cabinet, but the two men in front targeted Luemba's protection detail. Two pops and twin muzzle flashes dropped the agents before they could react, their bodies falling simultaneously, leaving Luemba standing alone. The double execution happened so fast and methodically that nobody in the room even reacted at first.

"Members of the cabinet," General de Souza said, addressing the assembly. "You are hereby relieved of your duties."

"João, what is the meaning of this?" Luemba said, using de Souza's first name in a last-ditch attempt at leveraging the decade-old friendship he'd had with the military man.

A man whom I had named as godfather to my child, Luemba thought with wounded pride. *A man whom I appointed as head of the military when the rest of the cabinet lobbied for another.*

"I'm sorry, Francisco," de Souza said with an expression that was anything but apologetic, "but your tenure as president has come to an end. Angola needs change, and that's not something that you're capable of."

Luemba had not navigated a civil war and twenty years of politics without learning a thing or two along the way. There would be no talking his way out of this situation. De Souza had flipped, and there was nothing Luemba could do or offer the man at this moment to make him flip back. A flashbulb image of de Souza's disappointed glare popped into Luemba's mind's eye. The memory was from two years ago when the general had expressed to Luemba his desire to participate "financially" as well as professionally in Angola's defense infrastructure contracts. When Luemba had eschewed the idea as a conflict of interest, his friend had bristled. The request had taken Luemba by surprise. João had been with Luemba for years. He knew better than anyone that

Luemba had run on an anti-corruption platform. Certainly, he couldn't go along with such a thing.

Apparently, my successor has no such qualms about offering such things, he thought as he swallowed hard and formulated his reply.

"And who, my friend, is going to usher in this change you speak of . . ." Luemba said, narrowing his eyes as anger supplanted his fear. "You?"

De Souza fixed him with a closed-lip smile. "I'm a military man, not a politician. My only aspiration is security and prosperity for all, something you were not able to deliver on your watch."

Luemba resisted the urge to lash out. His looked to the ground, where his faithful bodyguards lay motionless, each man with a crimson hole in the middle of his forehead, eyes open and lifeless.

If de Souza's orders were to kill me, I'd already be dead, Luemba thought. *Time is my best ally.*

"And what happens to the rest of us?" the minister of trade asked, hugging herself and trembling as she did.

"By orders of interim president Baptista, all of you are to be remanded into custody and taken to São Paulo prison, where you will await trial," the general said, then turned to his GOE team leader. "Cuff everyone in this room and prepare them for transport."

"You are taking me to prison, like a criminal?" Luemba shouted, indignation trumping his fear. "After all we have done?"

"Not you," the general said, not meeting his eyes this time. "I believe our president has something special in store for you, Francisco." The man used his first name not with familiarity but with disdain.

"And what is that?" Luemba asked, his voice no longer so steady.

"You will see in time," de Souza said, smiling. "Your vice president is already in custody. My understanding is there will be a very public interrogation of the facts."

Luemba felt his throat go dry.

He had no doubt that this would be followed by a very public execution.

This was how regimes changed in sub-Saharan Africa, after all.

26

**SITUATION ROOM
THE WHITE HOUSE
WASHINGTON, D.C.
1550 LOCAL TIME**

Ryan couldn't help but keep his eyes glued to the center screen, where the satellite feed still showed an aerial view of the United States embassy mission to Angola. The news that Ambassador Gonçalves, her executive assistant, and men from both the CIA and DIA were missing was not a shock, after what they'd watched. But it was a gut punch anyway. It was pretty clear that the crowd had thinned, but somehow it had also become more chaotic.

They've lost leadership, he thought. He clenched his jaw, because that meant that, as suspected, there was more to this story. *This was all for some other player to get our ambassador.*

There had been intermittent gunfire exchanged between the crowds on both sides of the compound and the Marine element still holding security from the rooftop, though there had been no additional attempts to enter the embassy grounds. The Marines had shown incredible fire control discipline, using fire mostly to push back the crowds from the breach points, but so far they had not killed anyone since the more intense gunfire during the assault and infil of the Marine Raiders. Those wounded or killed insurgents had been dragged away long ago now.

"Looks like they're losing some of their enthusiasm," Secretary of State Scott Adler said, noting the same thing Ryan had observed. "Maybe they've lost their courage after seeing some of their friends killed."

"Lost their leaders," Jay Canfield, his director of the CIA, corrected, again making the same assessment as Ryan had. "My gut says this was staged by someone else and whoever the puppet master is has long gone."

"Which begs the question not only of who, but why," Ryan grumbled. There was definitely something more at play, but he had no idea what. The what, he assumed, would help inform the who. "We need to find our people before the next stage in whatever the hell this is unfolds."

Canfield nodded, but then leaned over his computer, his eyes narrowing as some new intelligence data stream came in, Ryan assumed.

"The wounded and dead are all aboard the *Kearsarge*, Mr. President," General Bruce Kudryk said from where he, too, bent over a computer. "We can launch the Sea Stallions or additional Ospreys anytime to remove the additional embassy personnel."

Ryan pursed his lips, but said nothing.

After a few moments, Kudryk's boss, chairman of the Joint Chiefs Admiral Lawrence Kent, spoke next.

"Mr. President? Do you want us to finish the evacuation? Once the civilians are gone, the Marine Raiders can help sterilize the facility, then evacuate the Marine and security presence to the ARG as well."

Ryan felt his irritation grow into anger.

"No," he said curtly. "This is American territory inside a nation we have diplomatic relations with. We have no idea who is responsible for this, but it doesn't seem to be President Luemba and his government, so how does it look if we pack up, turn tail, and run?" He met Admiral Kent's eyes. "Evacuate the embassy of remaining civilians. Then fortify the position with additional Marines from the MEU if needed. But we will not surrender our embassy, and most especially not with our ambassador missing. I want our flag flying over the embassy, and you light it up when night falls. Are we clear?"

"Crystal clear, Mr. President," General Kudryk said, and despite the weight of the moment he wore a satisfied and proud grin.

"Mr. President," Canfield interjected, his voice communicating that he had something urgent to share.

"What have you got, Jay?"

"I don't have your who, but I may have part of the what," his CIA director replied tightly, looking up from his secure computer. He held Ryan's eyes. "There's just been an attack on President Luemba's office while he was in a cabinet meeting. There are several dead and it looks like Vice President Rosine de Carvalho was taken in a separate attack as she was leaving the National Assembly building. Obviously, a coordinated attack."

"This is a damn coup," Secretary Adler exclaimed. "Someone's overthrowing the government."

"Someone not friendly with the United States," Kudryk pointed out. "Why the hell attack our embassy? Why poke the bear?"

"Great questions," Ryan said. "But at the moment, none of them trump the question of who. China had a clear motive to attack our DIA operation. I don't believe in coincidences, so might Beijing be the puppet master here?"

"With what motive?" Adler asked. "We're way behind the Chinese in Angola, and they've spent billions shoring up a relationship with Luemba and his government. Why throw all that investment away?"

"Maybe Luemba was having a change of heart?" Arnie suggested. "We've been working pretty hard to get a foothold in Luanda."

Ryan looked up as the door lock released and Mary Pat Foley came through.

"I thought you were working this from McLean," he said, surprised to see her. How the hell had she heard about all of this already?

"Felt I needed to be here," she said.

Canfield gave her a quick update.

"Oh, shit," Mary Pat practically whispered.

"Yeah," Ryan said. "Is there any reason you can think of why the Chinese might be pulling these strings?"

Mary Pat considered a moment before answering.

"I need to dig deeper, Mr. President," she said. "On the surface it seems like they would be shooting themselves in the foot—trading an already great investment for something likely less certain, but there is a lot we don't know."

"Well, that's the point isn't it? And the understatement of the year," Ryan grumbled. "We don't need more questions, people. We need answers."

"Do you still want to hold the embassy, Mr. President?" Admiral Kent asked. A reasonable question if the country was about to explode into a shooting-war coup.

Ryan thought a moment.

"Yes," he said. "Larry, you've got the entire MEU out there in the ready group. Use them however you need to hold and protect the sovereign territory of the United States in Luanda. At least until we figure out what the hell we're dealing with."

"Will do, Mr. President. To be clear, you want me to land additional Marines? Any limits on the size of the force?"

"Use all of the resources of the MEU—the entire ground- and air-combat elements—however you need to ensure we keep our people safe," Ryan commanded. "Take surrounding areas in the blocks around the embassy if you need to form a defensible perimeter, but the American mission in Angola is ongoing until we find and safely return our ambassador and the other missing Americans. We're not going to tolerate this shit."

"Yes, sir," Kent replied, and Ryan was glad again he had surrounded himself with such amazing people. The admiral would get it done, and would do everything in his power to bring home the missing Americans and every Marine in the MEU.

"Answers," Ryan said again, slapping his palm on the table. "Now. We meet back here in one hour."

The room began to empty, and it was not lost on him that Mary Pat Foley kept her seat. After the door was closed, he leaned in, studying her face for a clue.

"Everything okay, Mary Pat?" he asked. But he could tell from her face and the pain in her eyes it was not. "Oh, God. It's not Ed, is it? Is he okay? Did something happen?" Maybe her husband had been in an accident or become ill.

She shook her head, eyes wet.

"It's not Ed," she said softly, resting her hand on his arm. "It's Kyle . . ."

"Wait . . ." Ryan sputtered, caught completely off guard. "Kyle? My Kyle? What happened?"

The invisible band around his chest made it hard to breathe. What on earth could have happened to Kyle? The last he had heard he was traveling frequently in his cyber job with the Navy, most recently working with Task Force 59 out of Bahrain.

"Jack, we believe that Kyle was one of the hostages taken from the embassy in Luanda."

Mary Pat sat, her hand still on his arm, watching him. A part of him wanted suddenly to burst out laughing. The joke was horrible, cruel, and inappropriate—but what other explanation could there be? But Mary Pat's wet eyes told another story.

"How?" he choked. "How is that possible? Why in the hell would he be in Angola? This is a mistake—or some sort of Chinese misinformation attack, or . . ."

He stopped and waited for her to speak.

"Jack, listen to me. Kyle took an assignment at the DIA. He's part of a cyber task force that addresses tech options to enhance our signals intelligence in denied areas. He and his team were in Luanda setting up hardware . . ."

"Wait," Ryan said as the pieces clicked into place. "You're telling me that Kyle was part of the three-man team attacked in Luanda?"

"Yes," she said gently. "Kyle was the sole survivor of the attack, and miraculously, he made it to the embassy that night. He was lodging there when the attack came. He's among the missing and is believed to be among the hostages taken from the rear of the building along with Ambassador Gonçalves."

He had never felt weaker or more out of control—not since terrorists had tried to kidnap his wife and daughter so many years ago. And now . . . now history was repeating itself, only this time with his youngest son.

"How did I not know any of this?" Ryan roared, his panic morphing into red-hot anger.

"I would have told you if I had known myself," Mary Pat said simply, "but I didn't. Kyle was offered the position and separated from the Navy to take it. I just got a call from the DIA's director of operations, who notified me, and I came right here to tell you in person. Kyle took the position only a few months ago and had requested that his decision be kept secret for now, something Dan respected."

"This . . . this isn't possible. We need verification." Ryan felt the room tilting and closed his eyes. He needed to tell Cathy, but what would he say?

She would be devasted by this.

"I know, and we're working on getting our facts straight. But don't worry, we'll find him, Jack."

Ryan took a moment to rein in his emotions.

Kyle had always been different—more private, more to himself. He had been a quiet loner all through high school and had finally found his place at the Naval Academy. Why would he give that up? He understood and even admired his youngest son for forging his own path, but resigning his commission to work for the DIA perplexed Ryan.

He opened his eyes and met Mary Pat's gaze.

"Whoever is responsible for this attack and kidnapping must be dealt with harshly and swiftly, Mary Pat. We will get our people back and those behind this will pay. I will used the full power of this office and this nation to bring justice. And if China is in any way complicit in this operation, they will feel the power of this office as well."

For a moment, Mary Pat looked like she might offer a counterpoint, but instead she just nodded.

"Of course, Jack," she said.

"I want the hostages found, rescued, and brought home safely. And I want read in on how you intend to do that, Mary Pat. "

"Understood," she said, softening again. "If you want, I can pull Clark off his assignment and task him with this."

"No," Ryan said, shaking his head. "We need him and Task Force 99 in place in case Syria escalates. And anyway, I have no intention of being quiet or secret here, so Clark's skill set is not what I need. I'll execute my executive power through the might of the *Kearsarge*'s ARG and her Marines. They're going to know we're coming."

Mary Pat gave his arm a final squeeze, smiled tightly, and then rose, heading for the door.

After she was gone, he leaned back in the chair, head back and eyes closed, and let out a slow breath. The love of his life was, at this very moment, waiting for him to return to the family house on the Chesapeake, but that wasn't going to happen. A part of him wanted to call her and tell the harrowing news now, but he decided against that. He needed more information and a plan. Something hopeful to offer Cathy to soften the news that her youngest child was in the hands of terrorists in Angola. But he could only wait so long—because their marriage was built on trust and honesty—and the longer he waited to tell her the truth the more she would feel like he was managing rather than supporting her.

Hopefully, Mary Pat would have solid intelligence for him soon.

If not, there was gonna be hell to pay.

27

PALÁCIO PRESIDENCIAL DA CIDADE ALTA (PRESIDENTIAL PALACE)
RUA PEDRO FURTADO
LUANDA, ANGOLA
2114 LOCAL TIME

Baptista stepped out of the SUV and gazed at the Presidential Palace. As he surveyed the grand facade with its stone columns, three-arch entrance, and upper-level balcony, he mused about how strange and ironic life could be. This building didn't exist when he'd been vying for power during the civil war. If his side had won, the palace would probably look completely different because he would have had presided over the design and construction as president. As it was, he'd been the outcast scraping out an existence in the shadows, while Luemba reigned in opulence. Baptista had never stepped foot inside this building, and his curiosity was beyond piqued. Make no mistake, for Baptista the Presidential Palace was as much the prize as the power that came with the office.

My days living in squalor are over.

With bodyguards flanking him left and right he strode toward the entrance, where General de Souza was waiting to greet him under the portico. De Souza snapped to attention and saluted Baptista.

"Mister President," the general said with a formal and serious tone. "Welcome to the Palácio Presidencial da Cidade Alta."

Baptista resisted the urge to grin like a child and forced his expression to be presidential. "Thank you, General. Status report?" he said.

"The traitors are in custody in the basement. My intention was to transport them to the São Paulo prison for incarceration until their public trial. Unless, of course, you have alternate instructions."

Baptista nodded thoughtfully and took a moment to appear to ponder the question.

The general was already demonstrating his worth by carrying out his orders methodically and smartly. While executing Luemba and his cabinet on the spot would have been the most expedient and simplest way to seize power, it was not a shrewd and sustainable strategy. For Baptista to legitimize his ascension and cement his reign as president, he needed to discredit and vilify Luemba and the cabinet. He needed to stoke public outrage by exposing the administration's corruption and lawlessness. Only by winning the hearts and minds of the Angolan people would he be accepted as interim president and duly elected in the next cycle. And it was equally important that—beyond the coup itself— Baptista operate under the rules and norms of the existing institutions of government. De Souza understood that Luemba and his conspirators must be afforded the semblance of due process under the judiciary branch so that Baptista was not viewed as judge, jury, and executioner himself. The last thing he wanted to trigger was another civil war. The current institutions of government were hard-fought and legitimate in the eyes of the populace.

He had zero aspirations of knocking down the halls of power only to rebuild them from scratch. No, Baptista's goal was simple—swap places with Luemba, replace the cabinet with loyalists, and leave the rest alone.

"A wise decision, General," Baptista said. "Make it so, but before transporting the traitor Luemba, I will first see him in my office."

This comment seemed to take de Souza by surprise, but he nodded regardless. "In that case, let me escort you and let you get settled before I have my men fetch the pres—" the general said, stopping midsentence before correcting himself. "The *prisoner.*"

"Thank you, General," Baptista said. "Lead the way."

Baptista entered the palace and was immediately impressed by the grand stature of the foyer with its towering high ceiling, white walls with gold embellishments, and exquisite carpets and flower arrangements. Either Luemba had fine taste and an eye for architecture and decor or the man had a very talented designer on his staff.

Most certainly the latter, Baptista decided, and became suddenly and acutely aware of how out of place and undignified he must look in his black-on-black tactical clothing and dirty combat boots. *By this time tomorrow, I'll have been measured by a tailor and ordered a dozen of the finest Italian suits that money can buy,* he mused.

"This way, Mr. President," de Souza said, gesturing to the left before they reached a decision point that would have revealed Baptista's ignorance of the palace's layout.

Baptista nodded and allowed himself to be led through a set of double doors, exiting the grand reception foyer.

"How are the troops reacting to the news of the president's arrest?" Baptista asked, the question loaded with subtext.

"So far, there has been limited dissent, but the day is still young," the general said. When Baptista didn't respond, de Souza added, "Don't worry, I'm prepared to do whatever is necessary to maintain discipline in the ranks."

Baptista both liked and appreciated the rejoinder, because the truth was, without the general, the coup would fail. De Souza was the most powerful figure in Luemba's government with control of the military. Had de Souza chosen to usurp Luemba and seize power for himself, he could have easily done so, and without Baptista's help. But this wasn't how de Souza operated. The general was a proud and accomplished military leader who'd dedicated his life to service. He'd achieved his life's primary aspiration by ascending to the rank of chief of the general staff of the Angolan Armed Forces. The reason de Souza had flipped on Luemba had nothing to do with power and everything to do with respect.

In de Souza's mind, Luemba failed to treat him as an equal—as a partner. Just because the general wasn't interested in swapping his uniform for a suit, it didn't mean he didn't have strong opinions and valuable insights on politics and governing. Courting de Souza from the sidelines and in secret had taken Baptista years, and standing here now looking into the man's eyes Baptista still couldn't believe he'd pulled it off. Five years ago, he told de Souza that President Luemba didn't respect or value the general's contribution in transforming Angola into the great and powerful nation it was today. After planting that seed, all he'd had to do was wait for Luemba to water and fertilize it until it took root and grew into a giant acacia tree in the general's mind—a prickly, thorny tree de Souza could not possibly ignore.

Hubris did the rest.

On reaching the president's office, Baptista crossed the threshold and stopped to survey the seat of Angolan power. He looked at the massive African mahogany desk with the vacant ebony-dyed, leather-upholstered executive chair behind it. He sniffed and was instantly repulsed by the lingering stench of the adversary he'd just deposed. Like a lion who'd just acquired a pride, he stalked around the desk and took a seat in the high-back chair to lord over his domain. Only now did he permit himself to smile in victory.

"It suits you," de Souza said, standing tall on the other side of the massive office in the same place he'd stopped upon entering.

Baptista's shifted his eyesights from the middle distance to the desktop, where framed photographs chronicling important moments in Luemba's life and of family members stood. The people in the pictures were all staring at him, their fake smiles a masquerade to hide their loathing and judgment.

In his mind, he could hear them shouting at him: *Usurper! Traitor! Imposter!*

His smile morphed into a snarl, and he leaned forward and toppled every single framed photo so that it lay face down.

"That's better," he said and felt a wave of relief.

"Mr. President, would you like me to send for the prisoner now?" the general asked.

"Yes," Baptista said. "And I want you to be here for it."

The general flinched at this, but bobbed his head in compliance and ordered that Luemba be brought up from the basement.

Baptista loved loyalty tests and demanded his partners and subordinates pass them regularly. He knew that de Souza and Luemba were once friends—good friends—with the general being named godparent of the president's daughter. Close friendships, even fractured ones, did funny things to a man's heart. Baptista could not risk de Souza going soft or changing his mind in the middle of the battle.

I need to see callous proof with my own eyes to be sure.

A few minutes later, the traitor Luemba was escorted into Baptista's office at gunpoint. The former president was handcuffed and had been stripped of his expensive suit coat and tie. Massive sweat stains encircled the armpits of his untucked white dress shirt, but he looked otherwise unmolested. On seeing Baptista sitting in the president's chair behind the president's desk, Luemba flared with outrage.

"You . . . of all people!" the deposed president seethed. "You won't get away with this, Baptista. You know that, don't you?"

Baptista stood and pointed to the pair of uniformed soldiers flanking Luemba. "Make him kneel."

The soldiers looked at de Souza. Then the larger of the two warriors stepped behind Luemba and slammed the butt of his rifle into the backs of Luemba's legs to drive the former president to his knees. Luemba grunted in pain, cursed in defiance, and even made an effort to stand, but a strong hand on his shoulder kept him down. Like an apex predator stalking prey, Baptista circled the desk and slowly descended on the kneeling man.

"You've let yourself go, Francisco," he said, looking down on his vanquished foe, who'd gotten fat during his tenure as the nation's leader. Physically, at least, the man kneeling before him bore little resemblance to the lean, fit, and ferocious warrior whose side had won the civil war over two decades ago.

Luemba spat defiantly on the toe of Baptista's right boot.

Baptista exhaled and shook his head in theatrical judgment. "Funny . . . my boots have been in need of a good spit shine. Clean them up, traitor. Use your mouth."

Luemba scoffed, but when he realized that Baptista was serious, he looked pleadingly to de Souza for help.

The general met and held his former boss's beseeching gaze.

For an instant, Baptista saw compassion flicker in de Souza's eyes. Then the general's expression hardened and his stare went cold. He signaled to the larger of the two soldiers, who obediently pressed the muzzle of his machine gun into the divot at the base of Luemba's skull.

Luemba resisted at first, but the soldier forced the defeated president's head down to the floor so he could commence the dirty business of licking Baptista's boots until they were clean, black, and shiny.

28

SOMEWHERE

Kyle desperately needed to urinate, but he'd decided to hold it until the muscles keeping his bladder closed failed. He would not dehumanize himself by pissing his pants so long as he was conscious and of sound mind and body.

But the discomfort was becoming unbearable, and he wasn't sure how much longer he could last.

Every second felt like a minute.

Every minute like an hour.

He had no idea how long it had been since his first interrogator had left. The man with the knife had said he would give Kyle an hour to think about how to make himself useful. Kyle felt like more time than that had passed, but his painful, bulging bladder was definitely skewing his perception.

He exhaled inside his hood and felt the black fabric lift momentarily away from the tip of his nose and cheeks before settling back into place.

The terrorist had said that when he returned, he expected Kyle to give up "something of value." That instruction alone wasn't particularly helpful to Kyle, but the thug's parting comment had been.

Kyle replayed that part of the exchange back in his head:

"For me to help you, I first need to know what it is that you want."

"Regime change," the terrorist had said, *"and for your government to let it happen."*

Epiphany struck and all the pieces clicked into place.

"I've been swept up in the middle of a coup," he mumbled inside his hood.

Then he chuckled because this wasn't a particularly complicated puzzle. The only reason it had taken him so long to solve it was because his skull had been bashed with a rifle and he was in the middle of dealing with hostage trauma. For some reason, he found his own dim-wittedness quite funny, and the chuckle turned into a slaphappy belly laugh—one that he quickly regretted because it strained his bladder to the limit with each abdominal contraction. He wasn't one to laugh easily or often, and there was no doubt in his mind that the strain of his situation was affecting him.

Footsteps in the hallway and the sound of the lock shifting on his door instantly transformed his laughter back into fear, and he fell silent. The door opened and every muscle in his body tensed with dire anticipation. The new arrival said nothing, just walked toward Kyle's chair—booted feet clomping on the floor. Kyle felt the hood shift as fingers grabbed the fabric at the top and yanked. Now free of the hood, the room exploded with light and Kyle squeezed his eyes shut against the brightness. But wanting to see, he forced his eyes open in a tight squint, and the looming figure standing directly in front of him grudgingly came into focus. An African man, dressed in all black, save for a crimson beret atop his head, stood facing Kyle. He was holding a mobile phone out in front of him, the camera aimed at Kyle's face.

"Open your eyes," the man commanded in English, but Kyle thought the voice might be different than his original interrogator.

"I'm trying," Kyle said. "It's very bright."

Kyle heard the simulated aperture *click* sound effect that mobile phone cameras made when taking pictures. Apparently satisfied with the pics, the terrorist disappeared the phone into one of the many pockets of his black cargo pants.

"I need to go to the toilet," Kyle said. "Quite urgently. Please."

The man snorted, but walked over and undid the rope binding Kyle to his chair. Then he helped Kyle to his feet and pointed to a five-gallon bucket in the back right corner of the room.

"There is your toilet."

Kyle raised his bound wrists to the man in a wordless request for the plasticuffs to be cut.

The terrorist shook his head. "No."

Kyle turned and walked to the bucket. Since his hands were bound in front of him, he was able to unzip his fly and relieve himself into the bucket without too much difficulty. What followed next was the longest-lasting urination session of his life. If not for the five-gallon capacity of the bucket . . .

"Hurry up," the terrorist growled.

Kyle resisted the urge to quip that, unlike a transmission, his bladder only had one gear and instead nodded.

Eventually, he finished, zipped up his pants, and turned to face the insurgent fighter. Without the distraction of a painful and distended bladder, Kyle was finally able to concentrate. The analytical part of his brain, which until now had been in hibernation mode, woke up and did what it did best—crunch data. Given the terrorist's English skills and confident air, one could easily mistake this man for the leader of the coup, but Kyle suspected otherwise. This man's demeanor and actions reflected tasking—tasking that would only be given to a senior and trusted lieutenant—but tasking nonetheless.

Also, Kyle was becoming increasingly certain that this man was not the same man he'd interacted with before. That man's command of the English language had been more natural, nuanced, and arrogant. This guy took a more direct brass tacks approach. Besides, the leader of a coup would be too busy playing field marshal to spend hours interrogating the hostages himself. It occurred to Kyle that, to legitimize himself, the coup leader would want to create one or more degrees of separation from the act. This could have explained why Kyle's hood had remained on for the duration of the last conversation, but had come off now.

"Return to the chair," the man said and pointed to the chair where he'd been bound.

Kyle momentarily bent at the waist to stretch his tight and aching hamstrings, then did as instructed. He used the opportunity to survey the room, which, thanks to the hood, he'd not been able to see until now. The space was spartan and unremarkable—little more than eight feet square—with a single wooden chair, a dirty concrete floor, and the waste bucket in the corner. A single light bulb, screwed into an electric light socket that hung down from the low ceiling on a wire, was the only source of illumination. Now that his eyes were light-adapted, he realized the room was, in reality, rather dimly lit.

After resecuring the rope binding Kyle to the chair, the man spoke.

"I told you when I came back you needed to give me information of value. Now, tell me something important," the lieutenant said, still trying to sell the lie that he was the same man and the boss, a lie Kyle wasn't buying.

"I'm sorry to disappoint you, but like I told your boss earlier, I don't have any important information to share," Kyle said.

Surprise rippled across the insurgent's face at the comment.

Clearly, he'd not expected Kyle to flip the script on him. A heartbeat later, the man's expression hardened, and Kyle could see him contemplating his next action. He'd most certainly been given authority to use torture to extract information, but his boss had also likely put restrictions on the severity and ways and means of that torture. Kyle guessed that brutalizing faces was off-limits so that the hostages could be put on camera. Then again, the thug had just taken Kyle's picture, so maybe Kyle's face was now fair game for mauling.

His heart rate picked up, as it seemed from the fire in the terrorist's eyes that a blow was certainly coming. Unfortunately, his instincts were right. But instead of striking Kyle in the face, the man pulled a baton from his belt and whacked Kyle's unprotected right shin dead center on the leading edge of the bone. The agony from the strike took Kyle by surprise, and he heard himself half bark, half wail in pain. For a split second, he thought the blow might have broken his leg, that's how acute the pain was, but when he looked down he saw his foot still flat on the floor and connected to his knee.

"Ask me a spuh . . . spuh . . . specific question, and I'll try to answer it," Kyle stammered.

"Do you work for the CIA?" the interrogator asked.

"No."

"Who do you work for?"

"I work for a government contractor that provides IT services to the State Department. U.S. embassies abroad account for eighty percent of our business," he said and could literally feel a massive hematoma forming in the middle of his shin.

"What are you doing in Angola?" the man asked.

"I just told you, providing IT services to the U.S. embassy."

"What kind of IT service?"

"We're building out and securing their network infrastructure in Luanda."

"Why?"

"Because the Angolan government just signed a multibillion-dollar communications infrastructure with the Chinese, and my government does not trust the Chinese."

The terrorist nodded as if he were some kind of tradecraft and geopolitical expert. After a pause, he said, "What will your country be willing to pay for your safe return?"

"Unfortunately for both of us, the answer is probably nothing," Kyle said, his shin throbbing more than he imagined possible from a single blow. "The current administration has a 'no negotiation' policy with terrorists."

The man's expression soured at this comment. "We are no terrorists. We are liberators."

Kyle was about to correct the man, but the last thing he wanted was another blow to his shin, so instead he nodded. "Like I said, I wish I had better news. Believe me, I want nothing more than to go home."

"If they won't negotiate you for money, what is your value to us?"

"They won't negotiate me and the other hostages for money, but they will negotiate," Kyle said. "Let's say you took four hostages. Then, your boss could trade us for four of your people who might be detained somewhere else."

"How do you know we have four hostages?"

Kyle shrugged, despite the ropes binding his arms. "Lucky guess."

The interrogator's eyes flared with anger when he realized he'd been tricked. Kyle braced for another shin strike, but the man just swung the club threateningly in a circle with his right hand.

"If what your boss said to me is true," Kyle said, meeting the man's gaze, "if regime change is the endgame and he wants to rule Angola, then tell him that trying to intimidate and threaten President Ryan into compliance is the wrong strategy. It will likely have the opposite effect."

"Explain," the man said, his curiosity seemingly piqued.

"President Ryan is a man of principle. He's also a former Marine, which means he doesn't back down from a fight. Your boss attacked the American embassy. Even though the embassy is located in Luanda, once the Stars and Stripes is raised, the ground that it is built upon becomes American sovereign soil. Do you understand what I'm saying? By attacking the embassy, your boss attacked America. In President Ryan's mind, America is at war with your boss and his Army. So you need to tell your boss that, right now, his very best option is to de-escalate and return all the hostages unharmed. If not, the President will order the U.S. military to come in here and exact retribution."

"How do you know so much about what the American President will or will not do?"

"Because I voted for him, and since that day, I've watched how he's reacted to every international crisis since he became President," Kyle said. "How else can I decide if I want to vote for him again?"

The terrorist lieutenant stared at Kyle a long moment, holstered his club, and turned to leave.

"Can I get some water, please?" Kyle called after him.

The interrogator waved his hand as if shooing away a buzzing mosquito, left the room, and locked the door.

Kyle exhaled through pursed lips, feeling lucky as hell he'd escaped the interaction with only a single injury. He couldn't see his shin because of his pant leg, but using the calf of his other leg he could feel that the swelling was already significant—a half-baseball-size lump formed on top of his right shin.

His mind went to Madison.

Even though they'd only just met, he'd felt an unusually strong connection with the embassy staffer. And if he was being honest with himself, maybe he could even call it an attraction. Kyle knew he was awkward at the male-female interaction, far more than most his age, but despite his flat exterior, it didn't mean he didn't *feel* things. His problem was always in the showing of feelings, or even talking about them.

Except with Mom . . .

The thought brought an unwelcome wave of the exact type of feelings he fled from and he shook the thought away.

He was almost positive that Madison had been taken and the thought of what she might be going through filled him with dread and anger. After coming to in the back of the cargo van, he was positive he'd heard her voice. He'd tricked his interrogator into confirming they'd taken four hostages, one of whom he already knew was Ambassador Gonçalves. If Madison was the third, that left one more person he still needed to identify. Hopefully, the fourth person was either CIA station chief Freddy Vincent or the embassy RSO, Julio Tejada, because if so, with some help, he might be able to orchestrate their escape.

The clock was ticking, and what he'd told the terrorist lieutenant about the President was true.

"Dad doesn't negotiate with bullies," he murmured to himself. "Never has, never will."

If there was one thing Kyle knew he could count on to be as immutable and unchanging as Mount Everest, it was that Jack Ryan would not compromise his principles. Not even if his own son's life was hanging in the balance.

29

PLANNING TACTICAL OPERATIONS CENTER (TOC)
USS KEARSARGE (LHD 3)
SOUTH ATLANTIC OCEAN
FIFTEEN NAUTICAL MILES NORTH-NORTHWEST OF LUANDA, ANGOLA
0545 LOCAL TIME

Captain Miles entered Planning and let out a sigh of relief. Captain Andy Ho, the commodore commanding Amphibious Squadron Six—or just Phibron 6—sat at the head of the planning table, but the room and table were packed full. The commodore had assembled the entire team to plan what would be the largest amphibious assault force Miles had ever been a part of, outside of training exercises. Captain Ho was a great officer and a talented tactician and strategist. The problem was, he had not come up through the Gator Navy. The officer had served a JO tour on an LPD, but after moving to aviation and serving as a helo driver in Seahawks, his return to the surface Navy had been mostly on ships in the carrier strike group. That wasn't necessarily a disadvantage in Miles's mind—hell, any outside-the-box thinking was good in this work. But that was only true when the officer was humble and knew what he *didn't* know. In this case, the commodore had very limited experience putting Marines on the beach. Sometimes, a commodore with less insight and humility would take charge and plan missions that, frankly, just could not reasonably be executed simply because of limitations on ships, aircraft, and sailors that they may not have foreseen due to lack of subject matter expertise.

Andy Ho was proving himself to be an excellent and humble leader—as evidenced by the full room. On his XO tour, Miles had served under a Phibron without that insight, and the inevitable conflict between that officer and the LHD skipper Miles had served under had been hard to watch.

"Thanks for getting here so quickly, skipper," Captain Ho said with a smile. "We're just about to dive in."

"Of course," Miles said, and took a seat beside Colonel Crocker. "I'll fill Chris in after, since I need him on the bridge with the THREATCON, what it is," he added, referring to his XO, Captain (select) Chris O'Melia. They were basically on a wartime footing now, and that meant he needed O'Melia or himself on the bridge or immediately available to deconflict anything coming in. He'd been in CIC himself, working closely with the TAO to monitor any emerging surface threats. They had also launched fast boats to interdict any civilian ships that might represent a threat, so there was an assload of moving parts in play.

"As you heard, Tony, we've been ordered by the White House to put a force of Colonel Crocker's ground combat element ashore to bolster our protection of the American embassy," the commodore said. "That means getting Marines from the 2/6 ashore, but also vehicles and the logistics of keeping them supplied. The center of the operation is American territory at the embassy, but we've been given permission to secure several blocks around the embassy as a perimeter to keep it safe. That means a lot of Marines, a lot of support material and personnel, and a big-ass beach-landing operation to get it all in place. As a result, I've asked BMCS Bryson here to be part of the planning as well as Lieutenant Jen Knowles, our LDO and ops officer for well deck operations. And, of course, my fellow aviator, Commander Abreu, our air boss, and his LCPO for flight deck operations, Master Chief Ashley Glover. I want everyone to speak freely so we can get this done right the first time, and just as important, I want all the shops to know the mission and what everyone else will be doing."

Miles felt the already considerable respect he held for Captain Andy Ho go up even further.

"Let's start on the beach and work backward," Ho said, gesturing to Colonel Crocker.

"Thank you, Commodore," Crocker said, and stood, clasping his hands behind him, his shoulders square. "Our mission is to secure the American embassy, and to do that with the number of unknowns and the current threat, the force we need is considerable. My planners will give you the details of the operation, now called Operation Sea Fury, in a moment, but the big picture is this—we are landing two of the 2/6's rifle companies with the third held in reserve. That, with two platoons from the 2/6 weapons company is already a force of nearly three hundred infantry Marines, not including the Marines from the 2nd LAR, who will crew up the four joint light tactical vehicles and two anti-tank LAV-25s we intend to land with their assigned Marines. This means we need massive support from the Beachmaster units to coordinate bringing all this shit ashore using LCACs and LCUs."

The colonel turned to a Marine captain seated at the table in front of where the MEU commander stood, looking like the warrior he was. "Allen?" he said, gesturing to the younger Marine officer.

"Thank you, sir," the Marine said, tapping a laptop and bringing imagery they were now all familiar with up on the big screen on the wall. "As the colonel said, this is the real shit and will have many moving parts. Ahead of the beach landing, we intend to insert the remainder of Major Merriweather's special operations company—Bravo and Delta teams—into the embassy itself to augment Alpha and Charlie and the rather scant Marine security detachment there. This gives them the firepower to protect the embassy during the infiltration, should the assholes behind all of this get some ideas while we're coming in. They will remain staged at the embassy for contingency operations and on standby for rescue operations once the American hostages are found. This will be supported by the air combat element with a footprint nearly identical to the first insertion."

"The President is very clear that he wants our operations run from the embassy itself—demonstrating our commitment to United States territory there," Colonel Crocker said from beside the captain. "To that end, we will also be inserting the H and S staff into the embassy for onsite command and control." The colonel turned to Miles. "I still intend to coordinate all of this from the LFOC for maximal comms and coordination with the ARG," he said, alleviating Miles's inevitable question. It made the most sense that the air elements would remain based aboard the *Kearsarge* and the *Arlington*, where it would be easiest and safest to rearm and refuel. The Marine captain confirmed his suspicion when the air boss chimed in to ask the question.

"Are we setting up a FARP with a fuel bladder on the beach?" Commander Abreu asked.

"Negative, sir," the captain said. "With the ship only minutes from the beach, just outside the territorial line, the safest thing here is to stage the entire air combat element off the ARG. We will have air support operations for both infiltrations using the Vipers, Venoms, and two of the F-35s from the MAGTF. Then we'll set up a rotation to have continuous air support backed by a Ready Five at all times while our ground element is on the beach. We'll get into air details and get your input momentarily, sir."

"Perfect, thanks," the aviator said and jotted notes in the little green notebook on the table in front of him. Miles watched his air boss whisper something to Master Chief Glover, and she nodded and wrote in her own green notebook.

The planner then began to detail the flow of Marines, followed by vehicles including twenty Humvees and the new JLTV mixed with some LAV-25s. "We have the A3 variant of the LAV-25s, so they're highly capable and we're sending two of the AT variants, since we have no idea who the hell is controlling the Angolan military right now."

"If anyone is," Miles's command master chief, Bill Earhart, said from the other side of the table. "They sure aren't doing shit to put any of this down."

The captain agreed.

"Which is why we're operating on the premise that some or all of the military, at least locally, is involved in the coup, or whatever the hell this is. That's courtesy of our intel working with the Navy side shop and is up-to-date. Which is why we want some anti-tank LAVs ashore," he said, referring to their tank-busting LAV variants. "We'll also have mortar and an anti-tank team with the weapons company and, of course, we've got our air assets."

Miles was proud of the team he had here—both Navy and Marine—but this was one gigantic operation with a million ways it could go wrong. They had trained for this dozens of times and had conducted full-scale exercises twice.

But the real world was always different, wasn't it? And as the saying went, no good plan survived first contact with the enemy. That was more true here than ever, since it was unclear just who the hell the enemy really was.

The Marine turned to Lieutenant Jen Knowles, Miles's LDO for well deck operations.

"Let's start running through the flow for the amphibious portion, okay?"

"Oorah," Knowles said, the Marine battle cry bringing a slight smile to the faces of the Marines present. The Marines and sailors had really come together the last few months. The Marines no longer saw Miles's sailors as taxi drivers and the sailors no longer saw the Marines as crayon-eating soldiers taking up berthing, making the chow hall line unbearable, and crowding the gym. They had come together as a team, and he'd seen groups of Marines and sailors out on liberty together in Portugal—the best evidence ever that they were gelling into a single fighting unit.

Miles listened intently and took his own notes in his own little green, government-issue hardcover notebook as the Marines and his LDO went over the flow of amphibious landing craft that would deliver Marines to the beach. They would get to the air element in a moment, but it was clear that the CH-53Ms from the *Arlington* would cycle to deliver a security force of Marines to the beach first, ahead of the landings, to support and protect the Beachmaster unit setting up to receive the Marines ashore.

The team dug deep, throwing out what-if scenarios, talking about weather and winds, and ship movements to facilitate launch and recovery. The LCACs were basically hovercraft and were launched and recovered with just inches of water in the well deck to prevent typhoons of water blowing dangerously around the bay when they came and went. The LCUs, on the other hand, needed full ballast to launch from deep water in the well, and the entire evolution required moving the boats and LCACs into and eventually out of the launch well quickly and safely. The well deck of an LHD or LPD was one of the most dangerous places in the Navy.

The team worked hard, and the Phibron had established and now maintained a culture where everyone participated, questioned, made suggestions, and improved the plan. Over the hour and a half, which went by in a flash, the plan came into focus, was revised, and came into focus again. Miles realized how incredibly proud he was to be part of this team. And he realized how insanely capable that team was. They were about to put a thousand American servicemen and -women in harm's way in a hostile country under fire. Thousands more would be supporting that from a vulnerable position just off the coast—the next briefing he would have with the ship's company to plan out their defensive posture to mitigate air and sea threats during the operation—and he truly believed they were as ready and able as it was possible to be.

Proud . . . trustworthy . . . bold . . .

Just as it said beneath their crest—the *Kearsarge* motto.

"One additional idea, Colonel Crocker?"

Miles saw the man who spoke was standing at the back of the room, squared away like the other Marines, but his name tape said NAVY.

"What are you thinking, Doc?" Crocker asked, addressing the man Miles now recognized as Commander Jim Schneider, the Navy surgeon in charge of the fleet surgical team for the 22nd MEU.

"Sir, I'd like to stage my team on the beach as well," Schneider said. "We can set up inside the perimeter—the blocks that will sort of become our forward operating base, with the embassy at the middle."

"The *Kearsarge* will only be a quick flight away, Doc," the Marine planner said. "Seems like a big risk with little reward."

"Maybe," Schneider said. "Unless this shit show explodes and we have trouble getting a CASEVAC bird onto the beach. If the Angolan military is involved, that means they have anti-aircraft missiles and tanks, too. I can mitigate that risk and shorten the time to give care by setting up ashore, like we're designed to do."

Crocker nodded, liking it, and Miles was impressed by the stones of the Navy doctor, who was choosing to be even closer to the fight to treat his Marines.

"There's room on the embassy grounds, for sure," the planner said.

Schneider grinned.

"I have a better idea," he said and walked to the screen, pointing with a finger at the complex of buildings just to the east of the embassy, edged by the tall building where Merriweather's Raiders had inserted their sniper teams on the first infil. "This is the Boa Nova medical school," he said, then turned and looked over his shoulder, grinning. "I can't pronounce the Angolan or Portuguese or whatever name. But in addition to offices, classrooms, and housing there is a hospital . . . here." The surgeon pointed to a modest four-story building in the center of the compound. "It ain't much, but they have wards, four ORs, and an emergency room and clinic, not to mention an ICU. More importantly, the hospital is not in use. They moved the whole operation to the Climed facility eight blocks farther east. Now, I'm assuming that this whole damn thing will fall inside the perimeter y'all set up. So, once we have the facility, it'll make a nice staging area for some of our vehicles and equipment, and I can set up the FST in it that will be perfect. If things go sideways, we can still operate and treat our Marines."

The surgeon turned, hands on hips, and stared at the room.

"Allen?" Crocker said, looking at the Marine lieutenant.

"I like it, sir," he said. "Once the ground force secures that area, we move the FST to that building by air. We give them their own security detachment, just like H and S."

"Ness?" Miles asked, addressing his air boss.

"Shouldn't disrupt us at all on the air side," Abreu said. "We'll cycle a single 53 over from the *Arlington* and have them on their way in minutes."

"Do it," Crocker said.

"Done," Doc Schneider said, and faded back to the wall.

A tap on his shoulder brought Miles's eyes back up, where he saw a second-class petty officer leaning in.

"Sir, the XO wanted to let you know our riders are arriving in a few minutes."

"Ah, great," he said, and Crocker looked over.

"Riders?" the colonel asked.

"Yeah," Miles said. "Washington thought we needed an intel task force to augment our N2 shop."

"Who the hell's idea was that?" Crocker said, showing annoyance that the Marine colonel usually excelled at keeping inside.

"No idea," Miles said. "CMC, can you greet our guests and get them out of the way?"

"Of course, sir," Bill Earhart said. "Perfect time for some pogue riders to come aboard to eat our chow."

The room chuckled and the command master chief excused himself.

"Okay, blue side," Miles said to the Navy side of the room. "What are we missing?"

They dove back in, looking for holes in the plan.

Because the operation was kicking off in the coming hours and mistakes in this room meant mistakes later that could cost lives.

And lead to a new war, where superpowers might be picking sides.

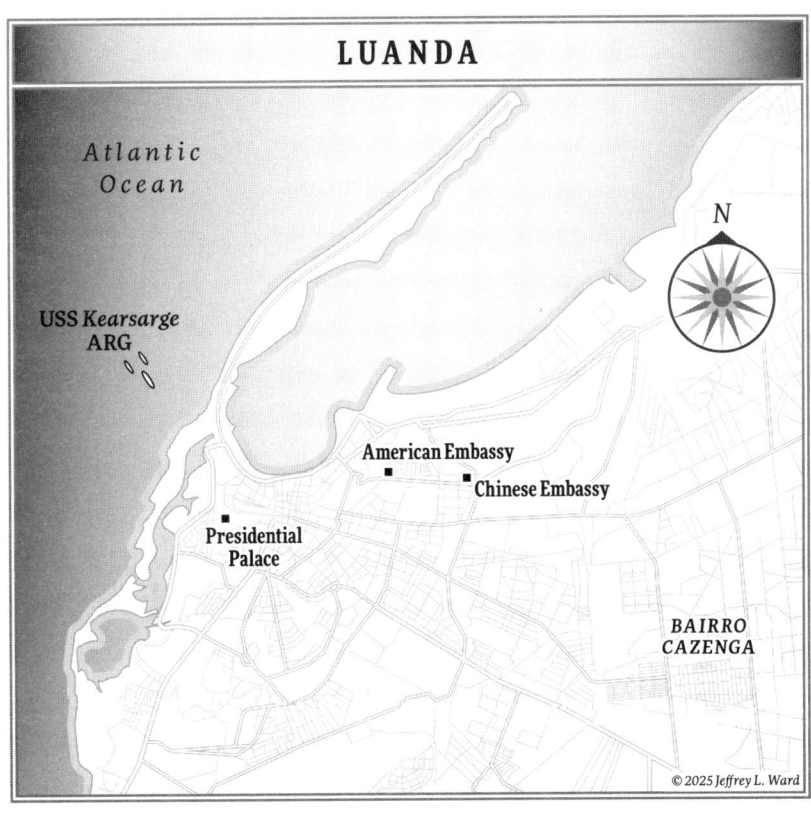

30

OVAL OFFICE
THE WHITE HOUSE
WASHINGTON, D.C.
2355 LOCAL TIME

Ryan was not one to pace, but at the moment he couldn't possibly sit, either. So he stood behind the Resolute desk, hands clasped behind him tightly and jaw clenched, looking out the middle of the three windows that opened onto the darkened South Lawn of the White House.

"It's late. You're exhausted. Are you sure this is the right time for this call, Jack?" Mary Pat asked, finally breaking the silence. "We have good people in theater right now, and perhaps, with more information, this call could be more . . . strategic, if you took it tomorrow. We still have five minutes to cancel."

He waited before answering, because she knew him very well and her instincts were probably right. Ryan had worked hard for years to rein in his temper, but his remaining weakness was when it came to his family. It was his responsibility to separate his personal needs and desires to the requirements of his office, because the executive power of the Office of the President was immense, and the repercussions of impulsive decisions often carried life-and-death consequences for many people in the world.

He had seen it firsthand, and the faces of the men lost in Operation Reciprocity under a different president would always be burned in his memory. That was a good thing, because those memories were a great litmus test whenever he felt himself leaning toward impulsivity. President Bennett had been a good man, but he had let his personal feelings at the loss of a close friend cloud his judgment. As a result, he had allowed Jim Cutter, the national security advisor at the time, to authorize the reckless covert operation and enter a deal with the devil with Colonel Cortez. Ryan had been the deputy director of intelligence at the CIA then, while his good friend Admiral Greer slowly succumbed to pancreatic cancer, but the operation had been authorized behind his back.

And good men had died . . .

"Jack?"

Ryan turned to Mary Pat.

"It's lunchtime in Beijing, so I think it's a perfect time for the call."

She rolled her eyes at his dodge. "You know that's not what I meant."

"I know," he said and let out a long sigh. "Look, you know me, better than almost anyone. You also know that I'm well aware of the risks of acting impulsively with my executive power, Mary Pat."

"I know you do, Jack," she said softly. "And I know you will always do the right thing. All I'm asking is that you should take a few more beats before this call. You have proven time and again that you put your nation and the people you lead before yourself. But, Jack, this is your son . . ."

"I know that," he snapped, more harshly than he intended. "But it's not the first time I've had to make difficult decisions while my family is out in harm's way."

Mary Pat maintained a neutral facial expression.

"This is different," she said simply.

Suddenly exhausted, Ryan slipped into his chair, behind the Resolute desk and across from his DNI.

"No," he said. "It's not."

But was she right? He'd made executive decisions many times from this office while his oldest son was out in the field, battling the evil they all needed to keep at bay. More recently, he'd made tough calls while his youngest daughter, Katie, was out on the pointy tip of that same spear. But their brother, Kyle, wasn't in the fight that he commanded. He was a prisoner somewhere—hostage.

At least I pray he is . . .

He squeezed his eyes shut a moment, then opened them when the phone on his desk chirped.

He pressed the button and held Mary Pat's eyes.

"Yes?" he said.

"I have the call coming through for you, Mr. President," the presidential secretary said.

"Thank you," he said as Mary Pat rose. "Put it through, please." He gestured to his closest friend and advisor to take her seat. "Stay, Mary Pat," he said. "I'll need your insight after and probably your accountability while I'm on the call."

Mary Pat retook her seat.

Ryan pressed the button to activate the speaker on the phone after the third ring.

"Secretary General Xu," he said, his voice even but firm. He wanted very much for the Chinese secretary general to know immediately how serious this call was. "I appreciate your taking this call."

"It is an honor to speak with you again, Mr. President," Xu said. The dance had already begun, Ryan supposed, since Xu had immediately reminded him of their last call. At that time, Xu had personally taken responsibility for the actions of the madman, President Li, who had brought their two countries to the brink of war over Taiwan. Xu had arranged for the safe extraction of both the American SEALs from the battlefield and John Clark's covert operations team aboard a South Korean freighter.

But if the CCP leader thought that meant Ryan owed *him*, then he had it very much backward.

"I'm afraid the circumstances of this call are far more grim, Mr. Secretary," he announced.

There was a short pause.

"More grim than two superpowers on the brink of war? This must be most serious indeed, Mr. President. How can I help you?" Xu said, still cordial, but a strain now evident in his voice.

"You can begin by telling me the truth about Angola, Mr. Secretary," Ryan demanded.

There was another pause, this one longer.

"I am afraid you will have to be more specific, Mr. President," Xu said, his voice now all business. "We have many interests in Angola, as I'm sure you are aware. But if you are referring to the horrifying attack on your embassy, I can do little for you other than to express my deepest condolences for this senseless—"

"We will get to the attack on our embassy, Mr. Xu," Ryan said, cutting the diplomat off. "But first we should discuss the preceding attack on Americans working in Luanda. I have two American telecommunications contractors dead—"

"If by telecommunications contractors you mean Western spies performing suspicious activities across the street from the Chinese embassy in Luanda, then I do believe I may have heard about this unfortunate event. Truly tragic, Mr. President. But if we are to have a real conversation here, it might be best if we both agree to complete transparency."

It was Ryan's turn to let a pause hang in the air, this time while his mind worked furiously to formulate a plan for this conversation. He locked eyes with Mary Pat, who raised an eyebrow, but offered little more.

This is my call . . .

"Very well, Mr. Secretary. If, hypothetically, we had American operators in Angola with the permission, I should add for the clarity of our hypothetical, of the Angolan government, and if, hypothetically, these Americans were working on a way to ensure effective communications that are free of the spy network we both know the CCP has established within *all* of the existing telecommunications networks inside the independent nation of Angola, are you suggesting that you believe the CCP would be within their rights to assassinate these Americans? Because I can assure you that I would very much consider that to be an act of war, Mr. Secretary."

Ryan realized that his voice had risen to just below a shout, and he struggled to rein his temper back in. He glanced at Mary Pat, who gave him a tight-lipped smile.

"Since, it seems, we are dealing in hypotheticals, Mr. President, I can assure you that what you have described would not warrant any action on our part. If, however, we were to detect spies from any nation, exploiting existing infrastructure legally placed in a host nation with their support and permission to spy on our interests, we would then consider a response to be not only legally warranted but ethically mandated." Secretary General Xu

Chao's voice was now rising as well, and Ryan could hear the controlled anger in it. "Hypothetically," he added, almost like an exclamation mark, after a moment.

"And a false flag operation to commit violence against our embassy?" Ryan demanded harshly. "Surely even you would consider such an attack on our sovereign territory anywhere in the world to be an act of war, Mr. Secretary. And, knowing me as you do, you must surely understand that I would respond swiftly and violently to such an act—a response that would indeed be *ethically mandated*."

He resisted the urge to rise from his chair to dissipate the angry and emotional energy that swelled inside him. His response would have been the same no matter who had been injured, killed, or taken. He was the President for all of the American people.

But this *was* in fact Kyle.

While Secretary General Xu formulated his response, Ryan added one more, less veiled threat.

"I should note that whoever is responsible for this attack will very soon feel the wrath of the American people. But the return of the hostages would go a long way to temper that response."

"I see," Xu Chao said finally. Then Ryan heard him draw a long breath. "Mr. President, I can assure you that were we to engage a perceived enemy force from any outside nation operating against our interests in Angola, it would be to protect our vested interests in the region and our national security. We would do so only in response to an aggressive act by another nation or organization. We want peace above all else."

"Your actions suggest otherwise, Mr. Secretary," Ryan growled. "Since we are being completely transparent."

"I am sorry you see it that way, but I must appeal to your reason here. I am sure this is quite emotional for you—as it would be for any leader—but I must ask you why on earth would we support an attack on your embassy, false flag or otherwise? So here is my transparency, Mr. President. Whatever cold war we are engaged in on the continent of Africa and most especially inside of Angola, the nation of China is winning."

"Now look—" Ryan began, shouting for real now.

"Hear me out, since world peace appears to hang on this conversation, Mr. President," Xu interrupted. "My point is, we are advancing our national interests in Angola very effectively with the administration that has been in power these last few years. It is no secret, so I will not deny it even though you are no doubt recording this conversation, that we have legally and legitimately invested enormous sums of money into Angola and those who are in power. What would be gained by attacking the American embassy under any circumstances, but certainly when things are going quite well for us in the region?"

"Perhaps you seek a change in power. Perhaps you are seeking to place someone who will better support your goals in the country?" Ryan posited calmly now.

"We are pragmatic above all else, Mr. President," Xu offered. "We do not wish war with the United States, as I believe I have proven to you already during the unfortunate incident in the Strait of Taiwan." That was a card, Ryan knew, that Xu had every right to play here. "But there is the simple cost-benefit ratio to look at, even if you find my promise of a desire for peace between our two countries hard to believe. To covertly support a coup and risk war with the West would accomplish what, exactly? We would be throwing away an enormous investment in favor of chaos and uncertainty, would we not? We have no need and less desire to see regime change in Angola, since our relationship with

President Luemba has been very, very fruitful indeed. Before continuing this path of escalating saber-rattling and threatening war, you best be sure that your sights are aimed at the right enemy."

Ryan leaned back. Xu was right—the Chinese had far more to lose than they did to gain with a regime change in Angola. In his emotional state, he had missed that all-too-important point, despite his best advisors pointing it out.

So just what the hell was going on? Clearly they were missing something. Perhaps the Chinese were not the puppet masters here after all, though certainly they might be guilty of willfully turning a blind eye.

"So, you are giving me your personal assurances that the CCP has nothing at all to do with the assassination of the American tech workers and the attack on our embassy? You know nothing about the deaths in Luanda and the hostages that have been taken?"

"Mr. President," Xu said firmly but calmly, "I have demonstrated my desire for peace with the United States to you in no uncertain terms with my actions during the unfortunate misunderstanding in the Taiwan Strait, have I not?"

"You have," Ryan agreed. "But that is not an answer."

"Then let me be clear," Xu said. "The People's Republic of China will lose hundreds of millions in investment in Angola and possibly lose a key strategic partnership with a regime change there. I can promise you in no uncertain terms that my country was in no way involved in the attack on the United States embassy in Luanda and that we are in no way involved in the attempted coup and chaos in Angola. For our own reasons, we are just as eager to get to the truth behind this disaster as you are. I will further promise that anything we learn that could lead to the safe recovery of American hostages will be shared with you immediately. We are ready and willing to assist you in any way we can."

Ryan let this hang as his mind reeled. Xu was right, he believed. He was barking up the wrong tree. It was not lost on him that Xu had *not* denied involvement in the attack on the DIA team in Luanda, but he would hold on to that for now. He made it a policy to never accept coincidences, but was it possible these two events were unrelated? Everything Xu said made sense.

"In the interest of maintaining the relationship with you that I believe we have established after the previous, unfortunate events brought on by President Li, I will offer you this. Take a very close look at the construction underway at the Base Naval de Luanda and decide for yourself if we would risk losing this opportunity."

"I will indeed, Mr. Secretary. We should both tread carefully in the coming days, if we share the goal of world peace."

"We should talk again, Mr. President. We are not enemies in this region, but rather we are simply competitors. I would not sacrifice peace for our interests in Africa, and I believe that the building of a relationship based on trust and respect between our countries is the key to world peace."

I bet you do, you slippery son of a bitch.

"We will indeed talk soon," Ryan finished, then disconnected the call with the press of the button.

Let the bastard sweat a little at least.

But the truth was, what Secretary General Xu Chao said made perfect sense.

He turned to Mary Pat, who, from the look on her face, already had her powerful mind working the problem.

"Thoughts?" he asked.

She let out a long breath.

"The MSS was almost certainly involved in the attack on our team," she said.

"I agree," he allowed. But the truth was, no matter how personal it felt, they would have disrupted a similar action on their network in a host country. Maybe not by assassinating foreign agents . . .

Though I don't know for sure that even that is true, he allowed.

"And while the simplest answer is almost always the correct one and, like you, I don't believe in coincidences, there may be something else in play here." Mary Pat paused a moment, as if deciding. "I do not believe they were involved in the attack on the embassy, at least at the moment, because everything he said about their investments and partnership in Angola is true," she continued. "But that doesn't mean that the PRC's relationship with Luemba wasn't in jeopardy for reasons we're unaware of, so I'm not prepared to give them a pass just yet."

"And I agree with that as well," Ryan said. "What was he talking about at the naval base in Luanda?" he asked.

"I'm not entirely sure, but I have a suspicion. Give me an hour or two and I'll get back to you."

"All right," he allowed, though it annoyed him to be kept in the dark. But this was the dance they did, to keep the honor of the office in place and preventing the temptations to abuse the power entrusted in him by the people. "We need answers, Mary Pat," he said. "And we need them now. Because the clock is ticking."

"I know, Jack," she said, empathy in her voice. "We are augmenting our footprint in the region, the Office of Naval Intelligence is involved, and we have the 22nd MEU landing in Luanda to secure our embassy and our interests any moment now. From there, the MARSOC element can react in minutes to an opportunity for a rescue and the ONI and CIA teams will find them that opportunity. We have good people, Jack, and they're doing everything that can be done."

Ryan suddenly realized he had not even considered, until this very moment, that his youngest daughter might also be in harm's way with all of this.

"We do have good people, Mary Pat. Do we have the very best from the ONI on this?"

She met his eyes with a steely look, and he knew she had heard the unspoken question.

"The very best, Jack," she said simply, and he supposed he had his answer. Still, if Katie was in the region, she and her team would be safe aboard the USS *Kearsarge*, the flagship of the ARG. Whatever terrorist element was attacking Americans in Angola, they couldn't possibly have the stones to attack the American Navy. And even if they did, they wouldn't have the means. The Navy had perfected the art of defense against terror attacks in the Red Sea and the Gulf of Aden. And Katie wouldn't be crazy enough to take her team ashore with the Marines.

Right?

"We need them to do more," Ryan grumbled. "And we need them to do it yesterday."

She nodded and headed for the door.

Ryan leaned back in his chair and sighed, allowing a few moments of grief for his son to envelop him. Then he wiped a tear from his cheek and reached for the phone again.

"Margaret, can you get me the First Lady, please?"

"Of course, Mr. President," she responded.

It was high time to let Cathy know what was going on with their son.

31

**CH-53K SUPER STALLION OF HMH-461
CALL SIGN IRON STALLION ZERO-ONE
FIVE MILES NORTH OF THE USS KEARSARGE (LHD 3) AT FIVE
 HUNDRED FEET AGL**
0737 LOCAL TIME

Katie looked at Conza—asleep across the aisle from her with his head leaned back against the orange nylon straps—with a mixture of envy and hatred. Forget about the white-knuckle fear she felt every time she flew—especially in a helicopter. It was still shocking to her that he could sleep in the rattling, noisy box of spinning parts that bounced around in the choppy air even if there *wasn't* a legitimate fear they all might die. As if to needle her further, Conza let out a long, slow yawn, eyes still closed, and readjusted his head slightly.

Another buffet of air hit the heavy helicopter, and having no armrest to grip like she'd had in the C-2 Greyhound that had delivered her a lifetime ago to the USS *Ford*, she instead gripped her own thigh and groaned. She looked across the aisle where Conza still slept and then glanced at the woman a few seats farther forward who looked at a tablet in her lap, apparently also unaware that they were all going to die. DIA agent Kaleigh Horgan was maybe six or seven years her senior, seemed quite relaxed, her legs, clad in gray cargo pants, crossed at the knee. But then again, she'd told them she had started her career as a naval flight officer and in her DIA job went by the nickname Goose as a result.

She felt eyes on her and turned to see Bubba grinning.

He leaned in to be heard over the noisy helicopter and through the headset built into the cranial helmets.

"Think a dip of Skoal would help, boss?" he prodded.

She didn't answer, but shot him an evil eye instead, then closed her eyes as the helicopter weathered another turbulent chop.

"We're on approach," the pilot said over the intercom, barely audible in the noisy bird. "On the deck in three minutes."

Katie swiveled in the uncomfortable seat to look out the rectangular, two-foot-tall window beside her. Of course, unable to look forward, all she could see was blue ocean whisking by uncomfortably close to the bottom of the helicopter—so close it seemed literally inevitable that they would crash momentarily into the sea. A moment later she saw wake from the ship, light green in the darker blue churned up by the powerful ship, and then the haze-gray steel of their destination as they passed along the port side of the USS *Kearsarge*.

Bubba had referred to the LHD as a "mini-carrier," and though she got the idea, there was nothing mini about the warship that she could see. The deck was maybe squarer and the superstructure more compact than an aircraft carrier, but to her the ship looked huge. Two F-35B Lightnings sat nose to tail, lined up along the starboard side as if to launch, and five others were parked tightly along the port side behind the superstructure at forty-five-degree angles to the port rail. As they passed, she saw the enormous number 3 on the side of the boxy superstructure.

"We're landing on number four," the pilot announced. "Need a quick turn to clear the deck for the Ready Five fighters."

She had no idea what number four meant, but turned to Bubba, hollering again over the noise.

"I thought the Marine F-35s took off vertically," she said.

Bubba just shrugged.

A moment later the huge Sea Stallion shimmied left and right once, then settled on the deck, and Katie blew out a breath she didn't realize she had been holding in.

"We'll egress aft, ma'am," the Marine who was suddenly beside her said. The aft ramp was already down, and the other Marine was handing their bags out to waiting sailors on the deck. "We're still hot, so keep your head down like we showed you and keep your eye pro on at all times."

"Thanks," she grumbled and unfastened her lap belt and shoulder harness with trembling hands. She stood up as Goose and Conza met her in the center aisle. "I hate flying," she said sheepishly to the DIA agent.

"So I see," Goose said with a grin. "Me too," she added.

Katie raised an eyebrow. "But I thought . . ."

"Totally kidding," Goose said and laughed over the whine of the engines. "But I do hate helicopters. They don't really fly, you know? They just sort of . . . beat the air into submission."

"Great," Katie said. "Welcome back from the land of nod," she said to Conza, who stretched beside her, then felt like a total dork for saying it. The former SEAL just smiled at her.

"Let's go, folks," the Marine urged. "We're on a schedule."

Katie followed Bubba to the ramp, where two sailors in overalls wearing cranials and goggles waited for them, two other sailors already hauling their bags across the deck.

"Keep your head down, Conza," Goose said as they stepped onto the flight deck of the ship. "I promised Lorie I'd look after you, and she's mean when a promise gets broken."

"I hear ya," Conza said, laughing.

Katie smiled. Apparently, whatever her fellow intel officer had going on with Lorie Tengco from the DIA was more serious than she thought, if Lorie was telling her colleagues about it. Her mind went to her broken weekend date with Dennis and she sighed. It was tough learning to navigate relationships in this job, she figured. But at least Dennis and Lorie would get it, right?

They hustled across the deck, rotor wash from the helo ro whipping her uniform fabric as she followed Bubba and the two sailors from the ship's crew at the front of their little human convoy.

Once inside the ship, the sailors secured the hatch, then one of them collected their cranials and goggles.

"Welcome aboard the *Kearsarge*, ma'am," the young sailor who collected them said.

"Indeed," said an older sailor, who approached from behind the junior sailor.

"Afternoon, CMC," the sailor said.

"Afternoon, shipmate," the man said. "You have everything you need?"

"Five by, Master Chief," the sailor said, and she could tell he both liked and respected the man who was clearly the command master chief for the ship. The sailor headed down the passageway.

"Welcome aboard, Commander," the CMC said, and she extended a hand, which he shook. "Lieutenant," the man then said to Conza.

"Thank you, Master Chief," Katie said. "This is IS2 Pettigrew and our DIA colleague, Ms. Horgan."

"Goose," the DIA agent said, shaking the master chief's hand.

"I'm Bill Earhart, the command master chief," the man said. "Captain Miles and the commodore send their greetings and apologize for not meeting you personally. Things are pretty shit-hot right now, so they're tied up. And the XO is on the bridge."

"Of course," Katie said. "We get it. We're here to help, not get in the way."

"Right," Earhart said, but she couldn't tell if he meant it or was just being polite. "Sorry there's no time for a tour, but I'll get Petty Officer Landon here to show you to your quarters." She did get it, of course. The crew and their embarked Marines were on mission and the last thing they needed was visitors.

But her team was here with a mission of their own.

"If it's all the same, CMC, we'd like to get right to work. We can find our way to quarters later, but I'd like to get set up in the N2 shop."

The CMC looked skeptical.

"Okay," he said. "We're a little unclear on what your mission is, to be honest, Commander."

She sighed. It was always like this.

Which was why she preferred working from her little office back in Maryland.

"We're here to provide intelligence in real time back to the decision-makers in the States regarding the situation on the ground," she said. That was right, wasn't it? Again, she could probably do that better from her office. "But we will data-share one hundred percent, so hopefully we can be a value add to your N2's mission as well."

"Okay," Earhart said, but he sounded unconvinced. He turned

to Petty Officer Landon. "Landon, take these guys to the N2 shop and get them with Lieutenant Billings."

"I don't have access to the N2, CMC," Landon said, unsure.

"You're all good, shipmate," Earhart said. "Lieutenant Billings will meet you at the door and take over from there. These guys have TS/SCI for our mission, so Billings will set them up with access. Then grab someone to help you and secure their bags in their quarters."

"You got it, CMC," Landon said.

Earhart gave Katie a tight smile.

"I'm sure the skipper or XO will come and find you when time allows," he said. "There is a lot of shit happening right now. Billings will get you up to speed."

"Thank you, CMC," Katie said.

He gave her a nod and then disappeared down the passageway.

"This way, ma'am," Petty Officer Landon said, and led them the other way, turning to enter a ladder well, where they ascended one level.

"Do you hate ships, too, Ryan?" Goose Horgan asked with a grin.

"Not as much as helicopters," Katie said, smiling at the jab.

"Good," Horgan said. "I mean, you are a naval officer, for God's sake."

After making more turns than seemed to make sense for the rather small space of the superstructure—and assuming it was just two P-ways in parallel, connected with crossing passageways like on a carrier—they arrived at a dead end and a black door inside of a larger steel hatch, which was secured open. There was a single iPhone in the crossbeams of the hatch.

The sailor she now knew as Petty Officer Landon pressed a call box beside the door and turned to her.

"You'll have to secure any electronics—including, like, Apple Watches—outside. Most people just set them on the hatch, but I can secure them in a lockbox if you like. I've never been inside, so I don't know what may be available in there," he added wistfully.

Katie and her team set their devices on the rails of the open hatch and she chuckled when she saw that Horgan's phone case had a sticker of a goose wearing a sailor cap on it.

The door opened, and an officer in BDUs, lieutenant bars in the center of his chest, looked out, blinking from the brighter light of the passageway. Katie remembered that feeling from her sea tour as an intel officer on the *Ike*. The low light of the N2 shop made you feel like a vampire, no matter what time of day.

"You Lieutenant Commander Ryan?" the officer said, closing one eye.

"Katie," she said, extending a hand.

"Nate," Billings said. "Come on into the dungeon."

That made Katie smile. They had called the shop the same thing during her deployment.

They entered the room, which was, to her surprise, a bit larger than the space she'd had on the aircraft carrier and rivaling the more modern spaces of the USS *Ford* during the Russian submarine incident.

As if sensing the memory, Billings eyed her closely now.

"You're the Ryan from ONI that figured out shit with the *Belgorod*, right?"

She clenched her jaw, but before she could give a self-deprecating answer, Conza chimed in.

"That's her," he said, slapping her on the back. "The myth, the legend that is rogue submarine hunter Katie Ryan."

Katie shot him a look.

"Right place at the right time and I had a great team," she said. "Including my top IS, who is here with me, IS2 Pettigrew."

"Mr. Pettigrew," Billings said, extending a hand.

"He prefers Bubba," Conza pointed out.

"Good to meet you, sir," Bubba said in his Louisiana drawl.

"I'm JC," Conza said. "Commander Ryan's lackey."

That finally got a smile from Billings, who shook Conza's hand.

"Or maybe her bodyguard," the intel officer said, eyeing the subdued Trident over Conza's name tape. "You're a SEAL?"

"Used to be," Conza replied good-naturedly, but Katie knew him well enough to suspect the question stung every time. "In my prime. Now I'm a one-legged intel dude." He reached down and tapped the prosthesis below his left knee.

"We think of him as our pirate," Bubba offered, getting an actual short laugh from Billings.

"And this is Goose, a member of our team from one of the alphabet agencies," Katie said, gesturing to Horgan.

"I'm usually more fun," Billings said, shaking the DIA agent's hand, "but we're in the eye of a storm right now. This is the first large-scale amphibious landing we've ever been part of outside of TRAINEX," he said, referring to training exercises. "Those are stressful enough, but now real bad guys may be shooting back, so we gotta lot of shit going on."

"And we're here to help, not get in the way, I promise," Katie assured the officer.

"Yeah, well, I guess I'm not sure what that looks like, to be honest," Billings admitted.

"Hey," Bubba said, not wanting to be part of whatever rice bowl drama might follow. "You think I can set up somewhere and get on the high side to start digging in?"

"Uh . . . Yeah, sure," Billings said. "Petey," he called out, and a young third-class petty officer leapt from a chair and joined them from the nearest of the four rows of parallel tables in the center of the room, each with four workstations and chairs. "Take Bubba here to the Bat Cave."

"Yes, sir," Petey said. "Follow me, um"—he looked at the rank on Bubba's blouse and his name tape, not ready to call him Bubba it seemed—"Petty Officer Pettigrew."

He led Bubba away.

"The Bat Cave is what we call the room where we run real-world intel comms," Billings said. "It's on the other side of the wall from signals, which we keep compartmentalized. Usually, this room, where we have all of our various analysts, is a bit more full, but I have guys up in Plans and the Marines are all in the LFOC. They have the right half of the room with those two rows, and blue is here on these two rows. My lead IS is in the Bat Cave."

"You don't mix in with the Marines?" Conza asked.

"Nah," Billings said and laughed. "It's a Marine thing. Let's go to our briefing room and you can tell me how you can help without getting in the way." He looked at Katie. "No offense, ma'am."

"None taken," she reassured the more junior officer. "We're here at the request of the White House to bridge any intel gaps on the geopolitical situation on the ground, not to mess up your intel flow with the MEU. Where that's a value add, we'll work closely, but otherwise try not to get in your hair."

Billings seemed relieved.

"Follow me," he said, and led her, Conza, and Horgan toward a door in the right corner of the room, across from where Bubba had disappeared up a couple of stairs on the far side of the room. As they followed Billings, Bubba stuck his head out of the dim room he had vanished into.

"Hey, JC," he said, then remembering they were in public, corrected himself. "I mean Lieutenant Conza."

"Yeah, Bubba, what's up?" Conza called back as they approached the door Billings led them to.

"They wanna talk to you back home," Bubba said. "The watch officer said they need you urgently."

"Both of us?" Katie asked, slightly irritated. She was the team lead after all, but then she reminded herself it could be anything—maybe something personal about family or something.

"They just want JC, ma'am," Bubba said, and Conza screwed up his face now, too.

"I'll see what it is and join you in a quick minute," he said.

She gave him a nod, and followed Billings, gesturing for Horgan to enter ahead of her.

Billings took a seat at the worktable between the currently empty workstations against the wall. He let out a long troubled breath and rubbed his hands on his face.

"Sorry you're catching us in the middle of a shit storm, Commander Ryan," the officer said. "I can give you a quick overview of what's developed recently while you were traveling."

"Sure," she said, eager to be up to speed.

Billings saw someone over her shoulder and gestured them in.

"Hey, Soo, come in here," he hollered. A younger officer, with a single ensign bar in the center of her BDU blouse, entered. "Ensign Soo is my JO. Jia, meet Commander Ryan from ONI, who is here to lend us a hand."

The small woman shook Katie's outstretched hand, but if she was skeptical about Katie's arrival to "lend a hand," she didn't show it.

"Take a seat, Jia," Billings said. "This'll be quick. So, first, from our standpoint on the ARG, the White House has ordered an amphibious assault to land Marines on the beach. They want us to secure a perimeter around the embassy with LAVs, JLTVs, air support, and an assload of infantry Marines."

"They're also moving the H and S to the embassy, sir," Ensign Soo said, addressing Billings.

"Okay, well, that's classic jarhead," Billings said.

"What's H and S?" Katie asked.

"That's the MEU's head shed, basically. It's the Headquarters and Service Battalion, but I'm guessing they're just putting the decision-makers ashore and keeping the logisticians here inside the LFOC. Colonel Crocker, the MEU commander, will likely stay here, but the H and S staff and relevant task unit commanders will likely be ashore." He turned to Soo again. "They're sending their intel shop?"

"Looks like it," the ensign said.

"What's the LFOC?" Katie asked, realizing she was already being a pain in the ass, but she didn't want a bunch of acronyms standing between her and a clear picture.

"Landing force operations center," Billings said patiently. "It's the Marines' version of our CIC where they run all the Marine-side operations. It's actually like a second CIC connected to our combat information center by a door." He glanced at his watch. "Okay, so look, let me get you an overview and we all can get back to work, because the H and S moving gives me more shit to deconflict."

"Of course," Katie said. "Sorry."

Billings waved the apology away and gave her something resembling a smile. The man looked tired.

"So, it seems that the attack on the embassy might well have been some sort of false flag designed to distract Angolan security forces from where President Luemba was addressing his cabinet. No idea who yet, but it would appear we're caught in the middle of a coup, because in addition to the ambassador and three others from the embassy who were captured, presumably as hostages to control our response, our mystery bad guys now have President Luemba as well as Vice President Carvalho."

"We got that brief en route," Katie told him. "Pretty ballsy move to pick a fight with America as a distraction to stage a coup. I mean, it kind of sets up a superpower as your enemy right from the start. Not a great way to rise to power with every American drone putting a target on your face."

"I getcha," Billings said. "But, you know, this may just be a culture thing."

"What do you mean?" Horgan asked.

"Hostages in sub-Saharan Africa are, like, almost a recognized currency," Ensign Soo chimed in, looking at the DIA agent. "And not just for political game play, but in business as well."

Billings nodded. "They damn sure overplayed that hand taking the ambassador and some of her staff, but in Angola this is sort of a day at work."

"Yeah, well they don't know President Ryan very well, I would suggest."

"Agreed. Hey, wait a minute," Billings said, narrowing his eyes at her name tape and making her pulse quicken.

What a dumbass for bringing Dad's name into this.

"Any relation?" Billings asked, raising an eyebrow.

"Look," she began before being gratefully interrupted by Conza, who poked his head in through the door, but didn't come in.

"Ryan," he said, his voice unusually strained. "A word?"

"Of course," she said, relieved at the interruption. She rose, and Goose Horgan followed suit. "We'll be right back."

She followed Conza out into the main room, where he led them to the corner, far from listening ears.

"Everything okay?" she asked, the look on his face raising alarms.

Conza hesitated a moment, raising her worry another notch.

"Not really, Katie," he said. "Look—no easy way to tell you, so here it is. Your brother Kyle is one of the hostages."

She blinked at him a moment because the words he said made no sense.

"That can't be right," she said. "Why would Kyle be in Angola?"

"All I know for sure is he was at the embassy because he was part of some DIA task force—the one that was attacked, presumably."

"Wait . . ." Her head was swimming now. "Kyle was the survivor from the attack on the DIA team?"

"It looks like it," Conza said. "The missing from the embassy include the ambassador and her executive assistant—which we knew—and then your brother and an agency guy."

She looked up at him and blinked again.

"I'm sorry, Ryan," Conza said.

She spun to face Horgan now.

"You must have known," she spat at the woman. "How could you not tell me?"

"Commander Ryan, I swear I didn't," Horgan said. "I would have told you. I'm a field agent and have little or nothing to do with the cyber joint task force. I did know the name, but to be honest I didn't even make the connection until right now."

Katie stared at the woman, blinking away unexpected tears at the thought of Kyle a hostage of the brutal terrorists that had assaulted the enemy and killed fourteen innocent people without the slightest hesitation She studied Horgan, who—to her credit—held her stare.

She believed her.

"Okay," was all she could muster. She turned back to Conza. "Did the ONI have anything new to offer on the location of the hostages?"

Conza looked resigned.

"We're the pointy tip for intel, Ryan," he said softly. "It's up to us and the organic CIA in country."

That made her perk up. The CIA had a small team in country and must still be working the problem, right?

"Did they evacuate the CIA team from the embassy?" she asked Conza.

"I can't answer that," Horgan said. "One of the hostages was part of the CIA team, and the rest of them remained at the embassy, operating out of there for now."

"Ground branch?" Katie asked.

Horgan shook her head.

"The missing OGA guy is a case officer and is among the hostages, presumably. They had analysts and a head of station. This is more of a listening post than anything, since we had a reasonable relationship with the government. We're way behind the Chinese, so monitoring what they were doing was the real mission. Not much cloak-and-dagger and no direct-action shit at all."

Katie wondered what must Kyle be going through right now. Kyle was quiet and pathologically stoic. She was probably closer to him than anyone, except maybe Mom. And she knew him well enough to know that while he showed little emotion, he had a ton of them. And he was a genius, but he was no Jack Junior. He wasn't equipped for this.

"Katie . . . ?"

She looked up at Conza and his kind eyes.

"I don't understand how in the hell a Navy lieutenant working in cyber ops was on a rooftop with a covert DIA team in Luanda," she said. "But figuring that out is important—not because he's my brother, but because it may help us unravel this mess." She turned on her heel and headed back into the room she had left. "Grab Bubba," she said. "I need him."

Her face must have shown how devastated she was because Billings and Soo stopped talking and their faces suggested they knew something was wrong.

"Is everything okay?" Billings asked with real concern.

"No," she said, "but nothing new. We need everything that you and the CIA team at the embassy have on the DIA operation that was running in Luanda ahead of all of this." She turned to Horgan. "And anything you can share is important, too."

The DIA agent nodded.

"Of course," Billings said. "We're pulling all that together right now, from the CIA and also the broader IC back home. We have a MARSOC Raider team on standby for hostage rescue, so that's our number one priority, once we support the landing."

"This is where we'll help you the most, Nate," Katie said. "Because that's where we'll focus all of our attention. It's going to be important that we share information in real time, minute by minute."

"Of course," Billings said. "You'll have full access here in the shop to everthing we have and we'll set you up at your own stations as well . . ."

He stopped when he saw Katie shaking her head.

"We won't be getting in your way here on the *Kearsarge*," she said. "But we'll have real-time comms open at all times."

"Where are you going?" Billings asked, confused.

"Wait," Bubba said from the door as he entered behind Conza. "We're going somewhere? We just got here . . ."

She ignored her IS and turned back to Billings.

"We're going to run our intel operation from the embassy," she said. "We need to infil with the H and S team. We're going to be part of the amphibious assault."

"Well, hold on a second," Billings said. "I can't authorize that. I'll have to check with—"

"I know," she said. "I'll take care of getting permission from the CO. Ensign Soo," she said, turning to the JO, who hadn't said a word since she'd returned. "Can you take me to the CIC? I need to talk to the skipper."

"You'll need to go to the LFOC, Commander," Billings said. "Only the MEU commander can give you permission for this."

"Fine," she said. "Sounds like I need to go to the LFOC, then."

Soo looked up at Billings for guidance.

Her boss just shrugged.

"Take her to the CIC first and let the skipper know, then maybe he can smooth it with Colonel Crocker."

"So, what," Bubba said, definitely not liking what he was hearing, "we're all going?"

"We're all going, Bubba," she said. "You and Lieutenant Conza figure out what you might need to bring, but we're falling in on the CIA EOC. We'll be leaving with the H and S team when they go ashore."

"When's that?" Bubba whined.

"Soon," Billings said. "That'll be third wave once the combat Marines are ashore, and the support teams are there. But if I know the Marines like I think I do, they'll be heading out around the same time."

"Why?" Bubba asked.

"Marines don't like to miss any fighting," Billings said.

"Wonderful," Bubba said.

Katie patted her IS on the shoulder as she followed Ensign Soo out of the room.

"And Goose," she said, stopping and turning back.

"Yeah, boss," Horgan said.

"I'll want everything you can find on this cyber team, okay?"

"Everything I know, right when I know it, Katie," the agent agreed. "We're all on the same team, I promise."

Katie hoped her eyes looked grateful as she turned and followed Soo across the room.

But her chest was tight, and her mind was racing with images of just what her brother must be going through.

She wondered about her parents. Surely if she knew, then her dad already knew as well.

How hard would the conversation with Mom be?

She clenched her jaw and followed Soo out of the N2, grabbed her electronics, and headed down the passageway.

She would do whatever it took to get all the Americans home—just like she always did.

But now it was deeply personal.

32

BRIDGE
USS *KEARSARGE* (LHD 3)
14.8 NAUTICAL MILES NORTHEAST OF LUANDA, ANGOLA
0816 LOCAL TIME

Miles found, for the first time in his career, he wanted to be somewhere else. Not somewhere else like away from the fight, but rather, very specifically, inside the LFOC. Watching the command and control of the insertion of the 22nd MEU onto the shore of Luanda from the screens in the Marine control center would be a sight indeed. But, as the skipper of the *Kearsarge*, he was right where he believed he should be, on the bridge of the ship that he commanded, with his XO ready to back up the TAO in the CIC. He was responsible for the safety of his ship and crew as they launched the largest real-world amphibious assault in decades and he could best do that from right here. He paced behind his OOD on the bridge, glancing occasionally at the controlled chaos on the deck.

Flight operations were crazy enough on an aircraft carrier, but nothing could match the ballet of moving parts of an amphibious assault launched from an LHD. The coordination involved to assemble and deploy Marines, launch aircraft to secure the landing zone with the Beachmaster teams, deploy LCACs and LCUs to get the Marines and their vehicles, weapons, and equipment ashore, and launch and recover the air support each of those elements required, was a task that defied belief. Adding the F-35s to the MAGTF had complicated things even more, since they needed more flight deck for launch, pushing the foul line back a full eight feet on a deck where distance between aircraft was often measured in inches. The presence of VMFA-214, the Black Sheep, added to their capabilities, but also limited the space from which to launch and recover the workhorse MV-22 Ospreys and the combat AH-1 Viper and UH-1 Venom helicopters, as his air boss loved to point out. Every evolution had its own requirements in terms of a ship's speed, direction, and, of course, how much flooding of the wet well was required for the maritime assets—which had its own impact on the ship's speed and ability to maneuver. Then add in deconflicting possible surface and air threats.

Miles smiled tightly as he watched the best damn crew he'd ever worked with as they did their jobs to make the impossible seem almost easy. He watched out the windscreen as two MV-22s left the deck, nosed forward, and headed for the beach.

"Bridge, Well Deck Control," came a call, and the OOD, Lieutenant Bryce Allen, picked up the call from his station.

"This is the Bridge," he responded.

"Bridge, Well Deck—LCUs are away. Adjusting for the LCACs."

"Well Deck, Bridge—Copy," Allen said and turned to Miles. "LCUs are away, sir," the OOD told him, his voice serious and tense.

"Thank you, Lieutenant," he said.

A moment later he felt a slight shudder as the ballast tanks were purged and the stern of the *Kearsarge* began to rise. The LCUs needed deep water in the well to launch. The LCACs floated on a cushion of air generated by turbine engines. The craft created winds of hurricane force in the well deck, so the less water inside to whip around as the craft "hovered" on top of the water in the torrent of wind. All personnel already had to wear full protection gear to safeguard against injury from the wind, water, and debris when the LCACs launched and recovered.

The *Kearsarge* was cycling her landing force first, with their sister ship, the San Antonio–class LPD, USS *Arlington*, close behind to launch two additional LCACs. The *Kearsarge*'s LCU would deliver the 2/6 weapons company plus one platoon of thirty-nine Marines from one of the 2/6 rifle companies, and a first wave of JLTVs, Humvees, and trucks, and two A3 variants of the older LAV-25s with anti-tank capabilities. Her LCAC would then deliver the rest of the rifle company, additional JLTVs, and additional Humvees. The *Arlington*'s LCACs would deliver the second rifle company and the additional vehicles and equipment.

The LCU was much slower moving ashore, so he could already see her maneuvering in the direction of the beach, knowing the LCACs would easily catch up. Shortly they would launch MV-22 Ospreys to deliver the Beachmaster unit and their security force to secure the beach landing zone. The landing would occur along the south end of the narrow peninsula that stretched north from the Fortress de São Miguel in downtown Luanda, with the main road of Murtala Mohamed Avenue running the full length to connect the city to the businesses, marinas, and restaurants along the stretch of beach that separated the South Atlantic Ocean from Baía de Luanda—Luanda Bay. The beach was long, wide, well-protected, and gave quick, easy access to the road. From the landing site, the force was literally a mile as the crow flies across the bottom of the bay to the U.S. embassy and barely two miles on the modern road, where Murtala Mohamed Avenue became 4 de Fevereiro Avenue, running along the bay. But that would be the dangerous part of the operation. If there was resistance, it would come on the highly dense urban infil to the embassy, a route that would make their Marines highly vulnerable.

Which was why Crocker had ordered mortar teams and two artillery batteries ashore in addition to the air support. Those batteries would arrive in the third wave, after the Marines secured a perimeter around the embassy. Which meant air support from the F-35s and the helicopter gunships was the key to the first assault.

"Bridge, TACC," came another call as his air boss in the tactical air coordination center prepared to launch the MV-22s and the Viper gunship helicopters that would accompany them.

"TACC, this is the Bridge," Allen replied.

"Bridge can you make your heading one-one-five degrees for air ops?"

"TACC, stand by," Allen said, and he looked at Miles, who held his gaze, not intending to make the decision for him. Allen nodded, accepting the autonomy, and spoke into the radio again. "CIC, this is the Bridge. Update surface contacts, bearing three-five-zero for new course one-one-five degrees true."

There was a short pause and then the CIC responded.

"Bridge, CIC," came the calm female voice of the TAO. "No new contacts. We still have two contacts designated Romeo Zero One and Romeo Zero Two maneuvering at slow speeds zero-eight miles north of the landing area in the mouth of the bay. No other contacts except confirmed commercial fishing vessels already on the track."

The Angolans had a Navy, but it was used mostly in a law enforcement role to protect fisheries and their commercial fishing operations. Still, they did have armed patrol boats and it was still unclear just who the hell was in charge of the military at present.

"Copy, CIC," Allen responded. Then to the bridge crew he said, "Helm, make your new course one-one-five degrees, maintain current speed."

"Helm, course one-one-five degrees, aye," the first-class petty officer at the helm, under the watchful eye of a senior chief, replied smartly.

"TACC, Bridge changing to your requested course."

"Bridge, TACC, copy," the air boss replied.

The course change was unnecessary to get the MV-22s airborne, Miles knew. But they also had two F-35s sitting on ready alert, prepared to launch at a moment's notice if the landing force needed air support early on. Those fighters would be airborne flying Combat Air Patrol (CAP) coverage once the assault was further along, but the air boss didn't want to complicate things yet. They were the only ship in the ARG that could recover the F-35s if there was a problem, so best to get the entire force launched first. This close in, the AH-1 Vipers and the UH-1 Venoms were more than capable of covering the force.

Miles looked forward, where Boatswain's Mate Ashley's team of aircraft handlers moved two Ospreys carefully from their tight row along the port side, where their wings had been swiveled ninety degrees over the top of the fuselage, the massive propellers in line, allowing the massive birds to be packed within inches of one another, a single AH-1Z Viper attack helicopter in the limited extra space between each. Two of the Vipers had already been moved to the starboard side just forward of the F-35 alert fighters, ready to launch as well. Master Chief Glover was on the deck in her yellow vest, supervising her team and pitching in as they positioned the two MV-22s, the "green shirt" sailors responsible for the aircraft launch already moving around the aircraft, readying them for launch.

He watched the ballet that was air ops on the *Kearsarge*. They would have the MV-22s airborne in minutes, and already he saw the line of the fully kitted-up Marine security force and the slightly less symmetric line of Navy sailors from the Beachmaster unit moving in quickstep to board the planes. This was the advanced party that would secure the beach landing site, covered by the AH-1s and the F-35s, which would launch next.

Even as they readied to launch, the activity below would be readying the LCAC to launch. On cue, the comms sounded again.

"Bridge, Well Deck Control—Hopper U6, away."

"Deck Control, Bridge—copy, Hopper U6, away."

Miles glanced left, where he saw the LCAC maneuvering already, accelerating toward the remaining wake of the newest LCU 1700, which he could still see off the port bow. On glassy sea with a modest load, the modern LCU could travel more than twenty knots. Today, they would be making less than fifteen, he assumed, which meant the LCAC, capable of speeds in excess of forty knots, would have no problem at all joining up. The two LCACs launching any time now from the LPD *Arlington* would join the formation easily as well.

By the time he turned forward again, the MV-22s were already loaded and spooling up, ready to deliver their Beachmaster teams to the landing zone.

The assault was on its way.

With his bird's-eye view, he felt his desire to be in the LFOC dissipate entirely. He leaned back in his skipper's chair and let his people work.

No matter where the Navy took him after this tour, no duty assignment would ever top commanding the USS *Kearsarge* and her crew.

33

PALÁCIO PRESIDENCIAL DA CIDADE ALTA (PRESIDENTIAL PALACE)
RUA PEDRO FURTADO
LUANDA, ANGOLA
0909 LOCAL TIME

General de Souza, the head of the entire Angolan Armed Forces under the new head of state, President Victor Baptista, strode swiftly down the hall, his blood pressure rising and sweat now dappling his forehead. It was not from fear that his new boss might punish him for this devastating turn of events. No, that was no issue at all. Without him, Baptista had no control over the military and therefore no control over anything. The loyalty the new president enjoyed was from de Souza alone, as the respected, perhaps even revered, head of the armed forces. The military itself? Well, the men and few women of the Angolan Armed Forces were loyal to him and whoever he then told them he served. No, he was at no real risk from Baptista, no matter how angry this news might make him.

His fear was of the Americans.

And that, perhaps, I have made a terrible mistake aligning myself with Baptista.

To be sure, he agreed with Victor Baptista's vision and his loathing of the West, but there was much more to his decision. He'd enjoyed a very, very comfortable life under President Luemba, but he had never been given the respect he deserved. More important, he'd never been given the *voice* he deserved. Luemba might value him as a soldier, but he treated him like a servant. In Baptista, he had a chance to have more than comfort. Baptista might see himself as the emerging leader, but he would never be more than de Souza's puppet. And if the Americans came ashore and decided to put down this coup? Well, then he would no doubt be hanged for treason. This was one part of the puzzle that needed to be fixed.

He approached the ornate door to the president's office and gave a curt nod to the armed soldier who straightened up and stared straight ahead as he arrived. Then he rapped once on the heavy wooden door.

"Come," Baptista barked, and de Souza opened the door and entered the office.

The room was ornate to the point of decadence, far more so than the presidential office at the government complexes, where such extravagance would be less well received. Baptisa sat behind the large oak desk, looking more like a revolutionary than a first-world president. That, he imagined, would change in time. It had for Luemba, after all.

Baptista stared at him as he approached.

"Is there a problem with our guests?" he demanded, worry on his face.

"No," de Souza said. "Something far more urgent, I am afraid." Baptista tossed a pen onto the desk, leaned back, and crossed his camo-pants-clad legs at the knees. "The Americans are coming."

"Coming where?" Baptista asked, standing now at the news.

"Surely they cannot have discovered where the hostages are being held. If they do, we lose considerable leverage, João," he said, the use of his first name bristling the general, but he refused to show it.

De Souza clenched his jaw at this, because, frankly, this was another problem with his plan. Baptista had the American hostages hidden by his PFU foot soldiers, and de Souza had not been involved. In fact, he had no idea where they were.

"That is something I cannot help you with, since you have elected to keep me out of that loop. But it is not the Special Forces team at the embassy I am concerned with, Victor," de Souza said, unable to resist the urge to return the favor of inappropriate familiarity. "It is far worse. The Americans are preparing to land Marines in Luanda. The amphibious ready group off our coast is deploying the Marines as we speak."

"What?" Baptista exclaimed, hammering a fist on the desk. "To what end?"

"To rescue their ambassador and the other Americans, of course," de Souza said, resisting the urge to roll his eyes.

"Then it is time to announce that we are hunting for them right now as well and expect to partner with the Americans. They must know that those holding their people will execute them if needed." He watched as Baptista paced like a caged animal now. The man was beginning to suspect what de Souza already knew—that he was completely out of his league.

"Will we, though?" de Souza said, a little more gently this time. He decided that managing Baptista now, in his agitated state, would take a bit more manipulation. "Mr. President, we may have underestimated the Americans and President Ryan's willingness to engage. Marines ashore in Luanda is a very big problem."

"Only if they know where we are keeping their people, General de Souza," Baptista said, glaring at him, but de Souza saw the uncertainty in his eyes. "That must not happen."

"Well, then, it is time to clip an important loose end, Mr. President," De Souza said. "We need to kill Luemba and the vice president immediately."

"Why?" Baptista demanded. "They do not know that we were involved in the embassy attack or that we took the Americans. They know only that we took power from them. We will claim, as we always planned, that it was their inability or unwillingness to stop the terrorists operating in our capital city that led to our taking power. Luemba was lining his own pockets, but not protecting our country."

De Souza thought a moment. That had been their plan all along, but his personal backup plan required that Luemba *not* be alive to implicate him in the takeover. If Luemba survived and the Americans put down the coup, then de Souza was a dead man.

"Then it is time to play that narrative now," he said. "But perhaps it is time for you to engage with President Ryan and begin negotiations." Baptista continued to pace behind his desk, clearly agitated. De Souza wondered if the man was up to such a diplomatic task. "It is time to be the president we all trust you can be. You have my full support. But you must buy us some time with the Americans."

"Yes," Baptista said. "I will reach out immediately. But, in the meantime, we must give the Americans pause."

"What do you mean, Mr. President?" de Souza asked, not liking what he was hearing.

"The Americans are weak, with no stomach for violence," Baptista said. "Let us show them our resolve. They have attacked our country without provocation or warning. Engage their landing force. If they suffer losses, it will make them worry. And I will demand an explanation of their invasion of our country without warning."

"They will claim we attacked first," de Souza pointed out.

"Only if they can prove that the attack on the embassy was from us, which they cannot," Baptista corrected. "I will demand they withdraw their Navy from our coastline, and I will promise them that we will work with them to find and rescue their hostages and punish those responsible. This will buy us time, and when I do 'rescue' and return the Americans, they will owe me. It will validate my claim to the presidency in the eyes of the people. And then we will try and convict Luemba and his vice president and hang them both. This will earn us the loyalty of the people."

De Souza clenched his jaw, but agreed. It was risky, but could possibly work. Either way, it would bolster his contingency plan, he supposed.

So long as Luemba was dead.

"It will be done immediately," he said. "But I recommend we move things along with the disposition of Luemba. The people need to know who is in charge, but also why."

"Yes. But first I will make contact with the American President," Baptista said.

General de Souza hurried from the room. He had orders to give to his two Navy attack boats at the mouth of the bay.

If this blew up in his face, he had a backup plan that would allow him to survive the fallout. It would require Luemba to perish with what he knew of what had happened—and the vice president as well. But de Souza knew he could make it work.

He was a survivor.

34

EMBAIXADA DA CHINA EM ANGOLA (CHINESE EMBASSY IN ANGOLA)
LESS THAN A HALF MILE NORTH OF THE AMERICAN EMBASSY
56WX+C5, LUANDA, ANGOLA
1001 LOCAL TIME

"The Americans are coming," junior analyst Wang said, urgency in his voice as he looked up from his computer. While they waited for the other two MSS field agents on the team to check in from where they were working hard to gain intelligence on just who in the hell was pulling which strings, Wang had been monitoring the American fleet now dangerously close to the coast of Luanda, while Sima pored over the regional intelligence briefs in real time for any information that might be useful. Their lead analyst, Zhang Li, sat beside Wang, looking through and vetting his own streams of intelligence for "other" sources. At the moment, Sima was more interested in what the American response might be than anything. He had considered calling Baptista and demanding answers from the horse's mouth, but so far had resisted for multiple reasons. The most pressing was that, with the Americans actively and openly operating in the area, he could not be nearly as confident about how secure any of his communications might be, especially with no confirmation yet on just how much damage the DIA team they had interdicted may have inflicted to their network. Add to that the fact that anything Baptista said would have to be taken with the proverbial grain of salt and the risk seemed, for the moment, to outweigh the benefits.

"They are sending additional operators to the embassy?" he asked Wang, who stared at him from where he sat. He could tell from his teammate's face, though, that there was more going on than just that.

"No, Liang," Wang said. "I mean they are *coming*. They are launching a full-scale amphibious assault. I am watching their LPD and LSD ships deploy landing craft as we speak. And they have Osprey delivering teams to receive them already."

"That's crazy," Sima said, confused. "The attack on the embassy is over. Why such a large, overt response?"

"Because the coup has happened," Wang suggested. "We know that Baptista has taken Luemba and the vice president. Perhaps they have come to put down the coup."

"With an entire Marine expeditionary unit?" Sima asked, not buying it. "That is overkill for such a mission, first of all—"

"Except we now know that most of the military is with Baptista," Wang interrupted.

"And secondly," Sima continued, giving him a look of displeasure at being interrupted. They were teammates, but there was still a hierarchy. "I don't imagine President Ryan being invested enough in who is in control. He is smart. He must conclude that a new leader is an opportunity for the Americans to improve their standing in Angola, and compete better for the rare earth minerals and access that I am sure they knew we are way ahead of them in controlling. Why take such a chance?"

"I have the answer," Zhang said, hunched over his computer, but one hand now pressing the earpiece of a headset that he had half on and half off his head, covering only his left ear.

"What is it?" Sima demanded, but Zhang held up a finger. After a moment, he took the headset off and turned to him, his face grim.

"Idiots," the MSS analyst exclaimed. Then he gave Sima a very serious look. "The American ambassador and three of her staff have been taken by the attackers at the embassy," he said. "They are being held hostage, but where and by whom are still a big question."

"What is the source of this intelligence?" Sima demanded. Surely Baptista was not that stupid. He was either reading the situation incorrectly, or the former PFU leader was, indeed, a moron.

Zhang gave him a wry grin.

"My source is the Americans themselves," he said. "Our Unit 99 has recovered signals from inside the Pentagon and I have confirmed it just now, decrypting messages between the embassy CIA team and Washington, D.C. There is very little more than that, but there is no doubt that is why the Marines are coming."

Sima pulled his hand over his face and sighed. This was a total disaster. There was no world left in which he could lend support to Baptista. That cost-benefit ratio just skyrocketed to an enormous number.

His phone chirped and he glanced at the screen.

Perfect.

He snatched the phone from its cradle.

"We have disturbing news," he said immediately, skipping any pleasantries.

"If it is the massive amphibious landing underway, then we are watching it ourselves in real time, Liang," his boss said sardonically. "Where do you think your imagery comes from?"

"There is more than that," he said. "The attackers have taken American hostages."

There was a long pause, and he could picture Director Chou closing his eyes and letting out a long, slow breath, as he so often did when receiving news he didn't like.

"Why in the hell would they do that?" he asked, but Sima knew the question was rhetorical.

"It may be time to reach out directly," Sima posited.

He waited patiently while Chou crunched the math of their situation in his enormous brain.

"No," he said firmly. "Cut off all contact, Agent Sima. This has become too dangerous. My call was to inform you that President Ryan contacted Secretary General Xu directly just a short time ago."

"What?" Sima said, unable to contain his surprise at such an enormous event. "Why? And why not President Huang?" the new president who had replaced the traitorous former president who had nearly started World War III with the Americans. Contacting him rather than the secretary general would seem to be the proper diplomatic course.

"They have a relationship after the debacle in the Strait of Taiwan," Chou said. "It is not important. But the 'why' is important. President Ryan made accusations of Chinese involvement in the killing of the American cyber team and suggested we may have also been involved in the attack on the embassy."

"That's ridiculous," Sima said, suddenly paranoid about

whether the Americans might have a better signals intelligence operation in place than he had given them credit for. He would be careful what, exactly, he said.

"Perhaps so," Chou agreed. "But I want you to close up shop, Sima Liang. Shut down all contact. If you have information useful to the Americans in recovering their missing people, send it to me immediately and we will share it with them."

"Of course," Sima said, wondering if Chou was also concerned about listening ears, or if his plan really was to offer Baptista's head on a platter in a gesture of peace with the Americans. It didn't matter either way. They didn't know shit, and if he could no longer be in contact with Baptista or those presumed to be in league with him, that had little chance of changing. "We will see what we can find out and pass it on immediately. This is most unfortunate. We were unable to contact them during the attacks to offer our assistance due to their comms being overwhelmed. We will work on this and pass anything we can to you."

"This is most unfortunate indeed, Liang," Chou said.

Then the line went dead.

Sima replaced the receiver and then looked at the two men staring at him.

"What are we to do?" Wang asked softly.

"Nothing," Sima said. He reached into his desk and retrieved the burner phone. He handed it to Zhang. "Bleach this phone for me," he said, and collapsed into his chair. "And then, we do nothing."

35

BRIDGE OF THE LEAD ANGOLAN NAVY'S DVORA MARK III FAST PATROL BOAT D-01
8.5 KILOMETERS WEST-NORTHWEST OF BAÍA DE LUANDA LIGHTHOUSE
TRAVELING SOUTHWEST AT OVER FORTY KNOTS
1042 LOCAL TIME

Capitão de Corveta (captain) Nando Katanga rested his hands in his lap so that the crew could not see that they were shaking. The twenty-seven-meter fast boat cut smoothly through the ocean swells, the special hull geometry allowing for constant seakeeping and a dry deck even at high speeds and rough seas. No, it was not the sea state that had his hands shaking. It was the insanity of what they had been tasked to do.

He could see, in the distance, the speck that was the small armada of American landing craft, heading east at much slower speeds. There was a cloudlike mist that surrounded the speck—which he could now see were several specks at once—that gave the target an eerie, almost supernatural appearance, and Katanga felt his pulse quicken.

"Range—eight thousand four hundred meters to the nearest

target," the sailor manning the remote weapons system announced. In this case, that sailor was Primeiro-Sargento Sala, his lead NCO.

"What is the position of Zero-Two?" Katanga asked. He had no view aft, where the second Mark III should be trailing in his four-o'clock position. Once they fired, his sister attack boat would surge forward, ready to engage with their top-mounted Typhoon cannon and bow-mounted 12.7mm heavy machine gun. Katanga's bow gun had been replaced by the gimbal-mounted sensor system required to aim and guide his four AGM-114 Hellfire missiles. Once his missiles hit their targets, he would then swing in to join his fellow officer and good friend, Capitão de Corveta Ferriera. Together they would strafe the landing craft and then haul ass back to safety in the bay, hopefully before being destroyed by aircraft from the American warships. Katanga had no idea how long it would take for them to get their helicopters into the air, but at forty to fifty knots, he imagined he and Ferriera had some small chance of escaping.

"Zero-Two is bearing one-three-five at a thousand meters," Sala told him.

"Very well," Katanga said. "Turn to port by thirty degrees and slow us down," he ordered the helmsman, squeezing the young man's shoulder.

"Yes, sir," the sailor said, his voice tight. Everyone aboard knew what they were doing and he imagined all were terrified.

I will fire my weapons and then turn and run. I will see Daniela and our kids again.

Perhaps the turn and change of speed would confuse the Americans, who most surely had been tracking them.

"Prepare to fire both missiles," Katanga said.

They were able to fire only one at a time, so it would take a moment to prepare the second one in the launcher. If they didn't get it off within thirty seconds, he had already decided they would abort and retreat. He had no doubt that when, as mission commander, he called the retreat, Ferriera would gladly join them and run away to shore beside them.

No one understood what they were doing, attacking the American Navy. They had been told that the Americans would be surprised because they were too arrogant to imagine the Angolan Navy to be a threat. He was told to believe that they would be in such shock they would not respond. He was told that they would be so busy trying to defeat the missiles and rescue their wounded, that the Mark III would slip away.

He knew this was to make sure they followed their orders. The Americans might be surprised, but they most certainly would respond. The sooner he could run for shore the better the chances they would survive.

"Do not illuminate the target until the last moment, Sargento," he said, using Sala's abbreviated rank.

"That is certainly a very good idea, Capitão," Sala replied with a grin. He glanced at his display. "Capitão Ferriera is matching our course and speed."

Katanga clenched his jaw again and looked out at the spiraling mist around the American landing force, now thirty degrees off his starboard bow.

"We will fire in one minute," he said, staring at the swirling mist of death out his windscreen. "Then we will run." He let out a long slow breath. "And while we run, we will pray."

36

CIC
USS KEARSARGE (LHD 3)
13.4 NAUTICAL MILES EAST-NORTHEAST OF LUANDA, ANGOLA
1048 LOCAL TIME

Katie stood patiently beside the door she had entered through, hands clasped in front of her, as the beehive of activity swirled around her. As she did, she resisted the urge to glance at her watch. If she was going to clear her team to infil with the MEU head shed—what the intelligence officer from the Joint Intelligence Center (JIC) had called the H and S battalion—she needed to get it approved pretty damn soon. She was told by Lieutenant Billings that the fastest way to get approval was to find the XO in the CIC. Her presence there, as an intel officer "augmenting" the N2, would be less obtrusive.

At the moment, that didn't feel true at all.

But she also got that, no matter the weight of her mission, she was still a guest, a "rider" on the lead ship for the amphibious ready group that was in the middle of one of the largest real-world amphibious landings of Marines in a generation of warfighters. She stared at the back of Commander Chris O'Melia's head, ready to catch the XO's eye with urgent raised eyebrows the moment the lanky officer turned in her direction.

"TAO, Surface," an officer standing behind a sailor seated at a workstation with a large monitor in front of him said, turning to the officer seated beside the XO.

"Yeah, waddya got, Mike?" the TAO replied. As he did, he glanced up at the large-screen monitor that showed a myriad of green squares and red triangles all over a green silhouette map of the coastline of Angola and the South Atlantic Ocean. In the center was a box labeled OS, which she guessed from previous conversations meant "own ship." "Shit," the TAO said before the surface warfare officer could reply. "What are our two Romeos up to?"

"We tracked them headed north and then they made a sweeping left turn," the other officer said. "They're at high speed, traveling in what looks more like a combat spread than something two fishing boats might do. And now they're headed directly at the landing force. Range to the lead LCAC now down to nine thousand yards."

The TAO looked at the XO.

"Sir, I want to launch the 60s to interrogate the targets," he said.

"I concur," the XO replied and reached for the radio himself. "Bridge, CIC—this is the XO," came the tense voice of Chris O'Melia. "I need the skipper."

Only a moment passed, during which time a Marine lieutenant stuck his head through the door that connected the CIC to the LFOC.

"Hey, what the fuck are those two boats—"

"We're working it, Ted," the TAO replied sharply. "We gotcha, bro."

"CIC, Bridge—this is the captain."

"Skipper, surface contacts Romeo Zero-One and -Two are maneuvering on an intercept course toward the landing force at high speed," O'Melia said. "TAO recommends launching the 60s and I concur."

"Do it," the skipper agreed immediately.

Katie saw that there was precious little chance of a conversation with the XO right now, but she also realized that it had fallen off her priority list as well. If those were military fast boats headed toward the landing force, they all had much bigger problems.

"What kind of weapons do the Angolans have?" she asked the room, but no one turned to look at her except an enlisted sailor manning one of four stations along the bulkhead beside the entrance door. Her station had a screen, but more interesting was the fighter jet–style joystick in the center of the station.

The young woman spoke softly.

"They briefed us that some of their fast boats have surface-to-surface missiles, ma'am," she said, her voice as tense as Katie now felt. "They're a variant of the Hellfire known as the AGM-114 Lima. They also have a twenty-millimeter cannon and machine guns."

"The Seahawks are away," someone in the room announced, which she assumed meant that the MH-60 helicopters were airborne now.

"Thank you, Air," the TAO replied.

"What kind of defensive weapons do the LCACs have?" Katie asked the sailor beside her, whose name tape read CUMMINGS.

"Just guns, ma'am," Petty Officer Cummings said. But then she gave a dark smile. "But they also have us."

"Cummings, give me a firing solution on the Sea Sparrow in case I need it," the TAO barked, and the sailor beside her went to work.

"Yes, sir," Cummings replied smartly.

That was a weapon Katie had heard of. The RIM-7 was a shipborne, anti-air and anti-missile weapon, based on the old AIM-7 Sparrow air-to-air missile. The *Kearsarge* had the next evolution, the RIM-162 Evolved Sea Sparrow Missile, or ESSM, which could engage maneuvering supersonic missiles, firing from her forward launchers. Clearly the TAO was read in on what the threat may be, if Cummings was right about the AGM-114s.

"Romeo Zero One is now painting the lead LCAC," someone across the room suddenly announced, loudly and with more than a little emotion. "TAO! Missile in the air. Missile in the air targeting the landing force."

"Guns . . ." the TAO barked.

"I have him, sir," Cummings said, her hands flying across her station at lightning speed, then grabbing the joystick. "Tracking . . . Firing, sir."

"Missile away, good track on the TAS," someone else said from somewhere beside Cummings.

Katie felt her throat go dry and she looked up at the big screen, where a red line now stretched off from the OS box, continuing as a dashed line toward what she assumed was the projected point of impact with the missile screaming at the landing force. Her mind flashed back to the USS *Washington*, where she'd met Dennis, the XO of the submarine nicknamed the *Blackfish*, and had lived through an attack very much like this one, only underwater.

At least now I'm not aboard the target.

Then she instantly felt guilt at the selfish thought.

Because there were a few hundred Marines aboard those landing craft who would perish if they were struck by an AGM-114L Hellfire missile.

"Locked," Cummings announced.

Katie looked at the big screen, where the tracks of the enemy Hellfire and their counter-missile were displayed. The seconds felt like minutes as the two missiles converged, though she knew the Sea Sparrow was traveling at Mach 2–plus. A new view on one of the smaller monitors now showed the maneuvering fast boat, crisply magnified to the point where it looked to be out the window instead of miles away.

The two tracks converged and a moment later Cummings announced, "Good kill," but before anyone celebrated, another voice hollered out.

"Second missile in the air from Romeo Zero One!"

"Firing," Cummings announced, this time the entire evolution taking but a split second.

"Launch the alert five fighters," came the next call, this one over the 1MC.

She watched again, sweated again, as the missiles converged.

"Air," the TAO barked after leaning in to the XO. "Charger, kill Romeo One, kill Romeo Two."

"Air, aye," someone across the room said.

Katie assumed that Charger was the call sign for the two MH-60S helicopters already in the air. She had no idea how long it took to launch the alert fighters—the F-35s sitting armed and ready on the flight deck—but it had to be a few minutes at least, right? The multi-mission Seahawk helicopters were just that—multi-mission for search and rescue, logistics, transport . . .

And ASuW, or anti-surface warfare.

That meant they were equipped with AGM-114 missiles as well, and no doubt a much more modern version than the Angolan fast boats had just fired at the landing force.

She watched the smaller screen as the video from the high-resolution cameras of the *Kearsarge* showed the lead of the two fast boats suddenly maneuvering, jinking back and forth at high speed. Suddenly a tongue of fire licked out from the machine-gun mount in the stern of the boat. In the background, she now spotted another, identical Angolan Navy craft also cutting back and forth. Then a line of fire stretched toward the boat from left to right on the screen and the entire vessel disappeared in a massive fireball as the Hellfire impacted. The monitor was whited out for a second. Moments later, the image cleared and she saw the remnants of the fast boat, listing badly and pouring out thick black smoke.

The camera continued to track the larger, moving boat in the foreground, and the destroyed fast boat in the background disappeared from sight. Then there was an abrupt flash of light from the left side of the screen and the second fast boat was engulfed in another fireball.

"Good kill," the sailor the TAO had called "Air" reported.

"TAO, Signals, SLQ-32 shows own ship painted from the shore."

The urgency in the sailor's voice was unmistakable.

"XO, N2 reported that they've got those two P5s on the beach. Are we cleared to engage? I can have Air route the F-35s to the site."

"Stand by," the XO said. He headed toward the door leading to the LFOC, where Katie could now see the Marine colonel peering into the CIC. Commander O'Melia hustled over to him, but before he reached him a voice shouted out again in the CIC.

"TAO, Signals—missile launch from the beach!"

"Guns," the TAO snapped.

"Got him, sir," Cummings said. Her voice was somehow more calm now, despite Katie's heart beating nearly out of her chest. She had no idea what a P5 was, but she knew that "own ship" meant the ship she was on right now, and that a missile was screaming toward them from the shore. "Firing."

She glanced at the main monitor, where two new, converging tracks now appeared—one reaching out from OS and the other from the shore across Luanda Bay from the landing site for the Marine landing force.

"Air, TAO—are the F-35s up?" the TAO demanded.

Katie understood immediately. They'd been fired upon now. With their ROE, they no longer needed permission to fire back.

"Up and ready, sir," the sailor replied.

"Destroy the shore-based launch site."

"Yes, sir," the sailor said, and leaned forward, talking now into the boom mic by his mouth.

Everything was happening so fast that Katie's head was spinning.

Just like on the Blackfish *and the* Jason Dunham.

She reached out a hand to steady herself on the bulkhead, just as the image on the small monitor—the one showing the burning, smoking remains of the two fast boats—was now replaced with a new image. Katie had seen enough air combat video in her job as an intel analyst to recognize the view through a heads-up display aboard a military fighter. This display was far more futuristic than most she'd seen, and she had no idea what most of the symbols meant. But when a green box with a diamond inside it stopped moving around and turned red, she thought she knew exactly what that signified.

A second later two missiles streaked toward the shore, where the now red box hovered over what she assumed to be the missile battery in Luanda.

"Good kill," she heard, and glanced at the other screen, where the two missile tracks now had intersected. She'd momentarily forgotten that there had been a deadly missile inbound targeting the *Kearsarge* from the shore battery.

"Missile battery destroyed," came another voice and she glanced back to the projected view through the Marine F-35B HUD to see the fire and smoke on the beach, where, she assumed, the missile battery had been just moments ago. "Looks like Black Sheep got 'em before they got the second missile off."

"Okay, people," the TAO said, clapping his hands together twice. "Great work, but stay frosty. This ain't over until our Marines secure the beach. Interrogate any and all surface contacts and stay tight with the JIC signals on any new threats."

There was a generalized murmur in the room and a couple of high fives.

"What do you want?"

She turned to see Commander O'Melia standing behind Cummings, his hands on his hips, staring at her. "Shouldn't you be in the JIC?"

"Sir, I'm Lieutenant Commander Ryan—" she began.

"I know who the hell you are, Commander," O'Melia interrupted. "But I got some real-world shit going on and this isn't where you should be. Why are you here?"

"Well, sir . . ." She was about to explain why she'd been sent to the ARG, but then corrected just in time, realizing that he meant why was she in the CIC during a battle. "Sir, I wanna get my team out of your hair and onto the beach, where we can do our job better. I understand that the H and S staff are staging out of the embassy, and I need permission—"

The XO jerked a thumb toward the door, open between the CIC and the JLOC.

"That's a Colonel Crocker question, Ryan," O'Melia said. "Only he can give you permission to go ashore. That beach is his—or will be in another twenty minutes, if I can keep us and the landing craft alive."

"Thank you, sir," she said.

"Don't thank me, Ryan," the XO said with a grim smile. "I'd personally rather get fired on by a dozen missiles than ask a Marine colonel to give me a ride somewhere."

She pursed her lips, trying to think of something clever, but the XO had already walked away to join the TAO.

Katie let out a big sigh and headed to the LFOC.

She had a feeling she was, literally, taking her team out of the frying pan and into the fire. But her brother and three other Americans were lost, held by bad people somewhere inside the city of Luanda, and she could best help them from the embassy.

She had no intention whatsoever of taking no for an answer.

37

PALÁCIO PRESIDENCIAL DA CIDADE ALTA (PRESIDENTIAL PALACE)
RUA PEDRO FURTADO
LUANDA, ANGOLA
1102 LOCAL TIME

Baptista slammed his burner phone down on the desk when it went, again, to the voicemail message that said no voicemails could be left at this number. Sima had told him that the Chinese support would be quiet, but that should not mean the man was unwilling to take Baptista's calls. He understood China wanting to stay in the background until the dust cleared—in fact that suited his needs just as well, making this all about who ruled the people of Angola instead of about competition for their resources from two superpowers. But surely Sima must see that he was now refusing a call from the current head of state.

Would the Chinese embassy have refused a call from President Luemba? And if not, how dare they refuse to take my calls?

With de Souza and his military backing his play, there could be little doubt that Baptista was, if not the *legitimate*, then at least the de facto ruler of Angola. His formal inauguration was but a formality at this point. He resisted the urge to call again. Calling again made him look desperate, and desperation would make him appear weak.

If they want our minerals and their naval base on our shores, they will come to me eventually.

There was a loud rap on the door.

"Come," he barked.

The soldier who entered looked terrified. This was no doubt because, as a member of the PFU who only today had become a soldier in the Angolan Army, he was one who knew full well what could happen when Baptista was presented with a failure.

"What is it?" he demanded of the profusely sweating young man who stood a fairly long reach from the desk Baptista sat behind.

"I have bad news," the man said, his hands trembling on the rifle he gripped, matching cadence with his trembling lip. Clearly the kid had drawn the short straw on being the one to share this bad news with Baptista, who kept his face stern while smiling inside. He loved to see the fear his presence produced. That fear had been a big part of his power up until this point. But there was no need for fear today. He suspected he knew full well the news his young fighter came to share.

"It is all right," he said. "Unless you are coming to report of your own failure, then you have no need for concern. I am for the people—you as well as everyone else. What do you need to tell me?"

The young man looked modestly relieved, but still nervous.

"Mr. President, I am sorry to tell you, but the attack against the American fleet has failed."

The man closed his eyes a moment, and when they opened again, those eyes were wet.

And now Baptista could not help but laugh. On hearing it, the soldier looked confused, eyebrows arching together in surprise.

"Come, come," he said, gesturing the man closer, and the soldier took two short paces toward his desk. "Surely you and the other men did not really think that two small boats with but a few missiles could possibly defeat the American Navy?"

"I . . . I don't know, President Baptista."

"Well, if you are to rise in the ranks of our Army—of the Angolan Army—soldier, then you *should* know. Our action was to give the Americans pause, and I assure you we did that." Baptista knew, of course, this would give the Americans more certainty, not reservation. He had paused nothing.

But, he *had* created a narrative.

"What of our boats and crew?" he asked.

"Gone, sir," the man said, and his shoulders visibly relaxed a bit. "They were destroyed by the Americans' missiles, I understand. No survivors, sir. And, when the Army—I mean, us, our Army, of course—when we launched a land-based missile, it was defeated. And then the American fighter jets destroyed the missile battery. Seventeen were killed."

Baptista tried to look solemn.

"Their sacrifice will be remembered," he said, and then held the eyes of the confused soldier, who had, of course, not seen this side of the leader he'd admired and feared before.

"Of course," the young man said, and lowered his eyes respectfully.

"Thank you for the report, soldier," Baptista said. He wasn't exactly sure what the new, shiny rank insignia on the crisp uniform denoted.

The man snapped to attention, gave him a crisp salute, and

turned and hustled from the room, clearly surprised to be leaving of his own power.

Baptista leaned back in his chair and smiled. De Souza's willingness to sacrifice men and naval fast boats was telling. He would certainly have known, even better than Baptista, that this was a suicide mission and that the men were a sacrifice. Yet, he sent his men to their deaths anyway, without question.

His loyalty to Baptisa and the new future of Angola was evident in that compliance.

A part of him hoped very much that he did not have to sacrifice de Souza as well, though that seemed like a false hope.

He picked up the phone from the ornate desk and pressed the first button at the top.

"Yes, Mr. President?" the voice said. The man in the outer chamber was a civil servant, not one of his own. He had been offered his life and a future if he continued to serve the administration, and he had gratefully accepted. Working with Luemba staffers was a risk, but there were things that Baptista's people simply did not know how to do yet.

But by tonight, I'll have my chief of staff appointed, he decided, and the role would be filled by someone he trusted implicitly.

"Frederico, I wish to speak to the American President," he said, summoning his best presidential voice. "Can you make this happen?"

There was a long pause, and he imagined Frederico was spinning out the consequences of failure in his mind. He had watched the palace chief of staff removed from the building in a body bag, after all.

"I believe so, yes," the man said, his voice trembling.

"Excellent," he said. "It is important that this happen quickly. As you speak with the Americans let them know that *President*

Baptista wishes to speak about bringing about peace. Tell them we are not responsible for the violence against their Navy or their embassy, but that we are hunting down those who are."

This pause brought a smile and a slight chuckle to Baptista.

"You . . . You are serious?" Frederico asked.

"Of course," he said. "You will find me to be a very serious fellow, Frederico."

"I will see it gets done immediately, Mr. President."

Baptista hung up the phone.

Transition was always difficult, but he would quickly learn who he could and could not trust. The greatest sadness, of course, was that so many of his most loyal followers in the PFU would have to be sacrificed.

But that decision was, after all, necessary for the greater good.

38

**SITUATION ROOM
THE WHITE HOUSE
WASHINGTON, D.C.
0517 LOCAL TIME**

Ryan watched the three screens that showed the growing force of Marines on the beach with his hands in his lap. It seemed every time he raised them to the table, the need to tap a finger or thumb to dissipate the adrenaline-fueled energy reached unmanageable levels. The screens gave a great, multi-perspective view of the landing of U.S. forces onto foreign soil that *he* had ordered. A high-fidelity bird's-eye view from the satellite tasked for this operation showed the beached LCAC and LCU landing craft and the Marines and machinery on the beach just west of the road that stretched the full length of the narrow peninsula forming the west side of the Bay of Luanda. Two armored Humvees and Marines sat on the road, barricading it from all movement north or south. Marines had also secured a comfortable perimeter around the beach landing with JLTVs, and two LAV-25s. Beside the close-up view of the beach landing, a second screen showed a broader view of Luanda, also in real time, with the narrow peninsula on which the Marines had landed to the left side of the screen and the dense city of Luanda proper across the bay to the right. In the center of the peninsula and north of their landing force, thick black smoke still billowed up from where the F-35B Lightnings from VMFA-214, the Black Sheep, had destroyed the missile battery site located at the Angolan naval facility, Base Naval de Luanda. Fire trucks and ambulances were seen there as well, fighting the ensuing fire and treating the wounded, which he hoped were exclusively soldiers from the battery that had attacked the *Kearsarge* ARG and not civilian collaterals. The techs had overlaid a dashed red line from the beach landing, through the city, to the multi-block area highlighted in green that represented the destination of the United States Marines of the 22nd MEU. At the center of that box was the U.S. embassy mission to Angola.

The third screen showed the battlespace imagery from the CIC of the USS *Kearsarge*, which Ryan knew was not far off-screen in the broader overhead view. There he saw only green boxes representing the ships of the ARG, though a few red contacts showed along the shore north of the city of Luanda with designators beside them as the battle team tracked them as possible threats.

"Looks like they're on the move, Mr. President," someone said—his chief of staff, Arnie van Damm, Ryan thought.

Ryan looked back at the center screen, which showed the much tighter shot over the landing site, where one of the Humvees now led a convoy comprised of several trucks, with JLTVs at the front and rear. A fourth screen now came to life, giving an overhead view of the landing site again as the center screen continued to track the moving convoy. He felt himself slipping into his old life of CIA analyst and later director, searching the images for clues of possible ambushes or other threats. So far he saw none, though the city of Luanda was so densely packed, it was nearly impossible to tell where a threat might emerge.

What he felt satisfied that he did *not* see was a military response to the landing or moving convoy.

"No movement from Quartel General do Exército, at least so far," General Kudryk noted, confirming Ryan's read of the situation. The base was just a few miles south of the route the convoy would take. The Marines would pass directly past the Estado-Maior da Marinha de Guerra, the headquarters for the Angolan Navy in Luanda, as well as the base for the Portuguese Military Cooperation. But these were both headquarter bases without much of a combat troop presence. Ryan was watching for mobilization toward their troops from the Quartel, or from the Presidential Guard Unit even more inland, where there seemed to be a large number of trucks and other vehicles present. So far, however, those troops were not responding. The Base Naval de Luanda was the operational naval facility just north of the landing force on the narrow peninsula, but right now it was a smoking pile of destruction, where the only activity seemed to be fire service and rescue personnel.

"Maybe our response to their attack on the landing force taught them a lesson," one of Burgess's staffers said softly from beside Ryan's trusted and talented SecDef.

"Maybe," Kudryk grumbled, unconvinced.

"The large presence at the Presidential Palace is staying in place as well," Jay Canfield, his CIA director, noted. "But who knows who they may have hidden in waiting."

"Or who the hell is even in charge," Ryan said. He was acutely concerned that they didn't know who, if anyone, was in control of the Angolan Armed Forces. It may well have been elements of the

PFU in the fast boats that had attacked their landing craft, and they may even have commandeered the missile battery at the Luanda Naval Base. They needed to know exactly who the real enemy was.

And if they are in control of the military.

"Mr. President?"

Ryan looked over at where the secretary of state called to him from across the table, his voice urgent and strained, a secure phone to his ear.

"What is it, Scott?" he asked, his pulse quickening at the look on Scott Adler's face.

Now what?

"Sir, we have a call holding from the Presidential Palace in Luanda. An urgent request to speak with you."

"President Luemba is okay?" Ryan asked, feeling some relief. Perhaps this coup, or attack on the United States, or whatever it had been was finally put down. Was it a coincidence that it occurred so quickly after his threatening call with the CCP's secretary general, Xu Chao? He clenched his jaw at the thought, but he would deal with that later. Right now, he needed the safe return of their hostages.

Including Kyle.

"I don't know, Mr. President," Adler said, his voice a tight cord of concern. "The call is from Victor Baptista—who is referring to himself as President Baptista."

Ryan felt surges of new fear and anger compete for his attention.

"We don't have diplomatic conversations with terrorists, Scott," he barked. "Tell him he can—"

"Sir, if I may," Adler said gently. "I agree with that policy one hundred percent. But right now, we don't really have much of an idea what is going on over there."

"Baptista is a leader of the PFU," Ryan snapped back. "We know that. And it appears that the attack on our embassy and the taking of our ambassador and . . . other hostages"—he had almost said *my son*—"was part of a violent coup against the elected president of an allied nation. I repeat, we do not—"

"Mr. President," Mary Pat challenged, and he turned to her, his face still red with anger. "I recommend we speak with him and hear what he has to say. We may gain valuable intelligence that we desperately need."

"Of course," he said. "But it can't be me. Giving him audience with the President of the United States legitimizes him as the leader of Angola. We can't do that." Ryan brought his hands up onto the table and drummed his fingers a moment. Then he turned back to Adler. "Scott, you take the call," he suggested. "Put it on speaker so we can all weigh in on whatever it is we get from this."

"Of course, Mr. President," Adler said, and squared his shoulders and blinked twice, the weight of this call not lost on him. "Put it through to the main number, Trisha," he said into his secure phone.

Then Adler leaned forward and tapped a button on the circular speakerphone in the center of the table. After a moment, a female voice said, "I have Mr. Baptista, Mr. Secretary."

Ryan smiled. He really had the very best people in the world. Even Adler's executive assistant knew not to call the man "president."

"This is the United States secretary of state, Scott Adler," Adler said with a commanding voice. "With whom am I speaking?"

"This is President Victor Baptista of the Republic of Angola," a heavily accented but quite-fluent voice replied. "It is urgent that I speak with President Ryan. I wish only to help and avoid any more violence."

Adler looked at him, and Ryan shrugged and gave him a nod.

"The United States recognizes only President Luemba as the rightful leader of the Republic of Angola, *Mister* Baptista. And our President does not legitimize terrorists. Now, if you would like to negotiate the return of the Americans being held in Luanda, I am all ears, of course."

There was a short pause that seemed rather well-timed to Ryan. Whoever Baptista was at his core, he was not stupid, and they would not underestimate him.

"Mr. Secretary, I am more than sensitive to the position you are in, and frankly I also understand your misconceptions of me—"

"Misconceptions?" Adler demanded, cutting off the soliloquy. "Is this not Victor Baptista, the known leader of the PFU terrorist group? I believe I know exactly who you are, Mr. Baptista. And I can tell you that if any harm comes to the Americans you are holding hostage, the world will soon know your name as well. Because I know my President well enough to promise that we will come for you."

"This is the misconception that I was referring to when I said I understand," Baptista replied coolly, and Ryan was again impressed. "Yes, I was for a long time affiliated with the PFU—which I will tell you is a nationalist political organization and, when I was part of it, sought only a better future for our country and our people. As the PFU became more radical—and more violent—I parted ways with them. I am now an independent political activist, nothing more. But your instincts are correct. While I cannot yet prove it, I do believe that the PFU may very well be responsible for the attack on your embassy."

"But not for the coup wherein you assumed unlawful control of the Angolan government?" Adler demanded sharply.

The man on the other end of the line gave a sad little laugh.

"Again, you have made assumptions that are not correct, Mr. Secretary," Baptista said. "There has been no coup. Rather, there has been a betrayal of Angola by former president Luemba. While Luemba may not have been directly responsible for the attack on your people, and by proxy an attack on America—whom I believe to be our best ally and partner, by the way—it is believed that he knowingly and willingly allowed the PFU, with the help of a foreign government, to perpetrate this horrible attack for personal gain. There were elements within our government and our military who got wind of this, and as a result Luemba is now under house arrest pending trial. I was asked, as a patriot, to serve only as an interim president in this time of crisis until such time as elections can be had to select our next leader."

"What foreign nation are you accusing here, exactly?" Adler said, looking at Ryan again and raising an eyebrow.

"In the interest of preserving world peace, I think it best I do not say until I have more evidence, which I expect quite soon," Baptista said coolly. "And then it is best I share that information only directly and privately with President Ryan."

"I see," Adler said, still controlling the conversation well. "I will be certain to pass that on to President Ryan. As you can imagine, he is quite busy managing this crisis personally. So, for now, just what is it you want from us, Mr. Baptista? If it is not to offer the return of our ambassador and other unlawfully held hostages, I am not sure what it is we have to discuss at this moment."

"I want exactly what you and President Ryan want, Mr. Secretary," Baptista replied without hesitation. "I want the safe return of the American hostages and the resumption of peaceful relations between our countries. I want justice for this situation—swift justice and punishment for those involved and those who, it appears, allowed this to happen. And I want a prosperous relationship with the United States, who I know will be a far more reliable partner with us than those who seek to use our country for their own gain—and to gain military presence and power projection into the South Atlantic."

"You are speaking of the Chinese?" Adler demanded.

"I have said too much already, Mr. Adler, but we are very short on time. I can help you find and rescue your hostages, if you allow me by partnering with me. While some of our military leaders have proven traitors to the Republic of Angola, the majority now serve our nation and are standing by to help. I want only to offer that help to you."

"And in return?"

"I want nothing in return but peace," Baptista said. "But it would do much to reduce the risk of violence and loss of life if you were to withdraw your soldiers from our city, Mr. Adler. This is a complex time in Angola, and I cannot guarantee their safety. There are many factions with varied loyalties in play right now."

"There is no way that will happen until we have recovered our people," Adler said, glancing at Ryan, who gave him an emphatic nod. Adler was proving once again why he had been the perfect pick for secretary of state. He was a brilliant diplomat, both tactical and strategic. "And I would like to point out that you attacked our forces—an act of war."

"Not me," Baptista said. "And not those in our great military loyal to the people of Angola. It is true that elements of the now violent and radical PFU had infiltrated the military—an unforgivable failure by Luemba's administration—but we believe we have most of the traitors uncovered and dealt with. Unfortunately, this is at the leadership level. It is undeniable that there may well be radical elements within our military not yet flushed out. We are working on this, but until we can purge these terrorists from our ranks, I fear there may yet be a real risk to your soldiers."

It was Adler's turn to let a silence hang in the air. After a long moment of allowing Baptista to sweat, he replied.

"If it proves true that rogue elements within the military are responsible and not you, then you will eventually have our thanks. If it proves otherwise, you will suffer the wrath of our angry nation, Mr. Baptista. In the meantime, I can assure you that our Marines are more than capable of responding swiftly and violently to any attacks on them while on this mission to recover our people and protect the American embassy—which we view as sovereign U.S. territory. For the safety of *your* people, I recommend you do everything in your power to discourage attacks on our Marines. We don't wish any more violence, but our Marines are more than capable of defending themselves. They are also lethal weapons for executing the President's policy decisions. If you truly want a productive relationship with the United States, then I suggest you do everything within whatever power you now have to make sure the Americans held hostage in Luanda are returned safely."

"I will do what I can," Baptista replied in an oily voice. "And our lines of communication, of course, remain open. As I learn anything I will use this channel to share it with you so that we can assist one another in our shared goals."

Without another word, Adler leaned forward and disconnected the call. Then he turned and held Ryan's stare.

"Very well done, Scott," Ryan said, and meant it. He rather doubted he could have handled the call nearly as well. Not only was Adler a far more talented diplomat with a much more even temper, Ryan had to admit that his emotions were clouded even further by the worry for his son. "What do we think?" he asked, addressing the room.

"I think he's full of shit," Kudryk said, putting a fine point on what most of the room was no doubt thinking.

Ryan nodded in agreement and turned to Adler.

"Probably," Adler couched. "But we really need to know for sure. I'm not certain it would be wise to burn this bridge just yet, not until we get confirmation."

"Well, we now have a lot of young American Marines in harm's way, who need us to be right about this," Secretary of Defense Burgess said. "If there are radical elements still within the Angola Army *and* radical PFU terrorists roaming around, this is a powder keg that will explode with just the smallest of sparks."

"Bob is right," Jay Canfield agreed. "But we need more information. I can't tell you that his claims about leaving the PFU are true, but I don't have anything to refute them, either—not yet. And we know that Luemba was in deep with China financially. Hell, that advantage by the Chinese is why the DIA team was there to begin with. I'm not saying Luemba was getting money personally, but China has invested billions into the Angolan economy, so either way his loyalty was skewed in that direction. And kickbacks are how business is run in sub-Saharan Africa, so it's certainly possible. Baptista may well be full of shit, as General Kudryk suggests. I'll get to work to figure it out."

"We don't have much time here, Jay," Ryan warned.

"I know, sir," Canfield said. "The ONI team is heading to the embassy to embed with my remaining CIA team, is what I understand. They know the stakes."

"Very well," Ryan said, signifying it was time to get to work. Inside, his gut was churning. With his fears about Kyle, he hadn't even thought about what might be going on with Katie. It had occurred to him that his daughter—being the naval intelligence rising star that she was—might be involved on the ONI side, but hadn't imagined that might lead her into a war zone of his creation. "Let's get to work, people."

The team rose, staffers grabbing files and bags for their bosses, and headed for the door.

Ryan tapped Mary Pat on the arm, keeping her until the door closed.

"You okay, Jack?" she asked, worry on her face.

The President looked like a man caught in a waking nightmare.

"Look, I know I shouldn't ask, but Cathy is going through hell right now and I need to be armed with knowledge. Mary Pat, is Katie on her way to the U.S. embassy in Luanda?"

Mary Pat shook her head and closed her eyes.

"Damn, Jack," she said. "With everything going on I didn't even think of that. I honestly don't know, but, well, she's Jack Ryan's daughter through and through, so it wouldn't surprise me. I'll find out."

"Only when time allows, Mary Pat," he said, feeling guilty. If not for his executive power he'd have no more way to get these answers than any of the other hundreds of parents of the kids he'd ordered into harm's way. "It won't change anything."

"Understood," she replied, then squeezed his arm. "We'll get him back, Jack."

"Let's get them all back," he said. "And let's do it five minutes ago."

She nodded and headed for the door.

Ryan sat in his chair for a few minutes more, completely spent emotionally, and exhausted physically.

Then he rose and headed out as well, returning to the Oval Office.

He had a lot of work to do. Not the least of which was checking in to see how Cathy was holding up.

39

U.S. EMBASSY
R. HOUARI BOUMEDIENE 32
LUANDA, ANGOLA
1312 LOCAL TIME

Katie found herself in what could only be called a war zone. Getting permission to come ashore with the Headquarters and Service Battalion had been much easier than anticipated. In fact, despite Colonel Crocker's stern look and apparent reluctance to send what he had called "REMFs" (rear-echelon motherfuckers) to the embassy, he had agreed pretty quickly and easily. It almost felt like the officers and crew were eager to get her and her ONI team off the *Kearsarge*. Now Katie tried with all her might to concentrate on what the CIA station chief was saying as they walked down the metal stairs from the roof and the sounds of the MH-60S helicopter that had delivered them faded away. It was not lost on her that she had put her team in danger, no matter what assurances the leader of the coup, Victor Baptista, had apparently given to her father. But either way, being here, surrounded by Marines, CIA case officers, and special operators felt infinitely more comfortable than watching missiles scream toward them from deep inside a Navy ship. When she'd pitched that to Bubba, he'd just rolled his eyes and Conza had laughed, admonishing her with "Jeez, Ryan, you're a naval officer, for Pete's sake."

He was right, of course, but being on land was just . . . *better.*

She had seen firsthand how dangerous and deadly conflict could be at sea—from the conn of the *Blackfish*, where she'd survived a torpedo battle, and from the CIC of the USS *Jason Dunham*, where she'd been a white-knuckle participant in a missile engagement. Naval service on the tip of the spear was not for the fainthearted or weak-kneed.

She tried to ignore the concerned look on Conza's face that was starting to irritate the shit out of her. She shifted her heavy bag on her shoulder as they reached the bottom of the stairwell and headed down a hallway to what she assumed would be a SCIF of some sort. She knew her irritation had nothing to do with Conza—he was just the closest person to focus her irritation on. She wanted to get to work, to unleash Pettigrew and his big brain, and to dig in herself and start solving the puzzle of where the hostages were and who had them. That always began with the "why," and that would take them to the "who" and then the "where." Together with Conza and Goose Horgan, they needed to start following the trail that would lead her to Kyle.

And the others, of course. They needed to save all of them, not just her brother.

It had occurred to her more than once that Horgan, being organic DIA, may have known already that her brother was among the missing. Conza had insisted that wasn't the case, but she wasn't sure.

Katie knew she had arrived at the embassy with a chip on her shoulder. She knew that it wasn't any of *these* people's fault that

Kyle had been taken, but she needed someone to blame. Someone within spitting distance. It wasn't right, but damn it, she was angry, and until she could direct that anger at an appropriate target, the dudes in charge of securing the embassy would serve as surrogates.

". . . obviously our current priority is locating the hostages," CIA station chief Freddy Vincent was saying, talking over his shoulder as he led Katie, Conza, and Bubba into the EOC, or Emergency Operations Center.

"The priority is *rescuing* the hostages," she said, correcting him, "not locating them."

"Right, right, of course, but in my mind that was implied. Before we can effect a rescue, we need to figure out where the hell they're being held," he said.

She pressed her lips together in a hard line, then said, "We're not doing *implied*, Freddy. I want everyone to be very explicit and clear on our goals and objectives. Otherwise, in my experience, it tends to lead to people operating with assumptions. And when we assume different things, do you know what happens, Freddy?"

"No, Commander Ryan, what happens?"

"As someone once famously said, when we *assume* it makes an *ass* out of *u* and *me*."

He let out a little chuckle, then, working hard to defuse the tension, said, "No assumptions. Gotcha." He then gestured to a man who'd walked over to join the conversation. "This is Julio Tejada, the embassy RSO. He's going to be your point man for all comms, tech, and coordination issues you might have while you're here."

"Commander Ryan, is it?" Tejada said, sticking out his hand to her.

"Yeah," she said, and shook it. "Just to be clear, the EOC is going to be our TOC for the duration of the rescue and counterterrorism campaign here in Luanda. We're going to rely on your site-specific expertise and local knowledge, but we're not observers and we're not your guests. Our task force from the ONI is running the show while the United States military has boots on the ground here."

"Understood, ma'am," Tejada said, then with the slightest hint of a smile added, "No assumptions."

"Now we're getting somewhere," she said, thawing just a little as she realized she'd be able to work with these guys.

"However," the man said, his eyes holding her, "I would ask you to remember that it is our people out there. They are not just our responsibility, but our family."

It's not their fault Kyle was taken, analyst Katie said in her head for the umpteenth time.

"Understood," she conceded with what she hoped was an apologetic tone. "And I apologize. We're all on the same team and have the same goals."

Tejada gave her a tight smile, then gave his teammate from the CIA a satisfied nod.

But warpath Katie wasn't quite ready to cede control.

"Freddy, when was the last time you slept?" she said, returning her attention to the station chief. Granted, she'd just met the guy ten minutes ago, but she recognized haggard when she saw it.

"I don't know, two or three days," he said, running trembling fingers through his hair.

She glanced at Conza, who clearly shared her concern. Freddy Vincent was cooked and no use to anybody in this state. He needed to lie down before he fell down.

"I appreciate you greeting us and providing the lay of the land, but you're no good to anyone like this," she said, never mind the fact she was sleep-deprived herself. "Why don't you get some rest . . . Tejada can hold down the fort until you're back on your feet."

Freddy looked at Tejada, who gave him a *I got this boss* nod. Then he exhaled, plastered on a smile, and said, "I appreciate that. I think I've, um, reached the biological limits of caffeine augmentation . . . And for what it's worth, I'm sorry about Kyle. I understand he's your brother, so I know you more than get what we mean about family."

She said nothing because there was nothing productive she could say on the matter.

As Freddy left to go get some sleep, she turned her attention back to Tejada. Unlike Freddy, Tejada wasn't jittery and didn't have bloodshot eyes, but she needed to ask the question anyway. "I'm going to ask you the same thing I asked Freddy. When's the last time you slept?"

"When I heard y'all were coming, I took a three-hour nap. I'm good to go, ma'am."

"All right," she said and went straight back to business. "As the RSO you're in charge of embassy security, correct?"

"That's correct, ma'am."

"I assume from the intact appearance of the EOC that the insurgents did not breach this space during the attack?"

"That is also correct."

"Do you have security camera footage for the duration of the incursion?"

There was no doubt in her mind that finding where the hostages were located started with who had them. No one was taking Victor Baptista at his word that some rogue third party was holding them and that he was only here to help. But, just like her admonition to Tejada, she couldn't afford to make any assumptions, either.

"Yes, and we took the liberty of reviewing and prepping what we thought were the relevant sequences that you guys would want to see," he said and motioned for her to follow him to a computer terminal, where he worked the keyboard with deft fingers. "This is stitched together using the feeds from multiple cameras . . ."

Katie watched as two pairs of insurgents in an embassy hallway breached a door and entered a room. They exited the same room several moments later dragging an unconscious man and manhandling a terrified woman at gunpoint.

"That's Kyle being dragged in front, and the female hostage is Madison Bennett," Tejada said. Then, anticipating her question, added, "Bennett is on the ambassador's staff. She's not one of Freddy's."

Katie glared at the monitor, where she watched as the terrorists carried Kyle's limp body down a flight of stairs while shoving Madison in the back with their rifle muzzles. They eventually exited the embassy, where they put black hoods on Kyle and Madison and loaded them into the back of a cargo van. A moment later, a second squad of terrorists arrived with two more hostages—also a man and a woman.

"Is that Ambassador Gonçalves?" she asked.

"Yes, and the man is Eric Ottinger. He's one of mine," Tejada said. "He's DSS and on the ambassador's personal protection detail and was with the ambassador at the time of the attack."

Ottinger had a dark stain on his shirt in the area over his left shoulder blade and the way he was hunching and moving made it clear he was injured.

"He looks like he might have been shot," she said, leaning in and squinting at the display.

"My assessment as well," Tejada said. "I'm not surprised. Eric's solid. He wouldn't have let them take the ambassador without a fight."

Just like with Kyle and Madison, the ambassador and Ottinger were also black-bagged and loaded into a van. Then the vans evacuated, leaving the embassy grounds and disappearing off frame.

The video ended.

"Please tell me you tracked the vans," she said, turning to Tejada.

"That's where our coverage ends, but the CIA had eyes in the sky focused on the embassy at the time." He closed the video player and opened a new file. "We've reviewed all the footage and we know where the vans unloaded them."

"Where?" she said.

A new static satellite image expanded on the screen—a bird's-eye view of Luanda—and it had a red pin location marker in the middle of high-density housing.

"This area is called Bairro Cazenga—it's the most densely populated of the nine cities, or what we could call municipalities, that comprise Luanda," Tajeda said.

"It's a fucking labyrinth," Conza said, speaking up for the first time. "We're never going to find them in there."

"Therein lies the problem. Cazenga has a population of over a million people crammed into fourteen square miles," the RSO replied with a solemn look.

"Did the bird have thermal?" Bubba asked, sounding hopeful. "If so, maybe we can we track their heat sigs."

Tejada flashed Bubba a wan smile, then hit a button on the

keyboard and the satellite image flipped to thermal imagery and the entire screen filled with thousands of human heat signatures.

"Shit," Bubba said, visibly deflating.

"Yeah, and we're only looking at a quarter-mile-by-quarter-mile area here," Tejada said. "This is a high-density urban environment the likes of which we don't have in the U.S. . . . and it gets worse."

"Worse? How could it possibly be worse than that?" Katie said, thrusting her pointer finger at the screen.

"Well, we were already pretty sure the outfit responsible for the attack was the PFU, aka the Patriotic Front for Unity, and hearing the name Victor Baptista from Washington simply confirmed our suspicions. I don't know how up to speed you are on Angolan history, but the PFU is the militant successor to UNITA. It's led by a man named Victor Baptista, and his stated goal is regime change. Consequently, I was also not surprised to track the vans to this area, because the PFU has been holed up and operating out of this neighborhood for years. Angolan counterterror—Grupo de Intervenção Rápida, or what we call GIR—has conducted multiple raids over the years, hitting suspected PFU safe houses hoping to nab Baptista. Rumor is they've always come up empty. What I'm about to tell you next is unconfirmed, but Freddy told me that a local asset reported the reason why is because the PFU has spent a decade building a series of tunnels underneath this area and they pop up all over the place."

A knot formed in Katie's stomach.

"Yeah, I know," Tajeda said, undoubtedly cuing off her grim expression. "In my opinion, this was the plan all along—breach the embassy, take hostages, and exfil the hostages to a location where they have the upper hand. They've foiled raids on their home turf, repositioning underground like gophers, and I assume that's their strategy now."

Katie shot him a look.

"Sorry," he said with a sheepish grin. "No assumptions."

"Tell me more about this Baptista dude," Conza said. "Is he your typical jihadi shithead or something else?"

"That's more Freddy's department," Tejada admitted, "but from the discussions we've had, I'd say the answer is no. First, he's not a jihadist. I don't even think Baptista is Muslim. His objective is purely political power. According to Freddy, the CIA was in league with UNITA when Baptista was a young man fighting in the civil war. Unfortunately, Baptista came out on the losing side."

"Which means two things," Conza said. "He knows how we think and operate, and he's probably bitter as hell that we abandoned the cause."

"According to the ODNI, Baptista claims he is no longer with the PFU—they became too radical for him," Katie reminded. "He claims he can use his former ties to help us secure their release."

"Yeah, well, like I said, that is more Freddy's department, but if you want my opinion . . ."

"I want everyone's opinion," Katie said.

"Baptista is full of shit," Tejada said. "We have him linked to PFU operations in our security briefs since I've been here, and I can assure you he is one brutal son of a bitch. Radical and violent PFU is nothing new, and it is certainly nothing a man like Victor Baptista would object to. Not to mention the fact that, after losing the support of the CIA and State two decades ago, he is certainly no fan or friend of the United States."

"So, what are you saying? That this is his revenge?" Bubba asked.

Conza shook his head. "Seems more likely that this is him taking another shot at what he failed to accomplish the last time, which is take control of the country. But instead of seeing us as a potential ally and partner, he considers us the enemy. Assholes like this love revenge, but everything is secondary to power. It was the same with the mujahideen in the Middle East."

"So, what we're saying is that the embassy attack was just one part of a larger plan to take over the government? The attack was part of the operation to grab President Luemba?"

Conza looked at Katie, then grinning, said, "I *assume* so."

She wanted to sock him for that, but also loved him a little for trying to help her keep in check. She tried to grin back, but only managed to shake her head. "Let's call it a hypothesis, which means that we have a lot of work to do, gentlemen. John, why don't you get with Captain Camperos and start working up a plan to hit the PFU safe houses in Bairro Cazenga. I realize it's not going to be easy with the tunnels and the fact this is exactly what they are expecting us to do, but we can't sit on our hands and do nothing, either."

"Agreed," he said, then with confidence added, "No offense to the Angolans, but the MARSOC Raiders are not the GIR. We're now well-equipped, with lots of high-quality operators, and don't forget highly motivated. I'll work up a package with Camperos."

"Good," she said, then turned to Bubba. "While John plans that op, you and I are going to chase down the network of connections this Baptista might have inside the Angolan government, and more important, inside the military. The Angolans have been pretty quiet and hands-off considering what happened here. And that would seem to have preceded his supposed 'invitation' to lead in the interim. I would have expected a much stronger reaction—police presence, SWAT, GIR counterterrorism units, or military special forces on the scene to augment our organic embassy security force." She looked at Tajeda. "I mean, you've been on your own since the riot, correct?"

Tajeda nodded. "Yeah, not what I expected . . . And my Angolan security liaison is not picking up or returning my calls."

A fresh adrenaline dump immediately energized Katie's weary bones. She clapped a hand on Bubba's shoulder. "We need to get after it, because if Baptista has been running multiple operations simultaneously, we might already be too late." She turned to look at Tajeda and then over to Conza and Horgan. "If this Baptista really is already in power, then that means that some or all of the Angolan military, at least here in Luanda, must be taking sides with him. Otherwise, he'd have failed already, and you'd be hearing from the leadership."

"What does that mean for us?" Horgan asked, and Katie could tell there was worry in her voice.

"It means we may be up against more than just a group of terrorists," Conza offered.

"It means it's a damn good thing that the 22nd MEU is on the ground with us," Katie added. "Because if we're rescuing our hostages from a well-equipped military, then that is a whole different ball game."

PART III

Guard against the impostures of pretended patriotism.
—George Washington

40

**OVAL OFFICE
THE WHITE HOUSE
WASHINGTON, D.C.
0724 LOCAL TIME**

Ryan sat behind the Resolute desk, phone to his ear, waiting for the outbound call to Cathy to connect. He felt more exhausted than he could ever remember. If the Oval Office were to suddenly burst into flames, he wasn't sure he'd have the energy to rise and escape. It wasn't that he was getting older, and it wasn't the weight of his executive power. It was those things being combined with the emotional and even spiritual burden of knowing his son was in the hands of savages, and so far, there hadn't been a damn thing he had done to change that.

And it is the weight of watching the woman I love struggling like I've never seen before.

In all the years he'd been in harm's way, Cathy had been the perfect wife and mother. She'd sacrificed and served the same way thousands of military wives and moms do every day—keeping her chin up and not complaining through it all.

My life and career may have finally asked too much of her, he thought, as it seemed like she wasn't going to pick up. He was about to hang up when he heard her voice, strained and low.

"Hello? Jack? Is there news?" she said, her voice ragged with emotion, and he could tell she'd been crying.

Maybe it was time she came to the White House so they could weather the remainder of this storm together.

"Not yet, my love," he said, trying to bottle up his own grief and guilt. "How are you holding up?"

"Doing my best," she said, then with an edge to her voice added, "I'm worried about our son, Jack. He's not like his older brother. He's not . . . built for this sort of thing."

"I know," he said, and her words felt like a gut punch because she was right. "But I think Kyle is stronger than . . . than we all give him credit for."

"I hope you're right," she said. "Does Katie know yet?"

"Yes, I think so," he said.

"What do you mean you think so?" his wife asked, her voice flat. "Did you talk to her, Jack?"

"No, sweetheart," he said. "She's working, you know. She's . . . out of town."

"Out of town?" Cathy said sharply. "Are you telling me she's in the middle of this shit, too?"

"No, no . . . She's an intelligence analyst. She's leading a team to help locate him and the others."

"That didn't stop you from sending her out on a submarine in the middle of a torpedo war with the Russians, or whatever classified bullshit happened," she snapped. Then, after a long pause, she said, "I'm sorry, Jack. You didn't deserve that. None of this is your fault. I just . . . I'm fine. I'll be fine, Jack. I promise. I love you."

"I love you, too," he said, then added, "I know it can be stressful here, but the East Wing isn't the same without you. Just say the word and we can have you here in a flash."

Ryan understood her need to be somewhere else, especially somewhere with the comforting memories of home instead of the White House. But, if he was honest with himself, it would be better for *him* if she came in.

"That's very sweet, and now I feel guilty. I should have asked you how you're holding up."

Ryan smiled. Cathy had always been the primary emotional caregiver for the whole Ryan family, including himself.

"I'm hanging in there . . ." He wanted to tell her that he was certain—certain in his bones—that Kyle was alive. But that was feeling, not fact. He wanted her to feel the same comfort he did, but he didn't want to give her false hope, even if he did need a little for himself. He split the difference and said, "I know he's okay, Cathy. We'll get him back. The entire 22nd MEU is in the city now with that goal as their mission."

"I know. Thank you, Jack. I love you."

"I love you, too," he said.

He replaced the phone and sighed, but before he could draw the breath back in, his phone chirped again and he pressed the intercom button.

"Yes?"

"Director Foley to see you, Mr. President."

"Send her in," he said, and rose from the leather chair, hope and dread competing for his heart's attention.

As Mary Pat walked through the door, he knew instantly from her face that this was neither bad news nor great news.

He slumped back into his chair and gestured at one of the chairs in front of the desk.

"Where are we, Mary Pat?" he asked.

She stood behind the chair, her body language suggesting she had little time for sitting right now.

"Just wanted to update you in person, Jack," she said.

He gave her a curt nod.

"The MEU is secure and they have established a perimeter around the embassy. It includes the academic center of the medical school to the east. The maternity hospital that is part of the complex is left in the control of the university, but with security inside. The FST team has set up a casualty receiving area inside the outpatient surgery center, which is now officially the MEU's cache. We have control of a two-block area."

"Command and control are inside the embassy?" he asked. He knew the answer, but wanted her to get on with it.

"Yes," she said. "And the in-theater intelligence footprint, where the organic CIA assets are now part of the joint task force headed up by Lieutenant Commander Ryan."

At the formal mention of Katie's name, he felt another twinge of guilt. He had not ordered his daughter into Luanda, but he was also not surprised that she ended up there.

"Where is . . ." He clenched his jaw. "Where are the hostages, Mary Pat?"

"Latest intelligence indicates they are being held somewhere in the Bairro Cazenga district, a very densely populated area where a complex tunnel system was developed over the years to shield the PFU from Angola's National Police—specifically the GIR, which have them designated as a terrorist organization." Mary Pat must have seen the despair in his eyes, because she quickly continued. "But our team is optimistic, Jack. The Raiders are standing by to raid safe houses the moment we have a target identified."

But will we find them in time?

"Jack, it seems clear to me that Baptista is *not* using the hostages for political ransom, but rather as a tool to legitimize his coup. He only undermines himself if anything happens to them."

"So you're certain that Baptista is holding them? Is that what I'm hearing?"

"No," she said, shaking her head. "But either way, it is in his best interest if they are alive and well. His goal is to manipulate you, not go to war."

Ryan nodded. It was sound logic. But in his experience, logic was not always the driving force in these situations.

"Thanks, Mary Pat," he said. "What is the timeline for the Raider rescue operation?"

"I don't know, but I will find out," she said.

"Make sure concerns about authorization are not slowing anything down, Mary Pat."

"I will," she promised.

"And I want to be in the Situation Room when it kicks off."

"Of course," she said. Then, after a moment, she asked, "How is Cathy?"

He forced a smile. "Managing . . . just like us."

She gave a curt nod and then headed for the door.

Despite his personal and very emotional investment in what was going on in Angola, he did have a nation to lead and problems in hot spots around the world he needed to address today. Not the least of which was a growing situation in Syria, which he prayed John Clark had well in hand.

His was a job that didn't allow for any breaks.

41

SENSITIVE COMPARTMENTED INFORMATION FACILITY–SCIF
U.S. EMBASSY MISSION IN ANGOLA
R. HOUARI BOUMEDIENE 32
LUANDA, ANGOLA
1812 LOCAL TIME

Katie and Conza sat with Goose Horgan, Bubba, Freddy, Tejada, and the two Marines—Major Merriweather and Captain Camperos—at the conference table in the embassy SCIF. Leaning in on her elbows, Katie stared at the star-shaped Polycom conference phone in the middle of the mahogany top as a disembodied male voice talked on speaker. The voice belonged to Henrique Gomes, deputy chief of staff to the director general of the Serviço de Investigação Criminal. Gomes was not an official CIA asset, but someone who—according to Freddy—was comfortable "sharing" on a regular basis. Katie had never had any dealings with the man to reference for comparison's sake, but Gomes sounded absolutely terrified. His rapid-speech cadence in hushed tones made her imagine the man hiding in a closet somewhere hoping to complete his call before being discovered. But thanks to Gomes's courage, they now knew the situation was worse than any of them had expected. Luemba was deposed and Baptista was in control of both the government and the military, and according to Gomes he was planning to proclaim himself interim president within the next few hours. The myth that he had been invited to serve as interim president by those who had arrested Luemba for treason was, not surprisingly, the first of what she imagined would be a myriad of lies by the former PFU leader.

". . . the coup was a complete surprise to José," Gomes was saying, referring to his boss, José Silva, the director general of SIC. "Baptista had dozens of collaborators hiding in the shadows in all branches of the government and the military. How he kept his plans so secret is a miracle. Nobody, and I mean nobody, saw this coming."

"What about resistance?" Freddy asked. "Is anyone standing for Luemba?"

"If there is any resistance, I've seen no indication of it. The entire cabinet has been taken into custody. They're being held under armed military guard, awaiting trial. Who is going to stand against General de Souza? He controls the entire military," Gomes said, then suddenly frantic added, "I hear someone coming, I have to go—"

The line went dead.

Freddy, who'd actually done as Katie had suggested and gotten some sleep, looked like a new man. He leaned forward, turned off the speaker, and looked at her.

She blew air through loose lips. "Well, guys, now we have the answer. Baptista is in control."

"Not if *we* stop him," Freddy said. "There might still be time to intervene."

"We don't get to make that decision," Conza said. "That's above our pay grade."

"Yes, buuuuut," Freddy said, drawing out the word, "it doesn't mean we have to sit here on our hands, either. There's plenty we can be doing while we wait for marching orders from Washington."

Katie agreed. "As far as I'm concerned, you're both right. Our first priority is to route this new information about the coup up the chain of command. The White House needs to know that Baptista executed a violent coup, not a peaceful ascension after a scandal. They need to know that the military is heavily involved."

"I think we could argue that Baptista staged the attack on the embassy with his asshole PFU buddies as a false flag to help him pull it off."

"And now you think he'll turn on his PFU buddies to hold on to the power?"

Horgan shrugged.

"Would that surprise you?"

Conza shook his head.

"No," he said. "I suppose not."

Katie let out a frustrated breath through clenched teeth. "I agree, but it doesn't matter what we can argue. We need to prove it, and the best way to do that is to hear from Luemba and the rest of the detained cabinet.

"Right now that is a stage two issue," Katie said. "We're in stage one, where our only priority is the Americans who are being held. Once they are safe, then Washington can decide what to do about Baptista."

"Well, that may well mean providing military and intelligence support for Luemba and his cabinet," Freddy pointed out. "We'll be tasked to support that."

Katie waved the point away.

"Stage two," she said again. "For now, we get to work prepping a rescue mission for the four hostages." She turned to Merriweather, who was the company commander. "Major, how long will you need to prepare after we get authorization from the White House to conduct a rescue op?"

"Ma'am, I already have authorization to conduct hostage rescue operations. The MEU's orders were broad and direct—secure the embassy and safeguard American lives by any and all means necessary. As far as Colonel Crocker is concerned, retrieving our people falls under that mandate."

Katie heard echoes of Jack Ryan in the major's words, almost as if her dad were speaking through the Marine officer from where he was sitting in the Oval Office thousands of miles away. She supposed that was exactly what was happening. "In that case, how long until your men would be ready to roll?"

Merriweather looked at Camperos.

The corner of the Marine captain's mouth curled into something resembling a crooked grin. "We're Marines, ma'am. We're always ready to roll."

Gotta love the Marines, Katie thought with a crooked grin of her own. "In that case, unless there's any objections, let's shift gears and start planning this op. Lieutenant Conza happens to have quite a bit of experience with this sort of thing—isn't that right, John?"

Conza, a former Tier One Navy SEAL with hundreds of missions under his belt, simply said, "Happy to help wherever and however I can."

From anybody else, she'd take the remark at face value . . . but for the briefest of moments, she saw a flicker of conflicted emotion ripple across the former operator's face. Conza's retirement from the teams had been prompted by injury. He'd lost his left leg below the knee and now wore a prosthesis. While he'd never explicitly said as much, Katie was certain that, had it not been for the injury, Conza would still be with the teams. Special operators, men like Conza—Navy SEALs, Army Green Berets, MARSOC Raiders, and so on—they didn't *retire* by choice. They *got retired*. She'd only recently started working with Conza, but she'd seen his mettle on full display during the shit show in Taiwan. Now she saw him silently wrestling with whether he should embed himself with the Raiders as a shooter on this op or stay behind and coordinate from the TOC. She could practically visualize the calculus in his head. His elite experience, skills, and muscle memory would make him a valuable and lethal addition to the mission in the field. His prosthesis was an operational handicap, but Conza certainly did not consider himself "handicapped." There was a difference.

Or was there?

Despite his Tier One pedigree, there was no question that his prosthesis would impact his mobility and endurance, as well as his speed and stability. Despite her athleticism, Katie recognized and accepted that *she* would be a liability if she tried to operate with the Marines on this mission. She wondered if he felt the same.

What happened next took Katie completely by surprise.

Major Merriweather turned to Conza and, with no detectable judgment in his voice, asked, "Lieutenant, are you planning to kit up and join Captain Camperos, or hang back with me and coordinate from the TOC?"

Conza's lips split into a big, good ole boy grin, the first she'd seen on this trip. "Well, Major, as tempting as kitting up sounds, I certainly wouldn't want to embarrass your boys out there. I imagine getting your ass whooped by a one-legged SEAL would sting the ego a bit, don't you think?"

Merriweather and Camperos both laughed, then the latter

said, "I could always have my guys take one boot off if you think that would help level the playing field."

Conza chuckled. "Nah, I appreciate ya, though. I hear they got flavored syrups for the coffee in the EOC. So I think I'll sit back and watch y'all on TV with a nice sweet, steaming cup of joe."

"Now you're talking like a Navy SEAL," Camperos said.

They all laughed again, and the matter was settled.

God, I love the Navy, she thought, wondering why anybody would work anywhere else.

"Excellent," she said, and turned to Tejada. "We're going to need to use the EOC as our tactical operations center for the op. I assume that's not going to be a problem?"

Tejada shook his head. "Not a problem at all. *Mi casa es su casa.*"

"All right," she said, shifting her attention to the CIA station chief. "Freddy, why don't you bring Merriweather and Camperos up to speed on everything we know about the PFU in Bairro Cazenga—how they operate, safe houses, and the rumored tunnel system. We want to make sure everybody is clear on the knowns and unknowns and the risk profile for the op."

And with that, she leaned back in her chair to listen to the CIA station chief brief the Marines while she said a silent prayer in her head that they were not too late.

42

**A QUARTER MILE FROM SUSPECTED PFU SAFE HOUSE
BAIRRO CAZENGA
EAST LUANDA, ANGOLA
2218 LOCAL TIME**

Captain Camperos sat in the front passenger seat of the lead joint light tactical vehicle, waiting with lights off. The JLTVs, which Camperos affectionately called by their nickname, Jolts, were parked in a line on the dirt road between two rows of shacks. At twenty-two feet long, eight feet wide, and fifteen thousand pounds, the Jolt barely fit on the road. Designed based on all the lessons learned from the global war on terror, the JLTV was the U.S. military's successor vehicle for the long-in-the-tooth Humvee. With its superior power train, suspension, egress system, and ergonomics, the Jolt beat the Humvee in fuel economy, range, mobility, and average speed over ground. Armor enhancements and the monocoque capsule design gave the JLTV greater survivability against IEDs, mines, and enemy fire.

On top of that, they also just looked cooler.

Sitting inside the lead Jolt, Camperos felt perfectly safe.

But the second he climbed outside, that feeling would evaporate.

He checked his watch. It had been nearly thirty minutes since the head shed had asked them to hold, and he knew his fellow Marines were getting anxious. Vehicles like the JLTV were as imposing as they were conspicuous. Everyone in the barrio knew the U.S. Marines had arrived. But the delay was necessary, and it was his fault. He'd called in the concern because it was something he wanted folks with brains bigger and sharper than his own noodling on.

He sighed.

"Is everything all right, sir?" the driver, Moose Elkins, asked.

Camperos seemed to agree, but didn't say anything.

He had a bad feeling about this op.

According to the spooks, the Angolan GOE counterterror unit had conducted multiple raids prosecuting the Patriotic Front for Unity in this sprawling neighborhood of low-income apartments and shanties trying to find and capture the leader, Victor Baptista. In those instances, the PFU didn't know the raids were coming. This scenario was different. The enemy had American hostages and had brought them to this neighborhood on purpose. In Camperos's mind, the insurgents were baiting them. Which meant that he and his Marine Raiders were probably walking into a trap.

"You seem quiet, that's all," Elkins said, pressing.

Camperos exhaled, then after a beat turned to look at the Marine sergeant. "Feels like we might be walking into a trap here, Moose. Satellite holds no thermals in the target house. I don't like it."

Elkins nodded. "The same thought crossed my mind, sir. Is that why we're holding?"

"Yeah," he said. "The head shed agrees and they're supposedly working on something."

When Camperos had expressed his concern, LCDR Ryan—instead of downplaying or dismissing his input—had immediately taken it seriously. He'd found that both refreshing and encouraging. There was something about Ryan that inspired confidence, but he couldn't quite put his finger on it.

Maybe it was the way she'd ordered the CIA station chief to take a nap and the salty spook had actually complied, he thought with a wry grin.

It had instantly become the worst-kept secret that her brother—the President's youngest son—Kyle Ryan was one of the PFU hostages. Given the family ties and dire urgency of the situation, Camperos wouldn't have blamed Commander Ryan for pushing hard and fast and expecting Camperos to "just shut up and do his job." But her reaction to his input had been the exact opposite. Apparently, she was working on *something* with the former Navy SEAL John Conza and Major Merriweather, who'd stayed behind with her to oversee the operation from the TOC in the embassy EOC.

"Raider One, Bullpen," a male voice said in his headset, using the call signs for Camperos and the TOC, respectively. Camperos pegged the distinctive voice as belonging to Conza.

"Go for Raider," he came back, keying his mic.

"Sending a map overlay to your tablet, let me know when you have it."

"Check," Camperos said and pulled the rugged tablet computer from a Velcro sleeve on his kit. He woke the screen up and opened the mapping application in his tactical management interface. The map was a real-time satellite image of the target set at a half-mile radius. Even though it was night, the image was enhanced with false color and contrast to make it easier to see and process what he was looking at. The cool thing about the application was that it functioned as a shared workspace—he was looking at the same view as the team in the TOC. An overlay appeared on the map—a half dozen yellow dots and a series of lines, some solid, some dotted.

"Bullpen, Raider One—I've got eyes on," Camperos said.

"The yellow dots are the locations of every Angolan counterterror hit against suspected PFU targets in the barrio conducted over the past two years. The solid yellow lines are tunnels documented in Angolan GOE after-action reports that were shared with Bullpen Actual. The dotted yellow lines are *possible* tunnels, generated by the team here that would be logical for efficient movement between safe houses. The numbers displayed above each line are the calculated distances between points in meters."

Conza hadn't yet verbalized Bullpen's recommendation, but Camperos was already thinking ahead, anticipating the plan while the former SEAL was talking. On-screen, his location and the rest of Alpha squad was represented by a green dot. Charlie squad, led by Captain Dane, was represented by a blue dot located four hundred meters north and east. The primary target—the presumed safe house, where satellite imagery had recorded two cargo vans delivering the hostages—was represented by a red square and located approximately equidistant between the two Raider teams.

Instead of breaching the target building directly, which is likely booby-trapped, he thought, rubbing his chin, *we could breach previous safe houses to gain tunnel access, then search for the hostages.*

"Our thinking is that the primary target building could be

rigged with explosives," Conza said. "They might have trip wires set up, or the PFU might have spotters watching you right now with remote detonators."

"That was my concern as well," Camperos said, and then shared his idea with Bullpen.

"That was precisely what we were going to suggest—Alpha and Charlie teams breach alternate target buildings, check for tunnel system access, and ingress the tunnel system. You'll likely lose comms and we'll lose your thermal signatures when you're underground, so it will be difficult and dangerous . . . but if the enemy is anticipating our primary action, this will throw them a curveball."

"Raider Two, One—what do you think of the plan?" Camperos said into his boom mic, calling Dane.

"Oorah," his counterpart came back.

"Bullpen, One—do you have recommendations for the alternate target buildings, or do we pick?"

"One, this is Bullpen," a female voice said on the line for the first time, a voice he pegged as belonging to LCDR Ryan. "We performed an activity analysis of the secondary sites using archived satellite imagery, looking at foot and vehicle traffic in and around each of the suspected PFU safe houses—that's what took us so long, in case you were wondering. Most were abandoned after the Angolan GOE raids, but a handful continued to have activity since. I'm lighting up three alternate target locations—designated X-ray, Yankee, and Zulu—that we recommend Raiders breach instead of the primary safe house."

Camperos watched as the new designators appeared on the map over three of the existing yellow dots. Next to him, Elkins was leaning over to look at the tablet, so Camperos tilted the screen so he could see. "Whadya think, Moose? Which of the alternates should we breach?"

"Mmm . . . I'd go with X-ray and Yankee."

Camperos nodded. "Two, One—are you on your tablet?"

"One, Two—yes," Dane said.

"Which two of the three alternate sites would you pick to breach—X-ray, Yankee, Zulu?"

"X-ray and, uh . . . Yankee," the Charlie team leader came back.

Camperos looked at Elkins. "Looks like you guys are of the same mind on this."

"What do *you* think, boss?" Elkins asked.

Camperos looked back at the map. The three positions roughly formed a triangle around the original target building with X-ray and Yankee both on the north side—the former to the northwest and the latter northeast—and Zulu the lone position to the south. He understood the logic Moose and Dane were likely using—breaching on opposing sides and hoping to meet in the middle. But that also put the entire force north of the drop location. What if the bad guys had taken the hostages south? With this plan, they'd have to travel under the potentially booby-trapped safe house to explore south if they came up empty.

But that's assuming the additional tunnels even exist.

He looked back at Elkins. "If both you and Dane agree, let's go with that," he said, then keyed his mic. "Bullpen, Raider One—recommend breaching X-ray and Yankee."

"Copy, Raider . . . Wait one," Ryan said, but Camperos sensed uncertainty in her voice. After a thirty-second pause, she came back. "We were thinking Yankee and Zulu, but you have the green light for X-ray and Yankee. Godspeed and happy hunting."

"Roger, Bullpen," he said, then, addressing his fellow Marines, said, "Raider, change of plans. Alpha will be breaching the alternate target location Yankee and Charlie will breach X-ray. Infil will be on foot. After breaching, commence tunnel search. If no tunnels are found, fall back to vehicles and regroup."

"One, Two—copy all. Standing by to infil on your mark," Dane answered.

Camperos took a mental snapshot of the map on the screen before returning the tablet to the sleeve. Then he crossed himself, switched his radio to VOX, and pulled the latch to open the front passenger door of the JLTV. His rifle up and ready, he stepped out into the night and made the call to rally his Raiders into action.

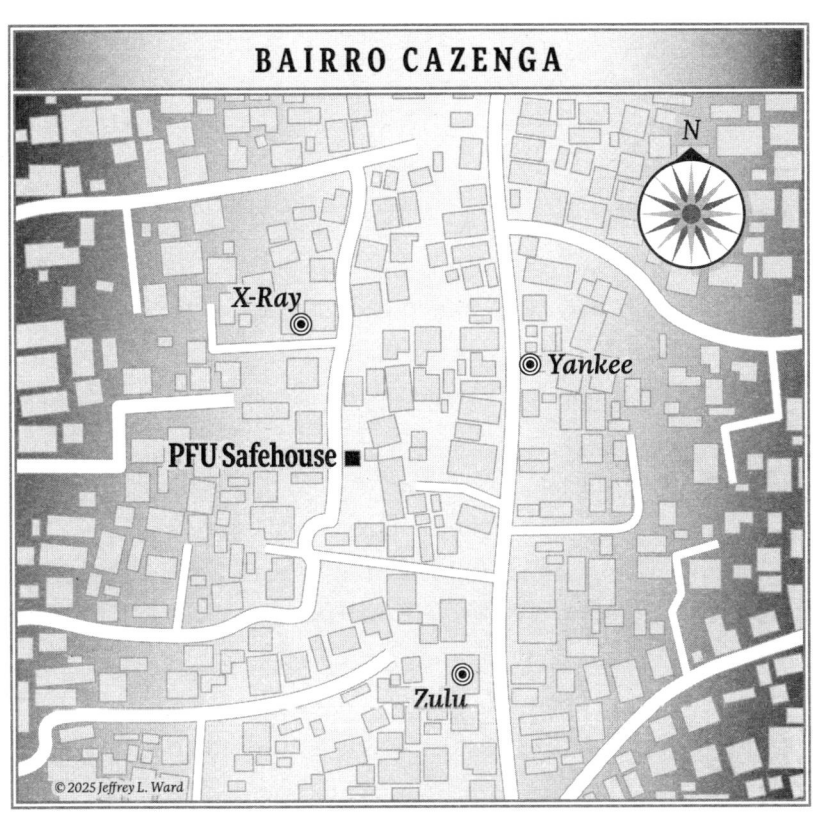

43

SOMEWHERE

Kyle's legs had fallen asleep from being tied to the chair for so long. When his terrorist interrogator returned, untied the rope, and forced him up, he immediately collapsed to his hands and knees.

"What is wrong with you? Get up," the Angolan said, giving Kyle a whack in the ass with the club he was wielding.

An epic wave of pins and needles spread across his glutes, quads, and hamstrings. "You left me tied up so long my legs lost blood flow. I need thirty seconds for my muscles to reoxygenate," Kyle said, glaring up at the man.

The terrorist looked perplexed for a moment, but instead of kicking Kyle or bashing him with a club, the man waited.

Kyle, knowing better than to press his luck, struggled to his feet as soon as feeling had partially returned to his legs. Trying to escape in this condition was out of the question, but at least now he could try to walk.

The terrorist hadn't been clear about what he wanted, having simply barked, "Let's go," after freeing Kyle from the chair. But he had left the cell door open, so Kyle took a tentative step in that direction, assuming he was being relocated.

"Go," the man said and prodded Kyle in the back with the end of the club, the man's patience and the moment of grace expired.

Kyle shuffled to the door, his feet and calves tingling and itching something fierce as he did.

"Where are we going?" he asked.

"No questions," the man said, his tone harsh and unsympathetic.

At that moment, something his older brother, Jack, had once said came back to Kyle: *"Pay attention to changes in the status quo, little bro. It usually means something big is coming."*

What was happening now most certainly qualified as a change in the status quo. Like an army of ants emerging from a trampled anthill, fresh fear crawled out from the center of his chest and spread over his entire body as he considered what was happening. He wondered if he was about to become a bargaining chip. Was his life about to serve as a demonstration of his captors' commitment to their cause and willingness to carry out their threats? Was he about to suffer the same fate as American journalist James Foley, who was kidnapped in Syria in 2012? Would Kyle's captors hack his head off with a machete on camera and post the video for all the world to see? The thought of Katie and his mom watching such a brutal and macabre thing made him nauseous.

Kyle paused at the threshold of the door leading to the corridor beyond.

"Turn right," the terrorist said.

But Kyle didn't move. His feet might as well have been bolted to the floor. The moment felt like an inflection point—the first and likely only opportunity he would have to flip the script. If he was going to act, the time to act was now. His terrorist interrogator had forgotten to put Kyle's black hood back on. The brain fog and vertigo from being concussed were almost gone . . .

He looked down at his hands . . .

His wrists were still bound with plasticuffs, and the skin beneath was bruised and had begun to chafe. He gritted his teeth and knitted his fingers together, forming a two-handed ball of flesh and knuckles. He visualized the strike: arms straight with elbows taut, but his torso and hips rotating, providing momentum and power as his human mace—

"Move," the terrorist barked at the same time a jab with the butt of the club in the middle of Kyle's back sent him stumbling forward into a dimly lit basement.

He quickly regained his balance and composure, but the opportunity was lost. He could feel it in his bones. Like an unconsummated first kiss at the doorstep, he'd hesitated a second too long, and the moment had passed him by. He glanced over his shoulder to see if he might have a second chance, but the man with the club was maintaining a full stride length's standoff distance. Kyle's arms would need to be five feet long to have even a chance of making contact.

He silently cursed himself for failing to act.

With blood flow restored to his lower extremities and feeling returned, the large egg on his shin throbbed now with every step—a painful reminder of what even a single whack from his torturer's club could do. Even if he successfully rushed the terrorist, he would take a blow from that club. And despite Kyle's several-inch height advantage, his adversary packed at least fifteen pounds more muscle than Kyle carried on his lean, runner's frame. He had not failed to notice the man's rippling, sinewy forearms and well-defined biceps during their first encounter. His courage simmered off like a pot boiled dry on the stove, and fatalistic defeatism settled over him as they arrived at the next cell.

"Stop here and put your hands and face against that wall," the terrorist said, pointing at the long concrete wall opposite the row of cell doors.

Kyle did as he was instructed, all the while wondering if this might be another opportunity to jump the terrorist while the man's back was turned. Keys rattled as the terrorist unlocked the door. Keeping his hands on the wall, Kyle craned his neck and looked over his shoulder, assessing the distance. As if feeling Kyle's gaze on him, the man with the club glanced over his shoulder and they locked eyes.

The unspoken message was clear as day: *If you try anything, I will beat you to a pulp.*

Then the terrorist jailer disappeared inside the cell, only to emerge a half minute later trailing Madison Bennett. The embassy staffer had a split and swollen lower lip, and her hair was disheveled. She wore a terrified expression on her face as she was shoved out of the cell from behind, but the instant she saw Kyle she perked up.

"Are you okay?" he asked her.

She nodded. "Are you?"

"Yeah," he said.

"No talking," their minder said, his voice a feral growl as he slapped the club into the palm of his free hand. Then the radio clipped to his waistband squawked.

The terrorist looked annoyed at first as he answered the caller, but then his expression changed to concern. After a quick and heated back-and-forth in Portuguese—none of which Kyle understood—the terrorist yelled at Madison to post on the wall beside Kyle.

Pounding footsteps echoed from somewhere and a moment later three Angolan men arrived, all dressed in dirty black combat fatigues, and each man armed with a machine gun. One of the new arrivals pointed his rifle at Kyle and Madison, one helped the leader open the two remaining cell doors, while the last man ran ahead and disappeared into what looked like a hole in the foundation.

"What do you think is going on?" Madison whispered.

"Looks like they're moving us," he whispered back.

"Why?"

"Not sure," he said, but his gut told him this was an emergent and compulsory action. "But maybe the cavalry is on the way."

Kyle and Madison both turned as the terrorists brought out the remaining two hostages from their cells—Ambassador Gonçalves and a man who Kyle didn't recognize—both of whom appeared to be in much worse shape than Kyle and Madison. The ambassador was hunched over, bent rather severely at the waist, clutching her abdomen. The male hostage had a ghostly pallor, slumped shoulders, and looked unsteady on his feet.

Madison immediately ran to check on the ambassador. At first, Kyle thought the leader was going to strike Madison with his club, but he didn't. Instead, he turned to Kyle and pointed at the other American, who looked like he was knocking on death's door.

"Help carry him," the lead terrorist barked.

Kyle held up his bound wrists. "How am I supposed to do that with my hands bound?"

Meanwhile, beside him, Madison was tending to Gonçalves. "Madame Ambassador are you injured?" she said, hunching to be at eye level with Gonçalves.

"He punched me in the stomach very hard and . . . and I think something is wrong inside," Gonçalves said, her voice pained.

The lead terrorist shook his head in irritation, but he walked over and used a pair of cutters to clip the plasticuffs from Kyle's wrists. Six feet away, Kyle saw his fellow American male hostage swaying and about to go down. He moved quickly and caught the man before he fell, hooking his right arm around the injured American's back and under the armpit. A beat later, he felt wetness soaking through his sleeve. He leaned back for a look and saw the back of the man's shirt was drenched in blood.

It's a gunshot wound. He's been shot.

Stoked by outrage, he turned to the leader. "This man is badly wounded. He needs a doctor."

"You shut up and carry him," the terrorist said, narrowing his eyes at Kyle. "Or *you* will need a doctor."

Teeth gritted, Kyle turned to his charge. "What's your name?"

"Eric," the American said in between labored breaths, the name barely audible.

"Eric, it looks like you've been shot. Have you been shot?"

Eric nodded erratically.

"Let's go!" the terrorist ordered and pointed to the hole in the wall with his club. "That way."

Eric's cuffs had already been removed, assuming he'd been cuffed, which allowed Kyle to hook the wounded man's left arm over his shoulders.

"Do you think you can walk?" Kyle said, taking a tentative step forward.

"Yeah, but I don't know for how long."

"Hurry, we leaving this place," the leader barked impatiently in thickly accented English from the three-foot hole in the foundation wall.

Kyle looked back over his shoulder at Madison and the ambassador. Madison looked up and stared into his eyes, silently reiterating the obvious—Gonçalves was also in a bad way.

He sent her a wordless answer: *We can do this, Madison. It's up to us now.*

"Okay, Eric. I got you," he said, turning his attention to the path ahead. "You can do this. Just put one foot in front of the other."

Based on his youth and level of fitness, Kyle pegged Eric as one of Tejada's boys, but given his injuries, Eric was definitely out of the fight. Kyle helped the DSS officer through the ragged hole in the concrete foundation wall and into an underground tunnel. As he shuffled forward, his analytical mind surveyed and assessed the tunnel's construction: earthen walls, floor, and ceiling with irregularly spaced wooden bracing and rafters. Based on the rough-hewn texture of the walls, Kyle surmised it was hand-dug. He automatically began to calculate how many laborers it would have taken—

"Move faster!" the terrorist leader shouted and prodded Kyle in the back with the tip of his club.

The man's self-assured, unflappable demeanor from earlier was gone. He was on edge, panicked even. It was obvious he'd been ordered to relocate his hostages urgently. This told Kyle that American forces—either SEALs, Marines, or Green Berets—were in theater. The head of the operation running this circus was spooked and relocating his buried treasure. Kyle could intentionally try to stall and slow their progress down, but that option was unnecessary and not great for Eric.

"If you want to go faster, then I'm going to need your help," Kyle said, calling a spade a spade.

The leader huffed loudly, but holstered his club. He walked back to take a position on Eric's opposite side and threw the wounded American's right arm over his shoulder. Together, Kyle and the terrorist enforcer supported nearly all of Eric's weight as they moved through the tunnel. After what seemed like thirty yards, Eric's toes were dragging in the dirt, and his chin was bobbing against his chest.

"If this man dies on your watch," Kyle said sideways to the terrorist, "there's going to be hell to pay."

The Angolan fighter turned and looked sideways at Kyle and for the briefest of instants, Kyle saw fear in the other man's eyes. Then, the terrorist's face hardened, and he said, "You better watch yourself, or you'll be next."

44

BAIRRO CAZENGA

Legs churning and head on a swivel, Captain Camperos led Alpha squad through the dark and deserted back streets of one of Luanda's poorest and most densely populated neighborhoods. The dirt road underfoot was so dry and hardpacked, it could have almost passed for pavement, and the Marine couldn't help but wonder if it ever rained here. The fetor of burning charcoal and garbage competed with unpleasant wafts of latrine gas as he navigated his way to the target . . . a task proving a little trickier than he'd anticipated.

The barrio was laid out in an irregular grid pattern. On satellite imagery he'd noticed how abutting sections of the neighborhood had both cross streets and through streets that didn't necessarily line up, nor were they always perpendicular or parallel to their cousins. He hoped if he made a wrong turn into a dead end that either LCDR Ryan or LT Conza—both watching him from the TOC via satellite—would say something. So he proceeded with confidence, trusting his memory, because a good Marine was sometimes mistaken, but never in doubt.

Unlike neighborhoods back home, Bairro Cazenga didn't have

streetlights—making the only source of ambient light the moon and the occasional window. A few of the buildings and homes appeared to have electricity, but most did not. Also, unlike American neighborhoods, none of the properties had front yards or walkways to access the dwelling. Every shanty was surrounded by an eight-foot-tall privacy fence made of wooden slats or sheets of corrugated metal that abutted its neighbor, creating a long continuous fence on both sides of the street that spanned the entirety of the block.

The effect was unsettling; Camperos felt like a rat navigating a maze, not knowing what lay in waiting around the next corner.

Adding to the creepiness, he'd not seen a soul on the streets since they'd left the Jolts. At the same time, he had the distinct and uncanny feeling of eyes watching him and his men from the shadows. He felt exposed and vulnerable. The walled-off streets put his team at risk of getting caught in cross fire, so he'd decided to hug the left side of the street along the fence line en route to the target. He was just about to request a sitrep from Bullpen when Conza's voice spoke in Camperos's headset.

"Raider, Bullpen—we have activity at Yankee and X-ray sites," the former SEAL said, addressing both Raider squads simultaneously. "At X-ray, we're tracking three thermals, but now they've disappeared. Our working theory is they egressed underground. We have four thermals at Yankee. Three were presenting as sleeping and one presumably on watch, but now they're all up and active."

"Copy all," Camperos said.

"Sounds like we're blown. They know we're coming," said Staff Sergeant T. J. Ward, who was moving in lockstep with Camperos on his right.

That's what happens when you hang out in armored vehicles in the neighborhood for half an hour before the op, Camperos thought, annoyed at the delay he'd single-handedly been responsible for.

"Raider, Bullpen—advise your intention. Breach or abort?" Conza said, putting the ball in Camperos's court, which took the Marine captain by surprise.

Wasn't Major Merriweather in the TOC with Conza and Ryan? Why wasn't he making the call? Delegating something like this down the chain into the field when the senior officer was supervising in real time was unusual. Maybe this reflected a difference in communities. Camperos had never operated with the JSOC SEALs before, but that community was famous for their "big boy"–rules approach to leadership and operations. Marines did things differently.

His boss, Major Merriweather, should be making this call.

Annoyed, Camperos halted his team with a closed fist and took a knee. "Bullpen, Raider—Raider is standing by for instructions."

"Raider One, this is an audible situation," Conza came back. "You're the quarterback, you call the play."

Camperos looked over his shoulder and locked eyes with Master Sergeant Enzo Fuentes, who was kneeling a few paces behind. The master sergeant's face held no fear. No uncertainty. He gestured in a chop toward the target, signaling his opinion on the matter.

Camperos keyed his mic. "Bullpen, Raider One—Raider is breaching."

"Bullpen concurs. Stay frosty," Conza came back.

"Two, One—sitrep?" Camperos said, checking on Charlie team, which should be several blocks away, getting into position to breach X-ray.

"Two is Dagger," Captain Dane came back, using the call sign signaling that Charlie team was in position and set to breach at X-ray.

Camperos popped to his feet and chopped a hand forward. Dane had not halted his team as Camperos had—and therefore was already in position—whereas Alpha needed a few more minutes before calling Dagger. But every minute counted, especially if the three shooters at X-ray had egressed underground into the supposed tunnel system like the head shed thought. Also, the Charlie and Alpha and breach sites were completely different scenarios. X-ray had no remaining thermals, whereas Yankee had four. Charlie team would breach without resistance, and so holding them for a simultaneous breach with Alpha was pointless. The bad guys were already tipped off.

Time to be fluid.

"Copy, Two—breach at will and pursue tangos underground if you find tunnel access," Camperos said. "But watch out for booby traps. Be advised, they might have left a present behind."

"Two," Dane came back, using his call sign as a tacit acknowledgment of the order to breach and be careful.

Camperos was worried about Dane's squad potentially breaching a house wired to blow, but he needed to commit all his brainpower and concentration to breaching and securing the Yankee site. The four thermals inside were most likely all bad guys, but without visual confirmation, Camperos could not rule out the possibility that one or more were hostages. Four hostages had been taken from the embassy, but the terrorist kidnappers had not communicated since. The head shed didn't know if all four hostages were still alive, nor did they know if the terrorists were keeping them in a single location or if they'd split them up.

It was uncertainty that made special operations so dangerous.

Overcoming that uncertainty is what made special operators so badass.

Camperos halted his team of seven Raiders along the fence at the front of the target house—four on one side of the gate and four on the other.

"One, Bullpen—you've got twenty-two feet between the gate and the front door of the target house," Conza said in Camperos's ear. "And what looks like four shooters in defensive positions. Two at the windows right and left of the front door and two in the back corners. Be advised, they are ready and waiting for you."

The unsolicited report from the head shed was exactly what the Marine captain needed to know. This was a double-breach scenario—which was much riskier and more dangerous than kicking down a door. Alpha squad had to first breach the fence, then cross the yard, before they could breach the door and enter the house. They would take heavy fire from the tango shooters in the windows unless . . .

Camperos turned and scanned the buildings across the street. Ordinarily, he'd have a sniper set up in an overwatch position in advance for a breach like this, but every structure in this area of the barrio was only a single story tall, providing no useful height advantage. Even if he could put a guy on the roof of the house across the street, the privacy fence made the angle shit.

Then another idea came to him.

He looked across the fence gap at his master sergeant. Using gestures, Camperos proposed that Fuentes send two guys over the fence into the neighbor's yard to the north and Camperos would send two of his guys over the neighbor's fence to the south. Then both those two-man teams would hop the fence surrounding the target house simultaneously at the back, gaining access to the yard, hopefully undetected, then breach from the rear, catching the enemy unaware.

Fuentes flashed Camperos something resembling a smile.

Camperos turned to brief his guys, but Elkins and Pavlo had been watching and were all over the plan.

"We got this, Cap. We'll lead and go in with flash-bangs. Wait three seconds after the boom, then y'all can make for the front door. Cool?" Pavlo said.

"Sounds like a plan," Camperos agreed with a half smile.

With that, Pavlo turned and quick-stepped after Elkins, who had already moved into position some fifteen feet away at a section of privacy fence belonging to the neighboring house.

Feeling hopeful for the first time all night, the Marine captain watched two of his best operators disappear over the top of the eight-foot-tall privacy fence like it was child's play. Then, gripping his rifle, Camperos turned back to center to wait for the percussion of combat to call him and the rest of Alpha squad into action.

45

EMERGENCY OPERATIONS CENTER (EOC)
U.S. EMBASSY MISSION IN ANGOLA
R. HOUARI BOUMEDIENE 32
LUANDA, ANGOLA

Katie eyed the vacant task chair in the embassy EOC. Nobody was using that terminal. Nobody would bat an eye if she took the seat. Her feet, knees, and lower back all ached and needed a break. But she knew if she dared sit in that comfortable-looking, ergonomically perfect chair, she'd be lights-out with her chin on her chest with drool running from the corner of her mouth in less than sixty seconds. So she forced herself to keep pacing.

But good God, did she want to sit down.

Over the past hour, they'd confirmed that the coup was real and Victor Baptista had taken control of the Presidential Palace and the military. President Luemba and his cabinet were in custody, but their custody status and location were unknown. Freddy's source on the inside said they had been locked up in the palace, but heard they were being relocated to São Paulo prison.

Is Baptista insane? Does he really think he can pull this off?

She blew air through her nose and turned her attention back to the monitors at the front of the EOC, streaming real-time satellite and drone imagery of the op happening in Bairro Cazenga. Over the past several months, Katie had done and experienced things—terrifying, white-knuckle, pucker-factor, off-the-charts things—she would have never imagined when she pinned on her "butter bars" as an ensign in the Navy. She'd stood on the conn of a fast-attack sub in a torpedo battle with Russian submarines a thousand feet below the surface. She'd helped coordinate tactics from the CIC of an Arleigh Burke destroyer in a missile engagement with a Chinese warship in the Strait of Taiwan. But this was her first time managing a special operations mission from a TOC in real time. Despite knowing she was orders of magnitude safer right now than she had been on the sub or the destroyer, this moment felt more harrowing.

Because this time she wasn't worried about her own safety.

This time, she was worried about Kyle.

She'd been running around, hair on fire, from the moment she'd left D.C.—so occupied with the urgent events that she'd not had time to truly process the stark reality of her brother's capture and all the emotions that came with that. With the MARSOC rescue intervention in progress, and her powerless to do anything but wait and watch, those emotions were bubbling to the surface. One way or another, she'd soon have clarity about her brother's fate, and that terrifed her.

Sometimes, not knowing was better.

At least then I can pretend everything is okay.

Her eyes went to Conza, who was totally in his element, radio-talking with Alpha and Charlie team leaders as the Raiders breached the X-ray and Yankee safe houses. Watching the former SEAL work reminded her of her older brother, Jack Junior. She wasn't read in on the nitty-gritty details of what her big bro did for a living, but she knew it involved clandestine operations. His build, his level of fitness, his firearms proficiency . . . even the way he carried himself these days *oozed* operator.

She wasn't surprised.

Like her dad, Jack wasn't afraid of a fight.

Like her dad, Jack ran toward danger instead of away from it.

With both her brothers on her mind, her thoughts naturally drifted to the past and how each of the Ryan kids had ended up where they had. Like most siblings, the Ryan children's relationships with their parents and each other had been impacted by birth order and age gaps. As the older kids, Sally and Jack naturally hogged the spotlight, vacuuming up Mom and Dad's attention with their antics and activities. Katie and Kyle, who were younger, sort of became like luggage on the Sally and Jack road show—bonding most strongly with each other instead of their busy parents and self-absorbed older siblings. As a result, to this day, Katie was convinced she knew Kyle better than any other soul on the planet.

She wiped her eyes with the back of her hand.

If she knew anything with certainty, it was that her brother was writing and running the algorithms necessary to survive and escape. Of course, the only problem was, the men who'd taken her brother were neither analytical nor patient men. They were men who chose violence over diplomacy, brutality over discourse. If interrogated, Kyle would be his own worst enemy . . . but through no fault of his own. His terse answers to their questions and demands for clarity would be misinterpreted as belligerence and disrespect.

Kyle being Kyle would trigger their worst impulses, and this realization terrified her.

She felt a gentle hand on her shoulder and turned to find Bubba studying her with a concerned expression. "You all right, boss?"

"Yeah, I'm fine," she said, forcing a closed-lip smile. "Just emotionally wrung out."

He nodded. "I know you're worried about your brother, but these clowns didn't take hostages just so they could execute them. Baptista needs them for negotiating leverage. It's like Monopoly, he's holding them to use later as his get-out-of-jail-free card."

"But that's stupid. My dad can't and won't trade Angola's national sovereignty for hostages," she said, doing something she never did, referring to the President as her dad while she was on the job.

"Are you sure about that, ma'am?" Bubba said with a questioning look.

"Well, yes, because Angola's sovereignty is not something we can barter. You have to control something before you can trade it. America doesn't possess Angola."

Bubba considered her comment for a moment, then said, "I disagree. The moment American Marines take control of Luanda, I think one could make a pretty compelling argument that we do."

"Mmm, I guess I never thought of it that way."

"From Baptista's point of view, the lives of the hostages might be the only card he can play that will force the President to recall American troops."

"And why stop there?" she said, her sluggish mind sparking with epiphany. "If I were Baptista, I'd demand the White House publicly recognize my legitimacy as a condition of their release."

Bubba touched his nose. "Winner winner chicken dinner."

She sighed. "Bubba, tell me something—why do there have to be so many assholes in the world?"

"Great question . . . And why do all the assholes always want to be in charge?"

She looked down at her feet, feeling defeated.

"This is probably inappropriate, but I'm going to do it anyway," he said, and stepping up, gave her a little sideways hug.

"Thanks, Bubba, I needed that," she said, patting his back before he let her go.

"We're going to get Kyle back, ma'am. I can just feel it," he said, giving her a goofy but heartwarming smile.

"I hope you're right," she said, her voice weary, "because the world is a better place with my brother in it."

"You look exhausted, ma'am," he said and gestured to the vacant task chair, which was practically singing a siren song to her in the corner. "Why don't you take a load off for a spell?"

"Oh, hell no. Ten seconds after my butt's in that seat, I'll be snoring," she smiled and shook her head. In her peripheral vision, she could see what looked like the heat signatures for Alpha squad getting ready to breach the Yankee site. "We should probably shut up and get dialed in. Looks like things are about to heat up."

46

**OFFICE OF THE PRESIDENT
PALÁCIO PRESIDENCIAL DA CIDADE ALTA (PRESIDENTIAL PALACE)
RUA PEDRO FURTADO
LUANDA, ANGOLA**

Baptista sat alone in the president's office, at the president's desk, with no one to talk to and nothing to do. The feeling was both unfamiliar and unnerving. For the past decade leading the PFU, he'd rarely been alone. His lieutenants and underlings swarmed him like moths around a light bulb. Now that his power and importance had increased a thousandfold, nobody wanted to talk to him.

Strange.

He'd ordered President Luemba's bedroom cleaned, stripped of all personal items and memorabilia, and the bedsheets changed hours ago, but no one from the housekeeping staff had reported the task complete as of yet. Starting tonight, and from now on, Baptista would reside in the Presidential Palace. The hour was late, and, admittedly, he was exhausted, but he refused to turn in for the night until he received an end-of-day situation report from de Souza. Without reassurance from the general, Baptista knew that he'd fret and worry all night long about the Americans and not be able to sleep a wink.

A knock on his office door gave him a start, and he twitched in his chair.

"Come," he barked, grateful that he was alone and no one had been present to see him flinch at something as benign as a knock at the door.

The door opened, and his nephew, Jorge Luis Baptista, entered looking nervous.

Baptista had no spouse or legitimate children of his own, but his brother, Michael, had two sons. Jorge was educated, hardworking, and had proven himself to be loyal. He was also the brighter of the two boys. Baptista trusted very few people in this world, but he knew he could always count on family, which is why he'd appointed Jorge as his chief of staff a mere three hours ago.

"I'm sorry to disturb you, Uncle—I mean, Mr. President," Jorge stammered, "but Chinese deputy ambassador Sima is requesting an audience."

"What time tomorrow does he want to meet?" Baptista said.

"Not tomorrow, sir. He's here. He wants to meet now."

This pronouncement blindsided Baptista, and his reflexive inclination was to refuse the request so as not to appear unprepared or too accessible. A president should never be eager or too accommodating, as this could be interpreted as a sign of weakness. In his country, he was at the top of the hierarchy, and everyone else's schedule should flex to conform to his whims. If Sima was the *actual* ambassador it might be different, but he was only a deputy. Baptista's gut told him he needed to flex, but if Sima had come here at this late hour seeking an audience, then whatever news he came to share must be important. He'd told Sima during their last conversation that any help the Chinese government could offer managing and deterring the Americans would be most appreciated, and that he, Baptista, would personally make sure that Sima profited financially from such an arrangement. The emissary's late-hour, in-person arrival must mean that Sima routed Baptista's request up the chain of command and was here with the answer.

With the power of the Chinese government and military on my side, the Americans will have no choice but to back off.

A hopeful smile curled his lips.

"Send Deputy Ambassador Sima in," he said, and sat up straight in his chair.

"Yes, Uncle—er, I mean Mr. President," Jorge said with a contrite bow before turning to scamper off.

Baptista decided he couldn't be too angry with Jorge for the slip. He'd encouraged the young man to call him "Uncle" for years. The practice was rooted in habit, not disrespect. It would take a couple of days for Jorge to break the old habit and form a new one. Jorge was family, so Baptista would afford the young man a grace period.

But his patience was not indefinite.

Sima Liang entered the presidential office, stopped several feet inside the door, and greeted the president. Baptista resisted the urge to stand to receive the Chinese emissary and instead gestured to one of the two ornately carved wooden chairs with red velvet upholstery on the other side of his desk. Sima walked to the right-hand chair and took a seat.

"A late hour for a visit, Ambassador Sima," Baptista said, speaking English to the Chinese official, as Baptista did not speak Chinese and Sima did not speak either Portuguese or any of the Indigenous African tongues.

"Indeed," Sima said without apology, fixing Baptista with a stern, no-nonsense expression.

"Do you have news from Secretary Xu and the Party?" he asked, vexed that he was having to ask the question and pull the information out of the man. "I assume that is why you're here—to update me on the support your country will be offering."

The Chinese man frowned and reached inside the flap of his suit coat jacket and retrieved the four hostage photographs that Baptista had provided him earlier in the day. The ambassador arranged them on the presidential desk facing Baptista. Then he pointed to the first image and worked his way down the row as he spoke.

"This woman is confirmed to be United States ambassador Patricia Gonçalves. This man is Eric Ottinger, a member of the embassy security staff, typically assigned to the ambassador's personal protection detail. This woman is Madison Bennett, a senior staffer from the State Department who works on Ambassador Gonçalves's policy team. But this man," Sima said, tapping the final photograph, "is not who he claimed to be on his passport and entry visa."

"CIA . . . I knew it!" A vulpine grin curled Baptista's lips. He'd held a twenty-year vendetta against the CIA for their betrayal and abandonment of him and UNITA and now he finally had the power to make them pay for that mistake. "When and if I need to make a statement, this is the man who will be sacrificed."

Sima shook his head. "No, this man is not CIA, and what you're suggesting would be very foolish."

"And why is that?" Baptista said, not appreciating the Chinese man's tone.

"Because the man you've kidnapped is President Jack Ryan's son."

Baptista's heart skipped a beat. "Excuse me?"

"Kyle Ryan, President Ryan's youngest son—Naval Academy graduate and officer. Our intelligence services tell us he is working for the Defense Intelligence Agency, but this has not been validated. His identity, however, *is* confirmed . . . which is a very big problem."

"What are we going to do about this?" Baptista said, feeling panicked for the first time in as long as he could remember.

"There is no *we*," Sima said, sitting back in his chair and knitting his fingers together in his lap. "This is what I have come here to tell you. My superiors are withdrawing all support and will disavow any connection to your actions and rise to power. We will not intervene in the inevitable and bloody conflict between your military and the Americans. We do not, under any circumstances, condone the taking or executing of hostages. My recommendation to you, sir, is that you return the four hostages to the American embassy immediately and stand down all military action against the American Navy and Marines."

"We had a deal," Baptista shouted, shaking his balled-up fists with fury. "You can't abandon me now. You're supposed to be helping me with the Americans!"

"We had an *understanding*," Sima corrected, "and that understanding was that we would not intervene in support of one side or the other when you challenged Luemba for power. It appears that you grossly misunderstood China's position. We do not, and never have, supported military action against the Americans, nor did we condone extreme tactics such as false flag operations attacking the American embassy or the taking of hostages."

"China is no friend to America. I never took Secretary Xu for a coward until this moment," Baptista growled.

Sima's face flashed crimson. "Do you not understand the

magnitude of your actions? You have kidnapped Jack Ryan's son, you fool!"

Hot anger flared in Baptista's chest and he sprang to his feet. "How dare you speak to me that way. Get out of my office."

"Happily," Ambassador Sima said and, getting up, strode out of the office without a parting glance.

Fuming and breathing heavily, Baptista leaned forward and put his palms flat on the desk. His laser beam gaze focused on the picture of the fourth hostage, the one that Sima claimed was President Ryan's youngest son. And as he stared at the young American's face, the gravity of his situation finally hit home.

Dear God, what have I done?

47

BAIRRO CAZENGA

Crouched outside the perimeter fence with his weapon at the ready, Camperos tapped the pad of his index finger against the side of the trigger guard, keeping time like a metronome. Four feet away, Master Sergeant Fuentes mirrored Camperos's posture on the other side of the still-closed front gate, waiting for the engagement to kick off. Any moment now, the two pairs of breachers from Alpha squad would be kicking off the assault and breaching the target house at the rear.

Confirming that his internal clock was properly calibrated, the next thing Camperos heard was Elkins's voice in his headset quietly counting down:

"Three . . . Two . . . One . . . Go . . ."

A split second later, the percussive whump of a flash-bang grenade shook the night, followed immediately by multiple bursts of rifle fire. Fuentes popped up from his crouch and kicked the privacy fence gate open. Camperos immediately shifted left in his low crouch to take a kneeling firing stance, sighting into the courtyard while shielding half his body behind the fence. Sighting now on the front of the target house, Camperos scanned for targets. Muzzle flashes flared in the two darkened windows on the front facade, pulsing like a strobe light in a haunted house on Halloween.

The front door swung open and an armed fighter burst out. He fled five feet, then whirled and raised his weapon. Camperos put his holographic targeting dot on the back of the man's head and squeezed the trigger. The round flew true, punching a hole in the terrorist's head and crumpling the man in the spot where he stood. A beat later, a second shooter tried to flee through the wide-open door, but this man was dropped from behind and fell at the threshold, his torso landing outside, with his lower body still inside the house.

The din of gunfire fell silent, and the house went dark.

Camperos popped up into a combat crouch and surged through the open gate into the front courtyard, scanning for threats. A figure sighting over a rifle appeared in the doorway, and Camperos targeted center mass. His brain immediately identified the shooter as a friendly—Elkins, from the looks of it—and shifted his aim off target.

Elkins put a round into the head of the terrorist squirming in the doorway, then announced on comms, "One, Yankee is secure. Four tangos KIA."

Camperos passed the report to the TOC. "Bullpen, Raider One—Yankee is secure. Four tangos KIA."

"Copy, Raider One. Be advised. Raider Two discovered tunnel access at X-ray site and led Charlie squad underground to search for hostages. We've lost comms with Charlie," Conza came back.

"Well, I'll be damned," Camperos muttered to himself. Then, stepping over the body in the doorway into the tiny dwelling, he replied, "Roger that. Alpha commencing search for access at Yankee."

He quickly scanned the interior of the house, which didn't

take but a couple seconds because there wasn't much to see: a kitchen table, some chairs, an IKEA-style cabinet in the corner, a propane grill, a stack of five-gallon water jugs, and sleeping mats, pillows, and blankets on the floor. He didn't even have to give the order; his men were already searching the floor for trapdoors using the tactical lights affixed to their rifles.

"Think I got something," Pavlo called from where he'd taken a knee on the plywood floor in the middle of a mess of bedding.

"Photograph the dead and bag their phones," Camperos said to Fuentes as he walked over to Pavlo.

"Aye, sir," the master sergeant said and delegated the order.

Camperos took a knee beside Pav, who had his rifle slung and was using a gloved hand to whisk dirt away, revealing a seam in the wooden floor. Elkins joined them and, using his Ka-Bar, wordlessly went to work digging into a parallel seam a few feet away. Camperos pulled a bowie knife from his kit and joined the effort to pry up what looked like an access panel in the floor. Working together, they got the rectangular piece of wood out of the floor, revealing a subterranean access. A staircase made of cinder blocks led down into the darkness below.

A pair of boots stepped up beside Camperos, and the Marine captain looked up to see Master Sergeant Fuentes shaking his head.

"What is it with bad guys and tunnels, huh? Do they all go to the same gopher training school?" Fuentes growled.

"Luckily, Uncle Sam decided to send in the world's most capable exterminators," Camperos said, getting to his feet. "Did you get everything we need?"

Fuentes nodded. "Two phones, one radio, and photographs."

"Good," Camperos said and keyed his mic. "Bullpen, One—we found tunnel access at Yankee. Intend to descend and commence hostage search and rescue."

"Copy all, One. Happy hunting," came the reply in his headset.

Camperos lowered his night vision goggles over his eyes and powered on the IR emitter for low-light augmentation. The bottom half of the staircase and the pitch-black landing at the bottom came into focus in green-gray digital monotone.

"Alpha squad, shift to NVGs with IR, and follow me," he said, bringing his rifle up and sighting down the staircase. "We've still got work to do."

48

PFU TUNNEL SYSTEM

Kyle glanced sideways at Ottinger, the wounded embassy bodyguard whom he was helping down the tunnel.

"Hang in there, Eric," he said out of the corner of his mouth. "Just a little bit farther and you can rest."

"I'm trying," Ottinger said.

"I know you are, and you're doing great. Just keep those legs moving. One foot in front of the other."

Ottinger's breathing was labored and also shallow. His forehead was dappled with sweat, and he was pale as a ghost. The security officer had a lean, muscular body, and Kyle could easily picture him as a distance runner or triathlete, but right now Ottinger exhibited virtually no muscle tone. Hell, he could barely hold his head up. The terrorists had done nothing to treat or pack his gunshot wound, and God only knew how much blood the man had lost.

"You have a runner's build. Do you like to run?" Kyle asked, trying to give the dying man something to focus on.

"Yeah . . ." Ottinger said, his voice not much more than a whisper. "Half-marathons . . ."

"Nice," Kyle said. "When I was at the Academy, I ran cross-country. I've never done a half-marathon, though."

"Tell me . . . about . . . a race you . . . remember."

Kyle smiled nostalgically and began recounting his grueling second-place finish at the Paul Short Run. However, he'd barely spoken for a minute when he felt Ottinger's arm go slack on his shoulder. The Angolan terrorist assisting Kyle in carrying Ottinger cursed as the security officer went limp, sagging between them like a rag doll. For a moment, Ottinger hung there, dead weight suspended in the air.

Then the Angolan fighter got angry and let go.

Instantly burdened with all of Ottinger's weight, Kyle lost his balance and went down. Harnessing some latent athleticism, he somehow managed to control the collapse and not fall on top of his fellow American while preventing Eric's head from slamming into a rock the size of a bowling ball on the tunnel floor. The midair contortions, however, tweaked his lower back something fierce. Wincing, Kyle untangled himself from Ottinger and rolled the unconscious man onto his back. The embassy security officer looked like death, and it wasn't just a product of the poor lighting in the tunnel.

Kyle had little formal medical training—just the combat medical course during his DIA indoc training—but he imagined the man was in shock.

Or he might already be dead.

Kneeling, Kyle checked Ottinger's vitals.

Weak pulse.

Shallow breathing.

He looked up at the Angolan insurgent and glared. The terrorist glared back, and they engaged in a game of "Who's going to blink first?"

"Is everything okay back there?" Ambassador Gonçalves called from several yards ahead.

"Eric is unconscious. He's lost a lot of blood, and I think his body has gone into shock," Kyle said.

"Leave him," the terrorist lieutenant barked. "We go now."

Kyle set his jaw. "Absolutely not. He's coming with us."

The Angolan drew his pistol and pointed it at Kyle's head. "I said, leave him."

Kyle recoiled.

Memories of Waddle and Cockburn—grinning and smack-talking—paraded across his mind's eye. He'd already lost two teammates in Luanda, and he'd be damned if he'd willfully sacrifice another. The idea of leaving Ottinger behind to die in this tunnel was repulsive.

The choice was binary.

There was no middle ground. No equivocating.

Still on his knees, Kyle shuffled forward and pressed his forehead into the muzzle of the Angolan's pistol. In the doing, he felt no fear, because he wasn't gambling. He'd run the calculations, knew the potential outcomes, weighed their merits, and made his choice.

"His fate will be my fate," Kyle growled, defiance incarnate.

The Angolan cocked the hammer of the Beretta pistol, his patience gone and murder in his eyes.

Pounding footsteps echoed in the tunnel ahead. "Stop!" a male voice shouted.

The furious Angolan holding the gun to Kyle's head turned to look at the newcomer.

"This one is nothing but trouble," he said, then switched to Portuguese and began to argue with the newly arrived PFU fighter, who was huffing and puffing from his run in the tunnels.

Their heated discussion didn't last long because the new guy said something that made Kyle's would-be executioner lower his pistol, then stare in disbelief at him. In that instant, Kyle knew unequivocally that his NOC had been pierced. The PFU had finally figured out who Kyle really was.

And that is an enormous problem—for me, but also for everyone else.

And for my dad . . .

"This man will help you carry your wounded," the lead terrorist said with a head nod at his compatriot. "We go now. Right now!"

Kyle recognized urgency and worry in the man's eyes.

The cavalry must have arrived, which meant the terrorists' safe house location was blown. How long would it take the American rescue squad to discover the tunnels and find the holding cells? Would they get lost in this underground labyrinth? And if they managed to stay on track, how long would it take them to close the gap? In that moment, Kyle realized he needed to slow things down and buy time, but he had do it in a manner that wasn't obvious.

The lower-ranking fighter knelt beside Ottinger and tried to get him up in an underarm carry, but Ottinger was completely incapacitated and flopped over like a limp noodle.

"That won't work," Kyle said, taking a knee and tapping the back of his neck. "Help me get him up onto my back in a fireman's carry. I will bear the load."

"Let me help you," Madison said, jogging over to his side, worry in her eyes.

He fixed her with a tight smile. "Thank you, but I can do this."

She started to reach for his hand, but stopped herself and took a nervous step back.

It took both Angolans and Kyle working together, but they got

Ottinger up and draped across Kyle's shoulders and hoisted Kyle to his feet. He was sleep deprived, dehydrated, and low on glucose, but Kyle did not falter under the load. With a primal growl, he took a step forward. Then he took another.

And another.

Summoning his inner warrior, Kyle set off down the tunnel with nearly two hundred pounds of American bodyguard on his back.

No matter the toll, no man would be left behind.

49

UNDERGROUND TUNNELS
BAIRRO CAZENGA

Camperos methodically descended the cinder-block "staircase," taking care with each step. The structure felt unsteady beneath his booted feet, with individual cinder blocks wobbling and the entire staircase swaying side to side.

Because the idiots who made this thing didn't bother to use mortar, he thought with gritted teeth as he scanned the tunnel ahead for threats.

Even with night vision goggles and IR augmentation, the tunnel was so dark he could only see roughly thirty feet ahead, which meant he could be walking headfirst into a trap. But if enemy shooters were hiding in the dark, they'd need night vision to see him, and Camperos calculated those odds to be in the single digits. The PFU fighters in the safe house they'd just eliminated had been poorly equipped, with no body armor, no helmets, and aged AK-47 rifles. His Marine training demanded that he prepare for the unexpected, but experience told him there was no elite hit squad hiding in the dark just out of range of his top-of-the-line NVGs.

As he reached the halfway point, he felt the staircase wobble, but not from his movement.

"Shit, this thing moves," Moose Elkins grumbled behind Camperos.

"Only two at a time," Camperos whispered into his boom mic, making a judgment call that would slow them down a bit, but also ensure everyone made it down without collapsing the damn thing.

On reaching the bottom, he quick-stepped five paces forward and took a kneeling firing stance along the left wall, scanning and covering the tunnel ahead. His rifle was equipped with an IR target designator—an infrared beam slaved to his gunsight only visible with NVGs—but he had the targeting aid turned off just in case. If the enemy *did* have night vision goggles, his targeting laser would ruin Alpha squad's stealth and serve as a nice handy visual aid for the bad guys to aim at.

Here I am, shoot me first.

He felt Elkins fall in beside him and take a knee.

Behind him, Camperos could barely hear his fellow Raiders as they methodically descended the cinder-block stairs with near-perfect efficiency and quiet. A double tap on his right shoulder from Elkins signaled that all members of Alpha squad had completed the descent and were ready to move out. Camperos shifted from his kneel into a low tactical crouch. He chopped a hand forward and led his eight-man search and rescue party into the black.

The cramped tunnel—which would have been deemed unsafe and condemned under U.S. building standards—could not have been more than five feet wide and six feet tall. The compact dimensions restricted their formation and movement to a single option—traveling in a column of four pairs. The tunnel's narrow geometry effectively neutered his main tactical advantage, which was his ability to divide Alpha into multiple, autonomous fire teams that could engage the enemy from different angles and positions. Hemmed in like this, the only viable shooters were the pair of Marines in the lead, in this case, Elkins and himself.

But Alpha's ability to execute on offense wasn't the only issue. Defense was also a problem.

In this damn tunnel, their ability to find cover, evade, and employ shoot-and-move tactics was nil. Equally bad, the entire squadron was a captive target. Any idiot with a machine gun could spray bullets down a tunnel and score multiple hits.

Adapt and overcome, his inner drill sergeant barked. *Yes, the tactical picture sucks, but you have a job to do, Marine.*

Camperos quickly recalibrated as his thoughts went to his mission objective—hostage rescue. Four Americans—including the U.S. ambassador and President Ryan's son—were counting on him and his team to get them out. The geopolitical situation in Luanda was deteriorating, and his countrymen and women had been taken as political pawns.

And pawns, he reminded himself, *are the pieces on the chessboard that get sacrificed in the name of strategy.*

Feeling a renewed sense of urgency, he quickened his stride. Beside him, Elkins, who was keeping pace, sped up to match. The column moved without talking, but the collective noise generated by eight fully-kitted-up Marines—the rubbing of fabric, jostling of gear, booted soles pounding the earth—reverberated in the tunnel. Moving at this clip, they wouldn't surprise anyone waiting in ambush.

But Camperos didn't have a choice.

He and his Raiders were playing catch-up.

With no map or intelligence on this tunnel system, he was navigating in the dark—both figuratively and literally. He imagined the satellite imagery of the barrio he'd studied on his tablet and went to work updating his mental map.

Alpha squadron had entered the tunnels at the Yankee checkpoint, and the tunnel entrance had been oriented on an east-west axis. It was also noteworthy that the safe house at Yankee had been an "end of the line" access point. After descending, there'd been only one direction to go—east. He added a little green dot moving east to represent Alpha on his mental map, then let his mental cursor slide several blocks north to checkpoint X-ray, where his counterpart, Captain Dane, had breached the other target house with Charlie team. He knew from Dane's last communication that Dane had also found tunnel access and proceeded underground. Unfortunately, he had no idea which direction Dane's tunnel—or tunnels—branched out from there.

Would this tunnel intersect the tunnel Charlie was searching? Or would both squads wander aimlessly in different sections of this underground warren without ever crossing paths? He assumed that the earthen interference would block anything other than line-of-sight radio comms while underground, but he decided that he should confirm as much.

He whispered into his mic.

"Bullpen, One—sitrep?" he said in a hushed tone, trying the TOC first.

No reply came.

He tried Dane next. "Two, One—radio check?"

Again, no reply.

He glanced at Elkins and said, "Did you hear me going out?"

Moose gave him a thumbs-up.

"As expected, Alpha has line-of-sight comms only," he said, addressing his team, and got multiple clicks back in acknowledgment.

After advancing about thirty yards, Camperos thought he heard something, halted the column, and took a knee. Sighting over his rifle, he looked for movement at the limit of his visual field, where the IR illumination faded, and details blurred into shadow. Just when he was about to get them up and moving, he heard the noise again—a faint chugging sound.

He turned to Elkins and signaled that the two of them were going to range ahead and investigate, while the rest of the team held in place. Elkins acknowledged him, and they advanced slowly and quietly, shoulder to shoulder, down the narrow tunnel. After ten paces, Camperos saw that the tunnel they were in appeared to bisect another tunnel at a perpendicular angle. He kept creeping forward with Moose, and as the resolution continued to improve, Camperos confirmed that a T-shaped intersection did indeed lie ahead. The chugging sound, which was coming from the left side of the new tunnel, now reminded him of a miniature stampede.

Boots on the ground . . . inbound.

He turned to Elkins, tapped his Peltor ear cup, and pointed forward and left.

Elkins nodded that he heard it, too.

The next question was whether the inbound group was friend or foe.

Camperos advanced them to within five feet of the intersection, then stopped and took a knee. Sighting over his rifle, he waited for the unknown party to cross the intersection. In their current position, he and Elkins had the advantage of surprise. The sound of footfalls got steadily louder, and an impending engagement seemed inevitable . . . But then the tunnel fell abruptly silent.

Camperos's pulse rate leapt, and his index finger began to absenlty tap out an inaudible rhythm on the trigger guard. His inner Raider worked the problem:

The inbound contingent is employing sound and light discipline—no talking and no flashlights. Also, halted as a unit.

If he were a gambling man, he'd bet all his chips that the other party was Charlie team. But he wasn't a gambler, so he decided to try something that would definitely prove what his gut was telling him before risking friendly fire.

With his left hand, he cycled on and off his laser target designator only long enough to flash the beam at the intersecting tunnel wall. Then he cycled it again, but this time left it on for approximately three times longer. For those in the know, Camperos had just used Morse code to signal "Alpha," which was one dot followed by one dash. The laser communication he'd just made could only be seen by someone wearing NVGs.

For a beat, nothing happened.

Then a green laser streaked down the perpendicular tunnel, originating on the left. The beam held steady for half a second, then secured. Next came a flash, followed by another half-second hold, followed by a flash.

Dash, dot, dash, dot.

Camperos translated the Morse code response in his head: *Charlie.*

He then turned to Elkins, who—judging from the smile on his face—had reached the same conclusion.

Feeling confident about the ID and that his fellow Marines were in radio range, Camperos keyed his mic. "Raider One at tunnel intersection, signaling for Alpha."

"Roger, One," a familiar American voice replied in Camperos's ear. "Raider Nine at the same tunnel intersection, signaling for Charlie."

On that confirmation, Camperos signaled for the rest of Alpha squadron to join as he and Elkins advanced to the intersection, where they met up with Master Sergeant Moore and three Raiders from Charlie squadron, bringing their numbers up to twelve shooters.

"Sitrep," Camperos said in a quiet voice as he hung his rifle and bumped fists with Moore.

"Been wandering around in this rat maze for fifteen minutes, but we haven't found jack shit," Moore replied in a hushed tone.

"Where's Dane?"

"At our access point, the tunnel had two branches. We split up. He took his stick north, and we went south."

Camperos squinted his eyes in thought while adding this connecting tunnel to his mental map. "Is this your first intersection, or have you explored other tunnels?"

"We've made several doglegs, but this is our first intersection," Moore said. "What about you guys?"

"Straight shot from our access point at Yankee to here," he said. "We've burned a lot of time and have nothing to show for it. Has me worried we've been outfoxed."

"Me too."

"Maybe Dane's having better luck than we are."

Moore shook his head. "Be careful what you wish for. Captain Hollywood has his bloody fang mouthguard in."

"God help us all," Camperos said through a chuckle, then swiveled to look down the unexplored tunnel for a beat before turning back to Moore. "I say you join us and we head down this unexplored section. We'll have to run into somebody or something eventually."

"Agreed," the master sergeant said, then cocked an eyebrow and pointed his rifle muzzle down the tunnel in a combination gesture that made his desire to lead the vanguard perfectly clear.

Camperos turned sideways to clear a path for the salty, battle-tested NOC. "By all means, Master Sergeant—age before beauty."

50

PFU TUNNEL SYSTEM

Carrying the still-unconscious Ottinger on his back, Kyle halted with the group at the bottom of a wooden ladder.

"Wonderful," he muttered, sweat streaming down his face. Now that he was stationary, his legs began to tremble under the load, and he knew he wouldn't be able to last much longer.

The lead terrorist climbed up the ladder and knocked on the bottom of a wooden panel blocking the exit. After a beat, the panel lifted, and the man was greeted by the face of an Angolan PFU fighter looking down. They talked in rapid-fire Portuguese, and Kyle suspected the topic of conversation involved how to get Ottinger up the ladder. His suspicion was confirmed when the leader called down to the two armed fighters who had been escorting their party through the tunnels and barked orders at the men.

The underlings slung their rifles and turned to face Kyle expectantly.

"They will help lift your man out. You cannot do it alone," the lead terrorist said, looking down from the cutout in the ceiling at Kyle. For a fleeting instant, Kyle thought he saw something resembling respect in the man's eyes.

"Let them help you," Ambassador Gonçalves said to Kyle with weary but resolute eyes.

Grudgingly, he took a knee, and the two fighters lifted Ottinger off his back. The physical relief he felt was indescribable, but he forced himself not to show that relief on his face. The two Angolans then proceeded to roughly manhandle Ottinger's limp body up the ladder.

"Please be careful with him," the ambassador said, and Kyle saw real concern on her face for the wounded bodyguard.

The terrorist leader at the top of the ladder grabbed Ottinger under the armpits and heaved as the two fighters pushed from below. In this moment of occupied distraction, Kyle's attention shifted to the pistol shoved in the waistband at the small of the back of the closest terrorist who was lifting Ottinger from below. This was an opportunity that would not present itself again. He could snatch it, shoot both the terrorists below, and possibly even kill the leader above. Working at machine speed, his brain analyzed the likely permutations, factoring in the unknowns. Even if he was successful in killing all three—which was unlikely given his limited marksmanship skills and zero combat experience— Kyle had no idea how many armed fighters were loitering in the room above. At least one, but probably more. The only tenable option was fleeing back into the tunnels, which meant leaving Ottinger behind. But it was possible Ottinger's heart had already stopped . . . Kyle had not checked his vitals recently.

He felt a gentle hand on his arm and turned to find Madison. She met his gaze with knowing eyes and shook her head once— the message crystal clear:

Please don't.

He exhaled with frustration, but answered with a subtle head bob.

No sooner had the opportunity for rebellion presented itself, the moment was over. With the hostage's hoist-and-transfer evolution complete, the two guards stepped down from the ladder and took up arms again.

"Hurry, climb. Ambassador, you go first," the terrorist leader called from above as Ottinger was dragged clear by unseen helpers from above.

Gonçalves ascended first, followed by Madison, then Kyle. When he was halfway up the wooden ladder, a concussive *whump* reverberated from down the tunnel in which they'd come. Kyle, along with the fighter escorts below, reflexively turned to look in the direction of the noise. Despite having never breached a door, Kyle knew instantly the detonation he'd just heard was a breacher charge.

Finally, the cavalry had arrived, and they were in the tunnels.

The PFU leader, looking down from above, must have reached the same conclusion, because he barked an order to the two machine gun–wielding guards below. The two men seemed uncertain, looking at each other instead of taking action. The leader pulled his pistol and pointed it down the ladder, aiming past Kyle at the underlings. Kyle, for his part, stopped climbing and held position on the ladder. Every second he could delay the evacuation was a second more he gave the special ops team to catch up.

"Go!" the terrorist leader shouted in English, and the junior fighters set off in a run in the direction of the holding cells. Then the leader grabbed Madison by the wrist and yanked violently downward, bending her at the waist so her face came into view. He shoved the muzzle of his pistol under her chin and glared at Kyle. "Exit now or she dies."

From the look in the terrorist's eyes, Kyle believed the man meant it. The PFU lieutenant's nerves were fraying under the pressure, and if he snapped, he would likely do something rash and unrecoverable.

"Don't shoot, I'm coming," Kyle said in a calm voice and resumed his ascent.

As he climbed out of the trapdoor, machine-gun fire reverberated below, confirming his hypothesis. The rescue team was engaging the guards and was only minutes behind. The terrorist shoved Kyle out of the way and quickly replaced the wooden cover. Then he barked orders at two armed fighters standing in the living room. The men got to work dragging a heavy-looking, cast-iron woodburning stove from the corner toward the trapdoor.

"Go! Get into the van outside," the terrorist shouted at all of them, but he was pointing his pistol at Madison.

Kyle scanned the dirty floor of the single-room shanty for Ottinger, but the security guard was nowhere to be seen.

"He is already in the van," the Angolan barked. "Now go. Run!"

Kyle jogged after the ambassador and Madison, who were scrambling out the front door of the tiny house. Outside, a black commercial van was idling with the rear cargo doors hanging wide open. Two fighters with AK-47s stood on either side of the doors, waving the trio of hostages to load themselves into the cargo compartment, where Ottinger was lying sprawled out on his back.

Kyle waited for the women to get situated before entering, but a hard shove from behind knocked him into the van, where he fell on top of Ottinger. A club strike whacked his ass and he jerked his legs in. The cargo doors slammed shut behind him. The leader climbed into the passenger seat, the engine roared, and the van spun tires as it accelerated away.

Wincing from the blow to his right ass cheek, Kyle climbed off Ottinger and onto his knees.

"Do you think he's . . . dead?" Madison asked, eyes fixed on Ottinger's slack-jawed, ghastly pale face.

Kyle reached out and placed two fingers on the bodyguard's neck. Anxiety spiked in his chest, as he couldn't feel anything. He shifted his touch to the other side of Ottinger's neck, pressing and probing deeper for a pulse. Just when he was about to speak the terrible truth, he felt one . . . feeble and irregular, but a pulse nonetheless.

"He's alive, but barely," Kyle said, meeting Madison's worried face. Feeling the terrorist lieutenant's eyes on him, Kyle turned to the man in the front passenger seat. "This man requires a hospital."

"No hospital," the terrorist said.

Kyle bristled. "If he doesn't receive medical treatment immediately, he will die."

"What does he require to live?"

"Trauma care and probably a blood transfusion."

The terrorist shook his head.

Kyle tapped the memory of a DIA training course covering field medicine he'd taken at the Farm. "At minimum, he needs to have his wound packed to stop the bleeding and a bag of saline to raise his blood pressure."

"Can you do this?" the Angolan fighter asked.

"I . . . I'm not a doctor."

"That is not what I asked you. Can you do this?"

Kyle hesitated, but felt Madison take his hand and squeeze. Normally, he considered unsolicited touches of any kind off-putting and uncomfortable. But this act of solidarity had both a calming and empowering effect on him. "If you get me a medical kit, I can do it."

"Good. We will be at the palace in less than ten minutes. They will have such a kit there," the man said and turned his attention back to the road.

"By palace, I assume he means the Presidential Palace?" Madison whispered, looking back and forth between Kyle and the ambassador.

The ambassador nodded, but from the expression on her face, Kyle couldn't tell if she considered this a positive or negative development for their safety and longevity in the world.

Kyle's brain automatically tried to run the math, but there were too many unknown variables to know for certain. He looked down at Madison's delicate hand still holding his own and expected her to release her grip the second he did. To his surprise, she didn't pull away, and neither did he. Was it possible that in the greatest moment of crisis and uncertainty he'd faced in his entire life on this planet, that in that chaos he'd found a kindred spirit?

Or was this moment nothing more than some preprogrammed, vestigial primate reaction to fear and trauma?

Time would tell.

But until then, he decided for once in his life he would stop analyzing and just take comfort in the moment and her touch.

51

OFFICE OF THE PRESIDENT
PALÁCIO PRESIDENCIAL DA CIDADE ALTA (PRESIDENTIAL PALACE)
RUA PEDRO FURTADO
LUANDA, ANGOLA

Just when Baptista thought the day couldn't get any worse, something truly terrible happened.

"Mr. President," Jorge said, barging into Baptista's office wide-eyed and breathless. "They're here . . ."

"Who's here?" Baptista asked, confused.

"The hostages," his nephew said, then lowered his voice to a near whisper. "The American Marines showed up in Bairro Cazenga and started raiding safe houses. They found the tunnels, so Bruno brought the hostages here."

"What!" Baptista launched out of his chair, a tornado of rage and fury.

Jorge cowered and backpedaled out of his path.

"Idiot. Where is he now?" Baptista shouted as he stormed past Jorge toward the office doors.

"He's . . . he's in the grand foyer," Jorge stammered.

One of the things Baptista had always prided himself on was

his ability to manage his temper and not lose control even in the worst situations. When he punished his subordinates or exacted retribution on his enemies, he always did so with a cool and level head. Even his executions were both rational and calculated. But right now, that part of his intellect was—like Jorge—cowering in the corner. When he confronted Bruno, there was no telling what Baptista would do because, right now, wrath was in control.

He marched down the long hallway and shoved open the double doors leading to the grand foyer. Like a scene out of his worst nightmare, Bruno Kalemba stood with pistol in hand, lording over the American hostages. Three of the hostages were huddled together, while one lay dead in the middle of the ornate presidential carpet. At first, Baptista nearly had a heart attack thinking the dead hostage was President Ryan's son, but the man's face didn't match the picture in the file. Baptista's attention flicked to the lean American male standing with the two women, and he saw that Kyle Ryan was, thank God, still alive. Next, he identified Ambassador Gonçalves and studied her for visible signs of physical abuse. Finding none, he locked eyes with the fourth and final hostage, the young female State Department staffer. She was of no import, but he noted that she had a swollen and bloodied lower lip, which further stoked his rage.

Baptista turned to Bruno. "Why the fuck did you bring them here?" he shouted in Portuguese.

"You told me to keep them secure at all costs. What choice did I have? The American Marines found our safe houses and the tunnels. I barely managed to exfiltrate the hostages in time. There was nowhere else to go," Bruno said, defending his actions.

"Nowhere else to go?" Baptista said, incredulous. "You could have gone *anywhere* in the city—anywhere but here! This was the only place in the entire country that was off-limits. Until this moment, I had plausible deniability, but now you have single-handedly ruined everything, you fucking moron!"

"I'm . . . I'm sorry," Bruno said, his face a portrait of fear as the realization of the grave mistake he'd made finally registered.

Out of the corner of his eye, Baptista noticed the ambassador staring at them intently. Gonçalves was fluent in Portuguese, and she'd listened to the entire exchange. Now he'd been the one who'd screwed up. He took a deep breath and let it out raggedly, trying to wrestle control of his emotions. To get out of this mess, he needed to think.

Switching to his native Kimbundu, he turned back to Bruno and pointed to the dead American hostage on the floor. "Did you execute this man?"

Bruno, who at least had the wherewithal to answer in kind, said, "No, sir. He's not dead. This man was shot in the back during the embassy raid. He needs a doctor."

"Then why is he lying on the floor in the middle of my foyer? Get him a doctor."

"Yes, sir, I didn't know if you wanted—"

"If I wanted him to die?" Baptista shouted, cutting him off. "Of course not, you idiot. These hostages were meant to be returned unharmed to the Americans as an olive branch . . . but you've ruined that plan. Now they know I'm involved. They have seen me talking with you. My plausible deniability has been destroyed."

"There is another option, sir. If they are dead, they cannot talk."

Baptista thrust a finger at Kyle Ryan. "Yes, by all means. Why don't you start with President Ryan's son."

Bruno's mouth dropped open, and he looked at Ryan. "That man is President Ryan's son?"

"Yes, you unwittingly kidnapped President Ryan's son from the embassy," Baptista said, suddenly overcome with sardonic laughter at the absurdity of it all. He tried to stop, but couldn't—a part of him aware of how maniacal and unhinged he sounded, and another part of him embracing the vibe.

And when he'd finished laughing, he felt better.

"Give me your gun," he said, extending his right hand to his most faithful and trusted lieutenant of twelve years.

Bruno hesitated a beat, then handed the Beretta to Baptista.

Baptista took the weapon, pulled the slide back to verify there was a round in the chamber, then shot Kalemba in the forehead.

Ambassador Gonçalves shrieked in horror as Bruno's body dropped like a felled tree.

The deed done, Baptista shoved the smoking pistol into the waistband of his pants, and turned to address the Americans in English.

His eyes fixed on Gonçalves as he said, "I'm sorry you had to see that, Madame Ambassador, but it was just brought to my attention that you and three other Americans were kidnapped from the American embassy and held hostage by a terrorist organization known as the Patriotic Front for Unity. I've just killed the leader of this radical group, and now all of you are rescued. Until my military can put down the remainder of the PFU threat, you will remain here in the Presidential Palace as my guests. My men will keep you protected and secure until I can arrange safe passage back to your embassy."

He turned to the pair of presidential guards who were posted inside the entry doors, and in English said, "Escort our American guests to the Presidential Security Suite in the basement and attend to their every need. Provide them with food, water, and medical attention."

The guards, he knew, were not fluent in English. The statement had been theater, of course. He repeated his instructions in

Kimbundu, albeit with certain key modifications. He also ordered that they summon six more guards to assist in securing the prisoners. The lead guard acknowledged the orders, saluted Baptista, then made the necessary radio calls.

"President Baptista, you have my gratitude for rescuing us and offering us refuge here in the palace," Ambassador Gonçalves said, trying very hard to sound dignified and genuine, while not looking at the executed body of Bruno Kalemba sprawled on the floor and oozing blood and brains four feet in front of her, "but if I may offer an alternative—with a phone call, I could arrange for the U.S. Marines to provide both security and transport logistics for our return to the embassy—"

"Oh, it is much too dangerous and unstable in the city at the moment for that," he said, cutting her off, while signaling to his guards. "I insist you remain here, in the safety of the bomb shelter in the basement of the palace, until the PFU threat is neutralized. I assure you, your safe return home is my highest priority. I will keep you informed of our progress securing the city. In the meantime, my security staff will escort you to the shelter and tend to your every need."

On cue, a half dozen uniformed security guards arrived in the foyer. Four of the men formed a diamond around the Americans, while two of them worked together to pick up the near-dead man off the floor. As Baptista's "guests" were escorted away, Kyle Ryan turned and locked eyes with him. The young man's hard, defiant glare both amused and unnerved Baptista.

Baptista held the First Son's eyes and nodded.

Ryan did not return the gesture.

Jorge, who had been keeping his distance, now walked up to stand at Baptista's right side.

"Uncle, what can I do to help?" the young man asked, and in

this moment, Baptista was touched by his nephew eschewing the *Mr. President* honorific for the familiar.

Baptista turned to him and said, "Have Bruno's body removed, the carpet cleaned, and order General de Souza to my office."

"Yes, sir. Is that all?"

"No . . . Summon a doctor and do whatever it takes to keep that wounded American alive."

Jorge looked confused. "Do you really intend to let the Americans go?"

Baptista didn't answer for a long moment, then, speaking the truth, said, "I haven't decided . . . We'll have to see what the rest of the night brings."

52

EMERGENCY OPERATIONS CENTER (EOC)
R. HOUARI BOUMEDIENE 32
LUANDA, ANGOLA
2344 LOCAL TIME

Katie paced back and forth behind the row of terminals, watching nothing happen on the satellite feed on the large-screen display until she couldn't take it anymore.

"Guys, I don't have a good feeling about this," she said, hands on hips.

"I totally get it," Conza said, stepping up beside her. "It's a terrible feeling being trapped in here, powerless to help, while the guys are out there in harm's way, but trust me, they've got it. This is what they train for. This is what they do."

"No, it's not that," she said, her frustration rising. "I'm saying we should have seen or at least heard something by now. It's been too long. Something must be wrong."

Conza smiled. "Ah, yeah, I hate that feeling. Happens to me all the time, but that's normal. My theory is that when you're in the TOC, your internal mission clock runs fast. Things always take a little bit longer to unfold than expected."

She knew his attempt to calm her nerves was well-meaning, but she wasn't looking to be placated. "My internal mission clock feels pretty calibrated. Try them on the radio, please."

Conza eyed her for a second, then keyed his mic. "Raider One, this is Bullpen—sitrep?" When no reply came, he tried Dane. "Raider Two, Bullpen—sitrep?" After an ample pause, he turned to her. "They're underground, ma'am. As aggravating as it is, we're stuck in a waiting game."

She stared at the screen, which showed a real-time streaming bird's-eye view of Bairro Cazenga. She focused on the on-screen designators marking target safe houses Yankee and X-ray, where Alpha and Charlie teams had breached and accessed the PFU's underground tunnel network. She had no idea which direction the tunnels ran from these checkpoints, nor how far the tunnels stretched. Did they go in straight lines, or did they bend and dogleg this way and that? Was there a tunnel connecting X-ray and Yankee? How many tunnels were there? How many other access and exit points existed besides the ones they had intel on?

She walked over to stand next to Bubba, who was sitting at one of the terminals.

"I want to zoom out," she said. "The satellite feed, I want to double the viewing radius."

"Okay, no problem," he said, working the trackball and keyboard. The picture feed zoomed out—the houses and buildings on-screen shrinking as the view expanded to include more area.

She stepped back and studied the screen, her eyes interrogating the new areas that had been outside the frame before. Methodically, she studied all the new heat signatures, watching their activity for anything that might catch her eye. Then she looked for vehicle traffic, as there hadn't been a single vehicle entering or exiting the area they'd been observing before.

"What are you thinking?" Conza said, stepping up beside her.

"I'm wondering if these tunnels snake out farther than we estimated. What if we missed something because we misjudged the size of the playing field?"

"It's certainly possible, but until Raider One or Two check in, I think it's safe to assume the action is still underground."

"Bubba, zoom out again, double the radius," she said.

"That's a four-mile radius," Conza said. "All due respect, there's no way the tunnels—"

"Zoom in on that vehicle," she said, cutting him off and pointing emphatically at the giant wall-mounted display. "The one at the top of the screen, hauling ass and heading east."

Bubba worked the controls and zoomed in on a lone vehicle, a medium-sized cargo van, heading east. "Looks like a delivery van."

"What's a delivery van doing making deliveries at this hour?" she said, her sluggish brain suddenly energized by an adrenaline dump.

Bubba shrugged. "I don't know."

"I want to track that van, but I also want to rewind. I want to see where that van came from. Did it originate near the op area? Can you do that, Bubba?"

"Yeah, I can do that," he said, working the controls again. "I'm going to leave the live feed on the main display and pull up archived data on my terminal. Does that work?"

She nodded, hoping her hunch was wrong, but suspecting she wasn't.

"How far back in time do you want to go?" he asked.

"I don't know—five, ten minutes," she said. "Just rewind so we can follow where that van came from."

He did as she asked, and they watched the delivery van travel in reverse and stop in front of a house in the neighborhood, but outside the target area they'd been watching closely. From there, he skipped back thirty seconds and hit play. They watched a group of heat signatures hurriedly exit the house, half of whom were loaded into the van.

"That has to be them," she said, her voice tight in her throat as she watched. "I think that's Ottinger—the one they're carrying. He's not putting off a lot of heat. Is he dead?"

"I don't think so, but from what I'm seeing, he's definitely unconscious," Conza said. "The others look intact, so that's good."

"Yeah, except our Marines are still underground, and the rescue failed. Our people are being relocated," she said, trying to keep her cool and failing. She looked back at the main screen to make sure they were still tracking the van. "Don't lose them, Bubba. We need to know where they're being taken."

"We won't lose them," Bubba said. "I promise."

"The van's still heading east," Conza said.

"Where do you think it's going?" Katie asked.

"That road they're on is Hoji ya Henda Avenue," Tejada said, joining the conversation. "It runs all the way to the government district. Pretty much a straight shot to Cidade Alta."

Katie swallowed. "Cidade Alta, that's where the Presidential Palace is located, correct?"

Tejada nodded in agreement.

"If that is their destination, how long until they get there?" she asked, watching the van move steadily east.

"They have only maybe five kilometers left," he said. "At this hour, with no traffic, they will be at the palace in ten minutes, maybe twelve."

She turned to Major Merriweather. "Major, do you have assets we can use to intercept that van?"

A pained expression spread over the Marine Raider commander's face. "Raider element has our JLTVs in Bairro Cazenga. Even if they exited the tunnels right now, they'd never catch that van. The rest of the MEU assets are set up here, around the embassy. This four-block area is our FOB . . . There's a chance we could mobilize an infantry team to intercept, but it's a snowball's chance in hell. It will take at least five minutes to put Marines in vehicles and get rolling. At that point, it becomes a simple geometry problem, and the geometry is not in our favor."

"Damn it!" She slammed the base of her balled fist down on the side of Bubba's terminal desk. She was furious that they'd come so close to saving her brother and the others, only to be foiled at the eleventh hour and fifty-ninth minute. She took a deep breath and collected her thoughts before turning back to the Marine major. "If I'm right—and my gut tells me that I am—that van is taking our people to the Presidential Palace. In my book, the second that American hostages are off-loaded from that van and marched into the seat of Angolan executive power as hostages, Baptista trades the title of president for terrorist. Maybe this is the opportunity we've been waiting for. Major, we need to talk to Colonel Crocker. I think it's time to take control of this situation once and for all."

"What exactly do you have in mind, Commander?" Crocker asked, once called up on the screen, but the glint in his eye told her that he was already on board with the plan, and now it was just a matter of getting permission.

"We surround the Presidential Palace and demand the release of our people. Call it intuition, but I suspect that if you guys park the MEU and a bunch of JLTVs on Baptista's front yard, he's going to think twice about not cooperating."

Crocker smiled, something she imagined he did only rarely.

"I'll need authorization for this," he said. Before she could interject, he added, "And I will get it. Well done, Commander."

The MEU commander disappeared from the screen, no doubt to contact the Pentagon or the White House—likely both.

"This is far from over, Commander," Merriweather said from beside her.

"I know, Major," she replied. "But we're getting closer."

She felt her mind clear and her resolve sharpen.

Kyle was alive and so were the rest of the Americans being held. It was time to put emotion aside—to channel her inner Kyle and let logic and math decide her next step. Because no one was being left behind today.

53

**SITUATION ROOM
THE WHITE HOUSE
WASHINGTON, D.C.
1752 LOCAL TIME**

Ryan watched as the best team of advisors in the world did what they did best—argued pros and cons, looked at all the variables, posed new what-ifs, and challenged each other to defend their positions. It had long been his policy to allow what, to an outsider, might look like chaotic arguing play out until it no longer seemed productive. They were nearly there, but not quite.

"Jay, you must have some gut feeling here about Baptista," Kudryk said, sounding frustrated.

"I do," the CIA director said. "I think he's an asshole. And I think he is a liar and an unreliable partner. I think he either was or still is a PFU thug, and that he is thirsty for personal power and wealth. But making a recommendation about whether to put troops into battle based on my intense dislike for the guy . . ."

"Is better than nothing," Kudryk said.

"It is the *same* as nothing," Canfield retorted. "It doesn't tell us whether he was behind the attack on the embassy or the coup.

What if he really was invited into an interim position of power by the military and the government?"

"Then we would be attacking the legitimate government of a sovereign nation," Adler, Ryan's secretary of state, said, finishing the thought for Canfield. "Without knowing if they were even involved in the violence against our embassy and kidnapping of our people."

"And we get back our people, either way," Robert Burgess countered. "They are being held hostage."

"At the Presidential Palace," Kudryk said. "If that doesn't tell us which side Baptista is on, then I don't know what does."

"What if they were delivered to the palace after being rescued by Angolan military from the PFU?" Adler asked, playing devil's advocate.

"Do you believe that?" Kudryk shot back. "Because I don't."

"If that was the case, then Baptista would have explicitly said as much so he could take credit for the rescue and build an important bridge to legitimize himself," Burgess said. "But he didn't. Which tells me that he *is* involved and is stalling for time to decide his next move."

Arnie van Damm looked at Ryan and then turned to Burgess.

"I think you know how the President feels about us assuming," he said.

Burgess sighed, resigned, but made one last play. "The only person who knows the truth about what happened is Baptista. And I think we all agree he's a liar."

"He's not the *only* one," Ryan said, speaking for the first time in a few minutes, which silenced the room and turned all eyes back to him. He stood, placing his hands on the back of his chair. "Who's the head of the Angolan military . . . What's his name?" Ryan asked, snapping his fingers.

"General de Souza," one of Burgess's staffers answered quickly. "That's right . . . de Souza."

"Yes, but de Souza already picked a side. Baptista could not have deposed Luemba without the military," Adler said.

Ryan nodded, his mind suddenly made up. "Then we need to talk to Luemba," he said and turned to Mary Pat. "Do we have any leads at all as to where Luemba is being held—or if he is even still alive?"

"Nothing definitive, Mr. President," she said. "But I can check with the ground team and see if they have anything."

"Do that," he said, then turned to Larry Kent. "Admiral, direct the MEU commander to deploy his forces to the palace, but he is not to launch an assault without direction. However, should they be attacked they have authority to direct any and all military response necessary to protect the Marines. And, should an opportunity arise to intervene and rescue our people, we will trust their judgment to execute an operation to do just that. Make sure he knows that we have his back on this."

"Yes, sir, Mr. President," Kent said, clearly liking that answer.

"And we will all be right here, in this room, to make critical decisions as the events unfold," Ryan added. "But we will not second-guess the commanders on the ground."

There was a murmur of agreement.

"Mary Pat," he said, turning to his closest friend and advisor. "A word?"

She followed him into one of the smaller breakout rooms. Ryan closed the door.

"What are the chances we can find out where Luemba is, Mary Pat?"

The director of national intelligence folded her arms and thought for a moment.

"Probably pretty good," she said. "There are several teams, including the NSA, piecing together satellite footage, signals intelligence, and other sources of raw data to reconstruct a timeline. We have a ton of data to sift through, but knowing what you need will direct the search."

"What I need is to know if Luemba is alive and where he is being held, if so," Ryan said. "And then I'll need to talk to the head of the intelligence task force operating out of the embassy in Luanda," he added.

Mary Pat gave him a soft look.

"As a father or . . ."

"As the commander in chief," he said. Then he leaned in and gave her a soft look of his own. "I think I may have an idea."

54

UNKNOWN BASEMENT
BAIRRO CAZENGA
LUANDA, ANGOLA
2359 LOCAL TIME

Camperos placed his holographic targeting dot center mass on the insurgent and pulled the trigger. The three-round burst made solid contact and dropped the shooter as the man attempted to reposition from the stairwell entrance to behind a stack of rough-cut timbers, where other enemy shooters were covering and engaging from. Camperos recognized the lumber as the same kind of wood used for beams and bracing in the tunnel system. The entire basement appeared to be a material staging area for tunnel construction.

Unlike the shanty houses that Alpha and Charlie squads had breached to access the tunnels over an hour ago, Master Sergeant Moore had navigated them to a subterranean egress point in the basement of what appeared to be a commercial building or an apartment. Unfortunately, the access point was under guard.

"When you said that we'd run into somebody or something

eventually," Moore said from where he crouched beside Camperos, "was this what you had in mind?"

"No. I was hoping we'd find the hostages," he said, pulling back behind a stockpile of cinder blocks, "but I guess that's what I get for—"

A barrage of enemy rounds slammed into the cinder blocks on the other side, interrupting him midsentence.

Moore popped out and squeezed off a quick volley of return fire before ducking back into cover. "What were you saying?"

"*I said* . . . that's what I get for letting you lead," Camperos answered with a sideways grin.

Moore shook his head as more enemy bullets slammed into their opportunistic cinder-block bunker, sending plumes of dust and chunks of concrete in all directions. Camperos and Moore had been the first pair to enter and clear the basement, but they'd been immediately pushed into cover by a PFU security force. The rest of the team was stuck back in the tunnel, unable to bring their numbers or firepower to bear effectively.

"As much fun as this is, I'm thinking it's time to turn the tables on these guys," Moore said, pulling a flash-bang grenade from his kit.

"Agreed," Camperos said and pulled an M67 fragmentation grenade. "How about a one-two punch, then we mop up."

"Oorah," the salty NCO said.

"Just keep it out here," Camperos warned. "The hostages could be on the other side of that door."

Moore nodded, pulled the pin, and lobbed.

Camperos squeezed his eyes shut, and a heartbeat later, the grenade detonated with a flash and a concussive *whump*. The Marine captain opened his eyes, pulled the pin on his M67, and stepped out from beside the pile of cinder blocks to aim while the enemy was still disoriented and reeling from the flash-bang.

Warning his fellow Marines, he announced, "Grenade" into his boom mic.

He lobbed the M67 behind the stack of lumber where the enemy shooters were hiding. Then he dove for cover behind the cinder blocks with Moore. A moment later, a thunderclap shook the basement with a concussive shock wave that dwarfed the flash-bang. The noise-canceling tech in their Peltors protected their hearing from the deafening roar, while the cinder-block barrier shielded them from the shrapnel burst.

Camperos and Moore popped to their feet in unison and looped around their cinder-block stack and assaulted what was left of the PFU security force behind the lumber pile. All three of the enemy shooters had been badly wounded by shrapnel and only one was able to lift his weapon. Camperos ended him with a headshot, while Moore put the other two fighters out of their misery.

With the immediate threat neutralized, they swiveled simultaneously and scanned the doorway leading to the staircase out of the basement. Seeing no immediate threats, Moore surged to the opening, stopped, and took a knee, sighting up the stairwell. Camperos took an offset position behind and signaled for the rest of the Raider element loitering in the tunnel to fall in for exfil. The remaining ten Marines poured out of the tunnel and quick-stepped across the basement. The first two Raiders surged past Moore and Camperos, taking the lead and ascending to the first switchback landing. The next pair of Raiders followed with expert efficiency and would assume the lead for the next flight up while the previous pair covered. The methodical ascent out of the basement happened without further incident. By the time Camperos and Moore reached ground level, the Alpha and Charlie squads had the interior of the first floor—which was unoccupied and under construction—completely locked down.

There were no more shooters present.

However, there were also no hostages. Either the hostages had never been there and the Raiders had stumbled into the wrong hornet's nest or the terrorists had already escaped with the hostages to another hiding place.

"Bullpen, this is Raider One—Alpha squad and four members of Charlie have exited the tunnels. No joy on locating the hostages. Repeat, hostages are still MIA. Location of Raider Two, Eleven, Thirteen, and Sixteen is unknown," Camperos reported on comms, while pulling out his tablet computer to locate his current position on the map.

"Raider One, Bullpen—copy all. We believe enemy exfilled the hostages via a previously unidentified exit and have taken them to the Presidential Palace. Raider Two is still dark," Conza replied.

Camperos looked at Moore and made no effort to hide the frustration he was feeling about failing their mission. "Do we go back under and search for Two, or do we wait for his stick to exit?"

Moore thought for a moment, then said, "Ask them if they observed the hostages being egressed or if this is a working theory. Maybe Dane's squad flushed them out but is stuck battling underground."

"Good thinking," Camperos said, then relayed the inquiry to Bullpen.

"Raider One, this is Raider Actual," said a new voice on the line, one belonging to Major Merriweather, who was the ranking Raider in the TOC at the embassy overseeing the op. "I want you to double-time it to the Jolts. Alpha team is being retasked.

Raider One, you will proceed with haste to the Presidential Palace, where you will augment and support Operation Iron Fist. The MEU has been tasked to surround and secure the Presidential Palace. If release of the hostages cannot be negotiated, the palace will be taken by force, our people liberated, and President Baptista taken into American custody."

"Copy all, Actual," Camperos said, hardly believing his ears. "And what about the other half of Charlie squadron? What are their orders?"

"Raider Ten will breach and secure the hostage exit site, now designated Whiskey. Coordinates have been sent to your tablets. We currently hold two thermals inside the target house at Whiskey. Once the threat is neutralized and the site is secure, Ten and his team will reenter the tunnels and conduct a search to locate Raider Two. Assuming Raider Two and his team are intact, Charlie will either join Alpha and the rest of the MEU at the palace or be retasked. Looks like we might have another assignment brewing for Charlie team. Any questions?"

"Copy all. No questions." Camperos turned to Moore. Grinning, he said, "Sorry to eat and run, but looks like I've got another party to go to."

"Don't worry, I fully expect to crash that party once we mop up here. Make sure to save me some beer and hot wings if you don't mind, Captain."

"Easy day," Camperos said and bumped fists with Moore.

He circled a finger in the air, rallying the members of Alpha team. Rifle up and head on a swivel, Camperos led his team of Raiders into the dark and deserted streets of Bairro Cazenga, where they would load up into their JLTVs and haul ass to the Presidential Palace and whatever shit show awaited them next.

55

PALÁCIO PRESIDENCIAL DA CIDADE ALTA (PRESIDENTIAL PALACE)
RUA PEDRO FURTADO
LUANDA, ANGOLA

General João de Souza was delivered to the front entrance of the Presidential Palace in his newly imported, Chinese-made Dongfeng Mengshi armored personnel carrier. The vehicle was big, heavy, and impressively made. Inside this beast, he was safe from bullets of every variety and caliber. Under ordinary circumstances, that gave him great confidence, but not tonight. Because the American Marines were mobilizing their forces, and the Dongfeng didn't stand a chance against an air-to-ground missile fired from an F-35B. Nothing in de Souza's arsenal could stand up against the war machines and weapons fielded by the American MEU that now controlled the ocean, the beach, and the airspace around and over the Angolan capital city. If the Americans decided to unleash hell on Cidade Alta, there was precious little the Angolan military could do to stop them.

And de Souza wasn't even interested in trying.

Baptista may be sitting behind the president's desk in the president's office, but the coup had already failed. The trick now was figuring out how to survive and emerge on the other side relatively unscathed.

"Wait for me here," he said to the driver and climbed out of the APC along with two special operators serving as his personal protection detail in case Baptista had designs on violently relieving him of command.

Jorge Baptista, the president's nephew and newly appointed chief of staff, was waiting outside under the portico. On seeing de Souza, he ran up to greet him. "General de Souza, sir, the president urgently requests your presence in his office."

At least this boy has not forgotten his manners or his place, he thought, his expression granite.

"Which is why I've come, Jorge," de Souza said, walking at a brisk clip to the entrance. "To meet with our fearless leader."

Jorge didn't have a response to that.

With his two bodyguards flanking him, de Souza entered the foyer of the Presidential Palace. Two females in housecleaning uniforms were scrubbing a section of the large, decorative oriental rug in the center of the entry. The bucket holding crimson-stained rags told him everything he needed to know.

Looks like somebody got in trouble.

Jorge jogged around de Souza and rushed ahead to the hallway leading to the president's office so he could get there first and announce de Souza, which made the general chuckle. When he reached the doorway to the president's office, Jorge was waiting expectantly with his hand on the knob.

"The president will see you now, General," Jorge said with a knowing look and pushed open the right-hand double door.

"Of course he will," de Souza grumbled under his breath.

Head held high and shoulders back and square, de Souza strode into the office he'd visited more times than he could count over the past decade. He stopped after crossing half the distance between the doors and the president's desk. To de Souza's surprise, Baptista was standing looking out the window with his back to the doors and to him. When Baptista did not turn, de Souza cleared his throat.

"When I was a young boy, my father used to come home from work and beat me whenever he had a bad day," Baptista said, talking to the window. "He had a lot of bad days, and therefore, so did I . . ."

De Souza said nothing, just waited for the usurper to turn.

"One day, after he'd given me a good pummeling, I asked him why he liked to hit me so much. He was surprised by my question. And his answer surprised me . . ."

The general waited several seconds for the revelation, but Baptista said nothing, thereby forcing de Souza to acquiesce and ask, "What did he say?"

Baptista turned and fixed de Souza with bloodshot eyes and a look that could strip paint off a wall. "He said, 'I beat so that when you grow, you won't be a weak and terrible coward like me, a man who is so afraid of getting knocked down that he cannot stand up for himself.' Then he embraced me and said, 'I beat you because I love you, son. It is the only way I know to prepare you for this cruel and violent world, where to rise as a man, you must be able to take a beating and persevere.'"

"That must have been terrible," de Souza said, holding Baptista's eyes.

"I hated him for many years . . . Until one day, I understood. It is because of my father's love and wisdom that I'm standing here, in this office, in command of this nation. I have taken countless beatings from countless adversaries, and I always persevere. When I am knocked down, I always rise and climb higher than before,"

Baptista said and paused for a long moment. "Nothing has changed. The Americans will try to knock us down, but we will rise from whatever punishment they inflict. This is our country, not theirs. We will refuse to bow to their demands. We will refuse to back down."

Interesting how "I" suddenly became "we," the general thought, suppressing the urge to smirk.

"Mr. President, the American Marines are mobilizing as we speak. I anticipate they will surround the palace, isolate you inside, and demand you release the hostages. If you refuse, they will storm the palace, take it by force, and take you into custody," de Souza said, trying to talk sense into the man. "The gambit is over, Victor. It's time to accept the facts."

"No."

"What do you mean, *no?*"

"I mean, the answer is no. I will negotiate a settlement with President Ryan. If and only if the Americans withdraw their forces from Angolan sovereign soil will I return the American hostages. I will not be bullied. I will not cede power. If President Ryan wants his son back alive, he will bow to my demands."

"Maybe you haven't been paying attention over the years, but President Ryan does not bow to anyone. Not to the president of Russia. Not to the president of China. And certainly not you, Victor."

He watched the man whom he had personally helped install as the new president. His fantasy that Baptista would be a puppet president, where he, de Souza, would pull the strings had all but evaporated. Baptista smiled at him . . . the maniacal, unhinged smile of a man on the ragged edge of sanity. "We'll see. General, fetch Kyle Ryan from the presidential bunker and bring him to me. It's time to find out if President Ryan loves his son as much as my father loved me."

"I will see to it, Mr. President," he said and turned to leave, pushing open the heavy door and ignoring the sycophant nephew, who snapped to attention as he hustled down the hall.

De Souza realized his own safety was only secure because of the loyalty of the military he commanded. But that meant nothing inside the walls of this palace, did it? Baptista was a madman and would murder him in an instant.

He had chosen badly. He had let his thirst for power cloud his judgment. He had convinced himself that only he could do what was best for Angola. But instead of challenging Luemba in a free election in the future, he had taken the shortcuts his own father had warned him of.

Now not only was his life in danger, but he had placed the future of Angola in the hands of a madman.

He could change none of that now. But he could survive, and if he did, then maybe he could turn this around.

But the Americans were coming, either way. His only chance to escape the noose he had placed around his neck required one more loose thread to be trimmed.

He pulled his phone from his pocket, the burner he had kept on him since all of this had started. He pressed the speed dial contact listed only as X, which would take him to another burner phone.

"Yes?" his most trusted officer answered immediately, the strain evident in his voice.

"Is he still at the São Paulo prison?"

"Of course," the man who had led his special operations the last three years said.

"Kill him," he said. "But it must not come back to me nor to Baptista, at least not yet."

Best to cover all my bets . . .

"Of course," the man said, sounding more relieved than anything. "The former president seems very distraught. It would not surprise me if he took his own life."

De Souza smiled.

"That would be very sad indeed," he said. "But it would not surprise me, either."

He ended the call and slipped the phone back into his pocket.

At least that was one variable he could erase that would implicate him. Perhaps he could sell himself as being caught up in the fray and waiting for the opportunity to act to save President Luemba. He imagined the grief he would display at not getting to him in time.

Then he smiled.

And if he were to kill Baptista himself, saving the hostages?

Well, the grateful Americans might even support him as the next leader of Angola—a true patriot of his people in a time of need.

He would not return to the presidential office unarmed. Perhaps the opportunity would present itself at the perfect time. The President's son could be the witness to his heroic act.

Yes . . . things just might work out after all.

56

EMERGENCY OPERATIONS CENTER (EOC)
U.S. EMBASSY MISSION IN ANGOLA
R. HOUARI BOUMEDIENE 32
LUANDA, ANGOLA

Katie's relief that at least three if not all of the four hostages were alive—and that one of the three was her brother—had now simmered into a feeling of helplessness.

That they were alive remained very good news, of course.

Keeping them that way might prove to be something else altogether.

As she paced, and waited, and paced some more—ignoring the regular looks from Bubba and Conza that showed equal parts empathy and concern—she realized that she was bringing nothing to the table. She was less than a passenger on this horrible journey. She was just an observer.

Conza was in his element, working comms and feeding intelligence in real time to the Marine Raiders in the field.

Bubba was working the intelligence—the data streaming constantly from satellites, drones, the CIA streams, and the LFOC on board the *Kearsarge*.

She was an analyst and, quite frankly, there was just nothing to analyze.

She was also the leader of the intelligence task force, but there were no decisions to be made.

She resisted the urge to sigh and stared for the ten-thousandth time at the grainy still photo they had pulled from the video feed—the one that showed Kyle and the others being led into the palace. Her mind went back to a hundred little moments, but she found the memories of their time at the Academy together to somehow be the most intimate. She wasn't sure how those memories felt deeper than a lifetime of Christmas mornings, summer vacations, and Thanksgiving dinners, but they did. Maybe because their time together as part of the Brigade was something that they, and they alone, had shared. Something outside the larger-than-life experience of being a Ryan. They had been in the same company at the Naval Academy as well, and the small-unit adhesion learned there was maybe a part of it, but it was more the stolen moments, when Kyle's otherwise stoic and emotionless face would break character into the gentle, knowing smile that few ever got to see other than her.

And somehow that closeness must have disappeared for Kyle— because I didn't even know he had left the Navy.

The thought brought her both sadness and anger.

She thought Kyle had learned, maybe because of her, that life could not be done well alone.

And yet here they were.

She stared at the still photo of the large man pressing a club of some sort into the small of her brother's back.

"Damn you, Kyle," she whispered under her breath.

"Commander Ryan?"

She turned to see Goose Horgan standing beside her.

"Sorry, Katie, but this is urgent," Horgan said.

"Of course," Katie replied, irritated that Horgan might think she was in some fragile state where she should be left alone. "We're all still on mission here. What's up?"

"Well," the aviator turned spook said, "Freddy has been working with NSA assets through the ODNI and it looks like we have confirmation of where Luemba and Vice President Carvalho are being held. Freddy has been working with his local managed assets, who finally resurfaced, and we know they are both there and still alive."

Katie thought about this revelation for a moment. That Luemba was still alive seemed a miracle, but it was also confusing and must mean something. If Baptista had really taken over in a violent coup, the norm in the region would be that Luemba would have died during the takeover. He could be holding him to stage a mock trial to legitimize himself. But witnesses were rarely a good thing. This was why there was still uncertainty about Baptista, perhaps.

Luemba and Carvalho know the truth . . .

"And there's a call for you, ma'am," Horgan said, interrupting her rumination. "Freddy received it through channels at the ODNI. They want to talk to you from the Situation Room at the White House."

Katie raised an eyebrow at that.

Another first after a year and a half of firsts, beginning with her first time being shot at. In her case it was with a torpedo while undersea on a submarine, and the year had only gotten crazier from there.

"They who?" she asked.

Horgan shrugged.

"I think maybe the President?"

Katie made a little *pffft* sound.

There were a million reasons that the President didn't get on the phone with O-4s out in the field, but in their case, there was an added reason. Their relationship might make some dads call, but not President Ryan. Like her, he kept family and service to the country separate—which was where she got it from, she supposed.

"Okay," she said finally. "Let's see who's calling."

"Freddy thought you might want to take it in private?"

Katie glanced at the picture of her brother, then over at the live satellite feeds. She should probably take it here, but it would be quicker to just go with Horgan. She followed the DIA agent to the back of the room, where Freddy was in the lone office set off from the EOC proper. He waved her in.

"Sit at my desk," he said. "We'll give you privacy."

"I think that's a bad idea," she said, slipping into his leather chair and reaching for the phone. "I know President Ryan pretty well. This won't be that kind of call. Please stay. This is probably something we all need to hear."

Hoping she was right, she pressed the speaker button on the phone.

"This is Lieutenant Commander Ryan," she said. For some reason her hands were shaking. This wasn't a call with her dad, this was a mid-grade naval officer talking to the President of the United States in the middle of a national security crisis.

"One moment for the President," a low, serious male voice said.

There was a click and then the secure line reconnected.

"Commander, this is President Ryan," the voice that was her dad's, but somehow not, said. She had heard this voice a time or two, when he'd taken calls in his official capacity from her childhood home on the Chesapeake. Then a bit of his dad voice crept in when he asked, "How are you guys holding up, Katie?"

"Very well, sir," she said, still nervous for some reason. "We're all relieved that the hostages—most of them, if not all—appear to be alive, sir. But there is clearly more work to be done. How can we help get them the rest of the way home, Mr. President?"

"That's why I'm calling," President Ryan said. "You've proven to have remarkable instincts the last two years, Commander. What is your gut telling you about Baptista?"

Katie thought for a moment.

"I wish I could say," she said carefully. "The consensus here is that he is what he has always been—a power-hungry thug. But, unfortunately, that doesn't mean that the story he's spinning isn't true. Regime change in this region often looks just like this. I wish we could speak with the military leaders."

"Or with President Luemba," Ryan said.

"That would be ideal. I was just learning from our DIA representative that Luemba's location and his incarceration status have been confirmed by the NSA and CIA."

"That's my understanding as well, but it comes mostly from the boots-on-the-ground intelligence apparatus that the CIA has running in Luanda. Commander, in order for me to make the best decision about what comes next, I need to understand and separate the good from the bad guys. Does the station chief there have the connections and relationships in place to facilitate getting a team into São Paulo prison, where Luemba is being held?"

She looked over at Freddy, who puffed out his cheeks as he thought about that. Then he offered her something resembling a nod.

"Yes, sir," she said, answering for Freddy.

"Good," Ryan said. "I have the DNI here with me as well as Director Canfield. We want you, the head of station, and your team to coordinate Luemba's exfiltration from that prison. Is the commander of the MARSOC element there?"

She snapped a finger to get Horgan's attention, who then spun on a heel to grab Major Merriweather.

I knew I should have taken the call out in the bullpen . . .

"Getting him now, Mr. President," she said.

"Good," Ryan said, and he sounded confident. And powerful. This was the Jack Ryan who wielded the executive power of the mightiest country in the world, not the daddy Jack Ryan who had read her bedtime stories. That they were really the same person never ceased to amaze her, more so as she learned how the world really worked. "Katie, we need to get Luemba out alive and ambulatory. We need him to fill in all the gaps we have about Baptista and General de Souza. Based on what we learn, the solution to this nightmare could very well be to return Luemba to the palace and to power."

"We'll do our best, Mr. President," she said, all anxiety and fear evaporating as her role in the moment crystallized.

"Let's get to work, Katie," her dad said, "the clock is ticking."

57

PENITENCIÁRIA DE SÃO PAULO
RUA DE ESPINHOS
LUANDA, ANGOLA

Former president Francisco Luemba sat on the uncomfortable prison bed—a metal cot that folded out from the wall—and wanly contemplated things beyond his fate. His outrage had turned to fear and his fear to resignation.

Now he was struggling with regret.

For once, he supposed, it was not his own fate he had regrets about. He was angry at himself for trusting General de Souza—a man he'd believed to be more than the head of the military, but also his friend and confidant. As a leader in Angola, he should have known better than to trust anyone.

That failure had cost him.

But it was not the price he would soon pay that weighed on him. No, to that fate he truly had resigned himself. The last few hours he had thought about his wife and children. In fact, he found he could concentrate on little else.

Luisa was a strong woman. Long ago, when he had been a better husband, she had been his best advisor and confidante. He supposed she had stopped advising when he had stopped listening, when his idealistic dreams had turned to practical needs and demands of the office. She had not shied away from the trappings of the path he had chosen, but she had always seemed just a little sad since then. Perhaps she would be okay. Perhaps she had already found a way to escape.

Luemba's children were all grown. Would Baptista go after them as well? Luemba decided the answer was yes because his adversary was an angry and violent man. But there was still hope. Maybe as president, Baptista would worry about the optics of such a decision. Perhaps de Souza would counsel against such a polarizing move as retribution and maybe, just maybe, Baptista would heed it.

I have hunted this bastard for nearly a decade, and he knows it. He will show me no mercy, but perhaps he will leave my children alone.

But Luisa? Luisa would be safe only if she found a way to escape the city.

The rattle of the cell block door at the end of the hall jolted him from his dark thoughts and sent his heart racing. Every time the door opened it happened, but this time his fear intensified. It was far too early for a meal, and he hadn't stepped outside his cell—not for exercise, not to speak with anyone, and not to hear any accusations. He had no idea what was happening, only what he could reasonably predict.

He had lost all hope for rescue.

It must be time. Time for his public humiliation, and then . . .

He closed his eyes, trying to push away the haunting images of the corpses from the executions he had overseen, including many of Baptista's PFU terrorists. He remembered how, in their final moments, the bodies had jerked and soiled themselves.

Soon I will be hanging from a rope . . .

Eyes bulging and body twitching while his family and countrymen watched his overweight body swing from the gallows, trousers stained with piss, and shit dripping from his pant legs.

"Mr. President," an unfamiliar male voice said, but without the respect the words usually carried.

Luemba opened his eyes to see an Angolan man he didn't recognize staring at him. In his right hand he held a pistol, only it was curious-looking with a strangely long and wide barrel.

"Who are you?" Luemba asked, deciding that he would be remembered, even if only by this man, as a strong president. His voice sounded convincing, despite his trembling hands pressed into his lap.

"I am no one of consequence," the man replied without smiling. "But President Baptista and General de Souza send their regards."

Luemba let out a long, fatalistic breath. "So, this is how it ends?"

"I'm afraid so," the man said. "Your trial would be nothing but spectacle. The nation deserves better—or so I am told. Suicide is the only solution. Overcome by remorse, you were not able to face humiliation in front of the country by confessing your sins. In death by your own hand, you honored yourself with absolution."

"I will not comply," Luemba said defiantly, finding some last measure of pride and resistance deep inside him. "I'll fight you, and you won't be able to make the wound look self-inflicted."

A vulpine grin curled the man's lips. "This is a tranquilizer gun. Once you're unconscious, I will manage the rest. When the guards find you, you will have hanged yourself in your cell."

The man took a step back and raised the odd gun. Every neuron in Luemba's brain told him to run, to hide. But he was in an eight-by-eight cell with only a cot and a toilet on the wall. There was nowhere to run or to hide.

So he stared at his executioner with defiance and pride.

Then another sound came from down the hall, and his killer heard it, too, turning in that direction. The assassin raised his tranquilizer weapon, pointing it back from the way he had come, but as he did a suppressed gunshot echoed and the top of the killer's head evaporated in a cloud of blood, bone, and brains. Then what was left of the man slumped to the floor, the tranquilizer gun clattering against the bars of Luemba's cell.

"Clear," someone called in English.

English!

Luemba rose from the bed, hands still trembling, so he shoved them in his pockets.

He heard feet shuffling quickly toward his cell. He could not see, and dared not stick his head against the bars. If he was seen as a threat he might be shot.

"Clear," a different voice called, closer now.

A heartbeat later, a uniformed soldier stepped into view on the other side of the bars, scanning over an assault rifle. An American Marine, if Luemba's uniform knowledge was to be trusted.

"President Luemba?" the man asked him, lowering his rifle.

"Yes," he said, trying to calm his nerves and sound presidential, but aware he had failed at both. "Who are you?"

The man smiled.

"Sir, I'm Captain Josh Dane of the United States Marine Corps. We're here to get you out of this prison. What happens next depends entirely on how your conversation with my boss goes."

"And who is your boss?" Luemba asked.

"The President of the United States—President Jack Ryan."

"Then we should go," Luemba said, feeling his first wave of hope since his arrest by the PFU terrorist. "I would hate to keep him waiting. Have you located Vice President Carvalho?"

"Yes," the Marine said. "And members of your cabinet. Honestly, we didn't meet much resistance except for this asshole." He gestured at the hired killer on the cell block floor. "We need to go—and right now."

There was a Klaxon-style sound and the magnetic lock of his cell released.

Luemba closed his eyes in relief.

"Thank you," he said, squeezing the shoulder of the soldier, seeing now that there were other soldiers spread out in the cell block hallway.

"You can thank the President," Dane said with a grin. "I'm just an instrument of his policy."

The Marines formed a box around Luemba and together they jogged to the door at the end of the hall.

"I . . . I need to call my wife," Luemba said, suddenly overcome with emotion.

"I understand," Dane said over his shoulder. "But that will have to wait until after the debrief."

Luemba wondered if he was dreaming. Perhaps the man who had come for him had succeeded after all. Perhaps this was just the last spark of a dying brain creating a fantasy to make the transition to death more palatable. He pinched his thigh through the orange cotton fabric of his jumpsuit, and the pain felt real and wonderful.

Apparently, he owed a great debt to the Americans and to President Ryan.

Which begged the question . . .

What have my "friends" from China been doing during all of this?

If he survived today, he would lead Angola differently tomorrow.

He hoped he would, at least. Maybe Luisa could help him keep that vow.

After departing the cell block, they moved quickly through the large but unimpressive foyer. It was not lost on Luemba that a cadre of disarmed Angolan soldiers were looking at their feet, none daring to look him in the eye. He felt a rage rise inside, an anger demanding that all of these men and women be punished, that their lives be ruined if not ended. But then a voice, Luisa's voice, came to him, asking if it was really their fault. In Angola, who really knew the truth, and he could only imagine what lies these people had been told. If he were in their shoes, would he risk dying for a man arrested for treason without even knowing the real truth? Or would he follow the orders of those above him, as they did from those above them?

"It is okay, my fellow Angolans," he said in Kimbundu. "We will make this right."

As he reached the doors, one young soldier, a woman—no older than eighteen—straightened up and saluted him. Luemba paused and saluted back.

A moment later, he was directed to climb inside a large armored truck.

In the passenger compartment, a woman—a very pretty American woman—sat on a bench seat waiting for him.

"President Luemba, I'm Lieutenant Commander Ryan of the United States Navy," she said, although, like the American soldiers, she was dressed in civilian clothes. Only, the vestlike kit she wore clearly did not fit and she had no helmet on her head. "I have some questions for you, and I need you to answer them clearly and honestly. We are asking Vice President Carvalho and your cabinet members the same questions in other vehicles. If we are satisfied with your answers, then President Ryan wishes to speak with you."

"I will answer all of your questions," he said, straightening himself up. "And then, if you are willing, I would like to meet with my people to take my country back from a traitor."

"If you answer truthfully, and if the President believes you, then I think you will find we are well positioned to help you with that request."

The heavy armored door closed and the APC pulled away.

"First question," the woman said. "Tell me everything you know about Victor Baptista and the events that led to your removal from power and imprisonment."

"First, tell me how you found me," he asked, wanting to gather his own details as well.

"There's no time for that now, Mr. President. Please, sir," she said, her voice almost desperate. "We're running out of time."

He nodded, accepted that he was no longer in control, and told his tale: "Victor Baptista is the head of the PFU, a political rival of the duly elected government for many years, and a traitor to this country . . ."

58

SECURE BUNKER
BASEMENT OF PALÁCIO PRESIDENCIAL DA CIDADE ALTA
 (PRESIDENTIAL PALACE)
RUA PEDRO FURTADO

"Madame Ambassador, can you drag a chair over here, please? We need to elevate his legs," Kyle said, taking a knee next to Ottinger, who was still unconscious, barely alive, and lying on the floor, where the guards had left him.

After being "greeted" by President Baptista in the palace foyer, armed guards had carried Ottinger and escorted Kyle, Madison, and the ambassador to a secure bunker in the basement. Kyle suspected that this space—a considerable upgrade from their previous subterranean accommodations—would serve as their new home and prison for the remainder of the crisis. Unfortunately, the upgrade in amenities was overshadowed in Kyle's mind by the geopolitical implications of being there.

"Thank you," he said as Ambassador Gonçalves dragged a metal chair with a padded seat cushion into position at Ottinger's feet. "Madison, can you get his other leg . . . Yep, just like that."

After getting Ottinger's feet elevated, Kyle leaned back on his haunches and turned his attention to the armed guard standing at the closed and locked door. "Do you speak English?" he called loudly to get the man's attention.

The guard looked at Kyle, but only stared and said nothing.

Kyle turned to the ambassador. "Can you please tell him in Portuguese that we need a doctor? We were promised a doctor and medical supplies. I don't know how much longer Eric is going to last if he doesn't get medical care."

The ambassador did as Kyle requested, and this time the guard understood. He entered a code to unlock the door, opened it six inches, and talked to the guard standing outside. Then the guard shut the door and spoke with the ambassador.

"He said a doctor is coming soon," Gonçalves said, her voice weary and coarse. Then, holding Kyle's eyes, added, "Eric's going to die, isn't he?"

"Without medical care, definitely," Kyle said. "I'm surprised he's lasted this long . . ."

The pained look on her face reminded him that this was a moment where he could have, *probably should have*, employed some tact and sensitivity in his answer. Katie referred to the technique as "sugarcoating" his responses, and she'd coached him tirelessly on how to do this during their adolescent years. He'd loved her for the effort, but hated the practice. Why would anyone in their right mind want to be misled and given false hope? But looking at the ambassador now, he understood why.

"That said, I still have hope," he added with a confident raise of his chin. "Eric's fit and, even in an unconscious state, has demonstrated a powerful will to live."

She managed a little smile, but her stitched forehead did not relax.

"Madame Ambassador, I know you were listening while Baptista and our previous jailer were talking, before the execution, obviously," he said. "What did they say?"

"Baptista was very upset and shocked that his man had brought us to the palace," she said, "but I suppose that was obvious even if you don't speak Portuguese."

Kyle nodded.

"He went on to say that by bringing us to the palace, his lieutenant had neutered any plausible deniability claims that Baptista could use to separate and distance himself from the incident, which appears to have been his plan all along—blame a rogue element of the PFU for the embassy attack and kidnapping and label them terrorists.

"I wouldn't be surprised if he planned to send in the Angolan military to rescue us and slaughter his people," Madison added. "Baptista executed his own man right in front of us, so it's not like doing such a thing would be beneath him."

"Agreed," Kyle said, glancing at Madison before turning back to the ambassador. "What else did they say?"

Gonçalves shook her head. "Baptista's clever. He saw me listening to them and switched to Umbundu, which I do not speak."

"It was Kimbundu, actually," Madison said.

Kyle and the ambassador both turned to her with surprised looks.

"I'm not fluent, but I've been learning it while I'm here," Madison told them, her voice clinical and unemotional. She looked at Kyle and her flat affect turned into a smile and she blushed slightly. "Languages come easily to me."

"What did they say?" Kyle asked, beyond impressed. He'd not often met a woman he could relate to—and never one as physically attractive as Madison. "Were you able to follow the conversation?"

"Well, Baptista wanted to know if the other guy had tried to kill Ottinger on purpose, and they argued about that. Then they talked about a way out of this mess, and the other guy suggested that if they killed us, then Baptista would still have plausible deniability because, you know, 'dead men tell no tales.' That's when Baptista freaked out," Madison said, turning to Kyle. "He knows who you are. They've pierced your . . . NOC, I think you spooks call it."

It was Kyle's turn to blush slightly. Clearly she knew nothing about him. If he was an operator, maybe he could have kept them both out of this situation altogether. His brother, Jack, would not have been taken so easily, he suspected.

"I'm no spook, I'm afraid," he said. "Just a cyber weenie."

Kyle had suspected already that they had figured out his real identity based on the way both men had looked at him during the argument. Thanks to Madison, this hunch was now confirmed.

"I'm surprised they managed that, but knowing that I'm a Ryan could work to our advantage," he said, his brain war-gaming out how to leverage his biological political capital, "if we play our cards right."

Just then, the lock on the door chimed, and the inside guard opened the door. A young Angolan man, dressed in clothes resembling a paramedic's uniform, entered with a very large first-aid kit, the size of a small duffel bag. He stepped into the room, but instead of rushing to Ottinger, he just stood there staring. Kyle noted the guy was so nervous that his hands were shaking. Anyone with legitimate emergency medical training and field experience would be acting, not standing frozen.

"Do you speak English?" Kyle said, trying to snap the man out of his stupor.

"Some English," the man said, and Kyle noted that his embroidered name tape read COSTA.

"Costa, are you a doctor?" Kyle asked.

"No, I . . . I emergency . . ." Costa said, struggling.

"EMT? Are you an EMT?"

"Yes . . . EMT."

"This man has been shot," Kyle said. "He has lost a lot of blood. We need to help him, or he will die."

Costa nodded nervously, but otherwise remained a statue.

Frustrated, Kyle walked over to him and grabbed the first-aid duffel. Then, hustling over to Ottinger, he said, "Come on, man, he needs you."

Costa walked hesitantly over to join Kyle as he unzipped the clamshell-style nylon bag and flipped open the two sides, which had neatly organized, integrated pouches and compartments.

"What can I do?" Madison asked, coming over to help.

"First priority is to get fluids into him," Kyle said, starting to inventory and lay out the contents. "Help me find the IV kit."

Madison started unzipping the rectangular compartments, while Kyle did the same.

"Is this it?" she asked, pulling a bag of clear saline out of a pouch and holding it up.

"Yes," he said, but he noted another bag, dark crimson in appearance, located in the same compartment underneath it. "What's that?"

"It looks like . . . blood," she said.

"Hand it to me," he said, then took it from her outstretched hand and scanned the label, mumbling as he did: "Hemopure intravenous . . . contains hemoglobin glutamer-250 bovine . . ."

"What is that?"

"It's a blood substitute. It appears this one is made from hemoglobin extracted from cows. I've read about these, but didn't know they were commercially available yet. This package says

South Africa, so maybe it's approved there," Kyle said, realizing that the bag of crimson liquid in his hand was the medical community's equivalent of the search for the holy grail and quite possibly the difference between life and death for Eric Ottinger.

"Should we give it to him?" she said, looking back and forth between Kyle and the paramedic, Costa.

Kyle asked Costa, "Have you ever used this before?"

Costa's eyes went wide, but he didn't answer.

Kyle grabbed the man's arm and shook him. "Hey, answer me. Have you ever used this product before?"

Costa shook his head.

Kyle gritted his teeth. He hated uncertainty, hated it more than anything in the world.

"Don't we need to know his blood type first? It has to match, right?" Madison said.

"No, that's the beauty of this stuff. It's just an artificial oxygen-carrying molecule. It doesn't have actual red blood cells, so you can give it to anybody. I read an article about how this stuff restored brain function four hours after death in rodent trials. It perfuses organs and reoxygenates them. It's amazing."

"Why isn't it used in the U.S.?"

"Side effects, I'm sure. Maybe it interferes with clotting . . . Or maybe the opposite. Maybe it causes clots, which can lead to a stroke. I'm not an expert. I don't know," Kyle said, staring at the bag.

He ran the math in his head. Most drugs that didn't get FDA-approved had side effects or contraindications that were serious but also rare. And the process of getting new drugs approved in the United States was much slower than elsewhere, which didn't always mean the drugs were bad or ineffective. Bureaucracy takes time.

Ottinger wasn't old, obese, or sick. But he was critically anemic from blood loss. To survive, he needed a transfusion, and that wasn't going to happen anytime soon. Hemopure was the next best thing, and maybe, based on the article he read, the *best* option in Ottinger's near-death state.

"I've decided. We're giving it to him," Kyle said and handed the bag to Madison while he fetched the rest of the IV kit. "Here, hold this while I connect the tubing."

"What do you mean, you've decided?" the ambassador asked. "We don't even know the risks. It might be banned in America for a reason."

Kyle met her eyes steadily a moment and then tried to be gentle and respectful, just like Katie had attempted to teach him.

"I understand, Madame Ambassador," he said. "And I'm as worried as you. But I've done the math . . ."

"The math?" Gonçalves said, her face confused.

But Madison got it, because she smiled and her eyes widened in realization.

"Madison has a gift for languages," he said. "You undoubtedly have a gift for diplomacy and human relationships, a gift I have never been accused of having. I have a gift for quickly evaluating a situation, the risks and benefits, the pros and cons, and applying mathematics to get to the best solution—even if it is only the better of two bad choices."

"How is that math?" Gonçalves asked, but her face softened.

"Everything is math," he answered, and turned to the IV setup.

After attaching the tubing and catheter needle, he opened the clamp and squeezed the bag. Once he'd purged the air from the line, he clamped the line shut and looked at Costa. The paramedic shook his head.

"Seriously, man. Are you not going to help?"

Costa exhaled loudly, seemed to find his courage, and reluctantly nodded. He pulled out a rubber tourniquet and tied it around Ottinger's biceps. Then he leaned down to inspect the back of Ottinger's hand, searching for a vein. The unconscious security officer had lost so much blood that his veins had no height and were practically invisible. Unable to find a suitable candidate, Costa got frustrated and threw up his hands.

"Fine, I'll do it," Kyle said and leaned down to try to find a vein. Finding nothing in the hand, he rotated Ottinger's hand and checked the inner arm below the elbow, He could see the vein, but not feel it.

"Have you ever done this before?" Madison asked.

"Once," he said, "but I did it in the back of the hand."

"I believe in you," she said, a comment he normally would have scoffed at, but for some reason, needed to hear—sugarcoating and all.

Holding the needle bevel-side up, he angled it at twenty degrees from the horizontal and punctured the skin just as they'd practiced on each other at the Farm. Of course, he'd been sticking a vein he could both see and feel, the size of a macaroni noodle, in a healthy, well-hydrated DIA agent.

"Aren't you supposed to sterilize that first?" Madison asked as he inserted the needle into the vein.

"Yeah, I guess, but I think that's the least of Eric's concerns at the moment," he said, annoyed that he'd missed a step. Pushing the procedural-misstep thought away, he backed the needle out and waited for blood to seep backward from the catheter tip. No blood came. He cursed and was about to pull the needle out and try again, but Costa put his hand on the back of Kyle's, stopping him.

"You are close," Costa said, and gently adjusted the needle. "Just a little change to angle . . ."

Kyle watched as blood seeped out, albeit with very little pressure, from the catheter. He smiled at Costa, who smiled back. They then worked together as a team to remove the needle while keeping the catheter in place and attaching the tubing. After that, Kyle removed the clamp, and the bag of Hemopure started to empty into Ottinger's circulatory system. Kyle and Costa exchanged a high five, while the ambassador brought a chair over for Madison, who was holding the Hemopure bag in place of an IV stand, which they did not have.

"You did it, Kyle," Madison said, grinning at him.

"We did it as a team," he said, and for a moment he flashed back to smiling at his sister on Worden Field when it was announced at the Color Parade that their company had won the semester-long competition for the color company pennant. He gave his best smile to the team he was part of now. "Squeeze the bag, Ambassador, and we can get it in more quickly. Then we'll hook up the IV bag to give him more blood volume. Together, maybe that will do it."

"How long does it take to know if it's working?" Gonçalves asked.

"I don't know," Kyle said, but he thought maybe he could see the slightest hint of color returning to Ottinger's cheeks. "I think all of his external bleeding has stopped, but after this bag goes in, we need to roll him over and inspect, clean, and pack his wound."

Before anyone could answer, the door chime sounded. All eyes went to the security guard as he punched in the code, unlocked and opened the door. On seeing who was standing outside, the guard snapped to attention, then stepped aside to clear a path for a middle-aged Angolan man dressed in an officer's uniform. The new arrival's uniform top was decorated with a stack of ribbons and medals the likes of which Kyle had never seen on any U.S. military officer, and his rank insignia displayed four gold stars.

The general entered the room and surveyed the goings-on. He first assessed the medical care being given to Ottinger, then locked onto Ambassador Gonçalves, then finally settled on Kyle.

"Lieutenant Ryan," the general said in English. "I'm General de Souza, chief of the general staff of the Angolan Armed Forces . . . Say goodbye to your colleagues. You're coming with me."

Kyle looked over at Madison, who held his eyes and gave him a weak smile of encouragement.

"It's going to be okay," he said, and then turned back to the general. "This man still needs a doctor, or he is going to die."

"Come with me, please," the general said, his voice softening this time. "I promise I am doing the best I can to save all of you. I have requested to the president that your colleague go to the hospital. If this request is denied, I will bring a doctor here."

Kyle raised his eyebrows in surprise. Was this man an ally? There was something in the general's eyes that didn't sit right with Kyle, and so he decided not to trust the man. But then again, he had once scrawled *Confide nemini* on his athletic jersey at the Naval Academy.

Trust no one.

Trust had never come easily to him.

59

**SITUATION ROOM
THE WHITE HOUSE
WASHINGTON, D.C.
1933 LOCAL TIME**

Ryan sat in the small, private office set off from where the rest of his team chattered in the Situation Room—running what-if scenarios about how this middle-of-the-night standoff with Baptista could play out. On the main screen, Marines held outside the Angolan Presidential Palace, ready to storm the building and engage the Angolan military on his order.

Like him, they were waiting.

Like him, the waiting would eventually take a toll.

He was acutely aware that he wasn't the only American parent who had an adult child in harm's way in Luanda. Every serving Marine, sailor, and embassy staffer had parents who might be fretting just as he was. But unlike him, these parents had no idea their loved ones were serving on the front lines of battle and risking their lives at this very moment. And, unlike him, none of these parents had the command authority to make commander in chief decisions that could either bring their loved ones home safely . . .

Or in a flag-draped coffin.

His executive power carried an incredible weight—one that the last few days had reminded him of in a deeply personal way. He hoped he would carry the memory of that with him to the next crisis, and the next . . .

"Mr. President?"

His heart skipped a beat at the voice, and he looked up to see one of Scott Adler's staffers—a young man of about thirty, who carried himself with the military bearing of a veteran.

"We got him, sir," the staffer said with a tight grin on his face.

"Luemba?" he asked, rising from the desk.

"Yes, sir."

Ryan strode into the main conference room, where the energy was electric. The central wall-mounted monitor displayed two windows. The right window showed the live satellite feed of the assets of the 22nd MEU surrounding the Presidential Palace. The left window was a teleconference with his daughter, streaming from what appeared to be her cell phone camera inside a vehicle.

"Mr. President," she said, not smiling with confidence, but one still short of victory.

"What have you got for us, Commander Ryan?" he asked, standing behind his chair at the end of the large table. He wasn't ready—or even able—to sit. He had thousands of Americans still in harm's way including half his children.

"Sir, we liberated President Luemba from prison," she said, her head and shoulders bouncing as the APC jostled along the road. "We're en route to the embassy and will arrive in a few minutes. I took the liberty to debrief Luemba and the vice president and asked the team at the EOC to do their best to vet the information—"

"Cut to the chase, Commander," he said, annoyed that she'd, once again, put herself at risk by charging into the field.

"Sir, it is our opinion that President Luemba was the victim of a violent coup to overthrow the democratically elected government of Angola. Victor Baptista used his PFU organization to stage the attack on our embassy and kidnap the ambassador and other hostages. Simultaneously, he brokered a deal with General João de Souza, the head of the Angolan military, to cede control of the military to Baptista. De Souza's forces took Luemba, the vice president, and the presidential cabinet into custody, charged them with treason, and jailed them at São Paulo prison. We believe the general is also responsible for the attack on the landing force."

"I assume you've documented all this and are uploading it to a secure server as we speak?"

"Yes, sir, Mr. President, but I wanted you to have command of the facts you need to make the best decisions possible," Katie said. He saw it in that moment—her fear for her brother and her desperation. It was buried in her eyes, but he saw it.

"Excellent work, Commander Ryan," he said and felt a swell of pride, though he was still irritated she'd not stayed behind in the safety of the EOC. But he knew that was the father in him talking, competing for control and a relevance with the commander in chief. As POTUS, he was grateful for her initiative—getting the intelligence needed as quickly as possible, and firsthand.

He scanned the faces of his team gathered around the table, all quiet now, knowing it was time for him to make the next call or to ask for opinions.

"I assume Baptista has tried to contact us?" he asked as he turned to Adler.

"Twice, sir," the secretary of state said. "And he claims he wants to negotiate for the safe return of the hostages. He *claims* he has rescued them, but that in order to return them we need to withdraw our Marines from Luanda and make assurances not to interfere with his government."

General Kudryk groaned. "Well, that's a load of bullshit."

"You're right, Bruce," Ryan said with a tight smile. "It is bullshit. And it suggests Baptista either doesn't understand the cards we hold or that he underestimates my resolve."

Grim smiles swept the table.

"I need to speak to the MEU commander," Ryan said. "What's his name?"

"Colonel Rick Crocker, sir," Admiral Kent said. "We have him on the feed already."

A new window popped up on-screen, and a "poster boy" Marine officer materialized, his jaw clenched and his eyes full of fury.

"Mr. President," Crocker said with a deferential nod. "We're prepared to take the palace by force if required. We also have a Raider team on-site, prepared for a more surgical infil and HRT if needed. We are prepared for all contingencies. We also have air support up and ready should the Angolan military attempt to mobilize armor or air assets. As of this moment, we're only facing off against palace security."

"Thank you, Colonel," Ryan said. "Do you have sniper overwatch in place?"

"I do, sir. We have lines on the entrance and the rear courtyard, but we can move shooters to target specific rooms, the Cabinet Room and presidential office, for example. Just say the word."

"Understood," Ryan said, then briefed the Marine colonel on several possible contingencies his analytical mind imagined could play out. When he'd finished, he said, "Stand by, Colonel, and remain fluid."

"Yes, sir, Mr. President."

He turned to Adler. "I think it's time to talk to Baptista."

Adler looked surprised. "You want to talk to him personally, sir, instead of using me as an intermediary?"

"Yes," Ryan said. "I want you to make him think he's earned an audience with me and therefore has gained the upper hand. I suspect we'll learn a great deal about our options for how to bring this coup to an end."

"I'll get him on the line and grease those skids, Mr. President," Adler said.

"Video chat, Scott," Ryan said. "I want to negotiate face-to-face with this asshole."

"You got it, Mr. President," Adler said and stepped out to set the stage.

Ryan exhaled, finally ready to take his seat. One way or another, he knew this would be over in the next thirty minutes. As he eased himself into the padded executive chair, he said a silent prayer that the strategist in him was nimble and clearheaded enough to make all the moves necessary to win the day and get everyone home alive.

60

PALÁCIO PRESIDENCIAL DA CIDADE ALTA (PRESIDENTIAL PALACE)
RUA PEDRO FURTADO
LUANDA, ANGOLA
0143 LOCAL TIME

Kyle took a deep breath.

This was it—the moment that everything that had happened in his life had either prepared or *not* prepared him for. His number had been called, and he was about to find out what Fate had in store for him. He felt a surge of fear, but also equal measures of duty and resignation. So long as he could manage the former and channel it into something useful, he might just have a chance.

He stood to face the commanding general of the Angolan Armed Forces. Challenging de Souza wasn't an option, as the general had brought two armed escorts, who looked ready and capable of killing on command. And he was beginning to allow himself to hope that, perhaps, the man might even be an ally. Was he a military man just caught up in a coup beyond his control?

He would know soon enough, he supposed.

As ordered, Kyle turned to say his goodbyes.

First, he looked at Ambassador Gonçalves. In her eyes, he saw both apology and gratitude that he'd been the one chosen to arbitrate their fate and that he'd accepted the burden.

"Don't worry, I'll be fine," he said, trying to put her conscience at ease.

Next, he locked eyes with Madison.

"Kyle, I . . . I believe in you," she stammered. Then a hint of a smile broke through her stoic facade, and she added, "No matter what happens, just do the math."

He looked deeply into her eyes conveying all things he wanted to say but couldn't. They were kindreds that way. He knew that sharing emotions for her was as difficult as it was for him, and yet in this moment, she'd told him that she cared and understood him.

"Time to go," de Souza said, his voice commanding.

Kyle smiled fondly at Madison—perhaps for the last time—and walked out of the bunker.

This hostage march through the Presidential Palace felt very different than the others. No black bag over his head. No painful binding on his wrists. No gun to his head, knife at his throat, or club whacking his ass. This time, he was being shown a certain measure of dignity. A certain measure of respect. A certain measure of *restraint*.

The power dynamic had shifted.

His captors did not want him to know this, but the subtext guiding their behavior and treatment of him communicated volumes. Right now, he realized he was being escorted to a negotiation, not an execution.

The execution would come later . . . if the negotiations failed.

Unfortunately for Kyle, negotiations were a battle of words. A linguistic chess game where turns of phrase and decoding body language dictated the victor. He was terrible at these things. A melancholy defeatism settled over him, but then Madison's parting words unexpectedly reframed the situation for him.

"Just do the math."

Madison was like him, but she worked in the State Department. She worked with the diplomatic corps. She knew what was happening. That's why she'd said what she said. Hope sparked in his chest. She was giving him advice. To play the game, all he needed to do was translate the wordplay into math.

That was something he could do.

The march through the palace took him up a staircase to the first floor, down a long hallway, and ended at a set of tall mahogany doors with ornate, polished brass handles. De Souza opened the doors and looked inside. Only after this quick safety check did he gesture for Kyle to enter and order his guards to wait outside. On crossing the threshold, Kyle immediately realized he'd entered the president's Cabinet Room. He'd visited the White House on two occasions. From the color palette to the massive oval conference table, to the grand picture windows looking out onto a courtyard beyond—this room reminded him of the Cabinet Room in the West Wing.

"Welcome, Lieutenant Ryan. I'm President Victor Baptista," said an Angolan man standing behind the middle chair on the far side of the table. To Kyle's surprise, Baptista was not dressed in a suit and tie. Instead, he wore black tactical trousers and a dark gray, ribbed sweater. Also impossible to miss, the Angolan president was armed with two pistols, a semi-automatic perched on each hip.

"It's just Kyle Ryan," he replied after a beat, his eyes shifting from the pistols to Baptista's eyes. "I separated from the Navy earlier this year."

For some reason, the clarification made Baptista smile. He

gestured to the empty leather executive chair on the opposite side of the table from his own. "Please, have a seat."

Kyle did as instructed, while General de Souza took the seat at the far end of the oval table, creating triangular geometry. The math of de Souza's seat selection was not lost on Kyle. Apparently, this was *not* a two-party negotiation. Through seat selection, de Souza subconsciously signaled he was no patsy and had his own agenda to satisfy.

An image of a three-legged stool flashed in Kyle's mind. Deceptive in appearance, a three-legged stool is stable, but only in equilibrium. Regardless of how strong the other two legs might be, if one leg falters, the stool will topple under the lightest of loads.

Kyle couldn't help but wonder which of the three legs in this dynamic would falter first.

"First, let me begin with an apology," Baptista said, knitting his fingers together. "None of us were ever supposed to be in this dreadful situation . . ."

Kyle listened and understood this statement for what it was—prevarication—so he said nothing.

"I think what we can all agree on is that the best course of action is to move on from the past and talk about the future . . ."

Kyle nodded, still listening, but his attention wandered to a large-format television monitor on the far wall that was powered on, but seemed to be in standby mode.

"As president, my only priority is to serve the people of Angola. To do that means I must put their safety and security above all else. It also requires rooting out corruption and malfeasance in the government. My predecessor failed miserably on both counts, which is why people have entrusted me as their champion of change," Baptista said.

Kyle turned back to Baptista and screwed up his face. "Funny—

from what I understood, the people of Angola haven't entrusted you with anything, because you were not elected. You've overthrown the duly elected president and seized power via a military coup."

Baptista bristled, but then flashed Kyle a bright smile. "The will of the people has been ignored and suppressed for nearly two decades under the previous shambolic regime. Only now will they truly be free to vote their conscience. Regime change was and is the only way to safeguard democracy."

"Mm-hmm," Kyle said. "And you're holding me and my fellow Americans hostage in the name of democracy as well, is that it?"

Baptista threw daggers with his eyes at Kyle, then said, "Everything that happened to you and your colleagues was carried out without my knowledge or approval. As soon as I learned of this travesty, I ordered you brought here. As you witnessed on your arrival, I punished the man responsible."

"So, that must mean that you had General de Souza bring me here to the Cabinet Room so you could tell me that you're releasing me and my colleagues and that we are free to return to the American embassy."

Baptista steepled his fingers and sighed. "If only it were that simple."

"But it is that simple," Kyle said and glanced at de Souza, whose face was a mask.

The usurper president shook his head. "Unfortunately, it is not. Because right now, the American military has invaded my country's capital city and appears primed to lay siege to the seat of Angolan power—the Presidential Palace."

This piece of information was new for Kyle. If the Marines had the palace surrounded, that provided him with immediate leverage.

"What do you want from me?" Kyle said, cutting straight to the point.

"I want you to tell your father to withdraw all American military personnel and equipment from Luanda and provide me with public assurances that the United States will not interfere with matters of Angolan sovereignty."

"Okay," Kyle said.

Baptista seemed taken aback, then grinned like a child, clearly surprised by the speed and ease of Kyle's acquiescence. "Excellent. I have President Ryan waiting on hold for a videoconference. All I have to do is press this button to connect the television—"

"I agreed to tell him, I didn't say that he'd say *yes*," Kyle said, interrupting Baptista before he connected the videoconference.

Baptista's smile evaporated. "What did you say?"

"I'll tell the President whatever you want, but that doesn't mean he'll do it. In fact, I can all but guarantee he will not comply with your demands. My father does not negotiate with terrorists."

Baptista's eyes narrowed, and a furious scowl transformed his face into something resembling an angry gargoyle. "So your father will sacrifice his own son in the name of foreign policy?"

"Are those the stakes?" Kyle asked, forcing Baptista to say it. "My life for your power?"

"Yes," Baptista said, crossing his arms.

Kyle looked at de Souza, who met his gaze but still betrayed nothing. "Then that's unfortunate," he said finally, "because it means that *everyone* in this room is a dead man. If that's your move, Baptista, none of us are walking out of this palace alive."

Baptista scoffed. "You're bluffing."

"I wish I were. I imagine you will make your demand and then the President will rebuff them. You will kill me—because I believe you are fully prepared to do that. Then"—he glanced at de

Souza and gave him a sad smile—"I imagine you will both die in the assault on the palace or, perhaps, be hung later for treason."

Baptista picked up the remote, pointed it at the TV, and pressed a button. The screen refreshed, and a video call interface appeared. Baptista clicked the remote again to join the meeting, and a live streaming view of the Situation Room appeared on-screen. The President sat in the middle, flanked by the most powerful men and women in government, and Kyle recognized all their faces—Mary Pat Foley, whom he had known since he was a kid; Scott Adler; Arnie van Damm; and Bob Burgess. His father looked older than the last time Kyle had seen him and also more severe—as if the muscles under the skin had become harder and more angular. He wondered if this was a product of the streaming software, the lighting in the Situation Room, or if his perceptual memory of his father was skewed to a kinder, gentler version that was more "Dad" than "POTUS."

Kyle sensed how his father's eyes locked onto him and, despite the distance, performed a wellness assessment before shifting to Baptista.

"President Ryan, thank you for waiting," Baptista said with a half smile. "Your son has agreed to help moderate this conversation to de-escalate the current situation and find a mutually satisfactory negotiated solution to the current crisis."

Kyle watched his father rein in his emotions before responding in an even temper and tone. "Kyle, son. Are you okay?" Ryan asked, looking at Kyle and ignoring Baptista's opening statement completely.

This surprised Kyle and almost made him get emotional.

Almost . . . but not quite.

"Some bumps and bruises, but I'm fine, Mr. President," Kyle said as his brain worked the problem. He knew he would have only a limited number of opportunities to speak and a limited amount of strategic and tactical information he could share each time, so he had to make them count. "But while I'm sitting here in the Cabinet Room, the ambassador, Madison Bennett, and Eric Ottinger are being held at gunpoint in the underground bunker. Ottinger is in critical condition and requires a medevac. But they are safe for now." He put a subtle emphasis on the word *safe*, hopeful that the President would understand that if he had to attack this room, the rest of the hostages would survive.

As he spoke, Kyle noticed two things. The first was Mary Pat Foley jotting a paper note and handing it to someone off-screen. The second was Baptista fuming in his peripheral vision, but the dictator did not cut him off.

This time . . .

The President turned his attention to Baptista. "Victor, you're not fooling anyone. We know exactly who you are. We know what you've done. The United States does not recognize your authority as president of Angola. It's time to stop this madness, release the hostages, and end the bloodshed before things spiral out of control."

"And if I refuse?" Baptista said, angling in and meeting Ryan's gaze head-on.

Ryan leaned back in his chair as if he were about to declare checkmate.

"As we speak, the Marines of the 22nd MEU are surrounding the Presidential Palace. We control your airspace and the harbor. I have F-35s in the air with missiles locked and loaded. The NSA is standing by to jam your radio comms and shut down all electronic communications. Also, I have multiple teams of MARSOC Raiders standing by to breach and take control of the palace. You can't run. You can't hide. It's over. You've lost. All the Marines need is my permission and the F-35s can deliver a precision bomb right . . . through . . . your window."

Kyle sensed those last words were for him, and he glanced at the tall window behind Baptista, just as he saw de Souza do the same. Was his dad telling him something or was it his imagination? He readied himself for what was about to come next, because the President's previous move, unfortunately, was not "checkmate." Baptista still had pieces on the board he could sacrifice.

Baptista popped to his feet, pulled both pistols, and pointed one at Kyle and the other at de Souza.

Only a half second behind, however, General de Souza stood and pulled his own pistol from the waistband of his uniform and pointed it at Baptista.

"Call off your Marines, or your son dies," Baptista said, his hands unflinching and his voice steady.

"Victor, enough. Drop your weapon," the general said, speaking for the first time.

"I knew you couldn't be trusted, de Souza," Baptista snarled, "but no matter, the Americans know you are a collaborator. Even if you shoot me, you'll still be executed for treason when they reinstall Luemba."

The general didn't reply, and silence hung in the room like a suffocating fog until finally Kyle spoke.

"Well, Dad, it looks like I got invited to a gunfight, but unfortunately forgot to bring a pistol," Kyle said with a wry smile, looking at his father on the screen. Then he glanced at the window behind Baptista and raised a questioning eyebrow.

To almost everyone on the planet, this comment would seem like a joke. But coming from Kyle, it was both a sitrep and a question. Mary Pat leaned in and whispered something in Ryan's ear. He didn't visibly react.

Then, with a defeated tone, the President said, "Kyle, as your dad, I'd do anything for you. But as the President of the United States, I'm held to a standard that requires me to be impartial and put the needs of the nation above my personal desires and loyalties . . ."

As his dad talked, Kyle realized the President was buying time, and he hoped his grandmaster father had understood everything and was making tactical adjustments. What he was waiting for was the opportunity to give permission.

And then it happened.

". . . and so, I'm sorry. I hope in your heart of hearts you can forgive me," Ryan said, unblinking. "Can you forgive me, son?" He let the question hang a moment and then added, slowly, his eyes telling Kyle what he needed to know. "Yes or no?"

"Yes," Kyle shouted as he rolled out of his chair and dove under the table.

Gunfire cracked as pistols were discharged. Kyle also heard the shattering of glass and covered his head with his hands.

Then he heard the wet thud of two bodies as they simultaneously hit the floor.

Kyle opened his eyes to find Baptista's dead eyes staring at him under the table. Half of Baptista's head was missing, undoubtedly from a high-caliber round fired by a Marine sniper outside—a shot coordinated by Mary Pat from the other side of the world. Kyle rotated on his hands and knees to look toward the end of the table, where de Souza had been standing. The general was down, lying on his back, writhing in pain. Kyle scrambled out from under the table, just as the general's two bodyguards burst into the room, weapons up and at the ready. One soldier ran to de Souza, the other aimed at Kyle, who slowly raised his hands over his head in surrender.

"Stand down," the general wheezed from the floor. "Surrender to the Americans."

The guard covering Kyle looked confused, but he lowered his weapon.

Knees shaking, Kyle turned to the screen. Then, looking at his dad, he tried something he rarely did and decided to make an actual joke. "Nice shooting, Tex."

The President's face, which had been a mask of tension and granite, finally relaxed and transformed to match the face of the man in his mind and memories. "That was very brave what you did, son. I'm proud of you . . . So damn proud."

Kyle resisted the urge to look down at his hands. "Thanks, Dad. I love you, too."

61

REAR LOADING DOCK
U.S. EMBASSY MISSION IN ANGOLA
R. HOUARI BOUMEDIENE 32
LUANDA, ANGOLA
0239 LOCAL TIME

Katie paced back and forth just inside the roll-up door to the loading dock, chewing the inside of her cheek. She was vaguely aware of Conza and Bubba passing a spit bottle back and forth and the shared tin of Skoal. She glanced at her watch, exasperated.

They should be here by now.

"Jeez, Ryan, you're gonna wear a trench in the concrete, if you don't stop," Conza said.

"She's gonna crash hard when that adrenaline wears off," she heard Bubba whisper to Conza, apparently unaware of the acoustics of the large loading bay.

That was true . . . she was surviving off thirty-minute power naps.

She turned, tried to smile, but whatever expression she sent instead made her teammate chuckle. Conza had been incredibly bolstering throughout this entire whirlwind operation, giving her the respect her positional authority demanded, while offering her the special operations guidance and experience she needed as backup. And somehow, he made it look effortless. She wondered how serious his relationship with Lorie Tengco was and hoped it was something that would help the battle-blooded SEAL find the happiness he deserved.

She looked outside, where two Marines, a security detachment assigned to the rear of the building, stood beside each other, chatting. Their weapons were slung on their chests, but their hands were on the grips, ready. For a Marine, danger was always lurking, wasn't it?

First to Fight, indeed.

A flashbulb memory of Dennis smiling at her popped unbidden into her mind, and she thought she knew why. She'd nearly lost her brother, and contemplating that future had been unbearable. Had she not been able to throw herself into her job managing operations in the EOC, the strain and grief of the last few days might literally have given her a heart attack. How did her mom manage the stress of a family of Ryans in harm's way so well? First Dad, then Jack Junior . . . and now Katie and Kyle both in the field.

How is Mom not a basket case? she wondered.

Cathy was truly an amazing woman.

Do I have that same strength of spirit?

She was starting to wonder. She'd been fretting over the impossible logistics of a relationship with a fellow naval officer, serving and deploying within a completely different community. If something made her romance with Dennis doomed to fail, she'd imagined it would be scheduling. But the last forty-eight hours had changed that. Something else was bothering her. Something difficult to articulate. Something much more visceral.

She chased the thoughts away.

Later . . .

A rumble drew her notice, and she spied a pair of JLTVs rolling down the narrow road between the embassy compound and the medical school behind it. She caught herself actually patting her hands together and bouncing up and down like a six-year-old as two kitted-up Marines opened the gate.

The JLTVs drove onto the grounds and pulled up to the loading dock.

Four combat Marines—Merriweather's Raiders lead by Captain Camperos, rolled out of the first vehicle. Then the second combat vehicle opened its doors and two other Marine Raiders exited, followed by the familiar, lanky figure of her brother. He squinted against the sunlight and raised his right hand to shade his eyes as he scanned the little crowd waiting inside.

Katie's heart leapt with joy on seeing his face. But she was immediately taken aback when she saw him turn and put his arm around Madison Bennett to steady her on exiting the vehicle.

Interesting.

The Marines escorted the duo to the stairs, while she was bouncing with excitement and anticipation. By the time Kyle reached the top of the stairs, she was sprinting toward him. When he registered her face, he flashed her a rare and precious smile. He let go of Madison and took two quick steps opening his arms—intent on giving, not just grudgingly receiving, a bear hug.

Knowing Kyle, she tried to keep the hug short, but to her shock, he refused to release her. She held him for what must have been an eternity in Kyle Ryan time. Then, finally, he broke the embrace and to really study her.

"What are you doing here, Sissie?" he asked, using a childhood name she'd not heard in decades.

"Well, when the President says jump . . ." she said and burst into a half laugh and half cry.

"You said how high?"

"Exactly," she said, finally spent with the emotional release.

"I should have known it would be you that came," he said. "Thank you."

She hugged him again, unable to help herself, but this time he only tolerated the standard two-second "Kyle hug." When she released him, he turned to Madison, who walked tentatively up beside them.

"Katie, this is Madison Bennett," Kyle said, and it was not lost on Katie that he took Madison's hand, not the other way around.

Is this bonding just the trauma of being prisoners together?

"I know," she said and smiled at the woman, who nodded uncomfortably with the same strained expression Kyle wore in social situations.

"The other vehicle with the ambassador and Eric Ottinger deviated from our return route. Do you know why?" Madison asked, her face clouding.

"Yes, they were taken to the Marine FST set up at the medical center next door," Katie said. "I just spoke with Commander Schneider, the surgeon in charge of the FST. Mr. Ottinger has received several units of blood and is awake. They are going to move him to the *Kearsarge* and do more testing and determine if he needs surgery. He said something about a tube of some sort . . ."

"A chest tube, probably," Kyle said, surprising Katie.

What did Kyle know about trauma surgery?

"I think that might have been it. Anyway, they said you guys saved his life. And the ambassador is also being treated. Schneider said she had a ruptured spleen, but was going to be just fine. He said they got her into surgery in time."

There was a flicker of relief on Madison's face, but then her affect went flat.

"Thank you very much, Lieutenant Commander Ryan," Madison said, somewhat formally for the situation. She glanced at Kyle. "I'm going to head inside and prepare myself for the debrief while you spend a few moments with your sister."

"No," Kyle said rather quickly. Then he gave the woman another, honest-to-God smile. "I'd prefer to stay together. I'll go with you."

Madison nodded, but seemed pleased.

"I'm glad you're okay, Kyle," Katie said.

"I'm glad you're okay, too, Katie," he said, then surprised her by adding, "I love you."

Sudden and unexpected tears filled her eyes.

"I love you, too."

"I've got to go. It's important that we have the debrief while details are fresh in our minds," Kyle said matter-of-factly and headed toward the door that led into the embassy proper. "I'll see you later."

"There he is," Katie murmured, grinning. Then, chasing after him, she said, "You do realize I'm the person running the debrief, right?"

EPILOGUE

**TWO WEEKS LATER
THE RYAN HOME
CHESAPEAKE BAY, MARYLAND
1908 LOCAL TIME**

The warm, comfortable noise of the Ryan dinner table, with all its memories and nostalgia, could not quite quell the emotional storm inside Katie. She sat quietly, a smile on her face, and soaked in the love at the table. But her mind was on a conversation she needed to have with the man seated beside her. She knew Dennis sensed that something was wrong. He'd gently asked once and probed a second time, but to his credit he had then respected and honored her enough to leave it be—to allow her to broach whatever the subject was in her own time. That made her care about him even more.

Which made the dread of the conversation even worse.

"So Kyle . . ." Cathy said with a coy smile. "Katie mentioned that you might have a plus-one tag along for the next Ryan family dinner."

"Oh, *did* she . . ." Kyle said and shot Katie his *Thanks a lot* glare she was so intimately familiar with. But she saw the glint in his eye.

"Go, little bro!" Jack Junior said from across the table, where he sat beside Dad, earning a vigorous head shake and eye roll from Kyle.

"I don't know what in the world you're talking about, Mom," Katie said, smiling innocently.

"And that is all you'll get out of her, I can promise," Sally said with a laugh, bouncing little Genevieve on her lap. Her little girl cooed and reached for Mommy's nose and Sally's husband, Davi, beamed at both of his girls. "I tried to get more out of her about *this* one a couple of weeks ago," Sally said, shooting a smile at Dennis, "and li'l sis was a brick wall. The Navy has trained her well as a spy."

"I'm not a spy, I'm an analyst," Katie protested weakly. "I think you have me confused with Jack."

"I have no idea what any of you are talking about," Jack Junior said with a grin.

The table erupted with laughter, making the looming conversation Katie needed to have with Dennis harder with each passing, tender moment. And watching her sister, Sally—the driven, career-oriented surgeon—cuddling with little Genevieve wasn't helping.

"Yeah, I've heard that line a thousand times," Cathy quipped and gave Dad a little punch on the arm. Jack Ryan leaned over and gave his wife a gentle kiss on the cheek.

Katie looked at Kyle, who wagged a finger at her, but it wasn't lost on her that he'd made no denials. She winked at him.

To her shock, he winked back.

"Well," Dad said, and rose slowly from the table. "The girls did most of the cooking, so how about the guys clear the table and clean up?" he suggested. "But, Dennis, you're excused from dish duty. You're still a guest—for now, at least."

Just getting harder and harder and harder...

"I wouldn't hear of it, sir," Dennis said. "Happy to help."

He stood and grabbed Katie's plate, placed it on top of his own, and to her surprise kissed her on the cheek.

Katie smiled, but avoided eye contact, and found herself having second thoughts about her second thoughts. Maybe she should just let things play out and see what happened. She'd never once in her life felt so at ease with a man. Dennis made her feel relaxed, and special, and pretty, and, well, *herself.*

But then, those were the things that made what she had to do so very necessary. She deeply cared for him—enough to know that the careers they'd chosen meant they were on a path that, regardless of their best intentions, would inevitably lead to pain and heartache.

"Can I talk to you?" Kyle asked, pulling her out of her head.

"What?" she said and looked over to see him staring at her sternly.

"I need to talk to you," he said.

She glanced through the door to the kitchen, where Dennis was scraping plates and laughing with Jack Junior about something.

"Don't you need to help clear the table?" she asked, wary of where this was going.

"On the porch," Kyle said. "Now, Commander."

Her brother turned and headed through the foyer toward the back of the house, fully expecting her to follow him.

Which she did.

They arrived on the large back porch, overlooking the Chesapeake Bay, which was glistening silver in the fading light.

"Are you okay, Kyle?" she asked. "I can only imagine what you're dealing with after everything."

"I'm fine," he said. "Though I understand for many people the post-traumatic effects of something like this may take considerable time to manifest. But right now, I feel like myself." He turned to her. He didn't smile, but his face was the happy Kyle she remembered from when they were kids. They had been joined at the hip back then, despite how very different they were. It was an unbreakable bond, she supposed. If she had lost him, she didn't know what she would have done. "It's you I'm worried about . . ."

"Wait . . . What?" she said. "Me? Why?"

"I know what you're going to do, Katie," he said simply. "And it's a mistake."

"I don't know what you're talking about," she said, but after all these years, he read her like a book.

"Yes, you do," he said simply. "You're going to break up with Dennis. Or maybe you're going to try and slow things down, to keep them casual for now, which will effectively have the same result."

Katie sighed. Everything in her life—from childhood all the way through the Academy—had been easier because she and Kyle did it together and they just always . . . *got* each other. There was no point in hiding anything from him.

"Relationships in the Navy are hard," she said, looking at the water. "I'm at the ONI, and if past is prologue, they're going to keep throwing hard and dangerous problems at my team. And Dennis has screened for command. Things are about to get very busy for him. Kyle, I have zero doubt he'll fly through PCO school and get his own boat—his own command. He'll be deployed or in work-ups constantly. And then what? What if he gets assigned to Pearl and I'm stuck in D.C.? Heck, they could send me to Europe for a NATO billet. Why does having a relationship have to feel like a logistics problem rather than love?"

Kyle stared at her, but said nothing. After holding contact for a long moment, she looked back to the eastern horizon at the darkening waters as the fading pink of the sunset was replaced by violet hues and tentative moonlight.

"You're looking at it all wrong," Kyle said simply, and she turned to look at him again. After a moment he, too, turned to look out at the bay. "When we were young—not like little, but you know, still kids—I used to wonder how Mom did it. She was so busy being a surgeon and worrying about her patients. She somehow made it look easy, even though Dad seemed to be on some new 'business trip,' constantly, and so often without warning. But we never felt neglected. We never felt she didn't have time for us. Then, later, when I began to understand the other stress she must be dealing with because of Dad's job, I thought, 'Man, I will never put a future partner through that.' The fear, the worry, the loneliness . . . What's the point of putting someone you love through all that angst?"

She held his eyes and felt her own become wet. She knew everyone else in their lives might be shocked at the depth of feeling her brother was showing.

But she wasn't.

"Exactly," she said, realizing he'd just proven her point.

"But I don't feel that way anymore," he said, blind-siding her.

"Because of Madison?" she asked, placing a hand on his arm.

To her surprise, he laughed—a real and rare out-loud laugh that he only treated her to.

"No," he said, but then considered a moment. "Someday

maybe, though." He turned to her again. "You changed my mind, or more specifically the look on your face when I climbed out of that van and saw you waiting for me at the embassy. It reminded me of the look on Mom's face when Dad would come home from one of *those* trips and she would look at him and cry. She wasn't sad, but she would cry anyway. Just like you did . . ."

She waited, confused.

"I think, after what I went through, that I understand it now. When you love someone, you want to shield them from fear, and risk, and pain. The easiest way of doing that is to separate yourself from them, from the people you care about most. But it's backward logic, Katie, because in doing that all you've done is traded love for emptiness. We need people in our lives who we fear losing, who we love so much that we worry about the risk and pain. Don't you see, that's why Mom and Dad work. That's why you and I are kindred spirits . . ." He took her hands, and the unprecedented gesture from her brother made her mouth drop open with surprise. "So, if you're thinking about trading love for emptiness, then I'm asking you to reconsider. If Dennis could be *that* person for you, then you'd be an idiot to not try."

Speechless, she stared at him in wonder, and the look made Kyle uncomfortable, so he let go of her hands and turned back to the bay.

"I love it here," he said softly.

She wanted to hug him, but she didn't think he would like that in this moment.

"Thank you, Kyle," she said. "You're a good brother."

"Any time," he said, then with a wry grin added, "It's not complicated. Two is greater than zero . . . It's just math."

He turned and headed back inside, and she watched him pass Dennis in the doorway. Kyle gave the submariner a curt nod as he passed, then closed the door behind him and disappeared inside the house.

"You okay?" Dennis asked, walking up to her. His eyes looked sad.

He knows. He isn't stupid . . . He knows.

"Yeah," she said with a close-lipped smile. "Can we talk?"

"Sure, I kinda felt like this was coming," he said regretfully while looking down at his feet.

She took his hands in hers and he looked up. She beamed at him, and he looked confused.

"I thought I knew what was about to happen, but now I'm not so sure," he said.

She met his eyes with hers, and realized how in his presence she felt warm, and safe, and . . . at peace. In her heart of hearts, she didn't want to be alone.

Kyle was right.

It's just math . . .

"Dennis, I think we have something real together," she said, "and I want to try and make it work . . . That is, if you want to?"

He looked shocked.

"That . . . that is not what I thought was coming. And, yes. I do want to see where this thing takes us, Ryan. I know relationships in the military are complicated . . ."

"I don't care about complicated," she said, and thought of how very complicated it must have been for Mom and Dad. Kyle was right about that. "And I know dating in the Navy somehow always turns into a logistics problem, but let's not worry about that."

"I'm a submariner—scheduling and logistics just so happen to be one of my specialties," he said, which made her laugh.

"Can we talk about how this—I mean, us—could work?"

"I would like that very much," Dennis said, and pulled her in for a warm hug. She shivered, not sure if it was from the cool night air or something else. "You're cold," he said, pulling away. "Let me go get you a jacket."

"No," she said, pulling him back tight into an embrace. "You can keep me warm."